Praise for

a can of peas

"Lake Emily is populated with fresh faces, intriguing relationships, and heartwarming stories that bring a community to life. Whether you live in a high-rise or a remote home, you'll recognize the people who fill this satisfying *Can of Peas*. Lake Wobegon? I'll take Lake Emily."

—JANE KIRKPATRICK, *award-winning author of the critically acclaimed Kinship and Courage series*

"Traci DePree has created a charming story that held me captive from page one and didn't let me go until the last page was turned. I laughed, and I cried, but mostly I fell in love with the characters and town of Lake Emily. I want to live there! Traci is a lively new voice in Christian fiction. I can't wait to read more of her work."

—DIANE NOBLE, *award-winning author of* Heart of Glass

"Traci DePree is a fine new writer, though I've been reading her work for years. She's one of the few who can make me cry with her well-written, poignant scenes that read like real life and also laugh out loud at sweet, funny situations. Enter the world of Lake Emily, get to know her people, and enjoy."

—LISA TAWN BERGREN, *award-winning author of*
The Bridge *and* Christmas Every Morning

I can't believe what a slice of *my* life growing up on a farm *A Can of Peas* depicts. Exchange peas and corn for wheat and milo, and Traci's farming community of Lake Emily *is* where I grew up, right down to the extension meetings. As I read, I felt as though I were reliving my childhood. Lovely!"

—DEBORAH RANEY, *author of* Beneath a Southern Sky *and*
A Vow to Cherish

"A charming story, gently told, *A Can of Peas* blossoms in the reader's heart, like the land bringing forth crops for harvest. I fell in love with all the people of Lake Emily, and so will you!"

—ROBIN LEE HATCHER, *award-winning author of* Firstborn

a can of peas

Traci DePree

WATERBROOK
PRESS

A CAN OF PEAS
PUBLISHED BY WATERBROOK PRESS
12265 Oracle Boulevard, Suite 200
Colorado Springs, Colorado 80921
A division of Random House, Inc.

ISBN 978-1-57856-523-8

Library of Congress Cataloging-in-Publication Data
DePree, Traci.
    A can of peas / Traci DePree.
        p. cm.
    ISBN 1-57856-523-5
    1. Inheritance and succession—Fiction. 2. Rural families—Fiction. 3. Family farms—Fiction.
4. Minnesota—Fiction. 5. Farm life—Fiction. I. Title.
    PS3604.E67 C36 2002
    813'.6—dc21

                                                                2002005872

Printed in the United States of America
2007

10 9 8 7

for

Rose Marie DePree

and

Willow Grace DePree

acknowledgments

No one creates a book alone. There are many people to thank for the creation of *A Can of Peas*. John, my dear husband, was my first reader and editor; he always believes and encourages even when my faith is lacking. Our children, Caitlin, Megan, Haley, and Willow, sacrificed much so Mom could write. You're the best.

Many thanks to Dianne Pinney, Jan La Fond, and Jean Haas for reading my rough draft and giving great advice. Todd Sullivan gave me a crash lesson in milking cows—his cow was the true voyeur! To the wonderful folks at WaterBrook who work tirelessly on my behalf.

Lisa Bergen, thank you for nagging me! Special thanks also to Erin Healy, for holding my hand through this whole process, even when life seemed determined not to let it happen.

And finally, many thanks to the people of Le Sueur, Minnesota, for being Lake Emily to me and more.

ROY MORGAN

It was an early June day in 1985. Ten-year-old Peter Morgan sat on the seat next to his Grandpa Roy as he drove the Chevy pickup along the dusty road. Peter's nose itched, and he gave it a scratch. Gravel pinged as it flew up under the truck.

They neared the rich green fields of peas. Peter could see the huge red combines from the canning factory moving like a procession of snails across his grandpa's land. The blades circled in precision like a pinwheel in a breeze, gathering the tender plants and pulling them hungrily into the machine's stomach.

Peter looked across the checkerboard of black and green and felt a warm contentment fill him. It was a perfect day, the kind of day when the sun shone bright and everything smelled new. The view from the cab stretched and yawned for miles. Peter could see the water tower at Lake Emily shimmering silver in the morning light, and the lake was a pale blue in the June sunshine. There was nothing like the harvest.

One of the big machines moved to the grain truck waiting at the side of the field and positioned the long auger's arm over the bed. Soon the peas came out in a flow of green. The door of the pickup squeaked as Peter and his grandfather got out to watch. Roy leaned against the grille while Peter climbed on the hood.

"Did you always want to be a farmer, Grandpa?" Peter asked, turning his head to look at the older man's strong profile.

Roy's gray eyes wrinkled into a smile. His gaze trained ahead, he said,

"I suppose I did, Peter. Same as my father. Some people are just meant to be out here in God's creation, breathing the spring air, working the soil."

"I wish my dad was a farmer," Peter said, sighing.

"Your dad has his own gifts, Peter, just as you do." Roy laid a comforting hand on his grandson's head, tousling his blond hair. Roy was quiet for a moment before he spoke again, "You see this field?"

Peter nodded as the scent of dark, rich earth and fresh-cut peas lingered in the air.

"People are like these here peas. They come in all sizes, you know. Some are big, some small. There's floaters and sinkers, but it takes all kinds, working together and helping each other out. That's what makes a family, a town, work." He glanced over at Peter as the combine finished filling the truck and started back up the rows. "Your father makes beautiful music—it's a gift God gave him." There was a long silence between them, filled with the rumble of the combines.

"What will I be when I grow up, Grandpa?" Peter lifted his blue eyes to his grandfather's.

"You'll be who you are now, plus or minus the choices you make along the way. Now, what you do, that's another matter altogether. You'll have to follow your heart…and God's leading. But it'll come to you, Peter."

Peter thought about that for a while before remembering the suitcase in his room, already packed for his father's next concert tour. "I don't want to go to Spain," Peter complained. "Why can't Mom and I stay here while Dad goes with the orchestra?"

"You'd miss your dad, Peter. Besides, he needs you," Roy said. "Before you know it, you'll be back here again. Maybe you can help bring in the corn."

I t's a crying shame," Lillian Biddle said in a loud whisper, hovering a bit too close to Peter Morgan. They stood on the dormant lawn on an unusually warm day in early April. Bare crab apple branches draped overhead, creating a somber, webbed shadow that encased the mourners who stood in scattered clumps across the lawn like faded dandelions. Steaming black coffee warmed hands, and napkins held sweet bars.

"You know, she'll have to sell the place now," Mrs. Biddle continued, "what with Roy gone. They hired my Bert over a month ago to do all the milking, ever since Roy's cancer got the best of him. A cryin' shame, a cryin' shame. I've seen it happen all too often. The man dies and the wife has to sell out, auction the equipment and move to town, even though she worked as hard as him to keep the place going. I remember," Lillian went on, "Cora Jorgenson, she was just devastated after Richard passed on. Heart attack in the middle of church, right after the benediction. They're Catholic, you know."

Peter didn't have a clue who she was talking about. His mind was on his grandfather—gone three days—and finding his grandmother in the crowd.

"When Richard died, Cora didn't have much choice. The bank was pushing to foreclose, could hardly wait till Richard was buried to get their hands on it. So she sold that beautiful farm. It had been in their family for four generations. But then during the farm crisis they had such a hard time of it. Almost lost the place then. I don't know how

3

your grandfather fared. He seemed like a levelheaded man, but then you can never tell."

Peter scanned the crowd, trying to catch a glimpse of his round-cheeked, gray-haired grandmother. Virginia had been so constantly surrounded by well-wishers that he'd had no chance to speak with her since he arrived in Lake Emily that morning. At least he'd been able to sit with her during the service, but there had hardly been an opportunity to talk then. Peter felt his wife, Mae, slip her hand into his. She was beautiful, her delicate figure draped in funeral black and a dark wool coat. Her long brown hair framed her fine-boned face and compassionate brown eyes. They'd been married all of six months. Six of the happiest months of his life, and then came the news of his grandfather's death.

"Couldn't she hire someone long-term? Like a farmhand?" Mae kept the conversation going. "To do the hard work for her?"

"Farming's all hard work, dear," Lillian scolded, then turned to Peter. "I suppose you'd know that—you visited the farm when you were growing up, didn't you?" When Peter didn't respond, she continued, "Oh, I suppose not—your father moved away first chance he got. Does he still play the fiddle? Boston. He was out in Boston for a time, wasn't he? Your grandma sure liked to brag about her David. He wasn't like my boys. It's a shame he didn't stick around after he finished high school.

"Besides…," she droned on. Lillian wore a blue polyester suit that was a good decade behind the times, with matching blue shoes, white hose, and a hand-knit shawl. She was a large woman, not heavy as much as big boned, with a sculpted, almost-pretty face betrayed by her overworked mouth. She was no doubt used to taking charge and keeping the menfolk in line. Peter had only met her on a couple of occasions before, but Lillian was a woman not easily forgotten. She'd come visiting whenever they were in town. Had probably diapered him as a baby. Maybe spanked him when his parents weren't watching.

Peter focused on Lillian's mouth, ignoring the words pouring out of it, wondering how she could be so oblivious of her effect on others. "A hired hand costs money. Virginia isn't one of those company farmers who have cash to throw around. What's the point of having a farm if you're paying someone else to work it? My Bert's been helping, but he can't keep that up forever. Farming's a family business, where everyone pulls together. Does for each other. That's what my boys would do…" Her words dangled in the air.

Peter followed her glance toward the old brick farmhouse where her sons, Albert and Alfred Biddle, stood talking, plates piled high with potato salad, Jell-O, and an array of hot dishes in hand. Peter had played with them on a couple of occasions as a boy. Their names, Peter's grandma had once told him, had been shortened to Bert and Fred shortly after they were born, when Lillian became outraged that the *Lake Emily Herald* listed the twins in the birth announcement as "the Als." Most folks still referred to them as "the Als," especially when Lillian wasn't around. They were a little older than Peter, in their early thirties, single, living at home. They worked the farm with their father, who couldn't bring himself to retire. Bert wore spanking new denim overalls with a gray suit coat. He had dishwater blond hair that stuck out in a curly mess, with a permanent ringed halo from wearing his seed cap. Fred wore a snug dark suit with a wide tie. His hair was cropped short. Both wore black work boots.

"I don't really know what Grandma's plans are," Peter said, taking a bite of the lemon bar he was holding.

"She'll have to face it sooner or later," Lillian persisted, her voice trailing off. She turned to say hello to another neighbor. Peter took the opportunity to pull Mae away in a quick escape.

The wind blew, rustling the dried leaves on the ground around the snowball bush as they swirled upward, then settled down again. Peter recalled the white flowers that would hang in thick, pregnant clusters in a month or two, their beautiful bouquets complementing the dark green of the leaves. His confirmation picture had been taken in front of that ageless shrub. The same year his mother had died. Laura had been so proud of him. He could almost see her green eyes and proud face shining in joy as she snapped the shutter on the Brownie camera.

Peter lifted his gaze to the house, a two-story square farmhouse with intricate woodwork along the eaves and a porch that wrapped around three sides. The bricks were a yellowish tan—Chaska brick, Grandpa always called it. Red shutters and a matching scroll-worked screen door accentuated the home with a crispness that was classic turn-of-the-century farmhouse.

Peter's childhood memories lived here. At least the good memories of visits between all their moves from one place to the next. Reading on the front porch swing on warm summer days while the smell of Grandma's cookies fluttered to him on the breeze. The cicadas' buzz in August and September as he watched Grandpa Roy combine beans or corn in the field, surrounded by a cloud of dust that obscured the big tires so the machine appeared to be floating across the golden acres.

In the summer, flower beds would flow around the lawn like streams of color, wide and rounded. One thing Grandma always complained about was a square flower bed—"too predictable," she would say. Peter wished that the ribbons of pink and purple and gold crocuses were already in bloom. He needed their cheer today. They would be followed by an array of rich perennials, each timed perfectly to bloom in full when its predecessor petered out.

Peter could still see his grandfather, pipe hanging from his bottom lip as he read the paper out on the porch, or sitting on the old yellow Minneapolis Moline tractor, a proud grin on his face as he rode in the Fourth of July parade. When Peter stayed over, Roy would play checkers with him long after he was supposed to be in bed. Peter sighed. There were so many things left unsaid. He wished he had asked his grandfather what it had been like to live in the same town his whole life, to live through the Depression and a world war, what it was like to know his place in the world.

Peter's gaze shifted to watch friends and family across the lawn. He didn't know most of the names or faces anymore, but they each had in turn offered their condolences as they passed. He caught a glimpse of Jerry Shrupp—J. D., Peter's father always called him. He had been David Morgan's closest friend in high school. *J. D. came, but Dad couldn't get back from another tour,* Peter thought bitterly.

Mae touched Peter's shoulder, reminding him of her presence. "Are you okay?" She smiled sweetly.

"I'm fine. I was thinking about Dad…" He let his words trail off, then gazed into her face. He cleared his throat. "I wish he could've been here."

"I know." She gave his hand a squeeze.

The screen door slammed, and Peter's grandmother emerged from the house, a weary expression on her wrinkled face. She was shaking hands with a tall, stoop-shouldered man. Peter noticed that a yellow calico apron with a *V* embroidered on the pocket had found her since she arrived at home. She was likely cooking something in the kitchen again, waiting on others in the midst of her own suffering.

Peter knew with certainty that his grandmother was better equipped to deal with the grief, better equipped to carry on after the loss of her spouse, than his grandfather would've been. If she had died, Grandpa Roy would've died himself, if not at once, then bit by bit. Peter had seen it in his counseling practice countless times—widowers, lost men without a compass, searching for what to do, where to go with the tail end of their lives, alone with empty expressions and emptier hearts.

Couples who spent a lifetime together drew strength and courage from each other. It was a silent arrangement, typical of those who had survived the Depression, and especially of farm families. They received no fanfare of flowery thank-yous, but theirs was a steadfast surety. A surety that, together, they would keep life on the straight and narrow. Perhaps it came with age, with the wisdom of seeing decades pass and gray hairs emerge, when health failed and the window toward eternity seemed clearer, vulnerability less an issue of manliness than of necessity.

Peter caught his grandmother's gaze. She waved and made her way toward them.

They met beneath the old cedar. Its rough-barked branches had weathered with the years. The dried blades of the previous year's tiger lilies surrounded the base of the trunk and whispered coarsely in the breeze.

"Grandma, how are you holding up?" Peter said, bending down and giving her a long embrace. When he pulled back, he could see tears shimmering in her eyes. "We're all going to miss him."

She sniffled and nodded her head before reaching for Mae's hand. "He's where he longed to be now," she said. "With the Savior he loved so much."

Peter felt a lump grow in his throat, and he was afraid his own tears would begin again.

"I'm so glad you're here," Virginia said. "It was a nice service, wasn't it? Roy would've liked it."

Everyone said that at funerals, Peter thought.

"Everyone has been so kind," she went on. "I wasn't prepared for that—how kind everyone would be…" Virginia's voice trailed off. "Did you two get anything to eat?"

"Yes, plenty," Peter and Mae said in unison. Mae went on, "You didn't do all that cooking yourself, did you?"

"Heavens, no, dear. The ladies' circle brought most everything. Seems we were just together for your wedding," Virginia said wistfully. "It was so beautiful. Roy really enjoyed his dance with you, Mae."

"I can't believe it's been six months either." Mae glanced at Peter. "Roy danced a mean polka. I'm glad I had the chance to get to know him a little."

Virginia smiled up at her, her pale blue eyes tired and profoundly sad. Mae was a good head taller than the older woman, her slim, tan frame a sharp contrast to Virginia's ivory, double-chinned form.

"Seems to be the way things go these days," Virginia said. "Families only gather at weddings and funerals. We need more weddings in our family…" There was a long silence. "So how is your job going, Peter?"

Peter glanced uncomfortably at Mae, then said, "I…uh…I got laid off, actually. About a month ago. It was all very political. That's why we moved in with Mae's mom and stepdad. I would've told you, but with Grandpa so sick I didn't want to worry you."

"I'm sorry, Peter," Virginia said. "Have you been job hunting then?"

"I've had lots of interviews and a couple of good offers," Peter said. "To be honest, I'm glad for the break. Work was pretty cutthroat, everyone competing for the big-dollar clients. I'm not sure it's for me anymore. I don't know." Peter shook his head. "Maybe I need to buck up and take whatever comes my way—"

"No," Virginia said. "Money, there's no lasting value in that. You should look for your heart's desire."

"I guess I need to find out what that is then," Peter chuckled, "because sitting in a chair listening to rich people complain about how depressing their life is just isn't doing it for me." Peter paused and gazed across the empty fields at a farm in the distance. It reminded him of the miniature farm set he'd played with as a boy. Two red barns, one bigger than the other, and between them three indigo silos, a long, low hog shed in white, and a small bungalow farmhouse. "I'd forgotten how beautiful it is here," Peter said almost to himself, breathing in the dusty tang of early spring.

"Remember the time your grandfather taught you to ride that draft horse?" Virginia said.

Peter's lips lifted in a smile as the lost memory came flooding back. He was ten years old and eager to ride. His grandpa had lifted him onto the big, strong back and told him to hang on to the mane. The Belgian had glanced at Peter with a knowing look in his eye, and his grandfather slapped his rump with a solid whack. That beast had taken off across the field at a full run straight through the soybeans, with Peter holding on for dear life. Peter could still see his grandfather's amused expression when the horse came back to the barn door.

"I'm so glad you're here," Virginia said, breaking into his reverie. "It's good to be reminded that people care."

"I'm sorry that Dad isn't here," Peter said, unable to keep the disappointment out of his tone. "He should have been."

"I told him not to come—he has commitments to keep."

"But he's your son. You need him here."

"I'll need him more later, after everyone's forgotten. Don't be so harsh on your father, Peter. He's a good man. He hasn't been the same since losing Laura."

"Grandma, Mom's been gone fifteen years. How long are you going to make excuses for him?"

"He's my son. David got to see Roy before he left, and he'll be back soon enough. I know his thoughts are here." Then she smiled and patted Peter's arm. "Did you see the bouquet of roses he sent on the dining room table? They're yellow—my favorite. Besides, when he gets back, I'll need his help to get the old place ready to sell."

Peter looked at her in alarm. "Sell? What are you talking about?"

"I don't have much choice," she said in reply. "I can't run this place by myself, and I can't afford to let it rot. Your grandpa and I talked it over before he died—that cancer gave us time to make plans. Besides, it's not as if the kids can take it over. That was what Roy always hoped for. Don't look so troubled, Peter. It happens all the time."

A dark feeling overtook Peter as he thought about someone else living in the old, beautiful house. This farm was the only stability he had ever known. The place they came back to between their moves from city to city after his mother died. "You should give it some time—"

"I've had time, Peter. Too much time. I wanted to move when Roy first got the cancer, but—" Her voice broke off, choked by emotion. She wiped her blue eyes with the edge of her apron, then looked at Peter. "He couldn't bring himself to leave. Roy loved this place. I guess we thought he'd beat the cancer…" She straightened her bent back. "The longer I wait the harder it'll be to sell. The fields need to be worked now to get peas in, and I can't do it. You wouldn't want to see these fat old legs climb into that big John Deere. Besides, it'll be nice to be in town, close to my friends. Most of them live there now. Truth be told, the farm keeps me from doing some of the things I enjoy. It's time for a change, hard as it may seem."

The lone bulb shone in Peter's eyes. He stood before the mirror, brushing his teeth, in the basement apartment in Mae's parents' home. One idea kept haunting him like an echo in a canyon. *Look for your heart's desire,* his grandmother's words of two days before reverberated.

What was his heart's desire? To sit in some stuffy office for the rest of his life? He'd had two offers to work as an in-house psychologist for prestigious companies in St. Paul, but he hadn't been able to bring himself to accept either one. And lately, whenever he considered it, the memory of harvesting peas with his grandfather filled his consciousness again. The image was so vivid. He could feel the cool April breeze caressing his cheeks, could hear the whirring of the blades as they cut the tender shoots, could smell the dark earth tinged with diesel fuel. He put his toothbrush away and meandered back to the bedroom.

Mae was settled in bed reading the latest best-selling romance novel. A beaded lamp glowed golden on the table beside her. Peter flipped back the thick comforter and slipped between the sheets, his head resting in his hand. He faced her and watched her lips move ever so slightly as her eyes scanned the page.

"What?" she said feigning annoyance.

"You're beautiful."

Her face flamed. A smile deepened the dimples in her cheeks. Her brown eyes sparkled beneath dark hair and perfectly sculpted brows. Peter reached up to kiss her softly on the lips. When he pulled back, she ran her fingers through his sandy hair.

"I've been thinking about Grandma," he said after a long moment.

"I know. Me too. It must be horrible to lose someone you love and especially to watch him die such a long, agonizing death. How long were they married?"

"Fifty-seven years. They eloped when she was nineteen." There was a long pause and he stared at the sheets, trying to think of a way to propose what was in his thoughts.

"You're thinking something else," Mae prompted, sitting upright. "I know that look."

"What look?" Peter tried to act innocent.

"Okay, out with it."

"I've been thinking about the farm, too," he began tentatively, finally meeting her eyes. "I've been thinking about taking it over."

"Taking what over?" She set her book on the side table and gazed suspiciously at him.

"The farm."

Mae laughed. "You're serious? What do you know about farming?"

"Nothing, really. Just the few tidbits I picked up from Grandpa."

"My point exactly."

"Grandma said it was Grandpa's dream to pass the farm on, and I think I'd really like it. Being outdoors, setting my own schedule. Putting down roots. I don't want to move around anymore—I had enough of that as a kid. I want to live someplace where people know each other. I spent my childhood jumping from town to town, not making any lasting friendships. I don't want that for our kids. And I can't stomach the thought of losing that beautiful old farm on the open market. It's my history…"

"Honey, it sounds very romantic, but don't you think you're being idealistic?"

"And I suppose living in a musty basement under your mother's watchful eye is ideal? And the way she treats you—"

"Hold your voice down," Mae shushed, then said, "I know you don't like it here, but it's only temporary."

"Until what? I've been thinking about it, and I don't want to resume my practice. Maybe that's why I've been putting off accepting an offer. Maybe God has something else in mind for me, and maybe I haven't been listening. I know this is quick, but I think it's right. The right thing for me. At least say you'll think about it. Pray about it?"

"Peter, I can't even fathom this. You're a professional psychologist. You have a good future ahead of you."

"It depends on what you mean by 'good,' doesn't it? Don't you remember how I was when I'd come home from work? How tired I was of the game playing, the backstabbing? I don't want that stress again."

Mae's expression softened. "I know it was hard—"

"Think about it?" Peter persisted.

"What about my job?"

"They have a flower shop in Lake Emily, and I'm sure St. Peter has a couple. Maybe you could work there. Or open your own shop."

"Now you're being silly."

"No." His eyes searched hers. "I'm dreaming. For the first time in my life, I'm dreaming." Peter sat straighter. "Can't you see? We have a chance to make a different kind of life for ourselves, a life that counts for more than a paycheck."

Mae sighed and uncrossed her arms. "Haven't you seen all those farm documentaries on public television? No one makes money farming," Mae said.

"I'm not afraid of a little hard work. We would learn as we go. Besides, we could be together. I wouldn't have to head off to the office every morning, get stuck in traffic, come home late. We could eat breakfast in Grandma's kitchen, take off whenever we want to. It would be an adventure."

"You are an optimist, aren't you?" Her eyes crinkled into a smile.

"I think we could really make a go of it, and Grandma will still be nearby if we need a little advice."

"You're assuming she'll be thrilled with your idea."

"You heard her—it was Grandpa's dream. She'll think this is perfect."

"It all seems so sudden. I can't believe you're ready to throw away all that time in college. Your degree will really come in handy milking cows!"

"You never know. There are probably a lot of depressed heifers—maybe I could help them work out their childhood issues."

That brought a smile to Mae's lips. "Peter, be serious."

"I feel right about this, Mae. I really do. The timing is perfect—I'm in the job market. We're young, eager… Besides," Peter continued, "the house is wonderful." He looked around their tiny room. "It sure beats this dump."

"It is a beautiful house, isn't it?" Peter knew by the twinkle in her eye that he had piqued her interest. "You're tempting me, Mr. Morgan." She quirked a brow teasingly.

"Who? Me? I'd never do that, Mrs. Morgan." He pulled her to him for another kiss.

"Ooh, Farmer Pete, your hands are cold!" She giggled.

"Think about it?" Peter asked.

"I'll think. But not right now," Mae said.

The next morning sunlight streamed through the single narrow window at the top of the wall, bouncing around the cabbage-rose wallpapered bedroom and filling it with a sweet welcome to a sunny spring day. Mae stretched, realizing Peter wasn't beside her. She lifted her head toward the door as her mother appeared with a tray bearing two steaming cups of rich coffee.

"Have you seen Peter?"

"He went for a run." Mae's mother, Catherine, was a smaller version of Mae—same dark hair and eyes. But where Mae preferred the casual, relaxed, outdoorsy look, Catherine was a dyed-in-the-wool Saks Fifth Avenue woman. Her nails kept their weekly manicure appointment, and her hair was obediently in place at all times. Mae couldn't remember seeing her mother without makeup on.

Mae sat up in bed and took the steaming brew her mother held out to her.

"I wanted to talk to you while Peter was out." Catherine sat on the edge of the bed.

"What about?" Mae took a sip.

"Well…there's no easy way to put this, honey," Catherine began. "You know your stepfather and I are happy to have you here for as long as you need. But it's difficult for us to sit by and watch Peter take advantage of you."

"Advantage? What are you talking about?"

"He doesn't seem to even want a job. How many has he turned down now?"

"Mother! Peter's not lazy, if that's what you're implying. He worked faithfully at Krentz and Krentz before they laid him off. It's not as if he had a choice in the matter."

"Dear." Catherine patted Mae's hand. "I know you love Peter, and I'm sure he tries his best. But we—Paul and I—don't see how he can provide the kind of lifestyle you deserve if he doesn't get out into the job market and start climbing that ladder. I knew he wasn't right for you when he first proposed."

"I can't believe we're having this conversation."

"But he's still waiting around, and for what? For you to support him? Or does he expect us to foot all the bills?"

"If you and Paul want us to move out, just say so." Mae felt her ears burn.

"No, sweetie, I'm not saying that. I think maybe you should talk to him, get him motivated…"

Mae chewed on her lower lip. "Okay, Mother," she conceded, wanting her to leave. "I'll talk to Peter."

"Thank you, honey. Really, it's for his own good and for your best interest," she said. "It's probably a self-confidence thing. Sometimes men need a little shove, that's all. You'll be glad in the long run." Mae resisted the urge to scream into her pillow.

Peter appeared in the doorway, his shirt and hair wet with perspiration.

"Who'll be glad in the long run?" he asked innocently.

Catherine smiled her dinner-party smile. "I better go get breakfast on for Paul. You know how he gets if he has to wait for his omelet." She gave Mae a pointed look and then walked past Peter without another word. Peter made a face at Catherine's back as she retreated up the stairs.

"What was that about?" Peter said when he turned back to Mae.

"Mother," Mae said the word tersely, then sighed. "Maybe you were right. Living with Mom and Paul is growing stale fast."

"What are you saying?" Peter sat on the edge of the bed and peeled off his T-shirt, wiping his face and head with it and tossing it onto the heaping laundry hamper.

"Maybe…I'm considering what you said last night."

"The farm?" His eyes were hopeful, like a little boy who'd been told he could have a new puppy.

"Maybe we should go out next weekend and see what Virginia thinks of this harebrained idea."

Business had been hopping all day. Mae had made six floral arrangements—one for a wedding anniversary, two for the births of new babies, and three for a funeral downtown.

Lynn, Mae's boss, came in the back room that was a hodgepodge of pots and vases, baskets, stuffed animals, and picture frames, all the accouterment of bouquet making. "Mae, we have four more orders, and the ones you've finished need to be out before ten." She handed Mae the order sheets with the specifications for each arrangement.

"I'll get right on it," Mae said, reading over the instructions.

"The way today's going," Lynn continued, "I'll need you to stay late tonight if we're going to be ready for the wedding tomorrow."

Mae felt her heart sink. She and Peter had planned a night out. "I'll have to call Peter," Mae said.

"Well, do it quickly." Then Lynn turned at the sound of the front doorbell and went to wait on a customer.

As Mae trimmed daisies for a spring bouquet, her mind wandered to the conversation with her mother that morning. Mae had known moving in with her and Paul hadn't been the best of ideas, and it wasn't just that Catherine disapproved of Peter and everything he'd ever done or said in his life. Truth was, it wouldn't have mattered whom Mae married, her mother would've found him lacking. She found everyone lacking. She had a way of turning the screws on Mae's daughter-guilt without even batting an eye, and Mae was tired of it. Tired of pleasing someone who wouldn't be pleased.

MEL JOHNSON

Seaman, first class, Mel Johnson pulled the envelope from his mailbox. The delicate script made his heart miss a beat. It was from Clara. The winds off the Atlantic blew his sandy-blond hair into his face as he made his way across the deck toward the stairs leading to his berth, but his mind was pre-occupied with going belowdecks to read the letter.

Clara Weis had always been a peach of a girl. He'd watched her pretty face grow small and distant as his bus pulled away from Lake Emily for boot camp. She'd been his best friend since eighth grade, but she wasn't the same tomboy he'd thrown a football with. Something had changed about her, and the longer he was separated from her the more certain he was that she was more than just a friend. Deep inside he knew Clara was the love of his life. He had written the letter asking her to marry him the day after leaving port in France on a cold March day. That letter still sat in the top of his trunk, waiting for their next stop when he could mail it. If only she would come to the same conclusion, would confess her love for him too, then this torture would be over.

He sat on his cramped bunk staring at Clara's beautiful handwriting on the envelope. He felt as though his heart would explode. Taking a deep breath, he tore it open and pulled out the dainty, rose-scented stationery.

"Dear Mel," it began. "It seems forever since we said farewell. So much has happened I barely know where to begin. Norman Brighton has asked me to marry him!" Mel's face felt hot. Tears stung behind his eyes. "I can't even believe this is happening," her letter continued. "We're planning a Christmas wedding complete with mistletoe and white candles. I hope you have a leave coming up—I would love to have you there…"

Mel couldn't believe it. Why had he taken so long to see what had been in front of his eyes all those years? Now only to lose her. He ran his hand through his hair and rested the letter on the gray wool blanket. He'd finish reading it later. Right now he needed some fresh air.

He headed outside. The Atlantic buffeted the ship as it headed into a stormy horizon. Mel stood on the deck, his hands wrapped around the railing. Sea gulls swooped and dove around him. Salt spray stung his face. He stood for a long time, tears tracing down his face, the ache in his heart wrenching. It was good that there wasn't anyone else around. He needed to be alone. Maybe he'd always be alone, the thought struck him. Clara was gone as surely as the French coastline.

When he went back to his room, he reached for his notepad.

"Dear Clara," he began. "I'm so happy for you. Norman Brighton is the best sort of fellow. I have always held him in the utmost esteem…"

two

The Lake Emily Methodist Church was a magnificent structure. Built in 1905, it was a massive sandstone building with a gray slate roof and a large, square bell tower at one end. The formal flower beds on the grounds were faithfully kept by the retired farmers' wives in the congregation, guaranteeing an abundance of pastel tulips each spring, deep violet pansies and purple irises in the fullness of summer, and orange, red, and white mums as fall trickled in.

Peter and Mae walked across the dark asphalt church parking lot that had been repaved in the not-too-distant past with new bright yellow lines. They made their way through the raspberry-colored door, into the cool foyer, a tiled chessboard in brown and ivory.

They passed the judgment of stern black-and-white photographs of confirmation classes from decades gone. Pausing, Peter pointed to the photo of his grandpa. A young Roy stood straight, in the back row with the other boys, wearing a black suit, his curly hair slicked down. The girls wore white pinafore dresses with dark, buttoned shoes peering from underneath full skirts. Big white bows pulled back perfectly curled ringlets. Not one wore a smile, and the pastor's expression was one of the fiercest piety, daring the children to defy him. Peter had gazed at this same portrait since he was a boy, each time trying to imagine his grandpa at thirteen years old, so somber and distinguished.

Holding hands, the newlyweds walked into the narthex where Mel Johnson, church elder and head usher, waited as he had every Sunday with an eager handshake and a deep-dimpled smile on his fissured face.

21

"What brings the Morgans from St. Paul this fine day?" he asked. Melvin always remembered his name and, Peter suspected, the name of everyone who walked through the doors.

"We're taking Grandma out to lunch."

"Good, good," Melvin said, leaning in close to Peter's ear. "Roy was a good friend. He wrote to me the whole time I was in France during World War II. I'll never forget that. We're going to miss him."

"Thank you, Mr. Johnson," Peter said quietly, meeting his eyes and smiling warmly. "How's Millie?"

Mel raised his eyebrows. "She's doing okay," he said. "She had a bad fall a couple of weeks ago, but she's recovering well. She keeps forgetting to take her medicine, but then I'm a little forgetful these days too."

"Tell her she'll be in our prayers," Peter said.

"Will do." There was that smile again.

"Is Virginia here?" Mae asked.

"She's in her usual spot, near the front with Clara Brighton." He pointed.

The line behind them lengthened. A few other parishioners offered Peter their condolences. Taking their bulletins, Peter and Mae entered the sanctuary.

Thick beams girded the rich honey-hued wood ceiling. A simple cross reached to the peak of the steep walls behind the altar. Stained-glass windows of the apostles lit the pews in expensive shades of blue, gold, and green as if watching over the congregants, each guiding them in their spiritual journey. The Morgans always sat in the pew that St. Peter was in charge of. The disciple had a pained yet prayerful expression, as a rooster stood crowing in the background. As a boy, Peter had figured it was one of Grandma Virginia's chickens and the saint was praying that it wouldn't peck him. Peter smiled warmly at the memory.

When they reached Virginia, she was surrounded by a group of gray-haired ladies talking in whispers. Peter placed his hand on his grandmother's shoulder, and Virginia looked up, wiping her eyes.

Peter and Mae scooted into the pew, and the pipe organ bellowed a rousing Wesley tune. Mae listened to Virginia's high, wobbly voice and Peter's rich baritone blending in a heartwarming duet. After the welcome and a song by the choir, Pastor Alan Hickey strode down the aisle.

"We have a special visitor today," he said in a booming voice as he reached a young family in the back of the church. He gently lifted a tiny baby from its mother's arms. "Dustin Riley is here for the first time. He just got home from the hospital—what day was it, Mary?"

"Thursday." The mother beamed.

"Dustin is the newest member of our church family." Pastor Hickey walked slowly up and down the center aisle, gently holding the baby in his big hands, giving each in the congregation a glimpse of the small, crinkled face. Eyes warmed with delight at the sight of the newborn, as hushed *oohs* and *aahs* accompanied his passing. The choir chided the pastor to bring Dustin up front. After they'd paid their homage, Pastor Hickey walked back down the aisle to a stooped, elderly woman with curly white hair and a thick gray wool sweater.

"Evelyn, would you return Dustin to his parents for us?"

Evelyn rose slowly, her shoulders hunched over, and the pastor laid the baby in her arthritic hands. She looked down, her face aglow with pride, and carefully tucked the blanket around little Dustin. Then she shuffled down the aisle, in no particular hurry, and paused near the waiting parents. Bending shakily, she gently kissed the tiny brow and gingerly handed him back to his mother.

Mae's eyes welled with tears at the sight. The frail elderly woman, so sweet and gentle, the baby so small and helpless. The old welcoming the new. This was the sense of belonging Peter had spoken of. She wanted this connection in her own life too, she realized, where people took the time to greet a new life instead of rushing past it with a bouquet of flowers and a hastily scrawled "Congrats."

As the organ played and the congregation filed out after the service, the pastor leaned his six-foot frame down to Virginia's ear, taking her hand in his. "Virginia, it looks as though you have company," he said loudly into her ear.

"I sure do," she replied.

"It's nice to have you with us again, Peter," the pastor said. "And Mae, isn't it?"

"Thank you," Peter returned.

The pastor turned to greet those in line behind them, and Virginia whispered to Mae as they moved away, "I hate it when he does that— I'm old, not deaf! He's going to break my eardrum one of these days!" Mae laughed. "Come, I want you to meet Ella," Virginia said.

They made their way across the foyer, and Virginia squeezed the arm of a woman in a sharp-looking lavender suit. She seemed Virginia's age, with silver hair pulled back in a bun. She had a bend to her back and silver bifocals that rode on the end of her slightly hooked nose. "Ella, I want you to meet my grandson Peter's wife, Mae."

Ella smiled broadly. She took Mae's hand in both of hers. "It's so nice to meet you, dear. Virginia has told me all about you. I'm sorry we lost Roy before you really got to know him." Ella reached to take Peter's hand. "Peter, you look as dashing as ever." She leaned in and whispered, "I'll take good care of Virginia for you."

"I know. She's in good hands," Peter said.

"You two, stop your whispering," Virginia said teasingly.

"How long have you been friends?" Mae asked Virginia.

"Ever since she stole my boyfriend and married him," Ella replied with a girlish gleam in her eyes.

"Oh, you!" Virginia said, scolding. "Ella and Roy fought like cats and dogs; there was never any hope they'd make a go of it."

"She's right, you know," Ella said. "Roy fared much better with Virginia than he would have with me. And I can't cook nearly as well as Virginia can. He'd have starved to death."

Virginia grew quiet, and Ella put an arm around her like best friends in grade school. "Besides, my Jerry needed someone to nag him!" Ella continued.

Virginia patted Ella's hand on her shoulder and said, "I'm okay, dear."

After a moment, Ella turned to Peter and said, "So you're taking Virginia to lunch."

"Yes. We need to talk about the farm," Peter said.

"That sounds interesting," Ella said, raising an eyebrow at Virginia.

VERNON ELWOOD

The January sun was painfully bright on that cold day in 1933. Frost from the night before christened the trees in white as if a painter had taken a brush and traced each branch. The woods sparkled like living jewels around the Millers' pond. The ice was perfect, not a ripple, and no snow to shovel. A great day for hockey.

Eleven-year-old Jim Miller and his buddy Vernon Elwood sat on a downed tree, tying the laces on their black skates.

"Are you ready for my big slap shot, Vernon?" Jim teased his lanky friend.

Vernon was concentrating hard, making sure his double knot was secure before he looked up and said, "You'll make the hockey team, no problem. You're such a worrywart."

"Who's worried? I'm hopin' you're ready to guard that goal."

Picking up his hockey stick, Jim flipped the puck into the middle of the pond, gliding from one end to the other, keeping the disk perfectly positioned in front of him. He floated gracefully, despite his bulky winter clothes. Up and back he skated, the stick switching from left to right, keeping the puck always under his control. He'd practiced every winter to perfect his form, and his diligence showed. He smiled up at Vern. "Hey, watch this!" he shouted. "I'm going to put it right in the sweet spot." He skated to the far end of the pond and stopped, facing the goal for the showdown.

A loud, ominous crack filled the quiet. Jim froze, and a terror flashed through him as the ice around him suddenly tilted and gave way. He reached out desperately, plunging into the black water, sinking deep into its freezing depths. It was colder than anything he'd ever felt before. His face and hands tingled like a thousand pinpricks. Struggling toward the surface, his coat a heavy shroud, he bumped hard against the icy ceiling. Desperate, he grappled to find the opening until he saw the sunlight off to the left. Jim swam with all his might, came up for a deep, gasping breath of air, and heard his name as if from far away.

"Jim!"

It was Vernon. He lay on his belly, his arms stretching toward his friend. Jim's hands were already numb, his legs dead weights. Through sheer force of will he propelled himself toward those arms, a last panicked, desperate act, an unspoken prayer on his lips that he wouldn't go back beneath the darkness.

Vernon grabbed Jim's hands. He balanced on the thin edge of the ice. His grasp ferocious, Vernon tugged Jim up with surprising strength, the two of them sliding back away from the hole. A flow of water followed them, still clinging to Jim's soul.

Silence surrounded them. They inched along the ice on their bellies until they reached the safety of shore, terrified of hearing that cracking sound again. Then they slumped, breathing hard, staring at the crater in the pond.

"We've got to get those skates off of you," Vernon said, working quickly as he knelt before Jim and untied his laces, then pulled the soggy black skates off. He peeled back Jim's socks and dried his white feet with his own red scarf before helping put on his boots. Vernon wrapped his dry coat around Jim's shivering, wet shoulders and helped him stand. The boys walked home in silence.

three

Jim Miller opened the Chuckwagon Café in 1952. Most days of the week he could still be found there, moving from table to table, trading news and jokes with the regulars and laughing his contagious laugh.

True to its era, the Chuckwagon was a white brick building with large windows covering three sides, all slanted outward at the top. The diner was the hub of information for the little town of Lake Emily. The regulars sat and talked about everything from the price of gas and soybeans to state politics and the school board's latest referendum. Sometimes Arvin, the reporter from the *Herald*, would hang around looking for last-minute tidbits to fill the week's pages.

Vernon Elwood sat on the third stool at the red Formica counter, sometimes three meals a day, in his coveralls and a Massey-Ferguson cap. If the restaurant was busy, he'd help out busing or washing tables. He sat there today, a cup of coffee steaming in front of him as Mae, Peter, and Virginia stood in the entry, waiting to be seated.

"Popular place," Mae said of the crowded, noisy café.

"It's the only restaurant in town, but it's the best one and the food's good," Virginia said, her voice trailing off. Her gaze drifted to a booth in the corner.

"Are you okay, Grandma?" Peter asked.

"I will be," she admitted. "I haven't been in here since Roy and I had Sunday dinner two weeks ago at that table. At least this week is over—it gets easier, right?" She clutched her hands in front of herself.

A man with thick eyebrows and gray hair got up from his place at the counter. "Virginia," he said. "I'm so sorry about Roy. I know how hard it is to lose someone."

"Indeed you do. Thank you, Vernon," Virginia said sincerely. Then she turned to Peter and Mae. "This is my grandson Peter and his wife, Mae. This is Vernon Elwood. He farms down the road from us."

Vernon offered his hand to Peter in a strong shake. "Good man, your grandpa," Vernon said. "Always had a kind word for everyone, and he played a mean game of hockey. At least as a boy he did." Virginia's eyes glistened. "Well," Vernon continued, "I don't mean to keep you folks. Let me know if I can be of any help, Virginia."

He returned to his place at the counter, and Virginia leaned close and said, "His family died in a fire years ago when your dad was in high school." Peter's eyes returned to the solitary man, who sat sipping coffee and chatting with the owner.

The waitress, a woman in her fifties with blond hair and suspiciously dark roots, caught their eye. "Over here, buddy," she said. She pointed to a booth in the corner.

"Perfect," Peter said as they followed her.

Once they were all seated, she passed out menus and began her spiel in a scratchy voice. "The special today is a beef commercial with creamed corn or coleslaw—$5.95. I'll get some water for you right away." Then she scooted away to the next table.

"So what's this about the farm?" Virginia asked.

"That can wait. Why don't we order our food first?" Peter said.

"Now you've got me worried," Virginia said, giving Mae a sideways glance.

"Well, all right…" Peter smiled nervously. "We've been thinking about something, and we wanted to talk it over with you."

"Okay," Virginia said.

"We didn't know what you'd think of the idea."

"Get to the point, son. You're as bad as your father."

"I'm getting there, Grandma," Peter protested. "You know that I've been looking for work, and I haven't found the right opportunity—"

"I'm sure something will turn up," Virginia interrupted.

"Well…after we talked at the funeral, I started wondering if there wasn't something right under my nose."

Virginia turned to Mae. "Do you know what he's talking about?"

"I'm afraid I do," she said.

"We want to see what you think of us buying the farm," Peter said.

There was a long silence. Virginia looked at Peter blankly. "What do you know about running a farm?"

Peter held out his hands and shrugged his shoulders. "I can learn. I work hard. I like the idea of being independent, no boss to answer to, no punching a clock—"

"Actually, the cows set the schedule."

"But I don't mind that, Grandma. I've never known what I wanted to do, but now I feel as if a light has gone on inside me. I went to college because I was supposed to. But I never loved psychology. This is the first thing that has ever excited me. The more I think about it, the more certain I am of it. I can learn as I go, learn from my mistakes. I'll take all the advice I can get. I know it's sudden, but Grandpa's death made this crystal clear for me."

Virginia looked at him long and hard and then let out a soft sigh. She turned to Mae. "And where are you in all this craziness?"

Just then the waitress returned for their orders. "Okay, honey, what'll it be?" she asked Peter, who blushed at her endearment.

"I'll have the special, but could I get mashed potatoes instead of the creamed corn?" Peter said, realizing he hadn't even looked at the menu.

"Sure thing." She shrugged her shoulders. She pointed to Mae with her pencil.

Mae ordered a Reuben sandwich, and Virginia opted for the roast pork dinner. Then the waitress disappeared again. They could hear her raspy voice call out the order to the cook.

Mae's eyes met Peter's. She began, "To be honest, I'm not as sure as Peter is. Living with my parents isn't working out, and I'm glad to see Peter excited about something. But I'm a city girl, and truthfully, I'm worried about fitting in, in a small town." She squeezed his hand.

"At least you're honest," Virginia said, tilting her head in thought. Then she stared Peter in the eye. "You remind me of your grandpa." Peter smiled, and then Virginia continued, "He was stubborn too. And he was a dreamer. But he loved farming. Maybe that's why you've always been my favorite—don't tell your cousins." She wrinkled her nose. "But I don't know…"

"You said it was Grandpa's dream to have someone in the family take over for him." Peter knew he was begging, but he couldn't help himself.

Virginia chuckled quietly. "Using my own words against me—it's not fair."

"We'd pay whatever you feel the farm is worth."

"Oh hush," Virginia said. She thought for a moment. "You are right—I would rather keep it in the family, but this would be a big change for you. You haven't grown up farming like most of the men around here. There's no telling if you'll still like it a month from now. Anything seems better if you're looking to get away from a bad situation in St. Paul. Let's not rush into such a big commitment so fast."

She paused to consider. "What would you say to a trial period? Say if you worked the farm for a season? I'd charge you rent, same as any other farmer. A hundred dollars an acre per year plus rent on the house and barn. I imagine we'll have to take out an operating loan, but the monthly check from the creamery and the money you get when you sell the crop should offset that. I can show you Roy's books so you'll know what kind of numbers we're talking here. If you can keep the operation profitable, and you and Mae"—she shifted her gaze—"decide you like the work and living in Lake Emily, we could talk about a long-term arrangement. But I don't want you to have unrealistic expectations. Farming isn't an easy life. There's long hours and plenty of rough spots."

She was actually saying yes. Peter sat forward in his seat, his face beaming. "That sounds great! What do you think, Mae?" He turned to his wife.

"Watch out, honey," the waitress interrupted, "these plates are coming in hot and heavy!" She set their meals in front of them. "You must love mashed potatoes." The waitress glanced at Peter.

There were two huge scoops of potatoes on his plate, one covered with beef and gravy on top of a slice of bread, the other with just gravy. Chagrined, he looked over at his grandmother as the waitress disappeared again. "I guess I didn't know what a beef commercial was," Peter admitted sheepishly.

"She didn't get us any silverware either," Virginia said. She scooted over on the vinyl seat and got up to rob some from a nearby table.

After Peter said grace, Virginia continued, "Now, where were we?"

"I think we're waiting to hear from Mae," Peter said.

Mae took a deep breath and began, "When Pastor Hickey carried that baby to the old woman—Evelyn, wasn't it?—there was something that really spoke to me. I felt God whispering in my ear that I need to take a new look at things. I don't know what that all means, but I'm not so afraid anymore. I guess what I'm saying is, I'm willing to give it a try."

"What about your job at the flower shop?" Peter asked.

"Seemed there was always plenty of work for me at the farm without traipsing to town for more—but then you young people do things differently nowadays," Virginia said.

"I'll look around and see what I can find nearby. I'm not in a hurry to start a new job, but I'm sure we could use the income."

Peter couldn't seem to stop smiling. "We're talking like this is a done deal," he said.

"I suppose it is," Virginia said.

"So when do we start?" Peter said.

"Bert Biddle has been taking care of things for a while now, so I guess the sooner the better. How does tomorrow sound? Bert can teach you the ropes better than I can—and he's a bit more agile at tossing bales around the hayloft and getting the cows into the barn." She winked. "Milking starts around six. That okay?"

"Is that A.M.?" Mae asked. Virginia and Peter both laughed.

"Would you like to come over too, Mae? Not at six, of course, but maybe after you get off work, while the men do their evening milking. We could have coffee and get better acquainted," Virginia said.

"I'd like that," Mae said.

"You're going to do what?" Catherine was incredulous. Mae had known her mother would react this way. It was the whole reason she'd wanted to put off telling her.

"We talked to Peter's grandmother, and we've decided to move to Lake Emily to run the family farm."

"Peter doesn't know anything about farming. This is a failed proposition before it even starts. What makes him think he'll make any money milking cows?"

"You're the one who said he needed to get out there."

"And work his way up the corporate ladder, not the hayloft! How could you have agreed to such a lamebrained scheme? You'll be miserable out in the middle of nowhere."

"I'll be happy as long as I'm with Peter," Mae retorted.

"For how long?" Catherine responded. "You're young. A husband can't be your happiness forever. At some point you're going to wake up and discover that he has flaws. You have so much promise. What about your cello? I thought you were going to pursue your music once you graduated from college."

"That was your dream, Mom. I don't have any passion for it."

"You limit yourself, Mae. And now you're going to waste away in some boring little backward town."

Mae didn't know what made her more angry—being told she had no common sense or being treated like a child.

"You're going to end up just like your sister."

"What does that mean?"

"You know how Trudy pushes me to see how much of her craziness I'll take."

"Craziness? Mom, she's a teacher. She loves kids. She's creative, intelligent, and happy. Why isn't that enough? You honestly think she lives her whole life to spite you?"

"She's irresponsible. I was hoping for better from you. Mae, farming is a hard life. It's…it's beneath you. Why would you want this for yourself?"

"It isn't only hardship, Mom. There's a lot that's good about farming—"

"Peter," Catherine exhaled. "I knew he'd bring you trouble. Doesn't he care about you at all, look out for what's best for you? This is going to tear your marriage apart."

"Mother!" Mae shouted as tears filled her eyes. "Peter's my husband and I love him. He isn't dragging me away against my will. I want to do this, so don't blame him!" Her face turned hot. She'd never spoken back to her mother. Her daughter-guilt pointed its gnarled finger at her. "If you're going to try to come between us this way, then I'm afraid—" Her words broke off. "I'm afraid—" She knew what she needed to say, and yet her courage waned.

"What?" Catherine's mouth hung open.

"That this is the end of our relationship." There. She'd said it, yet she immediately regretted her words.

Catherine sputtered. "You would put him before your own mother?"

"I don't want this any more than you do, Mom, but you're forcing me to choose."

"I can't believe you're saying this. I only want what's best for you."

"What's best for me is that I make my own decisions, Peter and I together, whether you agree or not."

P eter shut off the engine and sat on the gravel drive. It was 5:30
A.M., half an hour early for his first day of milking. There wasn't
another soul in sight. The sky was just beginning its morning show, and
the yard light began to dim. He got out of his old green Chevy truck
and stood, inhaling the day. The morning air was crisp and cool. The
sky was a pale canvas, ready to be painted in shades of orchid and pink.
Faint pinpricks of starlight shone through the lavender sky, and the
moon hung low in the west, ready for its shift to end.

Peter walked over to the old machine shop and opened the door.
The interior was dark, and he felt along the wall for the switch, flicking
it on and flooding the big room with yellow light from the overhead
bulb. This had been his grandfather's favorite place. He and Peter had
put together the bicycle Peter had gotten for his tenth birthday in this
room. The big John Deere tractor and the combine sat in their usual
spots at the back of the building, waiting their turn to come outside and
play. The wall on the left was covered in tools that hung on pegs all
neatly lined up, and a long worktable stretched the length underneath
it. Peter walked to it and ran his hand along the rough surface filled with
dents and scratches. Grandfather's worktable, where he had toiled all
those years, where he'd given his life. Peter reached for a wrench from
the Peg-Board, wondering if anyone had touched it since Roy had. It
was cold and heavy.

There was an aura of reverence in the room. This wasn't a job he
was taking on—this was his grandfather's legacy, something to treasure

and hold as a fragile gift. Peter put the wrench back on the hook and turned to face the quiet. "I won't fail you, Grandpa," he whispered, "I won't fail you." He closed his eyes, listened to the ticking of the clock on the wall. The scent of diesel fuel and motor oil lingered. Specks of dust glittered golden as they danced in beams of pale sunlight.

Then, turning out the lights, he made his way to the barn. The warm humid breath of cattle poured out when he opened the door. The sweet smell of hay and manure mingled in warm memories. Peter loved this smell. It reminded him of warm summer days playing in the loft of this barn as a kid, swinging out on a rope over the big open area below and dropping into a huge mound of hay. He would lie motionless in the softness as little pieces of the dry grass poked at him through his shirt.

The ceiling hung low in the milking parlor, ramparts of thick wood bracing against the weight of the hay above. The walls were painted in many layers of bright white, giving the interior a clean, cheery feel. Cows meandered in the main section of the barn while some lay on their sides, chewing their cud. One cow wandered over to Peter, and he patted her head. She nudged into him and licked his hand with her sandpaper tongue. Peter laughed. "You're hungry, are you?"

"Mornin'," a voice sounded from the door. Peter looked over to see Bert Biddle in white coveralls enter.

"Good morning." Peter held out a hand and the two shook.

"Your grandma called," Bert said. He was almost identical in looks to his brother—same tall, lanky frame and dishwater blond hair, although Bert's was covered by a green seed cap.

"I don't remember too much about farming, so you'll have to go slow," Peter said.

Bert nodded. "We should get going then," he said. "Here, put these on." He threw another pair of coveralls to Peter, walked over to the big silver tank in the next room, and began opening a valve. Peter tugged on the one-piece suit. It was snug in the seat, and the hem rode a good four inches from the ground.

"Are these yours?" Peter asked when Bert came back out, noting that Bert was about the same height as him.

Bert's eyes went to the hem. "Nope. They were Roy's." Then he said, "You can come with me. We milk 'em eight at a time, track 'em by their number." He pointed to the red tags that pierced the heifer's ears. "That way you know what their production levels are, as well as their breeding history, that sort of thing."

Peter touched the first heifer's tag and watched as Bert lined the girls up to come in. The cows began meandering into the parlor, but when the first ones saw Peter they backed up, causing a bottleneck at the door.

"What's wrong?" Peter called to Bert.

"You're going to have to hide," Bert said. "They won't come in if they see you. They like everything to be the same." Peter stood behind the door that led to the milk tank and waited while the sound of clanging filled the room.

"You can come back," Bert called.

When he returned, Peter saw eight heifers lined up in the stanchions, four on each side, with their necks held in place by steel bars that locked shut when they moved into position. They looked suspiciously back at Peter as if to say, "Who's the new guy?"

Next Bert motioned Peter to a five-gallon bucket of clear solution. "This disinfects the suction cups," Bert explained, setting a spiderlike device with four black tubes into the bucket to soak. "We wash 'em down," Bert continued, "with this." He held up a spray nozzle at the end of a long, curled blue hose. He positioned the nozzle under the first cow's teats and sprayed it. "It's an iodine-based mix that disinfects. Let that soak in for, oh, thirty seconds and then wipe it down like this." He took a paper towel from one of the dispensers that were mounted between the stanchions and began to wipe off the heifer's udder. When Bert had finished, he reached for the tubes in the bucket, shook off the excess liquid, and attached each cup to a teat. Bert went to the cow waiting stolidly in the next stall and repeated the procedure while Peter watched closely.

"You want to give it a try?" Bert asked.

"Sure." Peter soaked the tubes and then disinfected the teats, carefully wiping each off before attaching the suction cups.

"You have to push this button." Bert pointed. "It releases the line so the cups can lower and raise." Peter hadn't noticed the thin rope attached to the tube's main line. "Keeps it off the floor," Bert said. "When the machine senses that they aren't giving any more milk, that'll pull the cups off the teats automatically."

"That's handy," Peter commented. Bert gave a nod and moved to the fourth cow. Peter took up the pace, and soon the mechanical sound of pumping filled the barn. The white milk moved through the clear tubes in a steady stream as the cows munched contentedly in their stalls.

Peter and Bert stood back and watched, hands in pockets. "You've got sixty or seventy head right now," Bert said. "That's not a bad number. Roy always kept most of the heifers that were born to rotate into the stock. Culled the old ones. 'Course, you can milk them for a lot of years. My dad had some he milked well into their twenties."

"And the bull calves?" Peter asked.

"Auction."

Peter nodded.

"We've been artificially inseminating since the sixties. You can pick a stud from a catalog. Had pretty good luck with calving," Bert said, walking over to the first cow who had finished giving milk. He sprayed her with the solution again, then pulled a lever that released the bars holding her neck. The heifer moved forward, around the outside perimeter of the parlor and to the door that was open to the outside. "I wait until I have two or three open stalls to go get some more. Saves me some walking." He turned red and smiled bashfully. "You can hide between a couple that are still being milked when I go for the next few," Bert said.

One cow on the far side let out a big cow pie, and Bert grabbed a large squeegee and pushed the mess off to the side. When the third cow was done, Bert returned to the main barn and tapped a few rumps to get the ladies moving. Peter watched from around a heifer. They ambled into the parlor and stepped up into the open stalls, the bars clanging shut around their necks.

"They seem to know what to do," Peter commented.

"They like their routine, all right," Bert said.

Peter and Bert went back to washing udders, putting tubes on teats, and watching as the machine did the hard work.

Peter glanced out toward the barn and saw that one cow had come up to the doorway of the barn. She stood watching with interest. "She looks eager," Peter said.

"She's a tease. She'll be the last one," Bert said. "Does that every time. When I go to fetch them she'll go to the back and hide." He chuckled.

"Do you know all the cows that well?"

"Some of 'em." Bert shrugged. " 'Course, I know ours a lot better. But when you hang around 'em seven, eight hours a day, you learn their personalities." It was 10:30 by the time they'd milked the last cow.

"We have the calves to feed too, out in those plastic igloos around back," Bert said. "Then we'll feed the heifers."

They walked into the room with the big tank and mixed three bottles of powdered milk replacer with warm water for the calves, who took their bottles eagerly. Once that was done, Bert fired up the diesel engine of the old Oliver. Peter walked behind as Bert moved toward the long roll of silage covered with white plastic that stretched along the west side of the windbreak. The big bucket scooped the fermented feed and then backed up to return to the pasture. Peter opened the gate, and Bert dumped the silage into the feed trough. The cows eagerly lined up for their breakfast in a procession of swishing tails.

Peter and Bert walked over to the water trough. One black-and-white heifer dipped her head to drink. Liquid brown eyes gazed back beneath long lashes at Peter as she gulped. "They drink a lot of water"—Bert pointed to the floating valve atop the stock tank—"so you're gonna have to make sure the well's working. Had some problems with it awhile back."

Peter nodded.

By eleven they were done, and they began hosing down the stanchions and cleaning everything for the next milking.

Shortly before noon the big silver Lake Co-op Dairy truck pulled up to the barn. A short, round man hopped down and reached for a long hose on the back of the truck. "Ed," Bert called, "like you to meet Peter Morgan. He's going to be taking things over here," Bert informed the stout little man who held out a hand.

"Ed Smee," he said, his smile huge in his small, wrinkled face. "Nice to meet you. You from this area?"

"St. Paul actually," Peter said. The man looked at Bert as an expression of skepticism flickered on his face.

"I pick up the milk every other day. I test it before I pump to make sure everything's legal."

"Could I watch that?" Peter asked.

"Sure."

Peter walked with the man and stood to the side while Ed filled a cup with the foamy milk and began his test. "We do this to make sure there aren't any trace antibiotics, contaminants, that kind of thing, in the milk." Then he hooked up the hose to the tank in the barn. Peter could hear the phone ring in the other side. He walked over to answer it while Ed stood by the truck. But Bert had already gotten it. His face was red, and he clutched the receiver tightly.

"I said I'll be there in an hour," Bert said tersely before hanging up.

"You need to get going?" Peter asked.

"It's just Fred." Bert shrugged his shoulders.

"Say, thanks for showing me the ropes," Peter said.

"We need to clean out the tank once Ed's all done," Bert said. "I'll show you that. It's pretty simple, automated like a dishwasher."

When they got to the truck, Ed was putting the long hose away. "That ought to do you for now," Ed said.

"So we'll see you again day after tomorrow?" Peter said.

"Yep," Ed said. "At the crack of noon." He gave a little cackle, then turned to go. The bullet-shaped truck backed up and then pulled around in the circular driveway. Ed gave a quick wave before turning onto the dirt road.

"I was going to show you how to clean the tank," Bert said, leading the way back inside the barn.

Peter caught up with Bert and asked, "How long have you been helping my grandpa?"

Bert thought for a moment. "A couple of months, I guess. He got real sick in February or so. That was when he hired me."

"And Fred can handle running your place by himself?"

"He can handle it."

Mae's white Jeep Cherokee pulled into the gravel driveway and turned toward the big red barn. Peter had been working with Bert somewhere in its depths since the wee hours of the day. Its peeling paint revealed weathered wood beneath, but it had a new green roof. Faded white trim accented the building, with crisscross trusses on the split door to the left of the white silo and four-pane windows spaced evenly along its length. Virginia's gray-muzzled yellow Lab, Scout, barked a lazy warning. Mae put the gearshift into park and got out.

Mae felt good to be here. The two-hour drive from St. Paul had become a transformation of place and soul. There was a calm that never seemed to leave this place. Birds chirped and twittered in the grove, and a black-and-white cat sauntered across the lawn. The air was filled with the promise of coming spring.

Mae stood in silence, surveying the miles of farmland that would become a part of her daily vision. The sun brightened the misty river valley to the west, and horses grazed along the perimeter of the woods in the distance. This was God's creation, laid out for their pleasure, something to breathe in deeply and never take for granted. Mae needed a healing peace like this. After the run-in with her mother, Peter had told her how proud he was of her, but she didn't feel proud. She'd tossed all night, her mind rehashing their argument. She awoke in tears, and Peter had held her until it was time to leave for the morning milking.

The screen door screeched open, and Virginia stepped onto the back porch.

"Good afternoon, dear," Virginia called. She hobbled across the gravel driveway and stood gazing at the distance with Mae a moment, then sighed that heavy sigh and turned with a smile. "Come on in. I've got the coffee on."

The house smelled heavenly, of fresh coffee and baked goods. A plate of oatmeal cookies cooled on the counter. Mae gazed around the century-old home.

"Would you like a tour?" Virginia offered.

"That would be wonderful," Mae replied. "It was so crowded at the funeral I really didn't have a chance to see it."

"Not much has changed since we moved in," Virginia said. "Roy wasn't much for working around the house when there were tractors to repair and barns to paint or, for that matter, any other excuse. He was such a saver, not a spender really."

Virginia opened the door to the entry closet, and Mae hung up her Windbreaker. Roy's tan coveralls still hung on the hook. Virginia's hand tenderly brushed the dirt-stained fabric. "Roy would take his Carhartts off, and he'd wash his hands"—she pointed to the sink next to the closet—"when he came in from chores."

A sadness settled in Virginia's pale eyes. She looked up at Mae and lifted her lips in a faint smile. "I'm having one of those days, it seems. Sometimes I'm fine. I can go about life as if everything's the same, and then there are days like today... Everything holds a memory."

"We could go into town for coffee—"

"No. I don't want to run away today."

The first floor had tall ceilings and thick oak moldings and windows with beveled glass inset in the top. The window sills were adorned with colored jars that sent rainbows of light into the room. Doilies comforted the backs of the padded chairs. The kitchen had a cozy eating nook to the side and adjoined a larger, elegant dining room to the left with a built-in hutch that held pink-petaled china and thick crystal pitchers. "My mother's china," Virginia pointed out. The table was an impressive piece, a dark walnut, with intricately carved legs that resembled a falcon's claws holding a ball.

Virginia inched cautiously up the creaking stairs, a firm grip on the thick oak railing as Mae trailed behind.

"I put up new wallpaper in 1975," Virginia said, referring to the hallway. "I remember because that was the year Peter was born. It was one of the few chores I got Roy to help with. We had such a time putting up that old paper. Fought so much, we about lost our salvation!" She grinned and stopped under the entry to the hall and pointed at the door-frame. "Here's where David marked his height. Five foot eight—he so wanted to make six feet. But Roy and I are such short people, you know, David really didn't have much chance at that. Now, Peter, he got his height from Laura's side of the family."

Mae took a closer look. There were pencil marks of varying heights inscribed on the dark wood trim with "David" and a date written next to each. Mae put her finger on the highest mark that was labeled "S. M."

"It always irked David that his little sister, Sarah, was taller than him," Virginia said with a smile.

"I always wanted to be taller than Trudy too," Mae said.

They returned to the kitchen where Virginia readied a tray with two dainty cups and a carafe of coffee. Then she filled a sugar bowl and creamer pitcher, placed everything on the tray, and led Mae to the dining room.

"We can sit out here," she said. "It's so much nicer. Cream and sugar, right?" Mae nodded. "I'll have to remember that," Virginia said. After she'd filled the cups, she gazed up at the old hutch. "Roy bought me those," she said, pointing to a collection of Hummel figurines hiding amid the dishes—little ceramic boys and girls, some holding umbrellas, some sitting on stools in an assortment of childhood poses. "He was stationed in Austria, so every once in a while he'd see one in the window that caught his eye. And then after he got back, he'd still buy them. I have over thirty, all told." She laughed. "It was his weakness. Never did know when enough was enough. I have them packed away everywhere!" Her eyes took on a misty quality. "I miss him. I feel closer to him whenever I look at them. Isn't that silly?"

"Not silly at all," Mae said. There was a long silence.

"Tell me about you and Roy," Mae probed after a few moments.

Virginia's face took on the faraway expression, and her voice became warm, wistful. "I worked in the canning factory when we first met, then I taught school for a while in the brick one-room schoolhouse by the Miller place. Like so many during the war, Roy and I married before he went off for Europe. When he came home from the war, his older brother took over their homeplace, so Roy came here and worked for Wilbur Kreitzer as a hired hand." She took a sip of her coffee.

"Wilbur was a nice man, a bachelor all his life. When he was in his late fifties, he came down with Alzheimer's, although we didn't call it Alzheimer's in those days. It was old age. He ended up moving into town and then the nursing home. Wilbur sold us the farm." She smiled at some memory. "You could tell a bachelor had been living here for years. Oh, was he a pack rat! Stacks of magazines and newspapers everywhere. He hadn't done a thing to maintain the place—but that's a farmer, isn't it? Keeps the barn painted, but wouldn't hang a closet door to save his life. The house just stunk; it took me weeks with all the windows open to get the musty smell out! I had to burn the curtains and buy new ones. There wasn't a cupboard in the whole place, so I had these built special by Lew Olson—he had a shop in Rush River."

Virginia took another sip of her coffee and continued her story. "Roy was like a son to Wilbur before he went into the home. They did everything together—farmed, hunted, fished. I was glad for it—Wilbur was a wonderful man, and it kept Roy from getting in my way around the house!" She smirked.

" 'Course, I did the cooking for both of them when they were working. And how they enjoyed eating! I liked to see the smiles on their faces when they'd come in to a hearty meal. Wilbur always liked my roast chicken—of course, I raised them myself. I don't know, I guess it sounds silly nowadays, with women all working and everything. But taking care of those men was good enough for me." Virginia sighed and took a sip of her coffee.

"When did you start your family?" Mae prompted.

"We got married, and whenever the children decided to start coming was fine by us. Nature's course, I guess. I quit teaching right after Roy and I got married. In those days they frowned on married women teaching. Then we had David in 1950. The white bedroom was his. Sarah followed two years later. We wanted to have more." Her eyes were moist as if she would cry, and her expression was distant. "But I never could after that. I'm so glad you're going to be living here." Virginia rested her hand on Mae's. "This old house needs a family again. A farm is a wonderful place for children to grow up. Farm kids are better set to face the world, I think."

"I'm glad we're coming here too," Mae said. "Especially with you as our family."

"Roy would've been so pleased," Virginia said. "I was telling you about Wilbur Kreitzer, wasn't I? You'll have to keep me on track, dear. My mind does tend to wander."

As Virginia talked, Mae pictured Virginia as a young, slender woman, her hair dark and swept up 1940s style, Roy out in the field on his old tractor, plowing the rich black soil. Virginia watching from the kitchen window, the devoted partner. A true Minnesota farm wife—hardy, strong, uncompromising, faithful. She was Norman Rockwell's Thanksgiving portrait, but with the children grown and moved on to careers and families of their own, and now Roy's death, the table sat empty.

When Virginia grew quiet, they each took another sip of their coffee, and Mae reached to refill the cups. "You said you had chickens?" Mae prompted.

"Oh yes! Always. I had over three hundred birds! Mostly Leghorns. I sold close to forty dozen eggs a week. I always had a hard time getting them clean. They say vinegar is good for cleaning eggs. Are you thinking you'd like to raise some chicks?"

"I don't know. Maybe. Everything is so new to me. I wouldn't have a clue where to begin."

"Well, what kind of chickens would you get?"

Mae gave her a blank look. "Kind? You mean there's more than one?" she said. "What kind would you suggest?"

"I was raising both layers and meat birds—so I had good dual purpose breeds, but if you're going to raise some for meat, you'd probably want Jersey Giants or Barred Rock."

"I'm not sure I could kill an animal…" Mae was certain her face betrayed her squeamishness.

"Let me know when it's slaughtering time, dear. I can help you. I love to slaughter chickens."

"You love to slaughter chickens?" Mae asked, repulsed.

"Heavens, yes. I always liked it when they'd dance around right after you whacked their heads off." Then she smiled a wry smile.

"You're pulling my leg, aren't you?" Mae said, laughing.

"A little," Virginia said. "There's nothing as gratifying as looking in your freezer and seeing a whole shelf of birds you butchered yourself. And they taste so much better than store-bought. Now, Roy, he hated chickens. Always said anything that stupid deserved a break. Never would take care of them, except when the children were born. Then he'd say, 'Now, the chickens take sweet feed, don't they?' As if he didn't know they needed egg mash. He was trying to rile me into getting up and around." She ran her fingertip along the top of her coffee cup.

"Would you like more coffee?" Mae offered.

"No. I've had plenty," Virginia said, then she stood. "We really should go check on those boys. They should be done soon. They'll be looking for something to eat."

"We'll have to do this often," Mae said.

"Yes, we will," Virginia agreed. "We certainly will."

five

The next Saturday Peter wrestled the stuffed chair through the door. "Set it over here," Mae said. He plunked it in a corner before finally slumping to the bed, exhausted.

"For only being married six months, we sure do have a lot of stuff!" Peter wiped his forehead with his sleeve and sat up, reclining on his elbows and looking at the old, familiar place.

The lower half of the bedroom walls were covered in a white wainscoting, and a blue floral wallpaper, now yellowed with age, covered the top half of the walls. The darkened hardwood floor had been worn smooth by years of feet whispering across the shiny surface. Ancient lace curtains dressed rippled-glass windows.

"Has this room changed at all since your dad lived here?" Mae was wandering around the room gazing at the photos, trophies, and other memorabilia of a generation past.

"My mom added the wallpaper and curtains—they lived here for a few months after they first got married. But it's still pretty much a shrine to good old David."

"Don't be sarcastic." Mae looked over her shoulder. She walked toward a shadow-box picture that contained a small violin, a bow, and a black-and-white photo of a fifteen-year-old David playing with the symphony from St. Paul, Minnesota. Peter used to stare at that shadow box when he was a kid, reading the article over and over, wishing he could strum the strings on the little instrument.

"He was quite a prodigy, wasn't he?" Mae said. She gazed at a newspaper clipping with the title "Local Boy Receives Full Scholarship to Julliard."

"Yep," Peter said, remembering countless concerts, his father standing before a full orchestra as he led them in a symphony.

"I'd love to go to one of his concerts."

"We could probably get tickets when he's back from his trip," Peter said nonchalantly. He went over to the tall, darkened oak chest of drawers and stretched out on the floor to reach under it.

"What are you doing?" Mae asked.

"She always kept it here." He stretched his arm to the wall, feeling for the little key. "Still there." He stood up, holding a black skeleton key between his fingers. Mae came to stand next to him. "What's it for?"

"You'll see, my dear," Peter said, lifting his eyebrows.

He carefully slipped the key into the lock on the small top drawer. Pulling it open, he lowered his face and breathed deeply. The scent of faint gardenias filled his memory, and Peter felt himself choke up with the images it evoked of his mother. "This drawer always smelled like Mom." He lifted his head, and Mae bent for a whiff. Then Peter pulled out a floral-printed cloth–covered jewelry box. "Dad said he didn't want to haul her treasures everywhere with all our moves, so he kept them here." He met Mae's eyes. "I think the memories got too hard for him to face."

Peter lifted the lid and gingerly examined a pair of pearl-drop earrings, a school ring from Lake Emily High, and a gold chain with a pale aquamarine pendant.

"They're beautiful," Mae said, lightly fingering them.

Peter lifted the pearls. "She wore these at their wedding," he began. Then the ring, "This was Dad's high-school ring. He gave it to Mom when she was fifteen. And the necklace—my birthstone."

Peter set the box on top of the dresser and reached into the drawer again, retrieving an aged brown leather-bound journal and several embroidered handkerchiefs. "She would sit and write in the evenings after I was supposed to be in bed. I'd watch her pen float across the page and wonder what it was she wrote there."

Peter could still see her long blond hair hanging down. She'd tuck it behind her ear unconsciously, her concentration on the page. Then she'd look up at Peter and smile. "You're supposed to be in bed," she'd scold gently.

"But I didn't kiss you good-night," Peter would say, knowing full well that he had. She'd reach up and peck his cheek and then tousle his short hair.

"I wish she'd known you," Peter said, gazing at Mae.

"Someday I'll meet her," Mae said. She reached out and took his hand.

That night after supper dishes were done and Virginia had gone up to her bedroom, Peter grabbed Mae's hand and whisked her out the door to the porch.

Mae's eyes glowed. "What's this all about?"

"Take a deep breath," Peter said, pausing. Mae drew in the cool air that held a tinge of sweetness. "Isn't it incredible?" he said.

"You're cute."

"Come with me." He pulled her along. The sun dipped low in the orchid sky, and wispy clouds feathered across the horizon in bold shades of pink. Pine trees had shoots of new growth like sparklers on the Fourth of July. The brown grasses were gone, replaced by a pale carpet of green. "By July this field will be full of fireflies," he said, looking over at her. "When I was little I would catch enough of them to make a lantern." He stopped and turned around. "I've always felt as if God was right here. So close I could touch him."

"It's beautiful," she breathed, resting her head on his shoulder.

"Let's go in the barn." They strolled hand in hand as the sunset bathed the barn in pumpkin orange. All was quiet except for the sparrows that flitted from post to post, annoyed by their intrusion. From inside, Peter could see the herd through the open door, conspiring together under an old oak, their rumps to the north in a line of swishing tails.

Peter and Mae climbed the ladder to the haymow, a hushed cathedral with shafts of dusty light seeping through cracks in the walls. The sweet scent of hay filled his senses. He reached for a bale and pulled a four-inch cube from the end. "A treat," he said to Mae. Then they climbed back down and out to the pasture. Peter gave a handful to Mae to hold out to the animals. A black-and-white Holstein, more pepper than salt, ambled over. Peter patted its neck, and the heifer rubbed her head into his shoulder.

"Will she hurt me?" Mae asked, standing back.

"She's gentle as a lamb."

The cow turned her head to look at Mae.

"What's her name?"

"She's a cow—they don't have names."

Mae put her hand tentatively on the heifer's side and began stroking. The cow flicked her tail at Mae's back. "Hey!" Mae yelped and jumped. Peter laughed. "Why did she do that?" she asked.

"She thought you were a fly. Try not to tickle her. Don't be afraid. She won't hurt you."

Mae inched closer and rubbed the animal on the hip. "You really like all this, don't you, Peter?"

"Yeah," Peter admitted. "It's like finally coming home."

A pair of swallows swooped out of the barn and rose into the evening sky.

Peter stood and stared at the black field.

"You know what puzzles me?" he said.

"What?" Mae moved next to him and wrapped an arm around his waist.

"How my dad could leave this."

"I don't know," Mae said. "It certainly seems perfect."

Virginia and Mae had already made five stops, looking at strangers' homes for sale. Peter had told them to go ahead without him since he needed to finish milking.

They had tried to convince Virginia to stay on at the farm, at least during their trial period, telling her it was too soon, she shouldn't rush things. But Virginia insisted, "I'm moving whether you take over the farm or someone else does. I'm not going to sit on my hands and wait for who knows how long. If there's one thing I've learned, it's that I have to keep going or I'll start feeling sorry for myself." Then they argued that it would cost her too much with all of Roy's medical bills, to which she replied, "We had good insurance. That was one thing Roy wouldn't skimp on. He didn't want to leave me destitute. We had a little nest egg, so you have no cause to worry." That had essentially ended the conversation. Mae wished she could get her to change her mind, but decided if she couldn't she could at least stay nearby to help wherever Virginia needed it.

"This one just came on the market," the Realtor announced from the front seat as he pulled into the drive.

Virginia gasped when she saw the place. Mae quickly cupped a hand over the older woman's ear and whispered, "Don't let him know you love it—it'll take away all your bargaining power."

Virginia nodded and put on a stern expression, but the excitement never left her eyes.

It was a white Cape Cod with two narrow dormers peeking from the upstairs. The windows had green shutters with pine-tree cutouts, revealing the white clapboard beneath. The curved brick sidewalk leading to the front door was lined with thick rosebushes, their yellow buds just visible.

Ron Dugan, the tall, spindly Realtor, came around his Chevy Suburban to open the door for Virginia and Mae.

"She's a beaut, ain't she?" Ron said. "Bee-u-tee-ful."

"Not too bad," Virginia said. She glanced at Mae.

"The owners said they'd be willing to put vinyl siding up if repainting was a concern—"

"Heavens no!" Virginia said. "I hate plastic houses."

They reached the six-panel front door, and Ron unlocked it and held it open for them to enter. An open staircase greeted them. Hardwood floors warmed every room, with thick woven rugs scattered in conversation nooks. Virginia led the way into a den on the right. It was masculine in décor, with brown leather chairs, a Jesse James wanted poster on one wall, and a gun case with a collection of old pistols.

"Roy would've liked this," Virginia commented as she peered out the long side window to the driveway.

The kitchen, a small butter-yellow-and-white room, had a deep white ceramic sink and tall cupboards that reached to the ceiling. A lilac-enclosed backyard visible through the kitchen window gave the home a private feeling. "This isn't as big as the kitchen on the farm," Mae said, trying to sound disapproving.

"I'll be cooking for just me now," Virginia replied. "This is nice. I could get used to puttering around a little kitchen without having so much to clean." She opened the oven and gazed into its depths. "Self-cleaning. I like that." Mae shook her head at Virginia and nodded slightly toward the Realtor. Virginia cleared her throat. "Of course, I will be doing some entertaining too…"

Ron walked ahead into the dining room, the third room in the circle, where a round table sat in a bay window with padded seating built in around it. A large cuckoo clock sounded the hour on the wall across from it. "Roy bought me a cuckoo clock after the war," Virginia said to no one in particular, gazing at the tilting bird before it disappeared behind its door.

"I'd have to get a new table," she said, surveying the room again. "My big farmhouse table would never fit in this *tiny* room." She winked at Mae.

The last room on the first floor was the living room. It ran the entire length of the west side of the house. Dappled light shone through lace curtains, and a Ben Franklin fireplace sat ready on a brick hearth. Next to the arched doorway at the front of the room, two inset shelves held an array of fragile teacups and little ceramic dolls from faraway places. "Whoever lives here likes to travel, or at least they have friends who do," Virginia said. "You can tell so much about a person by what they keep in their home, what they have nearby to comfort themselves in their lonely hours." She fell silent for a moment before saying, "My Hummels would go nicely here, don't you think, Mae?"

Mae nodded mutely.

"When did you say this was built?" Virginia asked, turning toward the real-estate agent.

"In 1948," Ron said. "By the same people who are selling it, actually. It's a good, solid home."

"The inspector will be the judge of that," Virginia said. Mae quirked a surprised brow.

Ron seemed unflustered. "The wife is going into the nursing home in St. Peter. The husband said he'd rather be with his wife there than wandering around this old place by himself. The Kreniks, do you know them?"

"I've heard the name but can't say as our paths have crossed," Virginia said. "Maybe they're Catholic. How old are the hot water heater and furnace?"

Ron pulled out his paperwork, shuffling for the information. "Says here they're both two years old." He smiled a cheesy smile. "Can't get much better than that—they've had time to get broken in so you know they're solid but not worn out."

"H'm," Virginia replied as she walked to the stairs. The Realtor waited downstairs while Mae and Virginia explored.

A deep-red carpet ran down the center of the wooden steps. Virginia held on to the sturdy railing as they made their way past generations of family photos. The upstairs was all nooks and crannies, with deep, narrow closets and built-in dressers, sloping ceilings, and gingham curtains. Stuffed chairs relaxed in the dormers that overlooked the street. One bedroom held a shadow box of beautiful pocket watches. A big orange tabby lounged luxuriously on a handmade quilt on the bed.

"Isn't she pretty?" Virginia said. "I always wanted an indoor cat, but Roy wasn't too fond of livestock in the house." She chuckled and petted the thick fur as the cat rewarded her with a big purr.

"You'll bring your dog along, won't you?" Mae asked.

"Scout?" Virginia said. "It'd be cruel to bring a farm dog to town. He's used to having the run of the place; to confine him in a little yard—I'm sorry, but he goes with the house, if that's okay."

"I thought you might be attached to him," Mae said.

"That's a lesson you'll learn quick—farm animals have jobs. They aren't pets." She stroked the cat's fur one last time before they turned to go downstairs.

Ron was waiting at the bottom. "How much did you say they were asking?" Virginia asked.

"Sixty thousand," Ron said.

Virginia looked around.

"I have one more house on our tour," he said.

"No need," Virginia said. "Let's go fill out the paperwork on this one."

Ron smiled broadly at Mae.

"But," Virginia said, "I'm not paying a penny over fifty-five thousand. I know the market value; fifty-four five is generous. If these people think they're gonna nickel-and-dime me, I'll walk."

Mae's mouth dropped open as Virginia walked past her with a wily grin on her face.

JERRY SHRUPP

May of 1972 was warm and green, ready to welcome the summer. Seventeen-year-old Jerry Shrupp had been plowing in the fields all morning, a copy of Hot Rod *magazine tucked next to him on the tractor seat. He'd been thinking about his best friend, David Morgan, and wondering how two people who were so different could be such good friends.*

David was still struggling with what to do after high school. But not Jerry. Like his father and grandfather before him, Jerry knew farming was the life for him. There was nothing like being alone with the earth, feeling the wind ruffle his hair, watching a hawk float overhead or a mouse scurry down the row ahead of the big tractor. Farming never failed him. It always offered more than he expected.

But David had choices to make—leave Lake Emily for Juilliard or stay and farm with his own dad. If Jerry had been given a gift of music like David's, some ability beyond driving a tractor, perhaps it'd be a struggle for him, too. Jerry couldn't imagine having to decide.

Right now life was good. Jerry's grades were decent. He'd made the basketball team. If only he could get Mary Peterson to acknowledge that he was alive, everything would be perfect. She was the most beautiful girl in Lake Emily. She had the softest long, curly blond hair and dazzling blue eyes. Every boy in school drooled whenever she gave her sweet dimples a showing. Jerry had no chance with her—he knew it as well as he knew the farm. He was tall and gangly, and his bright red hair stuck out even though he tried his best to tame it. And he was a farmer. That didn't help him any. No girl, especially a girl as amazing as Mary Peterson, would look at him twice.

Suddenly the tractor lurched. Jerry's head snapped to attention as he saw the front wheel disappear into the drainage ditch. Jerry instinctively turned the wheel and slammed on the brakes as the tractor moaned and tilted in slow motion and began to flip. He scrambled to jump free, pushing desperately off the seat as he launched toward the safety of the dirt.

He landed on his back with a thud, and instantly a searing pain coursed through his body. Jerry looked over his shoulder to see the tractor overturned. Its rear fender pressed viciously against his right leg. The motor coughed and died. All was silent. As the panic of his predicament struck him, Jerry let out a howling cry. He dug his hands into the mud and tore frantically against the trap. He swung his head around, searching for an answer, crying out for help. He could feel the web of blackness lurking, surging toward him. And then there was nothing.

The sound of a vehicle on the dirt road brought Jerry back. A truck pulled ahead of the tractor alongside the ditch and backed up to the far side of the sleeping monster. Roy Morgan, David's dad, lay down in the wet ditch and peered hard at Jerry's eyes. "I saw the whole thing, J. D. We're gonna get you out of here."

"I'm okay," Jerry whispered. "I'm stuck."

"I radioed for help. You hang on."

Roy was sweating in the midday heat as he hooked the long chain onto the tractor. He quickly looped one end around the tractor's frame and the other end to the frame of his truck. Jerry could see someone else in the driver's seat. He was pretty sure it was Willie Biddle. Willie waited for Roy's signal, then slowly began moving forward. Jerry felt the tractor lift a fraction, and the pressure lessened on his leg. His vision was starting to fade again, the blackness a determined tide. He took a breath. Roy was right next to him as the tractor lifted higher and teetered. Jerry stared, eyes glazed and frightened. He felt Roy's strong arms pull him back in one swift move, out of the indentation his body had made in the wet, black earth. The truck dug in, the wheels spinning against the heavy load, and the John Deere crashed back where Jerry had lain.

Jerry looked down at his mangled leg. His jeans were torn and soaked with blood, and the skin along his calf was peeled back like an onion, the muscles torn and exposed. His stomach turned. He slumped back. The darkness was returning.

When he awoke, the sound of an ambulance siren pierced the afternoon, and then one of the attendants was looking into his eyes with a small light. "Hey, Jerry, looks like it's your lucky day," the man said.

"Lucky?" Jerry said.

"You're lucky you're not dead," he said as they loaded Jerry into the ambulance.

Jerry gazed back at Roy Morgan who stood there like any bystander, watching, his hands crossed in front of him, the copy of Hot Rod tucked into the crook of his arm.

While the women were out house hunting, Peter was bent under a cow's belly. He heard the barn door creak open on its rusted hinges, and he looked up.

"J. D. Shrupp!" Peter said. "What are you doing here?" Peter sat back on the stool and wiped his brow with his sleeve as the older man limped over and stood leaning on the gate between the parlor and main barn.

"Heard David Morgan's son was taking over the family farm, and I thought I'd come out to welcome him."

Peter stood, and the two men shook hands. Jerry tilted his gaze toward the heifer. "Did I catch you in the middle of something?"

"Checking for mastitis," Peter said, then explained, "Bert said she had it. He wanted me to know what to look for."

Jerry nodded. "I don't dairy anymore, but if there's anything you need to know, I'd be happy to lend a hand," he offered.

"I appreciate that," Peter said. "There's an awful lot to do."

"You'll get the hang of it."

"I hope so," Peter said. "Sometimes everything feels so foreign, and other times it's as if I've been doing this all my life."

"Give it time. After all, you are Roy Morgan's grandson. Farming's in your blood."

"You want to come in for a cup of coffee?" Peter asked.

Jerry shook his head. "Probably should head back out. Seems there's never enough hours in the day."

"I know what you mean." Peter walked him out to his Dodge pickup. "Thanks for stopping by."

"You tell your dad not to be a stranger next time he's in town." Peter tapped the side of the truck as Jerry backed up, then gave a quick two-finger wave and left.

Peter walked over toward the little room that held the milk tank to make certain the milk was at its constant thirty-eight degrees. It had been one week since he and Mae had taken up residence in the farm. He had caught on to the rhythm of milking, he felt, pretty quickly. A relaxed contentment filled his heart. He whistled as he patted the side of one of the heifers and walked around her, looking her over. Bert Biddle was in the next stall finishing up with the last cow for the morning.

Bert stretched to stand and took off his cap and scratched his head before he said, "Peter...um...I've been meaning to talk to you. You're pretty far behind. I mean, that is, if you're going to put in peas this spring. Your grandpa had a contract with the cannery... You don't have to honor it, but you'd have to have the peas in within the next week or so to meet your deadline. Most every farmer in the county is done planting." Bert lowered his head as if he was sorry to say it. Peter's mouth hung open.

"It's April. How can I plant when there's still frost on the ground some mornings?" Peter asked, his brow furrowed.

"That's peas. They go in as soon as the soil can be worked. I'm really sorry—I guess I just assumed you knew. I should've told you."

"No. That's okay, Bert. You know, I was around at harvesttime, but I don't think I was ever here when he planted."

"When you're ready, I can give you a hand. Fred has our planter all tied up, but at least I can show you what you'll need to do so you can get plowing, then planting. I don't know if you've got your seed yet…"

"No," Peter admitted. "I guess I'd better get on that."

Bert nodded as if to say "enough said," then he shrugged his shoulders and turned to go.

"Bert," Peter called after him. "After lunch?"

Bert nodded again and said, "I'll be here."

Once Bert had left, Peter felt embarrassed. He should've known when peas needed to be planted. There was so much to keep track of, it was all a juggling act—when to plant, when to harvest, tracking milk production and prices, when to hay… He'd have to work harder, apply himself more if he was going to make it.

The first thing he needed to do was talk to Grandma about that operating loan.

"We need how much?" Peter sat with his mouth open, his ears ringing at his grandmother's words.

"Grandpa usually borrowed around thirty-five thousand dollars each spring."

Peter put his head in his hands. He, Mae, and Virginia sat in the sunny kitchen nook.

"Is there any way we can plant without a loan?" Mae asked.

"You don't happen to have thirty-five thousand dollars in an account somewhere, do you?" Peter asked.

"I could sell the Jeep. It's nine years old but it's still worth something."

"Not enough," Peter said.

"I don't know a single farmer who doesn't take out an operating loan every spring," Virginia said. "You'll pay it back after harvest in October. God willing."

"It's just a loan, Peter," Mae said. "People take out loans all the time."

"For thirty-five thousand dollars?"

"When I find a job—that could help," Mae offered.

Virginia began to laugh then, a low murmur that came from deep in her belly.

"What's so funny, Grandma?"

"I'm sorry. Was I laughing?" Then she put on a straight face. "If it'll make you feel better, I'll cosign with you. I'm pretty sure the bank would have a hard time loaning that kind of money to someone with no collateral who hasn't farmed before."

"I can't ask you to do that," Peter said.

"Why? Aren't you planning on staying?" Virginia said, staring him straight in the eyes.

"Well, of course, but—"

"Then you don't have much choice."

He knew she was right.

"You'll get used to it," Virginia said. "Before you know it, you'll be deep in debt, and you won't even blink an eye."

That afternoon, after Peter had made his trip to the bank, he climbed into the tall, enclosed cab of the John Deere and settled comfortably into the padded seat. He swiveled to look at the plow hitched to the back. The smell of diesel fuel hovered. Peter pushed a lever, and the six blades turned down toward the earth, then he pulled it up, and they returned. He did it again—down, then up, down, then up.

A tapping on the cab door interrupted his playing. Peter looked up to see Bert, a questioning expression in his eyes. Peter shrugged and opened the door, a grin on his face. "Now, this is a tractor!" Peter said.

The furrow in Bert's brow only deepened. "I was gonna show you the planter."

"Yeah." Peter felt his face flush as he climbed down behind Bert.

The planter rested, unhitched, to the side. It had twelve yellow boxes in a row atop metal fingers that dug straight furrows into the ground. "The box will release a seed every six inches," Bert explained. He grabbed a fifty-pound bag of pea seed and showed Peter how to dump the shriveled, dry green peas into each compartment and how the funnel-like bottom deposited each seed in its destined hole.

"You've got to make sure the ground's not too wet," he went on, "or you'll get stuck out there. Or worse, your seed will rot. If it's too dry the soil will crack and the seed won't germinate well. And keep your rows straight—that's how a man is judged."

They made their way back to the tractor, and Bert showed Peter which controls to use to drop seed and to lower the arm that marked the soil where the front wheel would follow on the next pass. Finally, he said, "You're gonna want to check your bins often. There's nothing as bad as running out of seed and not knowing where that last one fell." Peter nodded, taking mental note of the detail. Then Bert turned as if to go.

"Uh…" Peter cleared his throat and Bert turned back.

"Yeah?"

"I know this is going to sound dumb," he paused. "But I was wondering if you could kind of…give me a game plan."

Bert gave him a puzzled look.

"What I mean is," Peter went on, "I only farmed with Grandpa here and there, whenever I was visiting, so I don't have a real overview of what gets planted and harvested when." He left it there, hoping he wouldn't have to say more.

"Sure," Bert said simply. "Peas get planted in March or April. Corn or soybeans go in May or early June. Harvest the peas in June and plant pea beans. Late June will be your first haying, then another at the end of August, and again in September or October, depending on how well you're able to keep up and what the weather does. I've been haying in November when winter's late in coming."

Peter gave him a dumb look.

"Would you like me to write that down for you?"

Peter smiled. "If you could."

"No problem."

Bert ambled back to his truck, and Peter climbed into the cab, kicked the John Deere to life, and headed toward the easternmost field. When he was all lined up, Peter lowered the plow. It bit deep, straining against the tractor as it turned the rich loam into an ocean of waves.

When he reached the end of the first row, Peter lifted the plow and turned wide to set up for the next pass, then dug the blades in again. Soon the rhythm of the work became natural, and Peter's nerves settled. He gazed beyond to the acres spread out before him, his tractor a dot on the landscape, and he was struck by the simplicity of it all. He was a man turning the earth so he could plant a seed. It was so basic, yet so filling, working the same land his grandfather had so diligently cared for.

If only Grandpa had lived to see it.

Mae had been pacing and looking out the window for Peter since nine that evening. She hadn't said anything to Virginia about her concern, but it wasn't like Peter not to come home without telling her. She'd seen him go into the barn to milk at half past five, but then he'd disappeared again. Visions of him injured in some field filled her mind.

Finally at ten o'clock she heard the back door open.

"Where've you been?" Mae said, her face creasing with worry. She took his supper from the fridge and put it in the microwave to reheat.

"I'm sorry." Peter came over to her and kissed her brow. "I'm still plowing."

Mae pulled back, not quite ready to relinquish her mood.

The timer on the microwave dinged, and Mae went to retrieve his steaming bowl of stew. She set it on the table and turned to get some silverware.

Peter pulled out two chairs, and they each took a seat. "It's going to take a few weeks of long days to catch up."

"What do you mean?" Mae asked. "It's not a race."

"Actually it is. Bert tells me the first one to harvest gets the best price, generally speaking."

"So what are you telling me?"

"When I'm not milking, I'll be plowing and planting. We've got over five hundred acres of peas alone, not to mention five hundred for corn and soybeans. I'm figuring I'll be able to plow sixty acres in a twelve-hour day, then plant at about the same pace. That's in addition to milking. I won't be getting home till late at night."

"Okay," Mae said in a small voice. Peter pulled her close and kissed her temple. "I thought something had happened to you," she said, her lower lip trembling.

"I should've told you. I wanted to get back out there as soon as I finished milking."

Mae got up and brought over a plate with bread on it and set it before Peter on the table. "Virginia's in bed already," Mae said. "We have the place all to ourselves."

"I'm going to have to go back out as soon as I'm done eating."

"Oh," Mae said. "Okay." She got up and walked to the refrigerator to pull out the milk. "You want some?" He nodded. She brought it over and poured a cup for Peter. "You know," Mae paused, "maybe I could help you milk."

Peter lifted a spoonful of the stew to his lips and chewed thoughtfully. He shook his head. "I appreciate the offer, honey, but I know it isn't your dream to milk cows. I can manage. Besides, Grandpa did it by himself all those years. I'm sure I can too."

seven

The last week of April brought with it a rise in the temperature and spring fever. Mae had left job applications at a number of places in town, among them the florist and the bank—even the school—but everywhere the answer had been the same. "Not much work to be had in Lake Emily." She'd come home discouraged. It wasn't as if she could drive into the cities for a job—the two-hour haul each way made that impossible. She would just have to wait and trust that something would open up.

Virginia had gone to town for a change-of-address packet from the Lake Emily post office, and Peter was out on the tractor. So Mae had the place all to herself. She'd thought for a moment about her neglected cello in the closet but decided on a walk instead.

Mae slipped on a summery calico dress and fastened sandals on her pedicured feet. She smiled as she stepped outside. It was a fresh morning. A low strip of fog that was already beginning to burn off lay in the valley, a rising curtain at the start of the day. The orchard was vibrant with spring leaves. Oaks whispered in the breeze. The windbreak to the west was filling in with sprouting underbrush. Scout bounded over, his tail wagging. Mae reached down to scratch his ears. "Want to go for a little walk?" she said. The dog tilted his head, then trotted beside her, his nose sniffing periodically at the ground as they went.

Mae rounded the tall cedar tree marking the southwest corner of their island between the fields and stopped to contemplate the distant river valley. On all sides the ground was black, but she knew that soon this view would change as ordered rows of peas and soybeans and corn took their places. She could see Peter, a dot in the field, plowing the rich soil. She was glad that he was happy here. His face had shone with joy as he'd told her about plowing the day before. Yet this was *his* dream. He'd made that all too clear in his refusal to let her help with milking. And now with her inability to find a job, she didn't know what her part would be here, how she could contribute.

The breeze rustled her dress, and Mae's long hair blew in her face. She tucked the strands behind her ears and wrapped her arms around herself. There was a solitude here more lonely than she had expected.

Mae's thoughts turned to her mother, as they did so often while Peter was busy working. Even when she was a little girl, she had longed for the kind of relationship she'd seen between her friends and their mothers. Catherine had been more concerned about keeping her next social obligation than spending time with her daughters. As the years passed, Mae had simply pretended to be close. It wasn't the truth. She could see that now. And yet the desire was still strong within her. Even pretending to be best friends hurt less than this chasm.

Peter had told her to wait, to see if a little time and distance would heal the wounds. It seemed a reasonable idea, to wait. And pray.

Mae stood gazing across this landscape so unaffected by heartache and grief. She prayed about her worries, about her fear that Peter was pulling away from her, about her uncertainty in this new place, wondering if she'd fit in. Then she prayed about the situation with her mother, that God would find a way to bridge the distance with his healing.

"God," she concluded, "I know that you can bring about a stronger, better relationship with Mom through all this and that maybe in the meantime I might feel some pain. Help me to see your bigger purpose, and if not to see it, at least to trust you in it all. And, Lord, help me here, to be the wife that Peter needs, to find my place…" A tear slipped down her cheek, and she made no move to wipe it away. Scout had come back to see what was keeping her. The breeze kissed Mae's face. The sun slipped from behind a cloudy mask, and a hawk floated overhead toward the woods to the north, his glide effortless.

The cows had been let into the west pasture. They stood in a clump, their tails to the breeze, heads down as they mowed the grass in big chomps. A heifer ambled over to the fence. She stared at Mae with huge, brown eyes, chewing a mouthful of grass and flicking her tail.

"Hello," Mae said. One of the cow's ears moved forward, and she lowered her head slightly. Mae reached over the barbed-wire fence, careful to avoid the sharp points. She stroked the heifer between the ears. The cow reached out her long tongue to lick Mae's hand. When she saw that Mae had no food for her, she moved away, back to her friends in their coffee klatsch.

Animals had no cares, Mae thought. They only wanted to be fed, to be in the sunshine in the company of good friends. It was something to think about for her own life. "Come on, Scout," she said as she started walking again.

The flies had come out in force in the past week, so Peter had put up a long yellow fly strip that hung from the kitchen ceiling by a tack. Mae glanced at it now as she went inside. Her stomach churned to see the thick collection of dead creatures across its gluey surface.

She reached into the refrigerator to retrieve some eggs, onion, and cheese for an omelet, then stepped on the stool to reach the salt to refill the shaker. She felt a sudden crawling sensation on her back and jumped in panic. A wood tick had climbed up her dress during her walk. She screamed, then fell backward, colliding with the fly strip just before landing on her bottom on the wood floor. She shimmied, desperately trying to dislodge the tick, but the insect held firm. She grabbed a rubber spatula from the drawer and slipped it between her shoulder blades to scrape it off, but the tick crawled just south of her reach. So she lifted the hem of her dress and went at it from the other direction, finally scooping it onto the spatula. When she saw its little body, she shivered and shook it off into the sink, then ran some water to rinse it down the drain. She slumped back to the floor and reached up to touch her hair. The gooey fly strip was firmly stuck there. She tried to pry it loose. Soon her hands were covered with the gold gunk, and she still hadn't managed to get it free.

A stinging started at the back of her throat as the tears began. Tears gave way to sobs, and her body shook with each renewed wave. Everything was so foreign to her, this new place with no friends to speak of, Peter gone all hours, and her mom… Why couldn't she have a nice, quiet breakfast in peace?

A quick rap on the back door interrupted Mae's tears, and the screen opened in its squeaky way. Bert Biddle poked his head in the doorway to the kitchen. "Anybody home?" he queried before his eyes focused on Mae's train crash in the middle of the floor. Mae felt her face flush a deep red. "Um…is Peter still out in the field?" he asked as if she were standing there baking cookies.

"He was in the west field not too long ago," Mae said.

"Do you need any help with that?" Bert said, his gaze somewhere on the top of her head.

"Actually…," Mae began.

Bert stood over her and gingerly began pulling the long strip from her hair. Then he handed the tangled strip to her awkwardly, his head bent down, before saying, "You might want to try some Fels-Naptha soap on that. Okay, then. I'll go look for Peter," and he disappeared out the door.

Mae carried the strip at arm's length like a stinky diaper and laid it gently in the trash can. It had left a thick, matted coating on her dark tresses and on her neck, her pretty dress, across her cheek. She tried to run her fingers through her hair and stretched yellow strands of gluey, fly-speckled goo in midair like melted cheese. She bent her head down, bracing her hands on either side of the sink, and let the tears come in a silent flow. Tears felt good somehow.

MARY PETERSON

Mary Peterson had gotten the job she wanted for the summer as a candy striper at the hospital. She hoped to go to nursing school after graduation, and this was her proving ground.

So what if Dean, her boyfriend, captain of the football team and the most popular boy at Lake Emily High, thought she was wasting her time dreaming about school. She didn't care what he said. Not anymore. Not since last night when she gave his high-school ring back. She was tired of always doing this, that, and the other thing because Dean thought it was keen. She liked helping people in the hospital, especially the old people and little kids. It was satisfying, as though she was doing something that mattered. Dean never thought about anyone but himself. All he ever talked about was, "When I get out of this backward town…" Well, Mary thought Lake Emily was wonderful. There was nothing like going downtown and running into people she knew, chatting about the weather, saying, "Hey." There was a comfort to it. It was home, where her family and the people she loved and the people who loved her lived.

She wheeled the lunch cart down the antiseptic white hall and scrutinized each order to be sure she gave the correct meal to each patient. Nurse Jones had been very clear about the importance of that, and Mary was nothing if not meticulous about following instructions.

She knocked on the first door as she read the name. JERRY SHRUPP. Didn't she know him from school? She poked her head around the door. "Jerry?"

His head shot up, and his eyes looked huge and round. "Hi. What… what are you doing here?" he said.

"I work here." She pointed to her nametag. "What happened to your leg?" She reached for his meal from the cart and put it on the wheeled table in front of him.

"I…uh…a tractor fell on me."

"A tractor! That's awful. You could've been killed!" For some odd reason, he smiled at that, and Mary noticed the cute freckles peppered across his nose and the way his bright red hair stood up in the back.

"So." She hesitated. "Your family has a farm?"

"Yep," he said. "I'll take it over someday, same as my dad did."

"It's good to know what you want in life, isn't it?" Mary stepped closer to Jerry's bed.

"Why? What do you want to do?"

She lifted her head and saw his earnest expression. "I want to be a nurse," she said. "I like to help people." She watched his face for any sign of disapproval, but he just grinned.

"Well then, you're off to a good start, I'd say."

Their eyes met, and Mary felt a tingle crawl up her neck. "I suppose. Dean didn't quite see it that way."

"You and Dean are still an item then?"

"No!" she said a little too adamantly. "I broke up with him last night." At that Jerry grinned so widely that Mary thought his face would split.

"Miss Peterson." The stern voice of Nurse Jones interrupted their conversation. Her tall, foreboding form appeared in the doorway. Mary turned, flustered. "People need their lunches, Miss Peterson."

Mary's face blanched as she tried to regain her composure.

"It's my fault, ma'am," Jerry said. "I've kept her here with my blabbing. I'm sorry."

Nurse Jones gave a snooty humph *to Jerry, then turned on her heel and marched away. Mary smiled gratefully and returned to her cart. "Thank you, Jerry," she said.*

As she was about to wheel the cart out, Jerry said, "You think you could come back? After your shift, I mean. I wouldn't want to get you in trouble." He smiled at her, and Mary felt her face flush.

"Yes, Jerry Shrupp, I think I'd like that."

eight

T he extension meeting is at Mary Shrupp's," Virginia said the following Wednesday evening as they finished getting ready. "It's a
bunch of old ladies. Are you sure you want to go?"

"I've never been to an extension meeting before," Mae said. "I'd like
to at least find out what it is."

"Think of 4-H for adults, only with coffee and lots of snacks," Virginia said. "They're all nice ladies."

Mae met her eyes in the bedroom mirror, and they exchanged a
smile.

"Am I overdressed?" Mae wore a long yellow skirt with a close-fitting,
flowery short-sleeved knit top that showed off her trim figure.

"You look very pretty." Virginia patted her elbow. "Come now, we
have to pick up Ella for the meeting. We always drive together."

"I don't know how late we'll be," Mae said to Peter when they came
downstairs.

"Don't wait up," Virginia warned. "When the ladies get to talking
there's no telling how long we'll go."

"I'll be out in the fields anyway," Peter said. "We'll see who gets
home first." He kissed Mae and then Virginia on the cheek, and they
went out the back door.

They reached Ella's pillbox house, and she came out as Mae put the
car into park.

Ella climbed into the backseat and said, "Hello, kids."

"Is that seat okay for you?" Mae asked Ella.

"I'm just dandy," Ella replied. Her eyes twinkled. "So you're going to be a Suzie Q?"

"I guess," Mae said.

Before long they were pulling up Mary Shrupp's long driveway several miles north of Lake Emily. Their big white farmhouse nestled in the wooded acreage. Mae could see a circle of faces through the living room windows.

Mary, who appeared to be in her late forties, a trim-figured woman with a sweet voice and an encouraging smile on her perky face, stood at the kitchen door. "Lay your coats on the bed in the room on the left," she said. "We're going to get started in a few minutes."

After resting their spring jackets on the heaping pile, the threesome walked down the narrow hallway to the living room. An assortment of white-haired ladies lifted their gazes. Mae suddenly felt very young and very overdressed. Not that the women weren't dressed nicely, but Dayton's was obviously not a familiar haunt to these ladies. Sears seemed more the pace, sprinkled with a few Wal-Marts.

"This is my grandson Peter's wife, Mae Morgan," Virginia said. "She and Peter are working the farm."

A murmur of hellos followed.

"Hi," Mae said tentatively. She took a seat next to Virginia.

"So has Peter farmed before?" Mary asked, a kindness in her vivid blue eyes.

"Not really," Mae said. "Actually, we moved from St. Paul."

That seemed to close the shutters. From the looks on their faces, the women were embarrassed at Mae's admission.

"He's catching on real quick," Virginia jumped in.

Mae shifted in her seat. She definitely wouldn't bring up that they'd moved from St. Paul with anyone else in Lake Emily.

"The meeting of the Suzie Q Extension group will now come to order," Minnie Wilkes began. "Madam secretary, please read the minutes from our last meeting."

Mary took over, reciting the events of the previous month's gathering—a cookie recipe exchange, a gift to the Lake Emily nursing home in the form of a fifteen-dollar bouquet, and their upcoming plans for a husband-wife video night featuring *Riverdance*.

After the minutes were approved, Mary suggested that the women introduce themselves to Mae. Mae recognized a few faces from the funeral, especially Lillian Biddle. When it came to her, Lillian said to the group as a whole, "My Bert is teaching Peter to farm. Says he's a pretty good learner for someone who's never farmed before. Kind of late getting peas in, but he's planting anyhow."

Mae blushed. She hadn't expected everyone to know their business. She wondered what the woman would have said if she hadn't been there.

Lillian went on, "I've seen him out planting all hours. His rows are a bit crooked, you ask me." She snickered.

"His rows are just fine," Virginia said. Mae wanted to crawl under her chair.

"Let's move on with the lesson," Minnie Wilkes said with a scolding glare at Lillian.

The topic for the evening was "Attracting Wildlife to Your Backyard." Mary had brought out a whole assortment of birdhouses and feeders that she set up in the living room. The women took turns touring the collection, gazing in the little holes where the birds would make their nests. They talked about types of seeds for each different species and whether squirrel proofing was really possible, the cost of birdseed, how to grow sunflowers…

"Did Bert find Peter this afternoon?" Lillian asked Mae as the lesson came to its end. The memory of the fly-strip incident returned, and Mae prayed that wouldn't become public fodder too. Her face flamed.

"Um…," Mae said. "Yes. I think so." There was a definite spark in the older woman's eyes.

"He was going to help Peter with something," Lillian explained, then the woman turned away as if a switch had been thrown, and Mae breathed a sigh of relief. "Did I hear that Jerry already has eight new calves?" Lillian said to Mary. "Are you going to take them to auction?"

"You'd have to ask Jerry. I don't really pay too much attention to the farm. That's Jerry's thing," Mary said. She got up and excused herself to get their evening snack set up.

Mae looked around at the faces and wondered if she could ever truly fit in. These women had known each other all their lives, gone to school together, grown up on nearby farms, had farming in their blood. Who was she to think she could waltz in and become one of them? Her mother's warning echoed: "You'll never be happy." Mae blinked her eyes and shook the thought away.

Within a few minutes the group gathered around a perfectly set table with pink floral teacups and a sparkling silver tea service. The conversation ebbed and flowed like an ocean surf. At times they talked as one, the camaraderie of familiarity interspersed with long pauses when everyone would look at their coffee cups, take a sip, in no hurry to think of a new subject to discuss.

"So…," Mary said. "How are things going for—it's Peter, right?"

Mae nodded, glancing over at Lillian, then began, "He likes it. He's been milking mostly, and plowing and planting. He said he should be done planting peas in a few days."

"Tell him to be careful of that tractor," Mary said. "Those machines can be dangerous. Jerry was almost killed on a tractor when he was seventeen—his dad had him plowing the field all by himself. Jerry thought he could plow and read at the same time."

"Now *he* had the crookedest rows in the whole county!" Irene Jenkins interjected. They all laughed.

"If it wasn't for Roy and Willie it might've been hours before they found him," Lillian said, to which Mary nodded and shifted her eyes to Virginia.

"If it hadn't been for them…" Her words trailed off, and her gaze returned to Mae. "Tell Peter to be careful."

"I will," Mae said solemnly.

Finally, closing in on midnight, the ladies made their last farewells and headed home. Mae, Virginia, and Ella piled into Mae's Jeep. "Lillian was tame today," Ella said to no one in particular.

"Yes, I noticed," Virginia replied, then leaning toward Mae, "We've learned to love her, warts and all."

"So, what did you think?" Ella asked Mae.

"I had fun," Mae lied. "I learned how to attract birds to the back-yard—that'll come in handy."

"We're just a lot of old folks. You won't hurt my feelings if you say you don't want to keep coming," Virginia said.

"Well…," Mae started, then looked over at Virginia's hopeful face. "It's a good way to get to know the neighbors."

Virginia smiled. "They're a good bunch once you get to know them. A good bunch."

The phone rang as Mae stood washing breakfast dishes the next morning. Vivid sunlight shone through the green and blue bottles on the window sill. Mae picked up the receiver on the old rotary-dial phone on the second ring. "Hello."

"Mrs. Morgan?" a tentative voice said.

"Yes…?"

"This is the post office in Lake Emily. We have your chickens in. You can come pick them up this morning."

"What chickens?"

"It's from Murray MacMurry. A box of a hundred, looks like."

"Oh." Finally a circuit connected. "I'll bet you're looking for Virginia Morgan."

There was a momentary silence, and then the man said, "Well… yes."

"Okay," Mae said. "I'll be right down." She hung up the phone. "Virginia," Mae called up the stairs. "The post office called. They have your chickens."

Virginia's face appeared above the top riser. "Oh my. I forgot to cancel the order! I got so carried away with everything that was happening that it totally slipped my mind."

"Let's go get them," Mae said. "We can keep them. Besides, this will be fun."

"Are you sure?"

"I said I wanted chickens. This just saves me from having to decide what kind."

"Okay, I'll be right down."

A few minutes later Virginia was ready, dressed for a trip into town complete with elastic-waisted polyester slacks and canvas sneakers. They hopped into Mae's Jeep and made for the post office.

"I don't know where my brain's been," Virginia said. "I ordered those Leghorns seven months ago, before Roy was even sick. I should've cancelled it as soon as we knew…" Her voice trailed away. Her eyes drifted to some distant spot. The silver water tower in Lake Emily glimmered in the morning light. The fields had taken on dark brown stripes where the plows had made their mark. Meadows were thick with spring grasses, and each yard they passed held bright-colored crocuses as testimony to spring's first blush.

"Well, I'm glad you forgot to cancel the order," Mae said. "You can teach me the ins and outs of chicken ranching."

When they walked into the post office, the cheeping of hundreds of baby chicks filled the small interior. The postmaster, a stoop-shouldered man with ears that stuck out, led them inside the depths of the post office. A solitary, soft downy yellow chick feather stuck to the back of his shirt. The place smelled of paper and ink, and there were stacks of mail and mailbags scattered throughout the small room. Against one wall dozens of boxes full of farm wives' hopes were piled high. Mae could see feathers poking out of various holes, and the floor of the post office was littered with a small pillow's worth of fluff.

Mae peered in one of the holes in the box he handed her. "You sure there are a hundred birds in there?"

Virginia nodded. "They pack them in tight so they will keep each other warm."

Mae carefully carried the creatures to the Jeep, waiting until Virginia was positioned before setting them on her lap to hold. "We need to get them some feed from the elevator," Virginia said, then recited a list of all that they would need. The cheeping surrounded them.

Mae pulled up to the gravel lot of the elevator where they bought wood shavings, a heat-lamp bulb, and fifty pounds of chick starter.

When the noisy entourage arrived home, Mae put the box of chicks on the kitchen counter, then she and Virginia went out to the old henhouse and began cleaning it out for the birds. Within an hour the room was Lysol clean. They hung the heat lamp so the chicks would be warm and spread the wood shavings as a carpet. Mae filled the feeders as Virginia directed, sprinkling the top with a handful of grit to help the animals' digestive systems. Virginia retrieved two

Mason jars from the root cellar and cleaned them out. Then she filled them with cool water, screwed on the waterer, and tipped them upside down. A few bubbles plipped to the top as the tray beneath filled with water.

Mae went to get the box full of Leghorns and, once she had the door of the house closed, she opened the top. The yellow chicks were crammed back to back in that space. Startled, they quieted and peered up as one. Mae put her hand in to help the first little bird hop out. It plopped onto the soft shavings, looked around, and then stood still, overcome by stage fright.

"You have to show them where the water and food are," Virginia said. "Dip their beaks in each, then they'll remember." Mae picked up the tiny, soft bird, putting its beak into the long galvanized tray of feed and the red water tray. The bird gulped happily.

"I have to do that with all one hundred?" Mae asked.

"They're not the brightest," Virginia chuckled. "It's a good thing I didn't order three hundred!"

They each took a bird in turn and dipped its beak in food and water, and soon the happy sound of contented cheeping accompanied the sight of tiny yellow chickens exploring their domain.

That night Peter, Virginia, and Mae sat in the kitchen nook eating a hearty supper of homemade chicken noodle soup and sourdough bread. Peter had been out planting since the morning milking. Sweaty grime lined his handsome brow. Mae gazed at him for a moment. For the past two weeks, he'd been either sleeping or out in the barn or the field for endless hours. Their time together had evaporated like rain on a hot asphalt road. Even as she sat staring at him now, she missed him.

"I suppose you have to get back out in the field," Mae said.

"Probably should," he agreed. Mae sighed.

"I think I'll go check on the chicks," she said. "You want to come, Virginia?"

"You go on, dear," Virginia said. "I've got packing to do." Virginia had been working at sorting through piles of belongings, tossing what she could, piling up boxes for Goodwill, and asking Mae what she would like to keep. Mae had offered to help her go through Roy's things, but Virginia insisted on doing it herself.

"Are you sure you don't need a break?" Mae had asked.

"I need to do this," Virginia said. "It's part of my grieving, holding the things he touched near me…and letting them go."

Mae slipped on her shoes and went out the back door.

Inside the white clapboard-sided henhouse was a warm sanctuary. The chirping fellowship that throughout the day had been a loud reverberation gave way to a worshipful calm, with soft peeps tossed about now and then as the congregation settled in for an evening of rest. The birds clustered in two circles under the glow of the heat lamps. Mae checked the feeders and waterers, making sure they were filled to the top so there would be enough to last till morning. A few birds stood from their slumber and came to peck at the feed, standing right on top of the feeder as they ate or ambled to the water to dip their heads into the tray, lifting their beaks high into the air to swallow.

Mae stood on the other side of the low divider, taking in the soothing scene before her. She heard the door click as Peter slipped inside.

"I thought you had to get back to work," Mae said.

"You sighed. Something's always wrong when you sigh." Peter came to her side and put an arm around her waist, then kissed her temple.

"You've been gone a lot lately."

"I know. But it's temporary. I should be done plowing the cornfields in another week or so."

Mae looked up into his blue eyes. "I love you, you know," she whispered.

"I know." He smiled at her.

"You're supposed to say, 'I love you too.'"

"You'd be expecting it. That ruins the whole thing."

Mae reached a hand to his stubbled chin and put her head against his shoulder.

"They're cute, aren't they?" Peter said of the chicks.

"They are kind of fun," Mae admitted.

"Don't get too attached. It might make slaughtering them hard," Peter warned.

"I know. But Virginia volunteered to help with that, so I'll get through it." She gazed at the birds, then met Peter's eyes. "I really like your grandma."

"She likes you too."

Mae's eyes rested on the red circles of light where a mound of chicks slept. One chick got up and pecked around the feed. "I'm learning more about myself than I ever knew before," Mae said.

"Me too."

"Like what?"

Peter took a deep, satisfied breath. "Like this was a really good idea."

Mae shifted uncomfortably, and her eyes met his. She couldn't bear to ruin the moment by voicing her fears, so she turned and nestled her back against his chest. Peter placed his arms around her waist, and they watched the chicks together, letting the stillness quiet them. Then they slipped into the night and back to their own circle of light.

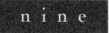

S o, Virginia," Mae said the next day while helping her fill a box with tablecloths and Christmas towels. "I've been thinking about putting in a garden. Is it too late to start?"

"Not too late at all," Virginia said.

"Do you have any books you could recommend?"

"On gardening?" Virginia had a puzzled expression on her face. "I suppose they have some down at the library. I've kind of let the garden go in the last few years. Harder for this old body to bend over and get at those weeds, you know. A few tomato plants and my flowers is all I can manage. What is it you want to grow?"

"I'd like to try a little of everything. I seem to have extra time on my hands lately…" Her voice trailed off. "It might be fun."

"I'd be happy to help. There's nothing like a bountiful garden to give a person a sense of satisfaction." Mae's eyes met hers uncertainly, and Virginia said, "Are you all right, dear?"

"I'm fine," she said, then turned and folded a red napkin. She didn't want to say anything, didn't want to complain, yet Virginia's eyes bored in.

"I suppose I'm just getting used to the long hours Peter's been working these days."

Virginia sat down on the bed. "It's an adjustment, isn't it?"

"I'm okay, really. You're the one who's going through the changes lately," Mae said.

"All of life is change. When we learn to stop fighting it, that's when we can start to be happy."

"I'll try to remember that," Mae said. "In the meantime maybe you can give me a primer on gardening."

That week the rain began. A week of heavy downpours followed by moments of sun, just enough to convince Peter that he'd be able to finish getting the fields ready for corn only to have his hope doused with another drenching. Peter stood looking out the window one afternoon while Mae made tuna melts. Rain splattered the windows in teary streaks.

Peter had spent the day researching farming financials to get a handle on how the farm had performed over the past few years. It wasn't looking good, and their newly acquired debt and the lack of employment for Mae nagged at him. One other thing that troubled him was how much it cost to keep Bert on. Peter needed Bert's know-how to learn the ins and outs of farming—he'd proven that already—but the money they paid him came straight from their profits, if there were any profits to be had. Peter wondered how his grandfather had managed to keep Bert on during the months that he was ill. But then he hadn't had much choice.

"You seem upset," Mae said, glancing up at his nervous pacing.

"I need to be out in the field."

"You can't make the rain stop, Peter."

"You don't understand. Everything has to be planted and harvested on schedule, or I'll have to buy the feed to keep our own cows fed. And that would mean a whole summer of work with no profits to show for it." Mae placed a steaming tuna melt on Peter's plate. "I've been thinking about Bert...paying him to help milk—" He stopped and shook his head.

"Is that a problem too?" She sat next to him at the kitchen table.

"I don't see how we can afford to keep him. The longer he stays, the less money we have in our pocket. It's as simple as that."

"Do you know enough about farming to let him go?"

"I think I've learned the routine pretty well. I can always call him for emergencies."

"Then let him go." She said it as if it were a no-brainer. But Peter had never fired anyone before. He didn't want to hurt the guy's feelings; it was simply a matter of finances.

"Call Virginia for lunch," Mae instructed. "And we'll pray that the rain stops."

Peter had been agitated all the next morning. The rain persisted. One of the cows hadn't been cooperative in coming into the barn, and he'd wasted a good half-hour in the downpour chasing her across the pasture. Now there was a leak in one of the hose connections to the milking machine.

"I'll run to the hardware for a new fitting," Bert said.

"No. I've got it," Peter insisted, avoiding Bert's eyes. He had to tell the man today that he was done. Peter's stomach knotted up, and he sighed as he examined the long clear tube closely.

"It'll contaminate the whole batch if there's a hole in it," Bert offered, as if Peter didn't already know that.

"Well, then I guess we shouldn't use it," Peter said defensively. Now why had he gone and said that? The man was just helping him out. Peter needed to get this over with quick, or he'd be a basket case before lunch.

"Um, Bert." Peter walked over to him, working to keep his tone level. "I've decided that...well...I can't really afford to keep you on."

Bert raised a surprised brow, and Peter hurried on, "I've kept you from your own farm long enough. I'm sure Fred's anxious to have you back, and I really think I can manage here on my own, for the most part. Although I may need to call on you if some emergency comes up."

Bert nodded. "If that's what you want."

"It's not a matter of wanting...I'm sorry."

"You sure you're ready?"

"There's only one way to find out."

On Saturday night Mae sat in the living room under the glow of a fringed floor lamp, studying her gardening books from the library. Virginia had long since gone to bed. Peter was out in the fields again, planting corn in the dark, making up for the eight days of rain that had kept him from his task. Mae could see the glow of the John Deere's headlight as it inched down a row in the distance.

One particular book, *The Have-More Plan,* had captured Mae's imagination. It was written by a couple from the 1940s who left their New York apartment for a new life in the country. It described how they raised all their family's food on less than five acres. There were photos of their little boy playing in the rabbit cages and the mother wearing a June Cleaver dress with a white apron while milking the family's dairy goat. Sheep grazed in their field while cows gazed placidly at the camera.

There was something enchanting about the whole idea—a family, a big garden, the orchard, animals raised naturally, a freezer filled to last through the long winter months. Mae pictured Peter and herself with a little boy or girl of their own, eating meals she had prepared straight from the garden. She'd go out and dig some potatoes to mash for that night's dinner, or she'd pull rhubarb in the morning and make a pie from it in the afternoon. The thought warmed her.

The garden would give her a way to contribute and keep her from sitting around waiting for Peter. That was what she'd been lacking lately—a purpose. Peter was busy night and day, and she was lost, without a focus. She had gone out job hunting a couple more times, but still nothing looked hopeful. Truthfully, she hated the idea of adding another work schedule to Peter's. A job would mean seeing him even less. At least now she had snatches of time with him. If she was gone all day, she wouldn't even have that. She shifted in her seat and gazed out at the tractor's light. Yes, a garden would give her something worthwhile to do.

"Are you coming to church?" Mae asked from the doorway as Peter turned over in bed. Sunlight streamed through the lace curtains, its dappled rays giving the white bedspread a honeyed effect. Peter moaned.

"I got to bed at four o'clock," he complained.

Mae glanced at the clock. It was half past nine. "That gave you five hours." She put on her earrings, then turned to brush her hair.

"I milked from six to nine, remember?"

"You haven't been to church in weeks."

"God'll understand. Let me sleep." He pulled the pillow over his head.

Mae threw her hands in the air and turned away. She hated going to church without him. She finished putting on her makeup and shoes, then said to Peter, "Will you be here when I get home? Maybe we can have lunch together."

Peter sighed and pulled the pillow down. "I have to get back out in the fields. I'll pack a lunch." The pillow went back up over his face.

Virginia was in the kitchen making breakfast when Mae came down. Her round frame moved from counter to counter as she went from buttering toast to frying eggs.

"I can do that," Mae offered and put two slices of bread in the toaster.

"You don't look happy," Virginia said.

"Peter's not coming to church again."

"It's only temporary. Until the field work is done."

"That's what he keeps saying."

"Be patient with him, dear."

Mae sighed. The toast popped up. Mae quickly buttered it and set it on the plate. "I guess I don't need to make any for Peter." Virginia gave her a sympathetic look.

"It's hard—the first year of marriage," Virginia said. "You're still figuring out how everything's supposed to work, finding out how to relate as husband and wife. Before long you'll find a comfortable place. It's give and take, but it's worth it."

Mae smiled and said, "How do you know so much?"

"Fifty-some years of married life tends to do that to a person."

A robin chirped high in the branches of the cedar near the barn. Mae was looking forward to this day. She laced up her faded Keds and walked to Virginia's garden plot. South of the chicken coop, it would get a full day's sunshine, and it was a low spot so it was bound to get plenty of water.

She could hear Peter fire up the old green Oliver tractor in the big, round-roofed Quonset hut and watched as he came chugging out of the darkness into the morning light. He had a two-bottom plow on the back that would rake its thick fingers through the dark earth, leaving it ready for tilling.

Mae stood and watched as Peter moved up and down the first row.

Peter stopped the loud diesel next to his wife and shouted, "I can hear some rocks in there. Why don't you walk behind and see if you can get them out."

So Mae followed, watching and listening for the telltale clunk of metal against rock. When she would hear it, she'd bend down, search the soil, and tug up the offending stone. Often it was a small piece no bigger than her fist, other times it was a small boulder that together they would wrestle to the sidelines. After several slow passes of following and digging, Peter and Mae had a good-size rock pile next to the chicken coop.

"How much longer?" Mae shouted to Peter over the sound of the tractor.

"One more pass."

Mae's back and legs ached, and sweat stung her eyes, but she felt good. Seeing her little patch of earth take shape brought a sense of gratification. She looked up at Peter, a smile on his determined face. She could see why he liked being outside—it fed a soul-deep part of a person. And when August and September knocked on her door, the produce from her garden would impress even the ladies at extension. Now, that would bring satisfaction.

She walked, ears attentive, eyes to the ground, as they made their final pass. When Peter finally turned off the tractor and climbed down, Mae stood and stretched her back.

"We're being watched," he said, pointing across the road with his chin. There sat two tractors, parked like pickups at a drive-in theater with Mae and Peter as the main attraction.

Peter waved, and the flannel-clad farmers returned hesitant two-fingered salutes.

Mae raised a brow as she stared back at them and waved. They started their motors and returned to their work.

Peter gazed at Mae and wiped her cheek with his thumb. "You've got a little smudge," he explained.

She turned back to her patch of earth and took a deep breath. "This is going to be wonderful."

Peter gave her a kiss on the cheek. "I better get back to work." He climbed up, and the engine roared to life as he moved back into the Quonset hut.

Mae went to get the old tiller. It was a dinosaur, so old that any brand name had long ago faded away. Mae filled the gas tank and gave a pull on the starter the way Peter had showed her. The old-timer coughed and choked. After several more pulls the engine fired, sounding like an asthmatic with pneumonia, wheezing and coughing every few beats. It smoked, but it didn't die, so Mae tilled. Slowly she moved up and down. Her arms and lower back throbbed from the exertion, but before long the dirt was soft and flowing through those blades like flour through a Mixmaster. At lunchtime Virginia came out, and together they admired her handiwork. All Mae had to do was buy seeds, and she'd be in business.

Virginia and Mae spent the afternoon shopping for seeds and seedlings, and then Virginia showed her how to plant, making sure she left plenty of space between rows for the plants to grow.

"It's hard to believe some of these things will take up so much space," Mae said, bending to pick up the garden trowel that lay in the dirt. "The pumpkins and squash alone take up a third of the garden."

"You'll be glad you trusted those seed packets when September arrives. They do tend to sprawl." Virginia gathered the empty packages and then took off her cornflower blue cotton gloves.

"Thank you for helping me," Mae said, tucking her hair behind her ear.

"It's good for me to get away from all that packing," Virginia said. "It can get a little intense in there."

"Could you use this?" Virginia said, holding out an old pewter jewelry box the next morning.

Mae gingerly touched a hand to the top. "You don't want to get rid of this. It's beautiful."

"That new house doesn't have room for my fifty years of junk. I have to pare back, or I won't have room to walk. Besides, it feels good to do a little purging; frees the soul."

"Well…," Mae said, turning it in her hands. "I'd be honored to take it then. Was it your mother's?"

"Oh no. Garage sale two years ago. She was asking $2.00. I talked her down to $1.50."

Mae's eyes lit up. "You'll have to take me along sometime. I never find anything this nice when I go."

"You have to hit the sales out in the country—they aren't picked over like the ones in town."

"How much more do we have to do?"

"I've got most everything in boxes. I hate to leave so much here for you to deal with, but I don't see how I can manage much more. I saved this for Peter." She withdrew an old pocketknife with an ivory handle from her apron. "It's Roy's pocketknife. Not worth anything, but Roy always carried it to open bales or feed sacks."

Mae looked at the old knife, a flat spot worn on the side. "Peter will love this."

"I've been thinking about that dining room table, too. Are you sure you want it? It's such a monstrous old thing. I don't want to burden you with it."

"No! I love that table. It's a part of the history here." She paused. "You didn't get it at a garage sale, did you?"

"No. Roy's dad built it when Roy was young. There were fourteen kids in the family, so he made it plenty long. They had benches on either side. I guess he figured they could keep adding kids that way without having to buy more chairs."

"Do you still have the benches?"

"Oh, they're in the attic somewhere. Buried in all the chaos. I don't even want to think about that project."

"We'll save that for after you're settled in town. Make an afternoon of it."

"More like a *week* of afternoons."

Mae laughed. "What would you like me to do next?"

"I think I'm about set for tomorrow." Virginia wiped her hands on her apron. "You could put a pot of coffee on. I'm going to miss coming down for coffee with you in the mornings."

ALAN HICKEY

Thirteen-year-old Alan Hickey was hovering near the comic-book stand while his buddy Jack kept watch. Alan's heart pounded. His palms were sweaty. The excitement of the moment pulsed through him, along with the fear he'd get caught. Quickly he slipped the comic book under his jacket and casually started walking for the door. Jack was right beside him. He looked over at the cash register where Mr. Ott, the pharmacist, stood ringing up a sale for a gray-haired woman.

The man lifted his head, and their eyes met for a moment. "You boys find what you were looking for?"

"Uh, no. But that's okay," Jack said smoothly, a plastic grin on his lying lips. Alan took a deep breath and opened the glass door. The little bell above tinkled, and he and Jack were out on the sidewalk.

"Did you get it?" Jack asked. Alan began to pull the book from his coat. "Not here!" Jack scolded. "Old man Ott will see you." They walked toward the park. Alan felt watched, certain that the people passing them somehow knew.

"You're a regular pro at this," Jack said.

"I don't know, Jack," Alan said. "I don't feel right about it."

"Are you gonna chicken out on me now? Come on, Alan. Don't be a mama's boy."

Alan clamped his lips shut.

When they got to the park, Jack pulled a package of Camels out of his shirt pocket. "I got these while you were busy with the kids' stuff."

Alan's eyes grew large. Jack peeled off the cellophane and handed Alan a cigarette.

"Here, light up," Jack said, offering him the matches.

Alan put the flame to the end of the cigarette awkwardly and inhaled. Immediately he began coughing, a deep hacking cough that he couldn't seem to stop.

"Ha!" Jack said, "You've never smoked before."

"I have too," Alan protested. Jack took a heavy drag on his own cigarette, then held it like James Dean.

"I need to get home," Alan said, suddenly feeling as if he couldn't get out of there fast enough. "I've got to deliver my papers."

"I thought you quit that job."

"It doesn't pay much, but it's better than nothing," Alan said.

"Whatever," Jack said. "I'm going to see what Dean Robleski is doing. I'm sure he's not delivering some lame paper." Jack turned and left.

Alan threw his cigarette down. He walked alone to the lake. The late afternoon sun glimmered like thousands of fireflies on the glassy water. Alan skipped a rock across its surface. He felt awful; a queasy sensation sat on his stomach, not from the cigarettes, but deeper inside. Mr. Ott's kind face haunted Alan's mind. He remembered when the man had helped him pick out a cross necklace for his mother's birthday. Mr. Ott didn't deserve to be treated this way.

"Alan," a voice sounded. Alan started and looked up to see Pastor Peterson's curious expression. "You seem troubled. Anything I can do to help?"

Alan shifted his gaze to the ground. How long had the pastor been watching? Then he said, "No. I'm okay." He ran a hand through his sandy hair. "There's something I need to take care of." He turned away and began to run. He ran as fast as he could downtown.

The bell tinkled when Alan came through the door. He was winded and stood trying to catch his breath. Mr. Ott looked up. "Alan," he said in greeting. "What can I do for you?"

Alan gazed at his wrinkled face. "Mr. Ott...," Alan started. He shifted nervously. "I..." He pulled the comic book from beneath his jacket. "I'm real sorry. I took this."

The man gazed at the book for a long moment before lifting his eyes to Alan. "What do you think we should do about this?"

Alan wasn't sure what Mr. Ott meant; he knew what he expected Mr. Ott to do—call the police—but he couldn't bring himself to say it. "I guess that's up to you, sir. I know that taking it was the wrong thing to do, and I'm real sorry."

"Alan, I've known you for a long time." Mr. Ott pursed his lips in thought. "Tell you what," he began, "I could use a soda jerk in the afternoons, after school."

"You mean...work here?" Alan asked.

Mr. Ott tipped his head. "I need someone I can trust to keep an eye on things for me."

Alan's face split with a smile. "Thanks, Mr. Ott, I'd like that a lot."

ten

The moving truck backed up to the front porch, and Pastor Alan Hickey along with several other volunteers from the Methodist Church, many of them boys that Virginia had taught Sunday school to twenty years before, began loading her life onto it.

Mae, Ella, and Virginia stood back, watching and directing when needed. In spite of all the commotion, it was a moment of reverence. Virginia's hands were clutched together in front of her, and she wrung them back and forth as fifty years of boxes came out of the house. "I hope I didn't forget anything," she said.

"You're not far away, if you did. You can always come get whatever you need," Ella said.

Virginia's eyes never left the big van.

"Are you okay?" Mae asked.

"You know what's funny?" Virginia said. "When you're young, no one tells you that you'll snap your fingers and the next thing you know, you'll be old. Alone. Starting over. No one tells you... You live like nothing will ever change, while all along nothing's staying the same. It's a funny thing about life. I look at you, Mae"—her gaze shifted from the van to Mae for a moment—"you and Peter, and I see me and Roy just yesterday. Bent over in our little garden, thrilled with the freshness of life. What happened to all that time we were going to have?"

Mae placed a hand on Virginia's hand.

"I don't have many regrets," Virginia went on. "I just wonder about all that time. Well, maybe I do regret not making more friends." Her gaze shifted to Ella. "Seems the few I have are beating me to the cemetery and leaving me all alone." She let out a heavy sigh.

"You still have friends," Ella said. "And I, for one, will not race you to the cemetery." Virginia reached for Ella's hand, giving it a squeeze before releasing it.

"Listen to me. I'm feeling sorry for myself. The truth is, we're all in the same predicament. Racing to hold on to a shadow. It's what makes eternity more precious—the fleetingness of this life." She smoothed her hands down her apron. "I better go make sure they get everything." She walked up to the kitchen door and disappeared inside with Ella close behind.

Mae remained where she was, gazing distractedly as Peter and Bert Biddle hefted a couch onto the back of the truck. What Virginia said clung to her, made her miss her own childhood already swept away like Virginia's belongings, reminded her of the weeks lost since she last spoke to her mother. The pain of regret hovered over her.

Lord, her prayer rose up, *help me to find a way to show my mother that I love her, that I forgive her. And help her to see that my marriage to Peter is a good thing.* Tears sprang to her eyes.

"We're ready to roll!" Peter's voice broke through Mae's thoughts, and she dabbed at her eyes.

She walked inside and found Virginia in the kitchen, wiping the Formica counters. "There were crumbs from breakfast," Virginia explained.

"Sounds like the men have everything loaded and are heading into town."

Mae, Ella, and Virginia squeezed into the Jeep, which was packed with Virginia's more delicate goods, houseplants, and bedding that she didn't want to have to dig for.

Virginia's thoughts turned to Roy. When they had first discovered that Roy had cancer, they had discussed the likelihood that she would have to move to town, that running the farm would be more than she could handle alone. But they hadn't discussed Peter and Mae taking it over. Would he be pleased with that decision? She thought he would, but that man could surprise her sometimes with his changing opinions. After all, hadn't it been Roy's urgings that encouraged David to pursue a career in music? Music, of all things, for a farm boy from Minnesota. But Roy had been right, hadn't he? He had known what was best for his son, what fulfilled him. And now Virginia sensed a similar drive in Peter. Maybe it was all in her imagination. But she could see that delight in Peter's eyes when he came in from a morning in the barn, as she had seen it in Roy's eyes for fifty-seven years.

When they came into town, Virginia gazed out at Lion's Park on the right. The lake shimmered with the morning light on the other side of the thick oak trees. Children were already bounding up and down the sandy beach next to the boat ramp. They passed the Methodist church on the left and the *Lake Emily Herald* office, its windows cluttered with piles of papers and office supplies. A metal box sat out front with papers for sale. The tiny white post office was already open, its flag flapping in the breeze. The barber pole turned at the shop next door, and Virginia could see Buzz Johnson inside sweeping the floor. The movie theater was dark at this early hour. Across the street the flower shop was just opening; thick bouquets of carnations and tulips loafed in the stands under the green awning. They turned left at Ott's Drugstore, making their way past Clusiau's Clothiers and the elementary school on the edge of town.

Virginia shifted her view toward her new house up the road. Roy had never seen the place, had never touched those walls with his presence. There were no memories waiting for her there, yet maybe that was a good thing. She wouldn't constantly be reminded that their time together was over. Virginia sighed and gazed out the side window of the Jeep.

"You seem quiet," Mae said.

"Oh, I'm an old woman learning how to walk on new legs."

"It'll take getting used to, living by yourself," Ella said.

"I don't know if it's something to get used to or something you just do." They passed houses like shoppers in the aisles until they pulled into Virginia's new driveway.

After a moment of silence, Virginia cleared her throat. "Well, we better make sure those boys don't break anything," she said and opened the door.

The cotton-candy sky had turned from pale pink to a deep lavender with thin wispy clouds that stretched in long tendrils along the horizon. Mae gazed out the Jeep window as Peter and she made their way home that night.

"I'm worried about Virginia," Mae said. "It's so hard to watch her struggling. I wish I could do something—"

"She's a strong woman, Mae. She'll be okay."

"You should've heard her while you were loading the moving van. She sounded so sad."

"We can still drive into town to check on her. Take her out to coffee, invite her to dinner after church. She's not alone. She still has us."

June came with warmer days. The house felt empty without Virginia. Mae tried to keep busy by playing her cello, but eventually she would find herself looking in Virginia's bedroom, only to find it bare. Peter had finished planting the corn, but there was no break in the work; as soon as that was completed it was time for the big machines from the cannery to come to begin harvesting the peas and hauling them into town.

Mae concentrated on her morning communion with God and the garden, even putting in a new bed of purple coneflowers and bee balm and black-eyed Susans on the far side of the vegetable garden. She made meals that she ate alone, keeping a plate hot for Peter in the oven. Lately he seemed so intent on growing the perfect crop that Mae was concerned about him. He had dark circles under his eyes, and when he did come in before ten o'clock he'd fall asleep in his chair within five minutes of sitting down. She thought about asking if she could help again, but his words of the previous time rang in her ears. "This isn't your dream. Grandpa managed all those years by himself; I'm sure I can too."

At least she had her chickens to keep her busy. The birds had more than doubled in size from that first day she'd brought them home from the post office. The cute downy fluff had given way to feathers, and they'd emerged from their fuzzy yellow facade as plain white, ugly, smelly birds who would tilt their heads and stare at Mae when she spoke to them.

She fed them twice each day, after breakfast and supper, and cleaned out their perpetually dirty pen a few times a week. They quickly came to recognize Mae as the one who quenched their ravenous hunger. The little creatures would scramble to the feed trays, frantically climbing on top of each other to be the first. Then they would follow her around the small yard in a cluster. When she would turn to look at them, they would stop and look around, pecking at the ground, acting innocent.

But they were just chickens. She longed for some human companionship. Of course she still had Virginia. She would go to coffee at her house, or Virginia would come to the farm every couple of days, but it wasn't the same as having her there whenever Mae felt lonely.

The ladies she had met at church and extension seemed to be very kind. Except Lillian Biddle. But it was too awkward to call a stranger out of the blue and invite her over.

Mae had grown up with a close-knit group of friends in St. Paul. They had graduated from high school together. They used to shop at the mall, go out to eat, get their nails and hair done together before they went off to their separate colleges. They'd grown apart some since then, but still they sent letters or phoned, and once in a while they'd have lunch together.

Mae decided to call Elizabeth to set up a lunch date with the old gang. It would give her something to look forward to. Maybe she would even invite them down to the farm sometime.

eleven

A low mist clung to the valley despite the growing warmth of the June day. Peter let the cows out into the pasture and brought the baler and hay rack around while Bert waited in the driveway. Peter turned off the tractor, jumped down, and walked over to him.

"Thanks for coming out. I don't know how I'd ever do all this alone. Fred coming?" Peter asked.

"Afraid not. He says we've got our own haying to do," Bert said, tugging on his cap.

"I'd be happy to come over and lend a hand once we're done here," Peter said.

"He's being stubborn again. Dad can help him," Bert mumbled. "Have you ever done this before?" He turned to face the equipment trailered behind the John Deere.

"Not since I was thirteen," Peter said. "It's like riding a bike though, right?"

"I reckon," Bert said.

Peter had mowed the week before and left the hay to dry, then raked twice to make sure the alfalfa was properly cured. The hay lay in neat rows. All that remained was to gather the heaps into square bales of emerald green and stack them in the barn.

"You want to drive or stack?" Peter asked.

"We should trade off," Bert said. "I'll stack first."

Soon the day turned warmer. Bert pulled bales off the baler and stacked them perfectly on the wagon. His arms rippled with muscles, and his trademark green cap had a ring of perspiration along its edge.

"You ready to switch?" Peter called back while the tractor idled.

"Let's finish this load," Bert said. The pile was high, a good ten feet off the ground, tall and straight. "Another row ought to do it."

Peter glanced back at the baler, churning out perfectly sculpted rectangles with green twine tied in two stripes along their length. A cloud of dust and hay particles floated in the air and stuck to Bert's sweaty arms. The field behind them was a stubbled beard. Bert moved effortlessly, accustomed to the backbreaking work. Once they finished that row, Peter pulled to the side of the field, detached the baler, and hooked the hay wagon directly to the tractor. Bert sat atop the heap, and they rode to the tall red barn to load the hay into the loft.

After lunch, Bert showed Peter how to stack, and within an hour Peter's back and legs and arms burned in muscles he'd never even known he had. Sweat ran in great streams down his back and face, the salt stinging his eyes. He wiped the sweat with his T-shirt and kept his focus, trying to catch his breath between bales. Peter had thought he was in shape, yet he was running to keep the next bale from falling to the ground as the machine force-fed him.

By the time the wagon was heaping high and they were heading back to the barn, Peter felt like a wrung rag. He lay flat on his back atop the pile, watching the clouds and letting the warm sun bake his face as a cool breeze lifted the sweat from his body. Never had he felt so spent. Or so good. The sweet smell of hay filled his lungs with its richness.

They pulled to a stop at the tall side door of the barn. Peter groaned, wishing they didn't have to haul each and every bale into the barn. He got up, arched his back, wiped the sweat from his face, and went back at it, tossing bales to the ground and then taking them inside.

"Tired?" Bert asked. He hefted a bale to the top of the stack in the loft.

"I'm okay," Peter said. He went to get another bale.

"So why did you decide to farm?" Bert asked.

Peter thought for a moment before answering. "I guess it seemed right. Like God opened the right doors at the right time and I walked through. And I didn't want to see the farm sold off without at least trying."

Bert nodded. "You glad you did?"

"So far," Peter answered. "But this going it alone...I'm not sure I can do it all."

"Partnerships have their ups and downs too," Bert said, hoisting a bale up, then walking outside for another.

"Have you always wanted to farm?" Peter asked. He pulled another bale off the pile on the ground and followed Bert into the barn.

"I guess so. Never gave it much thought," Bert said. "Something you do...like your dad before you." Peter tossed his bale up, and Bert tugged it to the top, setting it in line with the rest.

"So your family's been farming for a long time?" Peter asked as they went back outside.

"Fourth generation. My great-grandfather was given the place by the U. S. government after the Civil War. He fought in the Sioux Uprising in 1862 over in New Ulm," Bert said.

"It must be great to know so much about your beginnings."

Bert shrugged, then he stood and looked at the almost-empty hay rack. "I don't know. It doesn't do a whole lot to change my life. Just a nice story to tell, I suppose." He reached for another bale and hoisted it back inside.

When they were done, the stack reached almost to the rafters, its clean, straight lines pointing upward. Peter stood gazing at it for a while after Bert had gone home. The hay smelled of comfort and warmth and a winter without worry. A winter without cares.

It was raining. Mae had been running late all morning. She couldn't decide what to wear. Eventually she chose a long sleeveless sheath dress with straight lines and dressed it up with a pearl necklace. Her hair wouldn't cooperate, so she finally pulled it back and secured it in a messy bun. She ran outside to leave, only to realize that she had forgotten to feed the chickens.

Darting across the drive, dodging puddles in her black pumps, Mae tossed the frantic birds some egg mash. Then grabbing an empty feed bag to keep the rain off, she scrambled back to the Jeep and sped off for her lunch date.

She was a little nervous about seeing the old group. They hadn't been together since before she'd moved to Lake Emily. Marcia had sent a card congratulating her on "getting out of the rat race," and Karen had called to tell her that things weren't the same without her nearby. Yet Mae had a nervous ball in the pit of her stomach. She wondered what they would have to talk about. It wasn't like when they were in high school. Their lives were all so different now. Marcia was a financial consultant in a strip mall in Bloomington. Karen was a "makeup consultant" at Herbergers, meaning she sprayed perfume on unwary customers, and Elizabeth was a junior partner at an up-and-coming law firm in Minneapolis. It would be fine, she told herself.

Pulling into Applebee's busy parking lot, Mae checked her makeup in the rearview mirror. She felt a little queasy and put a hand on her stomach to calm its churning. Looking in the mirror one last time, she went inside. Everyone was already there—Elizabeth with her carrot-top mane and manicured nails, fair-skinned Karen, and Marcia in her outdoorsy Eddie Bauer fashions. Elizabeth waved Mae over to the table.

"Hey, farmer girl, it's about time you got here," Marcia said.

Mae scooted into the booth and said, "Sorry I'm late. I forgot about traffic. Have you ordered already?"

"I went ahead and ordered shrimp scampi for you," Karen said. "I hope you don't mind."

"No. That's my favorite," Mae said.

"Don't you look great!" Elizabeth said. "It looks like you've finally put a little weight on that skinny body."

"I don't know," Mae said, looking down at herself. "Maybe a little. Peter's grandmother is a great cook."

"Well, I'm glad," Elizabeth said. "You were making the rest of us look downright porky." They all laughed.

"Are there any cute single men out that way?" Karen asked.

"There are a few bachelor farmers I could introduce you to," Mae said jokingly, the image of Bert and Fred Biddle flitting through her mind. A fast-moving waitress went past with a huge platter of entrées.

"What is that smell?" Karen asked, lifting her nose into the air.

Mae sniffed, horrified as she realized that the odor of food was mixed with something distinctly in the chicken poop family. She glanced down at her mud-caked pumps in alarm and felt her face turn red. She put her elbows on the table and leaned forward, resting her chin in her hands as she shoved her feet far beneath her seat.

"I smell good food," Elizabeth said. Her gaze shifted to Mae. "So, Mae, tell us about your place. Are you going to be getting a new job now that you've moved?"

"I've been looking," Mae said, relieved by the change in topic. "But so far nothing's materialized. Maybe once the summer's over. It's a busy time on the farm."

"'On the farm'—that's so quaint!" Marcia said. "I can't imagine you living like that."

"Like what?" Mae said.

"Oh, in some giant old farmhouse, waxing floors, slopping the pigs. It seems so…I don't know…domesticated." The word came out like a slur.

"Now, hold on a minute," Elizabeth jumped in. "There's nothing wrong with being domesticated." There, at least Mae had one ally. "If that's the kind of life that makes you happy," Elizabeth finished. Her tone was vaguely condescending. Mae was batting a big zero. She shifted in her seat, and that scent wafted up again.

"So, Elizabeth." Marcia turned to the redhead. "I heard you have a big case."

Elizabeth's eyes lit up. "Do I ever!" she said, sitting up a bit higher. "The defendant is this fat little weasel of a man. Embezzling"—they all oohed at that—"but I'm pretty sure I can get him off. You ask me, I think he did it, but there isn't enough evidence to convict him."

All the other women were intent on Elizabeth's story. A few months ago Mae would've been as excited as they were at the juicy gossip, but for some reason today she wanted nothing more than to sit on her front porch and feel the breeze through her hair, to watch the blackbirds dive in clouds and cackle from the branches in the grove.

Elizabeth must've said something funny because everyone burst into laughter. "Mae, is something wrong?" Karen asked when she noticed Mae hadn't joined in their guffaw.

"Oh no." She smiled at the group. "Can you excuse me? I need to find the ladies' room."

Once inside, Mae frantically wiped off the chicken manure and mud that was caked on her shoes. What was wrong with her? She'd been looking forward to this visit, and yet now that she was here, she felt…disconnected. It wasn't as if anything had changed, really. Just her address. So why should she feel as though she didn't belong anymore?

She made her way back to the table, where her three friends were laughing. Elizabeth took a bite of salad from Karen's plate and smiled mischievously up at Mae. "You missed a good one, Mae," Elizabeth said. "Karen was telling us about her latest fling."

Karen raised an eyebrow. "I never called it a fling."

"She's dating the best friend of her last boyfriend," Marcia informed Mae.

"That's a touchy one," Mae said, trying to join in the jovial atmosphere.

"You aren't kidding," Karen said. "Especially when he saw us kissing before I'd had a chance to tell him I was breaking up."

"Shame on you, Karen!" Elizabeth and Marcia said as one.

Mae glazed over.

The afternoon filled with talk of shopping and boyfriends, the newest fashion trends and travel. Mae thought about the talks she'd had with Virginia, talks about life and loss, faith and courage, and she felt a deep sense that there should be more to friendship than chatter about makeup and weight-loss schemes. She wanted the kind of conversations Virginia and she had. Yet as she looked around the group, she realized she had never had a meaningful relationship with any of these women. She looked at her watch—three o'clock.

"I need to head on home," Mae said, feeling suddenly very tired.

"It seems like you just got here," Karen said.

"I know, but it's a long drive, and I have some things I need to do," Mae said.

"We'll have to do this again sometime," Elizabeth said.

"Yeah," Mae said, but in her heart, she knew something in her had changed.

* * *

The rusty beige station wagon with the flashing yellow strobe light pulled up to the mailbox. Mae and Virginia had been reading on the front porch, sharing coffee and chocolate chip cookies.

"I'll get it," Mae said, hopping up.

Virginia watched her walk, Mae's long dark hair swaying as she moved. When she returned, Virginia could see worry lines across her brow as her eyes scanned a letter.

"What is it?" Virginia asked.

"It's a letter from Mom," Mae said, handing the scrawled note to Virginia.

"This is personal," Virginia said, handing it back. "You don't want me—"

"I do," Mae interrupted. "Please read it. For me?"

Virginia looked down at the lined stationery. It began naturally enough, but soon the tenor changed.

> I had hoped by now you would've come to your senses
> with this ludicrous idea of yours. Your words cut me,
> Mae. They tear at my heart, and I can see now that you
> don't even care. Sometimes I think you wish I weren't
> your mother, that I was dead...

Virginia put the letter down, unwilling to read another word. She looked over at Mae and the tears tracing the soft contour of her cheeks.

"She's wrong, you know," Virginia said. She reached for Mae and held her in an embrace.

"This is the fourth letter like that," Mae said between sniffles. She pulled back. "Why does she do this to me? She says such horrible things. Whenever I do something she doesn't like, she accuses me of awful things. I just want her to love me." Mae's voice had turned hard.

"Everyone deserves a mother's love. Some mothers just…" Virginia's voice trailed off as she realized there was nothing she could say to justify Mae's mother's words. "Sometimes we need to find our family wherever we can. And I, for one, could use a granddaughter."

"Feeder pigs up three and a quarter, spring lambs down two." The Linder Farm Report was giving the latest ag report's price changes on the radio. Peter didn't have a clue what they meant, but Virginia had been giving him some lessons, and he'd gotten a couple of books from the library to bone up on his farming know-how.

Peter turned the radio off and sat in the old rocker in the living room. There was so much to learn it seemed daunting. Not only was there veterinary medicine and animal husbandry but also horticulture, engine repair and maintenance, business management, bookkeeping, and marketing to keep in hand. No wonder—as he'd discovered—so many of the farmers in Le Sueur County had college degrees in agricultural engineering. Even the Biddles had taken mechanics and agronomy courses to keep up with the newest technologies. Peter knew he could take a few courses at the University of Minnesota in Mankato, but there simply weren't enough hours in the day or dollars in the bank. He'd been calculating how many bushels of corn per acre at the current rate it would take to repay the loan. The pea crop had been mediocre at best, most likely because he'd gotten them planted so late. And what little money he did make from their sale he needed to turn around to buy the soybeans to replant those same fields.

"Whatcha reading?" Mae asked from her chair, her feet propped up on the matching stuffed ottoman.

Peter glanced up. "Financial stuff," he said as he yawned and returned his gaze to his magazine.

After a long silence, Mae said, "I'm thinking of inviting my sister to come for a visit. She's off from teaching for the summer, so I thought maybe she could stay for a while…say, July and August?"

"Okay." This time he didn't look up. He'd found an article on trends in the milk market and was trying to understand how to forecast the coming months. "Wow," he said.

"What? You don't want Trudy to come, do you?"

"Oh no. That's fine. I'm reading about the recent decline in the milk market. It doesn't look good, and even with production at full capacity, we'll be lucky to pay all our bills if prices don't go up soon."

Mae shifted in her seat. "It'll go up again, don't you think?"

"I don't know. I guess time will tell, but it's still a risk."

"I think I'm going to head on up to bed," Mae said. Peter looked up at her, wondering if she'd even heard what he said. She bent down and gave him a peck on the cheek.

"Good night," Peter said.

He listened to her footsteps on the stairs and looked back at his magazine, but his mind kept wandering to Mae. He couldn't help feeling that she resented it any time he talked about the farm. He wished she could share the burden with him, yet she seemed almost uninterested. Maybe it was his imagination, he decided. She certainly seemed to enjoy the garden and the chickens, and she had said she didn't feel at home with her old friends anymore. Maybe she really was settling in.

It was almost midnight by the time Peter made it up to bed. The hall light slanted on Mae as she lay sleeping. Her long dark hair glistened in the amber glow. She was so peaceful, so beautiful. Peter finished getting ready for bed and slipped under the covers. He turned toward Mae and studied the contours of her face, her high cheekbones, the curve of her long lashes, her pouty lips. He placed a hand on her hips and moved close, then bent his head to kiss her softly on the cheek. Her eyes opened sleepily.

" 'Night," she mumbled, then turned her back to him.

twelve

I'm here! Yoo-hoo." Mae could hear her sister's voice calling from the front porch when she arrived the next weekend. Mae made her way out the screen door, letting it slam behind her.

"Trudes!" she squealed as she leaned in for a hug. "I didn't think you'd be here so early."

"How's the little farmer?" Trudy said teasingly. Trudy had long, curly bright red hair and freckles that sunbathed across her nose like college students on spring break.

"Don't you look cute?" Mae said, pulling the edge of Trudy's skirt out. It was a full gypsy style. On anyone else it would've looked like a shower curtain; on Trudy it was a fashion statement. "They must love this in St. Paul."

"They love me for who I am." Her chin tilted up defiantly. "And thank you." Trudy turned in a full circle, letting the bottom billow out. "I like to wear clothes that could house small children in a storm." She smirked. "So where do I put my bags?" She nodded to her '79 silver Pacer with lime-green flower-power stickers that looked as if they'd come straight from a bathtub.

"I have a room all set up for you upstairs. There are five bedrooms, so if you'd rather have another one you can always move."

"Five bedrooms! You and Peter will have to get busy!"

Mae slugged her sister on the arm.

Trudy lifted the hatch, pulled out three heavy bags, and set them on the ground with a thump.

Mae lifted the nearest one. "Wow," she said. "That's as heavy as a bale of hay."

"A bale of hay—ha!" She slapped her thigh.

"You wait until I have you in the barn mucking stalls in that pretty skirt of yours!"

"*Mucking*—is that really a word?"

"Sure it is." Mae hefted another bag from the trunk. "Are you moving in? Why so many bags?"

"You never can tell," Trudy said.

"Hey, I'll show you my chickens after we get you settled."

Trudy raised a pale eyebrow. "This must be killing Mom."

Mae sobered and took a deep breath. "Mom and I are…" Her words trailed off.

"So that explains it."

"What?"

"Why she's suddenly taken an interest in my life. Her favorite daughter proved human after all, so she's calling her backup. I've been so freaked out! She's phoned four times in the last week to 'chat.' I'm thinking about screening my calls!" Trudy put an arm around her sister's shoulders.

"It was pretty serious, Trudy. I told her I was through with her. You know how she is… She was bad-mouthing Peter."

"I've had my run-ins with Mom—I know." Trudy lowered her arm and turned to face her. "So you were truthful. Is that the worst thing you can be with someone you love?"

"She is really hurt."

"Looks like you were too."

Mae looked away, afraid admitting her pain would bring on tears.

"Maybe this is a good thing," Trudy said. "I'm sure God has a lesson or two to teach her. She needs to know that you're all grown up. Of course, I will be charging you a fee every time she calls me!"

"I doubt she'd risk calling here. She wouldn't want to accidentally get me." Mae smiled and reached for another hug. "I'm so glad you're here," she said, hoisting a bag up the stairs to the broad porch.

"Give me a shovel, honey. I'll show you how to scoop that poop."

"Muck, it's called mucking."

"I was talking about Mom."

Saturday morning Mae woke as the orange ball of sun bounced over the horizon. Peter, of course, had been up since six o'clock. Cows needed milking more surely than the seasons changed. The coffee bubbled to the top of the old percolator, and its aroma filled the bright kitchen. Mae's stomach was upset, and she took a saltine down from the cupboard, hoping it would calm soon. Lately she'd been fighting this queasiness. She'd thought it was from nerves when she'd gone to lunch with her friends, but still it persisted. She made a mental note to get to bed earlier tonight.

As Mae stirred cream and sugar into her dark coffee, she heard footsteps coming down the hall. Trudy mumbled, rubbing her eyes, "What are you doing?" Her hair stuck out in every direction, and huge Big Bird slippers shushed across the hardwood floor.

Mae handed Trudy a steaming mug, to which Trudy added heaping tablespoons of sugar and cream.

"Are you always this perky in the morning? You weren't this way growing up."

"I was too."

"No. This I would remember." Trudy took a sip.

"Must be farm life."

"Oh great, so you're telling me this might rub off on me?"

"Maybe." Mae smirked.

"Okay, so what's on the agenda for today?"

"First thing, we're going to feed the chickens, and then we get to weed the garden."

"That sounds fun. Not."

Mae and Trudy had finished in the garden early and then had gone for a jaunt visiting the local antique stores. Mae had found a Yellow-ware bowl that she knew would look perfect in their white kitchen. And Trudy had purchased a Turkish tea set to complement her late-Bohemian style apartment, a wool Navajo blanket, and a Christmas cactus for her roommate in St. Paul. It had been a fun day of chatting as they browsed, walking from one place to the next. Trudy went through each store examining items carefully, but not buying a thing until the end of the day when she'd finally decided on what she absolutely had to have and then made them go back to three stores for the items that she'd said had "stuck in my brain."

Late that night Mae and Trudy sat together talking while strains of Mozart and Beethoven floated across the cozy living room. At around 9:30, Trudy stretched and yawned and said, "This farm life must be rubbing off 'cause I'm already zonked. I'm going to head on up to bed."

Mae stayed up, waiting for Peter to finish whatever was keeping him in the barn. She was tired, but she needed to tell him about her fun day. She had barely seen him all week.

Picking up a copy of *Country Life* magazine, she began paging through it, the fringed lamp casting a pool of light on the pages. Finally the back screen door creaked open.

"Peter?"

"Yep." He came around the corner, his face and hands covered with grime. "I'm going up for a shower," he said.

"I miss you," Mae said.

Peter ran a hand through his hair. "I'm sorry. The tractor needed some work—that thing is so old, I don't know how much longer I can keep it running."

"I'm not complaining," Mae said a bit too defensively.

"I miss you too. Let me get my shower and come back down. Then we can talk."

"Okay," she said. "I'll be waiting."

Hot water massaged Peter's tired muscles. It had been a long day. He'd replaced the starter on the tractor and then discovered that the fuel line had a leak. Then one of the calves developed scours, and he'd been keeping an eye on her. He'd reduced her milk replacer and she seemed to be doing better, but still it worried him. There were a lot of things that worried him these days. So many factors out of his control that could make or break this venture, everyday decisions that left their future hanging in the balance. At least today was done, and he could steal a few precious minutes with Mae before bed.

Peter came down the stairs and turned the corner into the living room. Mae's magazine had fallen to the floor, and her eyes were closed in sound, peaceful sleep. He sighed. So much for a night of talking.

"Huh?" she startled. "Oh, I fell asleep." Her eyes were half closed. Peter reached for the blanket that drooped over the edge of the couch and pulled it over her. "We were going to talk," Mae mumbled.

"We can set aside tomorrow night, have a special dinner maybe."

"Okay." She smiled sleepily. "I love you, Peter." He turned off the lights while Mae pulled the blanket tight around her shoulders.

"I love you, Mae."

One heifer had been acting strangely all evening. Peter was pretty sure she had bloat. Instead of her usual lopsided appearance, she looked like a balloon on four legs, and she moaned in obvious pain. He flipped through the notebook he kept to see if he'd made any notes about bloat, but he didn't find a mention. Finally he gave in and called Bert.

Peter had finished setting up the second round of cows when Bert slammed his truck door, his lanky legs carrying him to Peter in a few relaxed strides. "What's the problem?" he said in his quiet voice.

"She looks miserable." Peter pointed to the heifer.

Bert stood looking at her from the front. "Yeah, I'd bet it's bloat," he said. He reached into a tray along the wall and pulled out a bottle of milk of magnesia. "You'll have to give her this. Don't let her lay down. Keep her walking till she works things out and releases that gas." He took the bottle and gave the heifer almost half. Her long tongue sought for more when he pulled it away. "There you go." He handed the bottle to Peter. Peter sighed and patted the cow's side.

"Will she be okay?"

"Should be. She must've gotten too much grain somehow. You'll have to keep an eye on her. You could use baking soda and oil, but I think milk of magnesia is easier. If she doesn't get better, you'll need to call the vet to put in a shunt to let that gas out. You don't want to mess around with bloat. I can help you milk, if you'd like. So you can walk her," Bert offered. "She been milked yet?" Peter nodded as Bert walked over to release the headstalls of the patient cows awaiting their turn to be let loose from their milking.

Peter wished for the hundredth time he'd seen his grandfather work the barn and fields as the Als had seen their father—that kind of training would no doubt make everything second nature. But some days, it all seemed to come hard.

Yet Peter enjoyed working with the cows. They didn't criticize or disappoint, they just watched and came running delightedly when he brought their feed. It was a pure acceptance. They'd chew their cud, swishing their tails and meandering to the feed trough where they communed on silage and hay.

The sense of accomplishment when he turned out the lights each night was deeper than anything he'd ever felt before. Something here touched his very soul. Something indefinable about the deep-rooted connection he felt to what had come before, to those who had plowed this same land and worked this same barn. Peter fingered his grandfather's knife in his pocket, rubbing his thumb along the smooth side. Surely Grandpa Roy had felt this same kinship to the earth, to God.

Here God was a steadfast companion. He spoke to Peter each time the river valley was filled with fog on a summer morning or as he stroked a heifer's velvety nose. Peter often found himself praying about his concerns, asking for guidance. He certainly needed the help. He prayed that Mae was finding this same connection, and yet he wasn't sure she was. She seemed to have her good days, especially now that Trudy was here. But at other times she seemed distant, sad.

He knew his long hours of work were hard on her and she missed him. He missed her too and longed for the leisurely days they'd had together when they were dating in college, her a gorgeous freshman majoring in music, him a psych major. And yet the fear that he would default on his bank loan, or worse, that he wouldn't be able to keep paying rent to his grandmother, nipped at his heels, kept him in the fields too long, away from the very person he wanted to be close to.

Peter opened the doors so the heifers could go out to the pasture. The sick cow waited patiently, tied to the inner gate, while Peter wrote in his notebook, putting down Bert's instructions for bloat. Bert took over getting the next group of cows ready while Peter returned to the ailing animal. Snapping a lead rope to her halter, he walked her out into the pasture, careful not to let her lower her head to nibble on the grass. They strolled side by side for a good half-hour, and then he tied her to the gate and went back in to relieve Bert.

"Peter?" A female voice carried from the barn entrance.

"Over here," he said. Trudy's bright red mane floated above the partition as he placed the suction cups on a heavy udder.

She quirked a brow at him. "That looks fun."

"Want to give it a try?"

"Uh, no, thanks. Actually, Mae said supper's on, and she wanted to know how much longer you'll be. Something about a special meal?"

Peter ran his fingers through his hair. "Shoot!" He looked down at his watch. "I have a few more to milk. It's going to be at least half an hour. Did she seem mad?"

"Mae mad?" Trudy was obviously kidding. Her face sobered. "Maybe a little irked."

"Uh, excuse me," Bert interrupted. "I couldn't help but overhear." His eyes darted to Trudy's, and he nodded to her in greeting. "Hi." His face reddened from his neck up, like a flower blooming. He cleared his throat. "Uh...I can finish up here and walk the cow around for a little while." He nodded toward the heifer who was still moaning.

"What's wrong with her?" Trudy said, following his gaze.

"A little gas problem," Peter explained.

But Trudy was staring unabashedly at Bert again. Peter could've sworn he saw her flutter her eyelashes.

"Thanks, Bert," Peter finally said, standing. "You know I would've been in the doghouse."

"Yeah, doghouse," Bert said, still staring at Trudy.

"I owe you one."

Peter took off his coveralls and hung them on the hook by the barn door. He and Trudy neared the house, and sounds of Beethoven's Pastoral Symphony floated toward them.

"So…?" Trudy began.

"What?" Peter glanced at her, trying to guess what was on her mind. Not a clue.

"Who was the cutie?"

"Cutie? Who?"

"The farmer guy?"

"Bert? You're kidding, right?"

"Me? Kidding?"

"Bert is a neighbor—he's helping me out. You can't think he's cute. Trudy, he's a Biddle!"

"Honestly, Peter. If Mae had listened to that kind of talk, you wouldn't be married to her today."

"Hey!"

She turned her back to him and went in the back door of the house.

Mae was lighting candles on the table, her long hair glowing in their honey warmth. She lifted her head and smiled. "Good, you finished on time for once."

Peter went to wash his hands.

"Say, what would you two say to going to the nine o'clock movie? You're all done milking, right?" Mae said.

Peter hesitated. "I'd love to, honey, but one of the cows has bloat. I think I'm going to need to stay with her. Unless I can get her some relief before then…" Mae's face fell, and she turned back to the kitchen. "I'm sorry, honey."

Mae pulled the casserole from the oven. Her shoulders were rigid, and Peter knew she was trying not to cry.

"How about you, Trudy?" Mae said, turning to her sister.

"I'll go with you," Trudy said. "I don't have to wait for a cow to pass gas."

ALVA ENDICOTT

Alva Endicott rang the doorbell at Mrs. Cooper's apartment and waited for the aged widow to answer. Tonight was Tuesday, time for their weekly ritual. Alva was seventeen, a tall skinny girl who'd made friends with the eighty-two-year-old seamstress delivering meals and groceries to her each week. Alva had felt awkward at first. She'd never been around elderly people, but Mrs. Cooper made her feel at home right away. Soon Alva was coming over after school just to talk, to get the older woman's advice on everything from makeup to love.

Esther Cooper opened the front door and smiled at Alva. She carried her white pocketbook and wore a dramatic hat that would've made Greta Garbo jealous. Her makeup was extravagant, with dark red rouge and thick eyeliner, and her hands were covered with at least a dozen silver and gold rings with huge stones in gaudy settings. A large brooch in the shape of a flower with pink and white petals added the finishing touch.

"You want to drive tonight?" Esther held up the keys to the 1935 Ford.

Grinning, Alva grabbed them and said, "Sure thing, Mrs. Cooper." Once they had walked out front to the car, she opened the door for Esther.

Esther wasn't like other seniors Alva knew. She didn't care what anyone else thought. She was stylish, fun, and interested in everything, especially movies. Esther kept herself going, all right. Alva wanted to be just like her when she grew old.

"What's the show tonight?" Esther asked.

"Barbara Stanwyck in Stella Dallas. *I've heard it's a tearjerker."*

"I like Barbara Stanwyck. She has spunk."

"And class," Alva added as she started the engine. "She's so sophisticated and beautiful, and all the men adore her."

"What about Katharine Hepburn? I thought you said she was your favorite." The car glided through the quiet streets of Lake Emily. Alva looked ahead and saw the marquee for the theater lit up at the end of the street and a poster showing a sexy pose of Barbara Stanwyck in a red dress and beneath it a head shot of Stanwyck with John Boles. A group of teenagers milled outside the ticket window.

"Katharine Hepburn's too mannish for my taste," Alva said. "Barbara Stanwyck is strong but still all woman."

"They're both wonderful," Esther piped in. "But if you really want to know my favorite actor, it's that Gregory Peck. Those high cheekbones and his moody expressions melt me every time."

"Esther!" Alva said.

"I'm old, not dead," Esther said. They pulled into the parking lot and made their way inside.

It was Alva's turn to buy their tickets. The two women sat in the dark while the flickering screen cast its hypnotic spell. Stella Dallas made them laugh and cry, and at the end, when Stella stood outside alone in the cold as she watched her daughter's wedding through the windows, Alva sobbed in huge silent gulps.

"Her best movie yet," Alva said when the lights came up.

"That was worthy of an Academy Award, if you ask me," Esther said. "The academy always go for the schmaltzy stuff."

Alva laughed.

They made their way out of the theater, behind the crowd of moviegoers, the lights on the sidewalk guiding their way in the darkness.

"What's playing next week?" Esther asked as Alva started up the Ford.

"Captains Courageous with Spencer Tracy," Alva said. "Don't you think his eyes are too close together?"

Esther chuckled at that. "I guess I've never thought about it."

Lake Emily was dark, except for a few porch lights that collected frenzied moths in the late hour. Alva parked in front of Esther's apartment building and said, "You want me to walk you up?"

"Oh no, dear, you need your beauty rest. Best you head on home. Tell your mama I said hello." They both scooted out of the seat. Esther went to the front door, waving and then disappearing inside. Alva turned to walk the few blocks home.

The next week Esther didn't answer Alva's knock. Instead, a plain-looking woman in her late fifties came to the door. "May I help you?" she asked.

"Is Mrs. Cooper here?"

The woman's eyes clouded. "I'm sorry, but my mother died yesterday."

Alva's hand covered her mouth in shock, and tears filled her brown eyes. "But she…" Her words faltered, and Alva noticed that Esther's daughter was old enough to be her own mother. "Esther was my friend."

"Are you Alva?"

Alva nodded.

"Mom had a note and this on the table for you." She placed Esther's brooch—the one with the pink and white flower petals—in Alva's hand along with a note that read, "Remember to give to Alva next week."

Alva reached for the brooch and fingered the pink stone at its center. "Thank you," she whispered. "I'm real sorry your mother died."

The woman's eyes brimmed with tears. "I'm sorry for you, too."

Mae and Trudy stood in line at the Lake Emily movie house. It was an ancient building that had been beautifully maintained in its half-century of life. Tall white pillars stood in front alongside the ticket window, and the marquee was a runway of clear bulbs. A lush red carpet inside gave the theater a touch of Hollywood glamour. Mae got a small popcorn while Trudy ordered gummiworms.

Alva Endicott, Lake Emily's librarian, waited behind them. Mae had met her when she'd gotten her books on gardening. She had rhinestone-studded cat glasses on, and her silver hair was pulled back in a severe bun. Her hands were adorned with numerous rings, and she wore a pin with pink and white stones on her white silk blouse. "You're that new girl in town, aren't you?" Alva asked Mae.

"That's beautiful," Trudy said, gazing at the pin.

"Thank you," Alva said. Then to Mae, "Did you get your garden all figured out?"

"Oh yes. All planted and growing great."

"You'll like this movie," Alva said. "Not as good as they used to make but not too bad." She paid for her snack and walked ahead into the darkened room where the previews were already beginning.

Trudy led Mae to a couple seats right up front.

"I'm going to get a neckache up here," Mae whispered.

"It's perfect," Trudy said. "Like you're right in the action." She scooted down in her chair and laid her head on the seat back.

As Mae watched the love story, she found herself missing Peter.

There were so many things about him that she loved. He was devoted and hardworking, loyal, kind, funny. She needed to focus on those things, she decided, keep in mind why she fell in love with him in the first place. He would come around again once this season of hard work was over. She just needed to be patient.

Trudy and Mae had been working in the garden since breakfast, on their hands and knees, weeding and hoeing, watering with the long green hose and inspecting each plant carefully to check for pests and disease. Dirt filled every crevice of Trudy's hands and clung beneath her fingernails.

"I'm too old for this," Trudy said, arching her back. "My knees are killing me."

"You're twenty-nine."

"Exactly. I should be in that Adirondack chair on the porch, drinking iced tea and telling you what to do." Trudy wiped her forehead with the back of her dirt-covered hand, then pulled her long hair back. "I should've put my hair in a ponytail like you. It keeps getting in my way."

"I don't remember you being such a big whiner when we were kids."

"I'm not whining," Trudy whined, "just speaking the truth." The barn door slammed shut and Trudy glanced up. "Oh no!" she said.

"What's wrong?" Mae asked.

"It's that Biddle. I look awful."

Mae laughed.

Trudy's eyes followed his progress until he glanced her way. Her gaze locked with his, and he seemed to falter in his step. Maybe she didn't look as awful as she thought. Or maybe she was so ghastly she'd made him forget how to walk.

"Hello," he said. His voice sounded deeper than it had the night before, but the electricity between them was definitely the same.

"Hi," she said in a feathery voice.

"I…uh," he began. "I don't think I've seen you here before." That put a scratch on the record. He couldn't remember seeing her last night? Did he have some kind of memory disorder or something?

"Didn't I see you in the barn yesterday?" Trudy said.

"I would've remembered that. Definitely would've remembered that."

Trudy glanced over at Mae, who was sitting with her jaw dropped open like a startled trout. Trudy cleared her throat and shot Mae a "help me" look. Mae snapped out of her trance.

"I suppose I should introduce you. Fred Biddle," Mae said slowly, "this is my sister, Trudy Ploog."

"Fred?" Trudy said. "Now I'm embarrassed. I met your brother yesterday. Bert, right?"

"Yeah, Bert." The name was almost a mumble.

Trudy stood up to shake hands. "It's nice to meet you, Fred," she said, reaching for his beefy paw. He held her hand a little longer than he should have.

"Were you looking for Peter?" Mae interrupted.

"No. I was looking for Bert—we've got work to do." He shrugged his shoulders. "Well,"—his eyes darted to Trudy's—"I better get going. Chores to do at the home place. Trudy, was it?"

"Yes."

"You going to be around for a while?"

Trudy looked over at Mae who raised a questioning eyebrow. "The rest of the summer."

"I'll see you around then." He tipped the front of his seed cap and turned for his white Dodge pickup. The engine roared as he pulled a U-turn and left.

"What was that about?" Mae said, coming up beside Trudy.

"Now you shush," Trudy responded. "I can sense some possibilities around the corner, and I'd like to see what develops."

"Don't you mean you'd like to watch two brothers duke it out over you?"

"Mae flower! How can you say such a thing?"

"Come on, Trudes. What could you possibly have in common with those two farmers?"

"I guess we're going to find out, aren't we? You might be surprised what's lurking beneath those hats."

"Caps, they're called caps. And the surprise might be more than you bargain for."

"I'm fine with that."

"I knew I shouldn't trust that look in your eyes."

"What's the worst that could happen?"

"Well, there was the time that—"

"Okay, enough!" Trudy interrupted.

The acrid smell of chicken manure greeted Mae as she entered the hen-house. Mae plugged her nose and reached for the shovel to muck out the coop. The chickens had taken on a distinctly unattractive look—their white feathers seemed overlarge on their skinny bodies, and scrawny necks supported bulbous heads with big beaks. They were the quintessential junior highers—eager for attention, awkward, lacking confidence, lashing out at the slightest provocation. They scrambled about, eager for whatever would fill their gullets, competing for the myriad of flies that filled the coop.

Mae pulled the feeders out of the way and pushed the shovel into the corner. The birds scattered, complaining at being driven from their spot. One bird strutted around cackling loudly and looking accusingly at Mae. "Oh, be quiet," she said, taking a shovelful of manure to the wheelbarrow that waited outside.

The late-June day had turned hot, and Mae had taken to checking the waterers up to three times a day. She added another self-watering bucket to her mental shopping list. The animals seemed crowded in their little domain, often piled on top of each other. She thought about letting them run loose in the yard but knew that wouldn't work with the dog eager to eat them. She'd have to fence in a little yard for them to stretch their wings.

The chicken coop was a long, low building that had compartments along each side for nests. Mae put on her yellow gloves and began pulling out the old material, sneezing when the dust tickled her nose. Then she spread fresh shavings on the ground and in each little box.

After she was done cleaning the house, she went to the shed to get some metal posts and chicken wire. Outside the coop she diligently pounded in the green rods with the heavy post setter, lifting the gray handles to the top of her reach and then letting the tube slam down hard, pushing the posts farther into the ground with each motion. By the time she'd gotten all the posts in, she had worked up a good sweat. Next she unraveled the roll of chicken wire and attached it to the posts, careful to wire it securely. She snipped off the ends and stood to admire her handiwork. It was a small yard, but the chickens would appreciate it.

She went to open the coop door so the birds could explore their new domain, but the animals didn't notice their path to freedom. Mae stepped back and watched, thinking that they probably didn't want to walk past her. But they still pecked around their feeder and ignored the open doorway.

Mae crouched down and held out a hand full of feed to tempt them. The closest chicken was taking a drink from the waterer, her long neck tilted back as she swallowed. Finally Mae lunged. The bird squawked loudly and flew out of reach, and Mae landed with a thud on the shavings. The chicken stood on the other side of the pen and scolded Mae, spreading the news so all the other chickens would know how she'd been abused. The other birds looked on, horrified, their beaks ajar in shock.

"What are you looking at?" Mae said.

Virginia had been puttering around the house all morning. There wasn't much of anything to do—she'd baked another batch of peanut butter cookies for Mae and Peter along with a cherry pie. She'd cleaned the bathroom and kitchen the day before, not that they'd needed it. The laundry was done. Even her ironing was all hung and ready for wearing. She wandered into the living room and gazed around.

She could do some reading. She looked over the titles on her shelves, good books, but nothing captured her restless interest.

Picking up her framed wedding photo from the mantel, Virginia stared at the eager, joyful newlyweds. Roy had been so handsome that day. His face had those angular lines she had fallen in love with, and he had a little mustache that she used to tease him about; his hair was slicked back but there was a curl at the nape of his neck that refused to obey.

"I miss you," she said. Tears splashed onto the glass of the picture. Her only answer was the ticking of the cuckoo clock in the hallway. She wiped the tears off with the bottom of her shirt, then she sat on the couch, clutching the picture to her chest.

"What now, God?" She closed her eyes. "I know you have a plan for me in all of this. What am I supposed to do now?"

LEW OLSON AND
EARL CONNELLY

It was an unusually warm fall that year, 1940. Gardens were still yielding weeks after they were usually put to bed. People walked outside in their shirt-sleeves, thrilled that the Minnesota winter seemed unwilling to make an appearance.

Lew Olson had the duck boat all loaded with duck blinds, decoys, his shotgun and shells, and the picnic basket his wife had packed for him. He and Earl Connelly went duck hunting every year on Armistice Day weekend, and this year promised to be the best ever.

He drove up to Earl's in his Ford pickup.

"You're early!" Earl said as the screen door slammed behind him.

"Earl," Jean, Earl's wife, called from inside the house, "you forgot your lunch." She came out the door, a big black lunchpail in hand, the roundness of her final month of pregnancy accentuated by the apron tied high around her midsection. Earl jumped up to get the pail, giving his wife a kiss on the cheek before returning to the truck.

"Do you think I'll need a jacket?" he asked Lew.

"I didn't bring one. It's already pretty warm. You have enough ammunition?"

"You bet." Earl patted his box of gear as he loaded it into the boat in back along with his shotgun. He climbed into the passenger seat and rubbed his hands together, as he always did when he was excited.

They drove to the north shore of Round Lake and hauled the small boat into the marshy waters. Before long they were floating, quiet except for the rustling of reeds and cattails, eyes fixed on the bright sky as they navigated around the big lake.

Bang! *The first shot was fired, and a soft splash sounded up ahead.* "Got one!" *Earl said, a big grin on his leathery face.* "It'd be nice to have a dog to go get that for us."

"You're lazy," *Lew said as he reached for the paddles.*

"I'm not lazy. There's no sense in chasing birds if a retriever will do it for me."

By noon they had nine birds between them and decided to eat their lunches. "Jean isn't going to be happy with me," *Earl said. He took a bite of his corned beef sandwich.* "She hates cleaning ducks."

"You get your wife to clean birds for you?" *Lew said.* "My wife won't even touch them."

Lew surveyed the sky. Thick, ominous clouds brewed on the horizon, a roiling boil of blackness, and a chill breeze was kicking up. "Doesn't look good," *he said.* "Got some weather coming in."

Earl put his thermos back in his lunchbox. "Maybe we should start heading back."

"I think we can stay a little longer. With hunting this good, it's a shame not to try for our limit."

Earl nodded, and soon they were back to watching the sky. Boom! *Earl brought down another mallard.*

Within an hour the sky turned a greenish black, and strong winds began to blow, creating little whitecaps on the water.

"It's getting bad—we'd better head for home!" *Earl shouted into the wind.*

"Yeah, maybe we should," *Lew shouted back.*

Within minutes the wind had reached a howling scream, and huge raindrops were pounding the men. The temperature was plummeting like an out-of-control airplane. Then the rain turned to snow.

"We've got to get to shore!" Lew shouted, but against the sound of the wind he could scarcely hear himself.

The snow stung their faces and bare arms. Lew was shivering. He was sure Earl must be freezing too in his thin shirt, but he could hardly see him on the other end of the boat through the snow. They dug hard with their paddles. Lew could feel the surge from Earl in the back, but huge waves tossed the little boat around like a bobber with no direction. The flat bottom began to fill with the icy water. It sloshed back and forth, each wave soaking their feet. Finally, Lew put down his paddle and awkwardly made his way back to Earl.

"We can't fight this wind!" he screamed, cupping his hands around his mouth in hopes that his words wouldn't be lost. "Let's let it carry us in." He could see Earl shivering badly. His lips had turned blue. Earl dipped his head slightly in reply and slowly lifted his paddle to drop it back into the boat.

Lew returned to his position and held on as the swells carried them toward shore. Occasionally he would reach the paddle in to steer them. The waves loomed higher, some a good five feet from swell to trough. Lew looked at one as it arched high. He pushed hard against the paddle, afraid the wave would swamp the small boat. They turned, and the wave drove them forward, followed by another and another.

The temperature was still dropping. When they finally reached shore, Lew got out on wooden legs to pull the boat up, then moved hand over hand along the wobbly boat to Earl. "You okay, buddy?" he said into Earl's ear.

Earl gave him a puzzled look as if he didn't comprehend what Lew was saying. Earl's shivering seemed somehow lessened; Lew knew that was a bad sign.

"Come on, Earl!" Lew shouted. "Let's get moving." He pulled his friend to his feet and out of the boat. He was glad Earl wasn't a big man, or he never would've been able to get him up. "Can you stand?" Lew shouted, but *the wind howled louder, calling their names. It had been almost an hour since the storm had first hit them. Lew had lost all sensation in his ears and toes. And his shivering had turned to a dull, numb feeling.*

"We've got to keep moving, Earl. Jean needs you to come home to her and that baby!" At that, Earl took a halting step, then another. Lew rubbed his hands along his friend's stiff back, trying to generate some heat. There was no way he'd be able to get a fire going in this wind. He wished they'd brought their coats.

How could everything have changed so quickly?

Lew put an arm around the middle of Earl's back and shouted, "We're walking to the road. I have no idea how far it is, but at least we'll be moving."

They plodded against the swirling snow, heads down, toward the truck, they hoped. Darkness closed over them, and the eerie wailing went on. Each time they'd slow their pace, Earl would try to sit down to rest, but Lew would rouse him. Stopping meant death. Lew knew he'd never be able to look Jean in the eyes again if he returned without Earl.

They finally reached the road. Lew could not clear his mind of the swirling snow through which they stumbled. He didn't know which way led to his truck or to town. So they walked through the night, lifting their legs high through the hardened drifts of snow like ocean waves, sometimes running to bring up their body heat, never more than one step ahead of death. Lew's hands hurt until finally a deadened numbness overtook his right hand.

By morning, the winds had calmed and a deathly silence replaced the screams of the storm. Earl had barely said two words, but at least he was alive and walking. A snowplow pulled up alongside them.

"Lew?" It was Joe Walker, a friend of Lew's from Lake Emily. "Who you got with you?"

"Earl Connelly," Lew said.

Earl lifted his head slightly, his eyes glazed and unfocused. Joe said,

"You boys get in here quick. I'll get you up to the hospital." He helped them climb up to the crowded cab and handed them a flannel blanket. "He doesn't look too good," Joe said to Lew.

"He'll be okay," Lew said, wrapping the blanket tightly around his friend's shoulders.

Then the plow driver reached for a thermos and held it up. "Want some coffee?" He began unscrewing the cap and pouring the steaming brew into the red plastic cup, then handed it to Lew, who held it to Earl's lips.

"A lot of men died in that storm last night," Joe said as he started the plow up the road, lifted the blade, and retraced his path toward town. "How'd you two survive the night?"

Earl lifted his head, then said in a whisper, "Lew kept me going."

"Earl's too stubborn to die," Lew said. "Besides, he's still waiting to beat me at checkers."

fourteen

"I need to run to town for some dog food. Do you need anything?" Peter called up the stairs as he reached to put on a tired blue Minnesota Twins cap. Mae appeared above the top riser.

"Could you get some egg mash too?"

"Sure. How many bags?"

"One or two bags should be fine."

The screen door slammed shut behind him, and Peter walked to his truck. Scout followed, begging to go with him. Peter lowered the tailgate, and the old dog jumped up into the bed.

It was another gorgeous late-June day. The sun had warmed the inside of the truck. The corn was up. A yellow finch darted to the top wire of the fence. Scout barked, his gray muzzle pointed into the wind as he stood in the back with a big smile on his Labrador face.

It was nice to have a break from the constant demands of the farm. Peter felt more tired than he'd ever been. At night he would drop into bed, dead to the world within moments, only to have to get up again a few hours later to milk. He didn't remember his grandfather seeming this tired. He wondered what advice Grandpa Roy would have given him about that.

The six miles to town unfurled like a black ribbon. Peter raised his two fingers along the top of the steering wheel in a greeting whenever he met another oncoming pickup. He slowed as he reached Lion's Park and smiled when he saw the fountain in the park's center. He made his way past the cheery flower shop and the Used Books and Coffee Shop where a young couple sat under an umbrella at a French-styled table.

He turned right on Ferry Street. The Elevator loomed high, dominating the squat little town, its white square twin towers emblazoned with the words "Farmers' Elevator" painted in bold black story-high letters. Four small windows peered out from the top of each tower. He pulled into the gravel drive. Two farmers were talking in the parking lot.

"Hello," Peter said as he shut the truck door.

Both men tipped their heads in hello and followed Peter into the building. The place smelled of molasses mixed with hints of hydraulic fluid and lawn fertilizer. Two old men were playing checkers at a table near the coffee maker in the corner; both wore dusty seed caps with company names like Kent and Trelay on the patches on the front. Others leaned against the counter like drunks in a saloon, talking with each other and the man behind the counter whose shirt read "Jim Jenkins" in embroidered dark blue letters on his left pocket. As the screen door closed, every head turned toward Peter, and they stopped talking.

"Can I help you with something, Peter?" Jim said.

"Uh, yeah," Peter said. "I need two bags of egg mash and a bag of dog food."

"You're Virginia Morgan's grandson, aren't you?" the taller of the two who'd been outside said.

"Yes, my wife and I moved in this spring."

"Heard you're taking over the farm for Roy," the shorter said. "Got your peas and corn in pretty late."

"The rain held me back."

The man nodded as if that were reason enough. Then the shorter one said with an easy smile, "Saw you were putting in a garden."

"The wife is, really. I helped her plow it up."

"How'd you get her to walk behind the tractor and pull those rocks?

I've been trying to get my wife to dig up rocks for me for years." Everyone laughed good-naturedly.

"I won!" one of the checkers player in the corner shouted and rubbed his hands together.

"It's two out of three, Earl," the other said, getting up to walk over to the coffee maker. He gave Peter a long look, then said, "You new around here?"

"Yes," Peter said. "And no…"

"He's Roy Morgan's grandson," the taller man said again.

"I'm Lew Olson, and over in the corner is Earl Connelly," the older man said, extending a hand to Peter. He noticed the man was missing two fingertips.

"Happy to meet you," Peter said, shaking.

"So…you going to stick with dairying?" Lew asked.

Peter nodded.

"Must not like the prices these days," the short man said, his arms crossed and his hands tucked under his armpits.

"They aren't looking too great," Peter agreed.

"They've been dropping all year," Lew said. "Not a good time to be a dairyman."

"That's why I got out," the short man said. "Yeah. I quit on the whole thing last year. Sold the farm. Got a job in town. Let me tell you, life's been a whole lot easier ever since. My wife isn't nagging me about always being gone like she used to either."

"It's good for all of us that you got out, Marty," Lew said. "Means I don't have to compete with you to sell my milk to the creamery. Say," he turned back to Peter, "if you need anything, you let me know. Any Morgan's a friend of mine." Then he smiled with twinkling eyes.

Behind the counter, Jim looked up from his calculations and said to Peter, "I'll put this on your tab. I'll have one of the guys bring your feed to the dock."

"Thanks," Peter said, looking at the threesome. "Nice meeting you."

All the way home Peter couldn't get what the short man had said out of his head. *I quit on the whole thing last year. Let me tell you, life's been a whole lot easier ever since...*

Mae stood washing dishes in her bright kitchen. The sunlight bounced off the white tongue-and-groove cupboards and butter-yellow Formica countertops, making the room warm and cheery. She could see Trudy through the kitchen window. Her easel was set up, and she was intent on painting a pastoral scene. The silver milk truck was picking up another load of milk, and Peter was outside talking to the driver. One of the calico barn cats stretched and rubbed against Peter's legs. Peter bent down and scratched it between the ears.

Everything looked so ideal, and yet, Mae realized, it wasn't ideal, was it? She'd left everything that was familiar to her, and why? To get away from the pain her mother's constant criticism caused? Well, she hadn't exactly found acceptance here either. And she'd seen more of Peter before they were married. Now, when she did see him, he was stressed about the farm and about paying the bills.

Maybe her mother had been right after all. Mae sighed a heavy sigh and looked back out the window at Peter. She'd promised herself she would remember the good things. She just needed to try harder. And stop thinking about herself.

She watched the cat still rubbing against Peter's legs. Virginia's words from when they'd been house hunting came back to her—she'd said she'd always wanted a cat, hadn't she? Maybe that would be a good step. Helping Virginia instead of sitting around and waiting for Peter all day.

fifteen

Friday morning, Mae peered inside Virginia's front door. What was taking her so long to answer? Mae felt a sense of sudden worry.

"Mae, what's wrong? You look upset," Virginia said as she cracked the door. She was still in her nightgown and robe.

"I woke you up?" Mae moved back, glancing down at her watch.

"No. I'm just lollygagging."

"I'm sorry. I should've called. I assumed… I'll go and let you—"

"Come on in, dear," Virginia interrupted, stepping aside for her to enter. "It was about time I got myself dressed for the day."

"Did you sleep well last night?" Mae asked as they made their way to the cozy kitchen.

"Well, yes, actually, I did…" Her words hung as if she'd thought to say more but decided against it. Virginia filled a pot with water and put a filter and some Folgers into the tray. "So, what brings you to town this bright, sunny day?" Virginia said.

"Well," Mae began, "I was wondering if you would like to come with me to the pound."

"You want to get a playmate for Scout?"

"No…I was thinking that we could see if there's something there that you might like."

"Me?" Virginia looked into Mae's hopeful face. "I guess I never gave it much thought."

"A cat could be a great companion for you," Mae said. "I've heard

145

they can lower blood pressure…" Her voice trailed off. Her words sounded lame even to her own ears.

"My blood pressure needs lowering?" Virginia said, then smiled.

"I'm sorry. I'm not trying to push you into something you don't want to do. I thought—"

"I guess there's no harm in looking."

"Really?"

Virginia put a hand on Mae's. "Let me have my morning coffee and get dressed. Then we can go take a look."

The Humane Society was housed in the back of the Klein Veterinary Clinic, a big green house in the old downtown section. Mae and Virginia opened the front door, and a bell rang. Everyone in the waiting room looked up. Those sitting on the orange vinyl chairs included a freckle-faced little girl, her feet too short to reach the floor, with a baby bird in a box; an old bald man whose Boxer-type dog gave a low growl; and a petite woman who sat across the room with an odd looking cat—scrawny and low on fur. A fat tiger-striped feline that seemed to belong to no one in particular reclined in an empty chair next to the receptionist's desk, sleeping comfortably in a spot of sunshine, oblivious to anyone else in the room.

"Can I help you?" asked the sixtyish woman behind the desk in a pink smock with a bouffant hairstyle.

"Yes." Mae stepped up to the counter. "Um…are there any cats in the pound?"

The woman's eyes lit up. "Yes, we have a few. Mark!" she hollered down the hall. When a bespectacled man wearing a white lab coat poked his head out the door, she announced, "These ladies are looking for a cat."

"Oh sure," the short, heavyset man replied as he walked toward them. "I'm Dr. Klein," he said to Mae. "The cats are down here."

They followed Dr. Klein through the dark, winding hallway. The air smelled antiseptic, and the stainless-steel counters cast a Jekyll-and-Hyde aura. A lonely howling emanated from inside one room they passed, and a sniffling woman came out of another door, a cardboard box in her arms. They passed the surgery room, a room full of neatly shelved bags of dog and cat food and veterinary supplies, and stopped at a crowded little room lined with animal cages. The barking and yipping started as soon as they entered.

The doctor raised his voice over the melee. "We've got more cats than usual. A lot of dogs too, if you want to look at them."

Virginia glanced over at the bouncing, spinning dogs with their slobbering faces pressed against the bars, then shifted her attention to the cat cages.

A black cat with a white snip on the end of its nose hunkered at the back of its cage, hissing and arching its back. An orange tabby batted its paws through the bars playfully in an unashamed plea for attention, and a charcoal gray cat, more of a kitten, sat quietly, staring with wide eyes in a study of cat perfection. Other little kitties preened and stretched.

"A cat. Definitely a cat," Virginia said.

"They're cute," Mae said.

"Can I see the black one?" Virginia asked the doctor. He looked at Mae, a question mark in his thick eyebrows. Mae gave him a nod.

He opened the cage, and the cat took a swat at his hand. The doctor grabbed a leather glove from the top of the cage and reached back inside. When the cat took another swipe, the vet pounced, swooping the cat up with his gloved hand and grasping it tightly to his body. "He's pretty…feisty," he said, holding the struggling feline. "He was probably abused. Sometimes we have to put the ones like this down."

"He's beautiful," Virginia said. She reached to pet it, and the cat stared straight at her with pale blue eyes. "Those other cats will be easy to find homes for, won't they, Dr. Klein?"

"Yeah, I suppose," the doctor began.

"Virginia, maybe you could get one of the calmer cats that won't... terrorize you," Mae said.

"I know," Virginia said. "But I think he's cute."

"I'd recommend declawing," the vet said. "That will go a long way to saving your skin and your furniture."

"Can I hold him?" Virginia asked, reaching her arms out.

"Are you sure?" Dr. Klein asked.

She nodded. The vet carefully pried the cat's claws from his sleeve and held his legs down while Virginia slipped her hand around the midsection. She clutched the animal tightly, lovingly stroking the fur on his head and back.

"See," Virginia said. "He's already taking to me." A black paw arched toward her and raised a red line on Virginia's wrinkled hand.

"You said declawing?" Virginia said to the vet.

"We can do it in the next couple days, before you even take him home."

July sauntered in hot and muggy. The corn was knee high, and the heat of the season had settled in like a fat man on a rocking chair. Mae and Trudy would make breakfast around eight, then they would head out to the garden to weed and harvest whatever was ripe and to water. Today was such a morning. Trudy was hunched over, harvesting beets, with a wide-brimmed straw hat shading her freckled face.

"Mom called me again last night. Why did I give her my cell phone number?" Trudy said. "She's been asking about you."

"What did you tell her?" Mae said.

"I told her to call you herself."

"I bet she liked that."

Trudy pulled up a plump purple beet with a long taproot. "Wow, Mae flower." She held up the heavy tuber. "We done good!"

Mae smiled. "That's beautiful! Isn't this great?"

"I could think of funner things," Trudy laughed.

"We'll have beets for supper and then can the rest. Virginia left her pressure canner in the back of one of the cupboards. Maybe she can come over and show us how to use it."

"Okay, farm girl."

"I'm having fun," Mae said. "Besides, there's nothing wrong with being frugal."

"*There's* a flattering term."

A truck crunched onto the gravel, and the women looked up. It was Fred Biddle again, the third time in four days. Each time he had another excuse, but always he would find Trudy, and the two would go for a walk. Trudy waved as Fred brought the truck to a stop. She walked over to him. He hopped out and stood, shifting his weight on restless feet, his long body slightly hunched, his hands working over a cap in his hands.

"Hi, Fred. What's up?" Trudy asked. He seemed nervous, as if he were the star at a fourth-grade play and he'd forgotten all the words. His dirty blond hair was combed back, tamed for the moment.

Fred looked at the ground. "Well...I wanted to ask you something. You know the Fourth of July is the day after tomorrow..." Trudy moved a little closer, trying to read his darting eyes.

"Mae!" Peter came rushing out of the barn. When he saw Fred, he walked toward him. "Fred!" His eyes flicked to Trudy. "I think one of the cows has an infection. Would you take a look?"

Fred looked helplessly from Peter to Trudy and back.

"Her leg's swollen, and she's not putting any weight on it," Peter said, obviously panicked.

"I'll be there in a minute," Fred said.

"Go on," Trudy said, wondering why he was acting so odd. "We can talk later." She smiled into his eyes.

"Oh...," he faltered. "I guess I'll take a look." Fred retreated into the barn with a glance over his shoulder at Trudy.

"What was that all about?" Mae said, coming up behind her.

"Fred or that meddling husband of yours?"

"Trudy..."

"I think Fred was going to ask me out. Either that or ask if I knew anything about lighting fireworks."

Another truck sounded on the dirt road, coming in fast. Mae and Trudy turned to see Bert Biddle, his green Trelay cap firmly in place. He parked next to his brother's truck and stepped out of the vehicle.

"Bert, what's going on?" Trudy said.

Bert's face was red. "Going on? I was just... Is Fred here?" he asked, tilting his head toward Fred's truck.

"He's in the barn with Peter. Looking at a cow."

"Oh," he said, his eyes darting between Mae and Trudy.

"Uh, I better get back to weeding," Mae said, pointing over her shoulder to the garden. No one was listening.

"So, Bert," Trudy said, "what are *you* doing for the Fourth?"

Bert's face turned a darker red. "The Fourth? I...didn't Fred...? I'll probably head to the parade with Mom and Dad, like I do every year. There's food and music in the park, polka bands—"

"You like to polka, Bert?" Trudy asked.

"A little," he said, his head toward the ground. There was something utterly charming about his unassuming way. She almost expected him to dig the toe of his shoe into the ground and say, "Aw shucks."

"So…," Trudy probed. "Maybe I'll see you there?"

"Maybe."

"Save a polka for me…?"

He smiled shyly, then he said, "I'd better go get Fred. Ma wants him home."

Peter came in for lunch and washed his hands at the kitchen sink while Mae set the table. "That heifer has an infection in her leg," he informed Mae.

"What do you do about that?"

"Call the vet. He'll be out after lunch."

Trudy came down the stairs, having changed out of her grubby gardening clothes into a flouncy white top and bell-bottoms.

"Lunch is on," Mae said, and the three sat down at the Formica table in the kitchen.

"What's up with Fred and Bert?" Peter asked once they'd said a blessing over the meal.

"Were you this dense when you were dating?" Trudy asked, taking a sip of her iced tea.

"What?" He had a puzzled expression on his face.

"Trudy's toying with them," Mae said as she took a bite of her egg salad sandwich.

"I am not."

"Are too. It's pathetic, Trudes. You're a grown woman," Mae said.

"How quickly you forget, my little prom queen. It's rough out here in single land. Besides, I like them both. They're interesting."

"Interesting, how?" Mae probed.

"Well, I don't know exactly, but I'm finding out. I'm intrigued about what lies beneath those seed caps. People are a lot more than meets the eye. You know what I mean, Mrs. Farmer?"

"These things have a way of biting you back," Mae said. "I just don't want to see you with a broken heart. Again."

"Hey, I'm here for a few weeks. I'm getting to know the neighbors."

MARK KLEIN

Mark Klein had been out of veterinary school for nine weeks when he set up shop in Lake Emily in 1972. Dr. Gove, who had served Lake Emily for over forty years, had finally decided that Arizona was a better climate to grow old in, so he and his wife set off as soon as "the kid" dropped his medical bag inside the front door.

Mark's receptionist, Cindy Lowry, had come with the bargain. A slightly overweight woman in her midforties, she had a perky disposition that made Mark feel positively depressed by comparison.

The phone rang. "Klein Veterinary," Cindy chirped into the receiver. "Oh, you poor dear. Okay, I'll send Mark right over."

Mark raised an eyebrow. Cindy didn't seem to comprehend that he was her employer, even if she was twenty years his senior.

"You have to go out to Joe Walker's," Cindy said. "It's his dog, Major."

"Don't people usually bring the dogs to me?" Mark asked.

"You haven't seen Major—there's horses smaller than that dog."

"Did he say what's wrong?"

"Joe thinks he got into rat poison."

Mark wasn't looking forward to this. Rat poison killed more dogs than rats, it seemed. And the deaths were often slow and painful.

Mark put on his rubber muck boots and walked out to the new Ford truck, stocked with everything a vet would need on a house call. He started it up and headed to the Walker place.

The past six months had gone fast, and he was growing to like Lake Emily. The community of cats and dogs had adopted him as their vet, but the farmers in the area were still suspicious of this youngster with his "new ways" of doing things. He knew that everyone had to earn their way in Lake Emily, show that they were in for the long haul and not some fly-by-nighter. And he was determined to do just that.

When he reached the rural address, he turned up a winding drive that disappeared into six-foot-tall corn.

As Mark climbed up the steps, a flock of ducks landed in the marsh opposite the house, and Joe Walker cracked the screen door. He was a big man with a cane, hunched at the shoulders, and his skin had a grayish cast.

"What took you so long?" the man asked.

"I came right away," Mark said, entering the darkened room. Mark's eyes took a few moments to adjust. The small room was cluttered with unframed paintings leaning against the wall, clothes and magazines piled everywhere. An enormous black dog with a white muzzle lay on the floor next to an avocado green recliner. Major seemed to be unconscious, and his tongue lolled to the side as he moaned with each breath.

Mark withdrew his stethoscope and bent to listen to the dog's chest. The heartbeat was weak. "Do you know how much poison he ate?" Mark turned to ask Joe, who limped with his cane over to the chair nearest the dog. Lines marked the worry on his face.

"I have no idea. Is he going to make it, Doc?" The old man coughed, a wheezing hack that made Mark wonder if Joe would survive.

"He's really weak," Mark said.

"He started acting funny this morning. I thought it was old age, like me, you know. But then I found the door to the shed wide open and the rat poison spread all over. I should've tossed that stuff months ago," Joe said. "What was I thinking? Now Major's so sick." He looked over at the big form, and tears streaked his wrinkled cheeks. "He's all I've had since my Mabel passed." He pointed to a picture of a younger Joe, perhaps thirty, with his arms wrapped around a pretty blond-haired woman. It was taken on the beach with a boardwalk full of tourists in the background. She leaned into him, a flirty expression on her face as they gazed at the camera.

"She was a looker," Joe said. "And all mine for thirty-seven years." He gazed back at the dog and moved the cane to his other hand. He pulled a bandanna from his back pocket and wiped his face.

"Do you mind if I sit with you for a while?" Mark asked. There was nothing medically left for Mark to do, but he couldn't leave the man alone with the dying animal. He moved to a chair and watched the dog's labored, shallow breathing.

"Mabel gave me that dog as my retirement gift," Joe said. "He's a good dog, a good dog." He shook his head, then stared off for a long moment. "You know, I used to drive a snowplow for the county. That dog would ride next to me. He loved to watch the blade go up and down. I delivered a baby once, in a snowstorm. The story made the papers in Minneapolis. Bet you didn't know that." Mark shook his head.

They sat together, sometimes talking, sometimes watching.

Major died at a little after seven.

Mark hoisted the dog's big form out to the grave that he dug, and Joe said his farewells. When he was done, Joe's sad eyes looked up. "I guess I'm all alone now," Joe said matter-of-factly.

"Can I take you out for a cup of coffee?" Mark asked.

sixteen

The vet's red truck pulled up to the barn, and a short, stocky man got out. He looked to be in his early fifties, with thinning black hair and a sparkle in his brown eyes. He offered a hand. "Mark Klein."

"Peter Morgan," Peter said.

"You're Roy's grandson," the vet observed.

"Afraid so."

"You like being new in town?"

"I guess so. There's a lot to learn," Peter admitted.

"I won't hold it against you," the man said good-naturedly. "Been there myself."

"The cow's in here." Peter motioned to the barn door and led the man inside. "I noticed her leg seemed swollen this morning."

The cow was tied to the rail above the feed trough.

"H'm," the doctor mumbled as he moved next to the cow. She pushed her wet nose into his back as the vet ran his hand along the right front leg and then the other, finally returning to the original leg. The animal lifted it as if she was in pain when he touched the spot. "She's ouchy, all right. Any idea where she got that cut?"

Peter leaned closer and peered at where the doctor was pointing. "No. I noticed it this morning. I don't have any idea where she got it though."

Mark glanced around the barn, his brow knit. "You might want to look around, you know, babyproof the barn."

"Babyproof?"

"You don't have kids, do you?" Peter shook his head. "Keep your eye out for anything sharp," the vet continued. "She's going to need an antibiotic. I'll give her a shot today, but then you'll have to give her a shot for nine more days."

"You want me to give her a shot?"

"That a problem?" the doctor said questioningly.

"Uh...no...that's fine," Peter said.

The vet returned to his truck and dug in the drawers, withdrawing a vial of medicine and the biggest syringe Peter had ever seen. He could've put a whole mug of coffee in that sucker. "So where did you farm before coming to Lake Emily?" the vet asked as he pushed the needle into the pink bottle and began filling the syringe.

"I haven't farmed before," Peter confessed. "I'm kind of picking it up as I go."

"I see..." No doubt the man could read Peter's worried brow. "I'll show you how to give the shots. It's not hard."

They returned to the cow, who switched her tail at Peter, flicking him on the back. Mark moved next to the heifer's thick neck and grabbed some of the skin between his forefinger and thumb. "I pinch 'em before I stick 'em. It deadens the pain a little." After a moment, he jammed the three-inch needle into the cow's neck. Immediately the animal began bucking and swung her one-ton body toward the vet, who hopped nimbly out of her reach. When she stopped thrashing, Peter could see that the vet had still managed to get the needle tip into the animal's neck despite its coming off of the syringe. The tip stuck out just a little on the surface of her skin. "Grab her tail," Dr. Klein directed.

"Wh-what?" Peter wasn't sure he'd heard right.

"Hold her tail straight up in the air and push. It'll distract her from bucking." The stout man demonstrated, standing directly behind her rump and thrusting her tail into the air. Then he handed the ropelike tail to Peter, who tentatively moved into position. "Yep. Like that. And push."

The doctor moved to the needle and reattached the syringe, plunging the medicine in within a moment. "All done," he said as he withdrew the needle. "You'll want to put some iodine on that cut on her leg, then a full one of these each day." He held up the syringe.

"I have to do that nine more times?"

"Unless you want to pay for a vet visit every day. Welcome to farming, son." He patted Peter on the back. "Maybe you can get your wife to hold up her tail. I hear she pulls rocks from behind the tractor."

Peter turned red. "You heard that?"

"Lake Emily's a small town, son. Don't let it bother you. The rumor mill goes both ways." Peter wasn't sure what the man meant by that, but he let it drop. "It's a good thing you called. She would've been in trouble without the antibiotic."

"Can I milk her while she's on it?"

"You'll have to milk her to keep her flowing, but you can't sell it until the antibiotic is out of her system. Just put the tube into a bucket when you milk her. The creamery will be more than happy to test it for you. I'll stop out again next week on my way by and take another look at her, and answer any other questions you might have." He paused. "Give me a call if you need anything."

"Happy birthday to you. Happy birthday to you," Trudy sang in her best Marilyn Monroe voice as she came down the stairs the next morning. "Happy birthday, Mrs. Farm-er. Happy birthday to you." Mae sat at the kitchen table and lifted her lips in a weak smile. "What's the matter?" Trudy sat down with her.

"Peter didn't say a word about my birthday."

"Maybe he's got something planned for later. You know Peter, what did he do last year?"

"That's my point—if he remembered, he would've said something."

"I'll go set him straight." Trudy stood to go out to the barn.

"You will not!" Mae pulled her back down.

"Oh, I get it," Trudy said. "You're playing one of those wifey games. 'If you really love me, you'll remember my birthday. Otherwise I'll sit inside and mope all day.'"

Mae's face turned hot. "What do you know about it? You're not married."

"Sometimes you sit around here like a princess expecting him to drop everything while he's working night and day to make this farm a success."

"I looked hard for a job, and when I offered to help him with the milking, he refused! Besides, I do a lot around here."

"Sure. You tried real hard to lend a hand. Honey, you do what you want to do. Peter doesn't have that luxury. The chickens and garden are fine. But they're a hobby. You need to wake up and smell the roses—you've got one heck of a guy. Sometimes, Mae, you're just like Mom."

Mae was so angry she couldn't even think straight. Stunned, she stood and fled up the stairs to her bedroom. She sat on the bed. Trudy's words reverberated through her skull. How could her own sister say such horrible things? She wasn't like Mom. Mom was cold, selfish, indifferent. She treated Paul like an accessory.

Mae lifted her head and glared at the ceiling, wiping the tears from her eyes. What was wrong with expecting Peter to remember her birthday? It was about time he thought about her for once and not the next problem with the cows or the farm.

When Mae finally came downstairs, Trudy was nowhere in sight.

Breakfast dishes had been washed and put away, and the bright July sun shone through the window.

Mae was at the sink, getting herself a glass of water, when Peter came inside.

"Hey," he said. "Can you give me a hand with something?"

She turned awkwardly toward him, wondering if he could see that she'd been crying, but he'd already started back outside.

"Sure," she said in a small voice and followed him to the barn.

"You want me to do what?" Mae said. She put on green rubber muck boots that went up to her knees.

"Hold the tail like this." Peter demonstrated, forcing the cow to take a step forward until the halter strained on the lead rope that was tied to the gate.

"What if she…? You know." Mae's eyes were huge.

"You'll be fine," Peter insisted.

Mae raised an eyebrow, obviously not buying it.

"Please, honey, I can't do this alone." Peter wasn't above begging. "Otherwise she'll kick. A two thousand pound cow could really hurt me. It's like getting hit by a car."

She thought it over. "What am I supposed to do again?"

"Push like this." He showed her again.

Mae took hold of the tail and moved behind the cow while Peter went around to the animal's neck with the huge syringe. "Pushing?" Peter asked.

"Yes," Mae said, irritation in her voice. "Hurry up."

Peter pinched the neck just as the vet had shown him, then pushed the needle hard through the leather-tough skin. It seemed to take forever for the plunger to go all the way in, but soon it was out, and he was putting the cap back on. The heifer chewed her cud and glanced over at him curiously.

"Can I let go?" Mae asked. "Ew! I thought you told me she wouldn't —oh yuck!" she screamed. A plop hit Mae's boot. She moved to the side, her face twisted with disgust.

"Sorry," Peter said, a grimace on his face.

"Ewww," she said, her face a pale green. "It's not funny," she accused, looking down at her boots.

"Are you okay?"

"Yeah," she said grudgingly. "At least I didn't throw up."

"You look like you still might."

"I'm going outside." Mae left, and Peter could hear her turn on the spigot.

He untied the heifer's lead rope, snapped off the halter, and headed out to join Mae on the Adirondack chairs in the backyard.

"You sure you're okay?" Peter asked when he reached her.

"Yeah. I'm fine." She hesitated. "I'm glad the Als weren't there to see that one. Everyone in Lake Emily would have had a good laugh."

"I know the comment the vet made about you pulling up rocks bugged you."

Mae nodded her head. "It was humiliating. I wonder how many other things the people of Lake Emily know about us. Maybe they all know about my tangle with the flypaper strip too."

"They aren't that bad," Peter said. "You're feeling a little sensitive."

Mae crossed her arms over her chest.

"I saw Trudy drive off," Peter said, "Where'd she go?"

"Beats me," Mae said. She sighed heavily.

"What's wrong?"

"Just a difference of opinion," Mae said, turning to look away.

"Happy birthday," Peter said, leaning toward her.

Mae's shoulders slumped, and huge tears dripped from her eyes. "I thought you'd forgotten," she squeaked out.

"No, I didn't forget." He lowered his eyes to look into her face. "But would you mind if we celebrated tomorrow? I'm afraid I'm going to be running all afternoon. I'm not sure when I'll make it in tonight."

Mae wiped her eyes and shifted her head away from him. He couldn't tell if she was angry or just thinking. "Okay," she said finally. "We can celebrate tomorrow."

Later that day Mae heard Trudy's car door shut. The back door squeaked open, and Trudy poked her head inside.

"Are you mad?" Trudy asked.

"Yes," Mae answered.

"You can't stay mad at me on your birthday. I got you a gift," Trudy said. "Do you want me to sing to you again?"

"Get in here," Mae said.

Trudy came in bearing a large, brightly wrapped package. Mae's face cracked in a hint of a smile. "What did you get me?"

"Like I'm going to tell you. Open it, Mae flower."

Mae lifted the big box and gave it a shake. There was a faint bell-like sound inside. "Let me guess—there's a smaller box inside with a bell in it. You know I hate that."

"I know. Are you going to torture it or open it? Here, I'll get you started." Trudy poked her finger through the paper and tore a small section.

"Hey!" Mae complained. She pulled the wrapping back to reveal a beautiful red chintz apron with a heart and a dove appliquéd on the front. The dove held a small bell in its mouth, and the heart doubled as a pocket with "Mae" embroidered across its delicate surface.

"This is beautiful. You had this made for me?"

"Uh-huh. A fabric artist I know—she makes incredible purses too. But there's more." Trudy dug deeper in the box and pulled out a matching tablecloth and napkin set, each delicately appliquéd like the apron. "Now you can be the hostess with the mostest. Aren't they just fab?"

"Thank you," Mae said, her eyes getting misty again. "I love these. Thanks for remembering."

"It's nothing," Trudy said, reaching over to give her sister a hug. "Besides, it's your birthday. And that's not all I have for you, my sweet." She went back out the door and came in carrying a large grocery-store birthday cake. "You can't have a birthday without a cake." She set it on the table and pulled a box of candles from her pocket. "How many candles do you want?"

"Not too many."

seventeen

Mae stood in the barn door the next day. She looked fresh and beautiful on the warm Fourth of July day in a yellow floral spring dress and straw hat.

"I'm having some trouble with the well. We're out of water, honey," Peter said. He walked over to her and reached to give her a kiss on the cheek. Mae pulled away, hurt in her eyes. "I'm not trying to avoid coming. I *can't* leave now. It has to be fixed. The cows have to have water."

Mae sighed and glanced toward the Jeep where Trudy was sitting in the passenger seat, honking the horn and waving. "There's always going to be something, isn't there?"

"I know you're disappointed," Peter said. "I'll come as soon as I get it straightened out. I promise." He ran a finger along her jaw, lifting her eyes to his. "Please understand," he said.

"I do." Her shoulders drooped. "That's the problem—I understand fully. Tomorrow it'll be the tractor or you'll be out haying or whatever…"

"Can we talk about this later?"

"Sure." She turned away from him, and he put a hand on her shoulder. As soon as he touched her, she moved toward the Jeep, a brisk tone to her voice as she said, "We'll see you at the park. If you ever get there." She hopped in and turned the wheels, gravel spraying up as she left.

Peter stood watching Mae. She'd been moody all week, and now this. What had happened to their idyllic plan? A sweet life on a farm, slow and easy. Time to appreciate each other and grow in their pursuit of God. And yet there wasn't time for anything, it seemed. He was constantly exhausted, and she was constantly telling him he wasn't doing enough for her—if not in her words then in her actions. He'd tried to reassure her that it was only a temporary part of farming, that once the corn and soybeans were harvested, life would slow down. And she'd seemed to understand, but invariably the next day it was as if she hadn't heard a word he'd said. Didn't she know how important this was to him? Couldn't she see that he was carrying everything? The weight of the whole farm was on his shoulders. And what part of the burden was she carrying? She was too busy having lunch with her friends and going shopping with Trudy to even notice.

This wasn't the Mae he'd known when they were dating. That Mae had been understanding, compassionate, willing to try anything. He missed the old Mae.

Keeping this farm afloat required sacrifices.

Mae wasn't willing to sacrifice anything.

Mae and Trudy made their way through the festooned streets of Lake Emily. The American flag hung from porches and light poles, creating an endless profusion of waving red, white, and blue along Main Street. Children waved miniature flags on wooden sticks, their smiles wide in anticipation, and golf carts zoomed up and down the street selling pop to support the Rotary.

Behind a barricade, the parade was beginning its lineup with clowns, bright tissue-paper floats, Shriners in loud, tiny cars, and marching bands from every high school in the area.

Mae turned up the hill to Virginia's house and pulled into the driveway. Virginia had already set up lawn chairs on the sidewalk in front of her home. Mae tooted the horn as they got out and went to the screen door. Virginia met them.

"Handy that you live on the parade route," Trudy said.

"Isn't it though?" Virginia said, handing her a tray of glasses filled with frosty lemonade, sweat beading down the sides. "Can you take that out back? I thought we could visit some before the parade. Let me get some sugar for that," Virginia said, turning and retrieving a sugar bowl shaped like a strawberry. Trudy took the tray to the little white wrought-iron table between the chairs.

"Where's your kitty?" Mae asked.

"Probably hiding under the recliner," Virginia said, to which Mae raised a brow. "At least he's moved from under the bed. It's progress."

Trudy came back in. "The lemonade is on the table out there. Where's your bathroom?"

Mae and Virginia went and sat around her white patio table under a big green umbrella. The lilacs surrounding the property had long since lost their blooms. Now the thick hedge offered privacy while thick-trunked oaks and elms provided a deep shade to the parklike yard. "You look bothered, dear," Virginia said to Mae.

"Peter isn't coming today. There was a problem with the well… We were supposed to celebrate my birthday, which was yesterday." Mae didn't intend to cry, but the tears slid past her resolve.

"Roy and I used to have our rows over that kind of thing all the time." She put a wrinkled hand on Mae's. "It's the hard part of marriage and farming."

Mae reached inside her purse for a tissue. "Trudy said I'm just like my mom."

"Are you?"

Mae looked up as another round of tears coursed down her face.

"It's been bugging me all night. I promised myself I'd never be like my mom." Mae sniffed.

"That's a promise most of us make at one time or another and none of us can keep. Eventually we learn that our mothers aren't such bad people after all." She stirred sugar into the glasses and handed one to Mae. "Being a farmer's wife takes a commitment, Mae. It's not an easy life, but it's a full one. If you let it be. But you've got to be in it together, or it will tear you apart."

Mae sighed heavily, allowing the truth of Virginia's words to edge in. "I clean and make his meals, do his laundry."

"That sounds more like a housekeeper than a partner." She said it kindly, and yet the words stung. "Love him and enjoy the time you have together. But don't wait around for him to come to you. Go to him, Mae. Besides, why do you think all our women's clubs started—church Circle, Extension, the Monday Club—because our men were in the field or with their cows all hours!" She smiled.

Mae looked into Virginia's pale blue eyes and said, "I'll try."

Trudy walked out carrying a loudly purring cat in her arms. "Hey, guys!" She petted the cat's dark head. "Look who I have."

"How did you do that?" Virginia asked, her mouth agape.

"Do what?"

"Get Snip to come out of hiding and let you hold him?"

"You call him Snip? That's your problem right there. Snip has some real negative connotations—he was probably offended. Something to do with being neutered. He walked up to me and rubbed against my leg. But, you see, I'm not real needy, so cats are drawn to me. They want you to be standoffish like they are. It's a whole rejection psychology, really."

"Trudy, you're pulling our leg," Mae said. "Come on, how did you get the cat to come?"

"I said, 'Here, Fuzzy Pillow.' Now there's a name, descriptive and affectionate."

"Fuzzy Pillow?" Virginia said, looking at Mae with a grimace.

"Don't look at me! I don't answer for Trudy—she's her own piece of work."

JAKE JENKINS

A car to die for. Candy apple red 1963 T-bird convertible. Not a speck of rust. Original everything. Jake Jenkins had worked and scraped for two years, and now, on his seventeenth birthday, his dream had come true. He pushed the accelerator and made his way down Highway 36. The wind's hot fingers whipped through his blond hair as rock-'n'-roll blared from the FM radio.

As he came around a curve in the road, Jake could see dark black smoke curling from the old Elwood place. Flames licked the white siding on the second floor through the shattered glass windows.

Jake skidded the car onto the grass and ran up to the two-story house, the heat of the fire reaching out to push him back. He could hear the sounds of screaming and crying from inside, calls of the family in the flames. Without another thought, he pushed the front door in. Thick smoke came out in a dark plume, and Jake was forced to his knees to avoid breathing it in. Flames of orange glowed through the black smoke that burned his eyes with its poisonous breath. Jake called into the interior, "Where are you?"

A moan came from ahead and to the left. Jake crawled beneath the pillar of darkness toward the sound, feeling his way past a chair, a footstool, to a couch. The moan came again.

Jake knew the man. Vernon Elwood. He'd seen him sitting at the counter at the Chuckwagon talking to the owner countless times. Vern was lying on the floor, semiconscious. Jake took a deep breath and pulled the man's tall frame over his shoulders. He stood in a quick motion and ran, staggering under his weight, to where the open doorway had been. Jake

169

jumped down the steps, sucking in the clean air, and when he was beyond the reach of the heat, he laid the man on the lawn.

A scream sounded from upstairs again, along with a loud crash as something in the house collapsed. Jake took a moment to check on the man and made sure he was breathing. Another plea for help came as Jake returned to the house. The smoke was darker, and hot orange flames danced across the porch. With his arm, Jake shielded his face from the heat. The doorway and windows were engulfed. Jake ran around to the back to see if there was another way in, but it, too, was a wall of fire.

When he returned to the front, Vernon was coming to. He stared with horrified eyes. The voices of his wife and two daughters echoed from the flames. Vernon stood and swayed, then ran on weakened legs toward the house. Jake grabbed him from behind and dragged him back to safety as the older man struggled against Jake's grasp.

"I have to get them!" Vernon screamed. "They're still alive."

"There's no way in," Jake said, holding the older man firmly.

Vernon's eyes were wild.

A voice cried, "Daddy!" Tears brimmed in Jake's eyes.

Vernon struggled weakly against his strong arms, then he sobbed and collapsed to the ground, his eyes searching the upstairs windows. Flames poured out and upward. Then the house collapsed in on itself. Red and orange and black flamed higher as the devil sucked air from all around. The sound of sirens came down the drive. Heavy sobs racked Vernon's tall frame. Jake knelt beside him and wrapped an arm across his back as the firemen pulled up and unfurled their long black hoses.

They sat that way until only black smoking embers remained, curled remnants from the flames and heat. Nothing left of a life lived in that home except a broken, crumpled man in the arms of a seventeen-year-old boy.

eighteen

Sirens sounded promptly at one o'clock. The Lake Emily police force led the way as they had at the start of every parade since the town was founded in 1857—in shiny white cars now instead of the horses and buggies of their predecessors. Then came the VFW, generations of old men and young in uniforms from five wars, with flags held high. Citizens stood as they passed, the elders clasping hand to heart, reverent, distant expressions in their eyes.

Virginia had come to every Fourth of July celebration in town since she and Roy married. There were new faces, of course, the addition of food drives for the Lake Emily food shelf, but all in all it was the same parade each year.

The big red fire engines came along next, proudly shined to perfection by the volunteer fire department. Jake Jenkins tossed candy from his high seat in the cab and called to Virginia, "Who says only the kids get candy?"

She picked up a piece that landed at her feet and held it up to him. "My favorite!" A big grin spread across her face as she unwrapped the green apple Jolly Rancher and plopped it in her mouth.

Miss Lake Emily passed with her court of royalty, white-gloved hands waving in unison as they switched from side to side high atop the blue and gold tissue-paper float. She smiled with perfect white teeth and waved her best Queen Elizabeth wave.

"Virginia!" She smiled broadly in Virginia's direction. Virginia returned her wave.

The Shriners went past in their matching uniforms, the little tassels from their tubelike black hats flicking as their miniature cars careened up and down the street in figure eights. Barely missing, the cars passed each other in an alternating zigzag. Mothers shooed their children to the safety beyond the curb.

A polka band sponsored by the Community Bank *oompah*ed on a big hay wagon, and the Lake Emily Promenaders square-danced along the street. The women, in heavily petticoated, checkered skirts, twirled with each call as they do-si-doed and allemanded, while the men in string ties and cowboy boots kept their eyes trained on their partners, careful not to miss a beat.

A multicolored Chinese dragon wound side to side in a serpentine path, occasionally stopping to blow huge puffs of fire extinguisher steam from its nostrils, scaring the unwary and causing the crowd to break out in loud laughter and exuberant clapping.

The Girl Scouts took their turn, with a float highlighting their contributions to Lake Emily. They had a big trash can on their float with a sign that read "Keep Lake Emily Clean." The older girls skated alongside and passed out candy and fliers promoting scouting to youngsters on the sidelines. The Daisy and Brownie Scouts in their blue and brown waved from the revamped hay wagon.

The Boy Scouts came next, marching in disjointed military formation next to a float that had a collage of pop cans and stacks of newspapers. Their sign read, "Reduce, Reuse, Recycle."

Virginia loved these parades. The chance to get out and see old friends and young people. To celebrate summer in its fullness. Roy had always driven his old tractor in the Fourth of July parade. He'd made a wooden plaque that read "Minneapolis Moline, 1947, owned by Roy and Virginia Morgan." She wondered if anyone else would miss seeing that orange-and-yellow tractor chug up Main Street today. She gave a heavy sigh.

It seemed every thought led back to Roy.

Lion's Park was a river of people, some standing in line for the famed onion rings with a thick beer batter coating that the Chuckwagon served from a booth, some waiting for roast pork sandwiches, fried cheese curds, or thick lamb gyros with cucumber sauce. Trudy strained to see over heads as she, Mae, and Virginia moved toward a picnic table set up in a semicircle as the St. Peter Govenaires Drum and Bugle Corps performed their full act with precision.

Finally finding an open picnic table, the threesome sat with their deep-fried foods and overlarge Pepsi-Colas.

"Have you seen Bert?" Trudy whispered to Mae.

Mae lifted her chin to scan the crowd. "There's Bert's cap over there." She pointed toward the bandstand on the other side of the park. Her gaze returned to Trudy. "You're smitten."

"I am not," Trudy said. "I promised him a dance."

Trudy felt someone block the sun from her face, and she turned to see who was there. She put her hands over her eyes to squint at the intruder.

"Hey, Trudy," the deep voice of Fred Biddle said. "Mind if I sit down?"

"Not at all," Trudy said, motioning for him to take a seat. He nodded a hello to Mae, then Virginia.

"Been here long?" Fred said.

"Oh no. We walked over once the parade ended. Lake Emily really puts on a party," Trudy said.

"I suppose," he said. "Have you been to the midway?" He pointed over his shoulder to a collection of about a half-dozen rides and a few game booths. "They've got helicopter rides this year. Would you like to go?"

Trudy's face turned red as she felt Mae tap her leg under the table. "Um…sure. You want to come?" she asked Mae and Virginia.

"Sounds like fun. You go on ahead," Virginia said. Mae grinned a little too broadly.

"But…," Trudy faltered, "I promised Bert a dance."

"He's kinda busy with Mary Kinsey right now," Fred said, pointing with his chin. Trudy looked over at the bandstand again and could indeed see Bert dancing with a petite blonde.

"Oh," Trudy said, feeling disappointed.

Mae watched Fred and Trudy disappear behind the Tilt-a-Whirl a few moments before Bert Biddle came up.

"Bert," Mae said. He shoved a nervous hand into the front pocket of his jeans. "You looking for Trudy?"

"Um, yeah," he said, making eye contact at the last possible moment.

"You just missed her. She and Fred went to the midway for a helicopter ride." Bert's face fell, and the sound of chopper blades sounded in the distance. They both looked up as the rounded craft lifted above the trees and swooped south.

"Well, I guess I'd better be going," Bert said.

"Did you want me to tell Trudy you were looking for her?"

"No. No, that's okay. I think Mom and Dad are about ready to head home." He turned and walked away, looking as brokenhearted as a little boy whose cotton candy had been eaten by the circus elephant.

***

"Win the pretty lady a cute bunny?" A dark-haired carny with close-set eyes challenged Fred as he and Trudy made their way across the midway.

Fred smiled his best John Wayne smile, then swaggered over to the shooting gallery. Trudy grimaced. Next thing he'd get out his club and drag her by the hair into his cave.

"Watch this." Fred reached for the weapon and took aim. The little ducks started in formation across the front of the booth. *Bang!* The first shot went too far to the left. "Your sight's off on this thing," Fred complained to the man.

"Sight's fine," the man said, a glimmer in his beady eyes. "You've just got to aim straight."

Fred gave the man a menacing stare and then took aim again. The gun repeated over and over. When Fred was done, he'd knocked over twelve of the helpless decoys. The carny grinned a plastic grin, showing off two black spots in his mouth where teeth had once resided.

"Wow," he said. "Ain't he something?" This directed at Trudy.

"Yeah. Something."

Fred smiled and pointed to a giant blue monkey that the carny deposited in Trudy's arms. "Look at that," he said. She returned a polite smile, feeling suddenly self-conscious.

They strolled toward the helicopter at the far end of the midway, the monkey gazing awkwardly over Trudy's shoulder. "It's not really fair," Fred said. "I've been shooting since I was a little kid."

"That's mighty impressive," Trudy said a bit too sarcastically. Fred kept walking.

A skinny, bald man with a veiny nose sat next to the bulbous machine, which was roped off to keep spectators away from the flailing blades. He was smoking a cigarette and looking bored with life itself.

"Hey," Fred called above the sound of the motor. "You still taking folks up?"

The man nodded and tossed his cigarette to the ground, crushing it beneath his shoe. "Twenty bucks apiece," the man said.

Fred whistled low. "That much?" He reached for his wallet and slowly counted out forty dollars.

Trudy gave him a sidelong glance. He was cute, but she'd never seen this side of him before. He'd always been courteous and nice, but today it was as if he had something to prove, and it grated on her.

The man opened the door and grunted something about watching their heads and the monkey needing to stay behind. They climbed into the glass-enclosed cabin. It was deafening inside, so conversation was impossible. Trudy watched the pilot buckle himself in and begin flipping switches. She felt her stomach tighten. Why had she agreed to this?

Fred leaned next to her ear and shouted, "This is going to be great!"

She gave a nervous nod and felt the sweat bead on her palms. She wrung her hands nervously.

Fred sat back, crossed one foot over the opposite knee, and slid his hand along the back edge of Trudy's seat. She felt the skin on her neck crawl. Her knuckles were white as she held on to her seat. The chopper lifted into the air like a yo-yo on a frayed string.

Trudy peered out the window at the rides twirling around and the big blue monkey laughing at her from the safety below.

By the time the well drilling company came out to fix the well, it was time to milk again. Peter couldn't get Mae off his mind. She was going to be mad that he'd missed the day's festivities, but he couldn't have done things differently. He wished she understood that this was not a matter of choice but of necessity. Their ability to live and stay on the farm was dependent on his success.

His success. The words reverberated. Why did he feel so alone in this endeavor? Mae had been a real sport about moving here, and yet, he realized, she wasn't part of the farm. With milk prices still dropping like a toboggan on a hill, he didn't have room for the slightest mistake. Truth was, even if he did everything perfectly, Peter wasn't sure he'd be able to make ends meet.

Peter rushed through milking, readying the heifers in their head-stalls, moving with speed from one animal to the next. The cows strained to look back at him and stomped their feet, expressing their frustration at the change in pace. Soon the slurping sound of the machine as it filled with sweet creamy milk filled the silence.

Peter stood watching angrily, his sweat-soaked shirt cooling in the breeze. What if Mae never grew to like it here, to really be a part of the farm? Could they truly go back? St. Paul seemed like a foreign land to him now. The thought of living there again caused a physical ache in his gut. And there wasn't exactly a place to go back to now that Mae's mom was no longer speaking to them.

Peter thought of his grandparents for the millionth time, wishing he could find the way that had come so naturally to them. Wondering if he would ever find it.

The performances at the park went on all day. Festive polka bands played as plump women and scrawny men spun dizzily; guitar-wielding folk singers sang lonely ballads; marching bands from neighboring communities played for parents who stood in the back and led the crowd in, clapping at the end of each song. The Minnesota Zoo brought their traveling show with snakes and raptors, chinchillas and tarantulas.

Around dinnertime Mae and Virginia retreated to the quiet of Virginia's house. Virginia had made a cold pasta salad, and she sliced some garden tomatoes that she set out with shakers of salt and pepper. They sat in the shade of the backyard, sipping sweet lemonade, letting the day's excitement dwindle into quiet calm.

"Are you still upset with Peter?" Virginia asked.

Mae set her drink on the table and thought about it. "I don't know… The problem is, today he misses my birthday and the Fourth of July; tomorrow it'll be Christmas."

"That's true," Virginia said. Mae wondered why she didn't offer some explanation to calm her fears. "Roy missed Easter services more times that I could count. Every year I was angry at him." Her eyes met Mae's. "What I wouldn't give to be angry with him one more time."

As the sun began to dangle low, a vehicle pulled into the driveway, and the sound of a door slamming echoed across the pavement. "We're out back," Virginia called.

A few moments later, a fresh-scrubbed Peter poked his head around the corner. "Hi," he said tentatively, looking at Mae. She felt her insides jangle, and she lifted the corners of her mouth in an attempt to hide the surge of emotion.

"Would you like something to eat, Peter? I have a pasta salad and ham sandwiches still in the Frigidaire," Virginia offered.

"That sounds great, Grandma. Thank you," he said, taking the wicker chair next to Mae. Virginia gave Mae a knowing look and went inside. Peter reached for Mae's hand, but she pulled hers away.

"You're still mad." He drew closer.

"You expect me to say everything's all fine now, don't you? But it isn't fine, Peter." She turned her head. Hot tears stung the back of her nose.

His eyes searched hers. "I know you've been missing me, and I've been too focused on making this farm a success to notice. But you're not the only one who's feeling alone right now." Mae lifted her head to look at him, surprised at his admission. "I'm putting my all into this because I really want the farm to work, but you're not even part of it."

Trudy's words echoed, and Mae broke. Tears began to course down her face.

"I need you," Peter said.

"I'm tired of you always working…"

"I'm tired of always working too, and I'm tired of being resented for it."

Mae lowered her eyes. "I guess I have resented you for it," she confessed.

"And I was wrong to refuse your help…and I'm sorry. I've been trying to, but I can't do it all alone."

"You mean you want me to milk and hay…"

"Whatever it takes, even if it's running to the hardware for me or the bank…" His voice dropped off, and his eyes searched hers. "But…," he began, his voice hesitant as if he didn't want to say what was coming next, "if you absolutely hate farming…we'll quit. I'll take a job to pay back the operating loan, and we'll find something that works for both of us."

Her heart broke when she saw the tears in his eyes. "I'm sorry, Peter." Mae reached her hand across the table to him. "I don't hate the farm. I know you love doing this, and I've been…selfish. I want to be with you." She ran a hand along Peter's jaw, her thumb touching his tear. He kissed her palm. "I don't want you to give up, especially because of me."

He leaned in to kiss her. A soft, sweet kiss.

"We never got to celebrate your birthday," Peter whispered as he drew back.

Mae looked at him with doleful eyes. Peter reached into his pocket and pulled out a small box with a white bow. "I'm sorry," he said. He put the box on the table in front of her.

"I was too busy." He lifted her chin, looking her straight in the eyes. "I know you need me too."

She leaned in to his chest and let the warmth of his love caress her.

"Here you go," Virginia said loudly, letting the back door slam and setting down a tray on the table.

"Thanks, Grandma." She patted his shoulder.

"We haven't missed the fireworks," Mae said. "Virginia said we can go see them reflected in the lake if we go to Lion's Park."

"There's nothing like Fourth of July fireworks over Lake Emily," Peter said.

The night was dark and cool. Lightning bugs flickered here and there across the park's grasses. Blankets were spread in clusters with children lying in wait for the show to begin, their giggles wisping on the breeze. Peter and Mae made their way carefully through the patchwork of residents, choosing a spot near the water's edge and laying out their Hudson's Bay blanket. Virginia had said she was tired, but Mae suspected she was giving them a little alone time.

At ten o'clock promptly came the *boom, boom, boom* of the first fireworks, and for half an hour the crowd sat in awe. Flowering explosions of light lit the sky in green and blue and red and gold. The crowd let out the usual *oohs* and *aahs* as the big dandelions of color filled the sky. The deafening sounds seemed so close, and with the water's reflection amplifying their effect, it was mesmerizing. Peter reached for Mae's hand, and she felt a warmth move up her arm. She gazed into his shining eyes and felt as though he'd returned from a long journey.

nineteen

The sun was peeking over the eastern horizon, waiting for the all-clear signal when Mae walked out the back door. The morning air was already heavy and warm. Mae had on her overalls, a bandanna over her hair, green muck boots up to her knees, and a pair of yellow chore gloves on her small hands. Peter had gone ahead to round up the cows and get the first set lined up in their stalls. This was going to be fun, Mae decided. Working alongside Peter, the Tammy Wynette of dairy "standing by her man."

The dew was heavy on the grass, putting a wet gleam on Mae's boots. A killdeer complained loudly from the pasture at her intrusion. Mae watched the bird run along the ground, feigning injury to distract her from its nest.

Mae opened the crisscrossed door. The barn smelled of a faint chlorine mixed with sweet hay and earth and manure. It was a comforting smell. The black-and-white cows were lined up, and the machine's sucking sounds filled the room.

"All set," Mae said. Peter looked over, and the heifers strained to look back at her. Their tails switched at flies, and their liquid eyes were huge brown pools with long lashes.

"I'll show you what to do once I have a couple of open stalls," he said. Two of the spiderlike suction arms retracted, and Peter went over to spray the udders with iodine solution before pushing the lever to release the headstalls. The first heifer took a few steps forward, far enough to be out of the way of the stanchion bars, but then she stopped and stared at Mae.

"They'll need some time to get used to you," Peter explained. "You'll need to hide behind one of the heifers being milked."

"Hide?" Mae said.

"Duck down so they won't see you—they won't come in otherwise."

Mae went and stood between two heifers while Peter brought in two new ones. Mae gazed up at the tall heifer on her right and patted her soft side. The cow's eyes took on a panicked look as she twisted to see who was touching her, then she stomped her feet and began to pee. It splattered on the cement and onto Mae's overalls. Mae started to move out, but the two cows coming in saw her and immediately began backing away out of the parlor. Peter whacked their rumps, and Mae hopped back, resigning herself to the fact that she was going to get splattered and there was no way around it. She moved as close to the other cow as she could without panicking her.

"Come over here," Peter said once the headstalls clanged around their thick necks. "Spray the udders with this." He showed Mae the sprayer. "Then wait about thirty seconds and wipe them down." He walked over to the first cow, and Mae stood behind him and watched over his shoulder as he went through the routine of wiping clean the udders and teats and then attaching the long tubes. When he'd finished the first one, he stood up to let Mae take over the next one.

"Here goes," she said, feeling more than a little nervous. The heifer gazed at her suspiciously as she scooted closer. The animal shifted her weight to the near hoof. "Is she going to do something to me?"

He laughed. "You'll feel more comfortable in no time," he said. "Just be sure you don't put yourself between a cow and a wall or fence, and don't stand directly behind 'em."

Mae pulled the paper towel from the overhead dispenser and began to wipe the teats and put the suction cups on while Peter watched.

They soon had the routine down—Peter rounded up new animals, and the two of them split up the cows. As they finished setting up the last round of cows, Mae noticed that one heifer stood in the doorway watching the others get milked.

"Does she always do that?" Mae asked, gazing at the girl with an almost perfect white star on her forehead.

"She's our voyeur—happy to watch but she doesn't want to get milked herself. I'll bring her in after you leave."

Mae walked slowly toward her, and the cow backed up a good four steps. They stared at each other, and the heifer seemed to relax after a few moments, as if she'd evaluated Mae and decided she wasn't all bad.

Mae turned back to Peter. "I like her," she said. The corner of Peter's mouth lifted slightly, and he put his arm around her shoulder. Mae reached up a hand to his and tilted her head back to look into Peter's eyes.

"We're going to be okay," she said.

Brilliant Sunday morning light laced into Mae and Peter's bedroom. Mae slipped on her earrings, and Peter came from the bathroom, his hair wet from his shower, a towel around his waist.

"Back out to the fields?" Mae asked.

Peter stepped behind her and wrapped an arm around Mae's waist. "No," he said, kissing her shoulder. "We're going to church. Some things you just have to make a priority."

Mae turned toward him and gave him a hug. "I'm glad. You'd better get hopping—we have to be out of here in half an hour."

When Peter, Mae, and Trudy pulled up to the church parking lot, it was already packed. Peter parked on the street, and they went inside. Mae and Trudy went over to talk to Ella and Virginia. Mel Johnson, the head usher, was standing talking to a tall blond man who appeared to be in his late thirties. "Peter!" Mel said, extending a warm hand. "You know Jake Jenkins?" Peter shook hands with both men.

"I don't think we've had the pleasure."

"Jake's the fire chief," Mel said, "and an usher. We were talking about you."

Peter raised an eyebrow.

"Mel mentioned that you might be a good candidate to take your grandpa's spot on the ushering roster," Jake said. "I know it can be hard fitting it into a farming schedule..."

"No, no," Peter said. "I'd be honored. What do I need to do?"

"Mostly make sure the service goes smoothly—hand out bulletins, collect the offering, that kind of thing," Jake said.

"Put me down," Peter said.

"Will the first and third Sundays of the month work out?" Mel asked.

"I'll be here."

The corn grew tall as July rambled on. Cicadas with their loud buzz filled the afternoon air. Trudy was reading an art magazine on the front porch while Mae filled a glass with milk, trying to calm her churning stomach. She'd been so tired lately, and she wasn't sure why. She dismissed it as her early mornings milking with Peter. She felt her forehead to check for a fever. It felt cool. Mae took a long drink of the milk, and the churning calmed to a slow mixing.

"Mae?" Peter came in the back door. "I've got to get busy baling those north acres, and it looks like I'm on my own. What would you say to driving the tractor?" Then he caught the expression on her face. "You don't look so good. You coming down with something?"

"No. I'm tired."

"Why don't you lie down?"

"I'll be okay."

Peter scratched his chin. "Bert was going to come over, but he got caught up with something at their place."

"I'll be okay," Mae repeated, placing her cup in the sink.

"What's up?" Trudy came in from the porch.

"I asked Mae to drive the tractor for me, but she's feeling kind of sick."

Trudy inspected Mae's pale skin and weary expression. "You do look awful, honey. Peter, you're not going to let her drive. I can do it."

"Are you sure?" Peter said.

"Oh, like you're Mr. Experienced. You can show me what I need to do."

Peter looked over at Mae who slumped onto the stool as a wave of nausea swept over her. "Okay," Peter conceded.

"Goody!" Trudy clapped her hands. "Let me go get changed." She ran up the stairs.

"What was wrong with what she was wearing?" Peter said.

Mae shrugged.

"Honey, maybe you should go see a doctor."

"I'm not getting enough sleep. That's all."

"I get the same amount of sleep as you. Besides, what would it hurt to find out you're healthy? Then we'll know it's all in our heads—I have a psych degree to deal with that. Remember?" He smiled.

"You're very funny. My body needs to adjust, that's all."

After about ten minutes, Trudy reappeared. "I'm ready," she said, standing on the bottom step in denim overalls and a straw hat, her red hair tied into two braids.

"It's Pippi Farmstocking!" Peter said.

"Ha-ha-ha," Trudy replied. "Some people are so immature!" She led the way outside to the tall John Deere.

Trudy climbed up first, settling into the enclosed cab while Peter stood on the step outside and showed her how to shift and brake. "Turn the key while you push in the clutch."

"I've driven a stick shift," Trudy complained. She revved the motor.

"Easy!" Peter said nervously. "Set the idle up, then ease the clutch out. Okay. Steady." The tractor lurched forward taking a big hop. Peter grabbed tight to the cab's frame to keep from falling out. "You're going to have to be careful of the load on the back. It's wider than the tractor, so make your turns wide," he shouted above the tractor's noise.

"What?" Trudy hollered back.

"Turn wide!"

She turned the tractor around, the hayrack following behind, and Peter glanced up to see the ancient telephone pole dead ahead. "Turn!" he bellowed as the rack caught the pole and it began to lean like a cornstalk in the wind. Trudy slammed on the brakes. Sparks flew as electric lines pulled free and broke from the barn and shorted in a serpentine dance along the ground. Peter grabbed the key and turned the tractor off.

"Oops," Trudy said in a small voice.

"Oops?" Peter repeated. "Oops?"

"You already said that," Trudy said. Peter's face turned red, and Trudy said, "Okay, I can go with that." She stood to climb around Peter.

"Get out the other side. The power lines are still hot. If you touch them, they'll kill you," he warned.

"I'm sorry, Peter."

"Yeah," he said brusquely as he waved a hand at her. "I'd better go call the power company and see if I can get that old generator running. Maybe they can get here before milking tonight."

Mae was taking a nap when Peter came in. He went to the phone to call Bert for advice. His main concern was the milk tank and how to keep it cool. The last thing he needed was to lose a morning's batch of milk. He prayed the generator was up to the task.

"Bert," Peter said, "we've got a little problem over here…"

After explaining the situation to Bert, he called the electric company. They promised to be out "ASAP," which meant whenever they got around to it.

He'd gone out and baled the north field by himself that afternoon, too angry to ask for Trudy's help again. He drove a few feet, letting the baler drop the bales onto the ground, and then walked each bale to the hayrack and stacked a half-dozen at a time. It was tediously slow, but it kept him from yelling at Trudy.

Another day wasted. He'd have to head out again after milking.

Mae had said she'd be out to milk in a few minutes, so Peter went on ahead to get started. The generator seemed awfully loud in the unlit barn, but the milk in the tank was okay. The door was open, letting in the bright sunlight, but it still wasn't as bright as having the overheads on. Dust particles floated in the pillars of yellow as Peter bent to wipe down a heifer's udder.

"Peter?" Trudy poked her head inside the doorway.

"You!" he said.

"I'm really sorry." She stepped closer. "Is there anything I can do to make it up to you?"

"Well…," he considered, "I might have a cow that needs a shot."

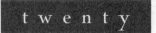

twenty

I t had been two days since the telephone pole incident. The power company informed Peter that he would be liable for the replacement cost, and then the insurance agent implied that he'd knocked the old pole down to avoid paying to replace it. Where would they come up with the five-hundred-dollar deductible?

Peter had hung up the phone after talking to the claims adjuster when Mae and Trudy came in from grocery shopping. Mae put a bag on the counter.

"Honey, we need to talk," Peter said.

"Which honey, me or Mae?" Trudy said cutely, setting two bags on the kitchen table.

"Can I talk with my *wife*, please?" His tone was not kind, and he knew it.

Trudy raised her hands in surrender and looked pointedly at Mae. "I think I'll leave you two alone."

"Peter, what was that about?" Mae asked.

"Why is she still here?"

"We talked about this, remember? I invited her for summer break. Besides, she's my sister. I like having her here." Mae opened a cupboard and began stuffing Campbell's soup cans onto the shelves. "You've been a grouch ever since the accident with the pole."

"Do you have any idea what your sister is costing us? She acts like it's no big deal." He put a hand on Mae's arm to turn her toward him, but she pulled it away.

"She didn't do it on purpose!"

"So we get to foot the bill."

"She's an elementary teacher; she doesn't have any money, Peter!"

"And we do?" The question floated on the air. Mae turned back to her grocery bags and pulled out a loaf of bread, pushed it into the breadbox, and slammed the door shut.

"I can't deal with this right now," Mae said. "When you're ready to stop your tantrum, we can talk." She went back out to the Jeep for more groceries. Peter stomped off to the barn.

Why couldn't she see this his way? She was being impossible. Peter went over to the dark heifer and patted her side. She nudged his shoulder, asking for a little hay. "I think you understand things better than I do sometimes," he said. "Women." She nudged him again, and he climbed to the loft and got her a wedge of hay. She eagerly took it from his hands and chewed while he watched.

Mae was waiting for him in the kitchen when Peter came in the back door. "Hi," she said.

"Hi," Peter answered, going directly to the fridge to make a sandwich.

"You've been stewing for quite a while," Mae said. He got out the mayonnaise and began spreading it on his bread. "Peter, look at me."

Peter lifted his eyes. "Yeah."

"I'm sorry," she said. "I promised you that I wouldn't let anything come between us. It's just that…well, Trudy's my sister. But if you want me to talk to her about paying for the pole, I will."

"No. I was frustrated," Peter said, setting the butter knife down. "You don't need to talk to her. We'll find a way to pay for it. Maybe the bank will extend us a little more credit." Peter ran a hand through his blond hair and sighed.

"I know the debt is weighing on you, and milk prices are low," Mae said. "But I'm in this with you."

Peter met her eyes. "You might have to remind me every once in a while."

"Mae!" Peter burst in the back door, a frantic expression on his face. "Come quick. The chickens are killing each other!"

Peter ran back outside with Mae hurrying after him across the drive and grass to the henhouse. What met their eyes inside was like something from a Stephen King novel. Four dead chickens lay bloodied, almost featherless, with limp heads. And the other birds were chasing a fifth victim, pecking and tugging on her plumage in a horrific bully fest.

"Why are they doing this?" Mae glanced around, trying to make sense of the mayhem. Both watering dishes had been knocked over and drained dry. The feed was almost gone too. Mae grabbed the waterers and said to Peter, "Get some feed!" She quickly filled the waterers and placed them back in the coop. The birds rushed as one to the trays, filling their beaks in exaggerated gulps. Peter set the feed dish down, and the animals clustered around that as well. Peter and Mae waited and watched what the birds would do next. Once the birds had their fill, they settled down to rest as if all was forgotten, no longer the murderous mob of five minutes before.

The surviving pecked chicken lay limp in an obviously exhausted state. She was bleeding where her tail feathers had been pulled, but she still had most of her plumage. Mae picked her up, and the stunned bird didn't protest.

Peter lifted the four carcasses and took them out to the burn barrel while Mae took her injured patient into the house to find a box.

"Whatcha got there?" Trudy asked as she came downstairs. Mae held out the bleeding bird. "Ew! That's disgusting. Are you going to butcher all your birds like that? 'Cause that seems really cruel."

Mae sighed. "She was pecked by the other birds."

"Really?" Trudy gave the hen another look. "Puts a whole new light on 'henpecked,' doesn't it?"

"You should see the four that weren't so lucky—at least this one's alive." She placed the bird in Trudy's arms.

"Poor birdie," Trudy said, petting her remaining feathers as the small, traumatized body rose and fell with each breath. Mae found a box in the basement, lined it with an old towel, and laid the chicken inside. The bird opened her eyes when Mae set some food and a bowl of water in the box, but she didn't lift her head. Then Mae found an eyedropper in her first-aid kit, filled it with water, and lifted the small beak to drip the cool liquid inside. The bird swallowed, its whole neck moving with the effort.

"This reminds me of when we were kids," Trudy said, "and you tried to save that squirrel Jack Linder shot with his BB gun."

Mae smiled at the memory. "Shirrel the squirrel recovered quite nicely," she said.

"After you fed it a hot dog and it barfed all over the couch! Remember how mad Mom was?"

"Well, of course. It was Italian leather!" They both laughed.

"I think this is a good place for you," Trudy said after a long pause. "You're a nurturer. Not like me."

"You nurture in your own way," Mae said.

"I suppose." There was a silence and then Trudy said, "I heard you guys arguing last night. I'm sorry about that. I want to pay for the pole."

"You don't have any more money than we do."

"Still, it's the right thing to do. I'm sorry it took me this long to fess up."

Mae reached across the counter and squeezed her hand. "You don't have to, but if you insist, I won't argue." They both gazed back at the sleeping chicken.

"So how long will she be a houseguest?" Trudy asked.

"Until she's up and healthy, I guess."

The next morning Mae came inside from the barn to start breakfast and heard a soft humming sound. There on her kitchen counter stood the plucked chicken tasting the leaves of Mae's African violet and strutting like a model on a runway.

"Okay, out with you!" Mae said. She reached to grab the bird, but it clucked away, run-flying at full tilt for the stairway. "Trudy!" Mae called. "Help!"

Trudy was instantly at the top of the stairs in her p.j.'s, her hair a giant bowl of frizz. "Head her off. She's coming up!" Mae shouted.

Trudy spread her arms and crouched low, duck-walking down the stairs while Mae covered the back escape. Trudy lunged toward the fowl, but it scampered between Mae's legs and headed for the kitchen.

"Maybe if we chase it into the oven…," Trudy said.

"Get on the other side of her," Mae said. The hen was strutting through the dining room, weaving between the chair legs.

"You could always wait until tonight when she's ready to roost," Trudy suggested, still low with her arms spread while Mae worked the opposite side of the table.

"And let her ravage the house all day? I don't think so."

Just then Peter came in the back door and both women shouted, "*Stop!*" Peter froze, eyes wide.

"Hold the door open, and get out of the way," Mae said.

Peter obeyed immediately, holding the screen door wide onto the back steps. Scout saw the open door as an invitation to come visit and bounded inside, a big Labrador grin on his face. The panicked chicken sprang straight up and flew to the top of the fridge as Scout started barking and jumping, his claws scraping the fridge door.

"Great! Peter, get your dog out of here," she shouted above the dog's yowling.

"*My* dog?" he said.

Mae gave him her best impatient look.

"Hey, I didn't bring a chicken in the house." He grabbed Scout's collar and led him outside. Mae realized Trudy had disappeared. She turned to face the now squawking bird who scolded nonstop from her perch. Mae stood there a full minute trying to think of what to do. Then Trudy came up the basement steps with a fishing net.

"I thought I saw one of these down there," Trudy said, grinning. "Okay, you go to the left and drive that birdie right into the trap." Mae complied, raising her arms to drive the chicken toward Trudy. The bird took awkward flight, losing altitude with each flap. Trudy gave a giant swoosh of the green net, and the chicken was theirs. Its feathers stuck through the mesh like a pillow losing its stuffing.

"You're a genius, Trudes," Mae said. She reached in and grabbed the mutinous fowl, pinning its wings back with her hands so it couldn't flap away again.

"And you," Mae spoke to the hen, "are officially declared healthy."

IRENE JENKINS

The corn was high, at least a good six feet, sun-dried to a beautiful golden with the warm September sun. Children's voices floated on the air, along with the constant crickets and the sweet calls of wrens. Irene Jenkins stood by the kitchen sink washing tomatoes for canning and gazing out at the beautiful scene before her. Her ten-year-old son, Jimmy, stood with his fingers pressed against his eyes, counting loudly to a hundred.

Irene had turned to check the water on the stove when the back door flew open. Jimmy came in, breathless and talking fast, his hands flying, pointing.

"Jimmy, slow down and shut the door!" Irene said.

"It's Jake. We were playing hide-and-seek, and he went into the corn. He must've because we can't find him anywhere."

"Okay," Irene said. "I'll come look. He's probably playing a trick on you." She dried her hands and turned off the burner before she went outside.

"Ja-ake," she called to her youngest son as she walked toward the fields that surrounded their property. There was no reply. "Jake, come out right now. Please," Irene raised her voice.

The breeze rustled the corn, and Irene began to feel worry creep up her neck. This wasn't like him. "Jacob," she called again, sternly now, peering deep into the darkness of the rows as she walked the perimeter of their island. Every row looked the same as the next. Jake didn't come. A thousand thoughts assailed her mind, and she felt her palms grow sweaty. How would they ever find him in the miles of corn? Her heart began to race, and a sick feeling boiled in the pit of her stomach.

"I'm calling the sheriff," she hollered to Jimmy and the neighbors' kids, who were also calling Jacob's name.

Jimmy's face took on a look of horror. "Are we going to find him?" He looked as though he was about to cry.

"We'll find him," Irene said, though her mind was bracing for the worst. "We'll find him," she said to reassure herself. She ran to the house and dialed her husband, Jim, at the elevator, then the sheriff's office. Jim was home ten minutes later, walking along the field, calling out his son's name as Irene had. The sheriff arrived and wrote down all the details, then he placed a call to the station and joined the vigil.

By evening most of Lake Emily had heard the news, and a contingent of over a hundred searchers had come to help. Minnie Wilkes and Virginia Morgan and the rest of the Suzie Qs had brought food to keep the volunteers well fed while their husbands, the fire department, and a slew of people Irene barely knew walked the rows of corn.

Darkness threatened, and Irene felt her hope dwindling. How could her baby survive the night all alone? Jake was afraid of the dark. Her hands began to shake with the thought of it.

"Irene." Virginia Morgan put a hand on her arm. "Would you like to pray with me?"

Tears brimmed in Irene's eyes, and she nodded her head.

"Dear Lord," Virginia began, "we need to find this little boy, and you know where he is. Please show us, and let him be okay. We beg you—let him be okay."

By now the tears were falling in earnest, a steady stream of pain. Irene lifted her head and looked at Virginia, who drew her into a long embrace. "Thank you," Irene whispered when they stepped away.

Irene returned to the window to look out at the yard. Virginia put on another pot of coffee and brought a cup to Irene when it was brewed. "You need to sit down," Virginia said.

"I can't," Irene said. Her eyes met Virginia's. *"My baby's out there."*

The back door flew open, and Jim burst inside. *"They found him in the corn!"* He grabbed his wife and held her tight. *"He's okay. They radioed. They're bringing him in!"*

Irene felt her knees weaken beneath her, and she let her husband's strong arms hold her up as sobs racked her body.

"Thank you," she mouthed to Virginia when she finally pulled away.

Police officers cleared the way for Rudy Schoen, a small, blanketed bundle in his thick arms. He laid the boy on the couch, and Irene knelt at his side, her husband standing behind her. Bright, frightened eyes stared up from a tear-streaked, dirty face. Irene touched his silken hair. She leaned her face next to his and wept.

Then her eyes scanned the others in the room who stood in witness of this miracle. *"Thank you all."*

twenty-one

T he July meeting of the Suzie Q Extension group was at Irene
Jenkins's house. Mae knocked on the back door and waited with
Trudy. It was a Colonial style, pumpkin colored with tan trim and dark
brown shutters. If the assortment of cars in the long driveway was any
indication, Virginia and the other ladies were already there. Irene smiled
as she opened the door. She was a tall, thin woman with hair graying at
the temples that she kept in a stylish bob.

"Come in," she said and stepped back for them to enter. The entry
walls were lined with family photos, and a small side table held even more
pictures. Grade-school shots of toothless kids, kids with braces, graduation shots, wedding photos. One picture caught Mae's eye. A handsome
young man in a fireman's uniform stood next to the shiny red fire engine.
His face was smudged with black soot, and he was holding some sort of
award. Irene noticed her gaze and said, "That's my son Jake."

"I think Peter and I met him at church."

"Probably. He's an usher." She turned her gaze back to Mae.

"This is my sister, Trudy," Mae introduced.

"Glad to meet you." Irene smiled and tipped her head toward Trudy.
Mae could hear the chatter of the ladies in the living room.

"Hey, everyone," Trudy said. She lifted her hand in a windshield-
wiper wave.

A murmur of hellos followed, and Irene suggested they go around
the room and introduce themselves. When they got to Lillian, she said,
"Are you from St. Paul too?"

"I sure am. It's a lot like Lake Emily," Trudy teased. Lillian's left eyebrow went up.

"I hate driving in the city. I always have Willie drive if we need to go up there," Lillian said. "The last time I was at the state fair, this man pulled out right in front of us. Willie had to hit the brakes so hard I was certain we'd plow right into the back of him, but did he notice? He looked at us as if we were from Mars."

Trudy nodded and shot Mae a look that said, "Is she for real?"

"I'd like to call the meeting to order," Minnie Wilkes said, "if that's okay."

They took roll call and talked about the trip they were planning to Red Wing, unable to decide whether they should go in August or September or wait until after the fall harvest. After endless discussion the topic was finally tabled, and the meeting moved on to the lesson for the night—a primer on canning tomatoes.

Mae had wondered why these women, who had no doubt spent their whole lives canning tomatoes, needed a class in the subject. But Virginia had told her it had become an annual rite in the group whenever they met at Irene's. That woman could can anything that would fit in a pint jar, she'd said.

They moved to the kitchen and stood crammed around the stove. A huge black enamelware pot of water boiled on the front burner.

In the sink, a mound of freshly washed tomatoes waited for canning, each bright red and perfect, not a blemish in sight.

"First," Irene began, "you bring the water to a boil. While that's heating up, you can wash off your tomatoes and core them. You can see I did that ahead of time so we could get out of here before midnight." Gentle laughter went around the group. "Dip the tomatoes in the hot water for a few seconds." She walked to the sink, filled a large spaghetti strainer with the delicious-looking fruit, and dropped it into the rolling water. Within moments she drew it out again and put the tomatoes into a big bowl of ice water. "You want to shock the skin off of 'em." She held up a tomato with a peely skin and neatly slipped the skin off in one piece and then squeezed the extra juice into an empty ice-cream bucket.

"I like to can the tomatoes like this, whole. Less hassle. Put your peeled tomatoes in a pot and warm them up while you wash your jars and lids and get the boiling bath ready. I'm going to use my pressure cooker," she said and lifted it up for all to see. "Mae, would you be a dear and keep an eye on those tomatoes while they simmer? Keep stirring them so they don't stick to the bottom of that kettle." She handed Mae a wooden spoon. Minnie and Trudy pitched in, peeling the rest of the tomatoes in the sink, squeezing them of their juices, and adding them to the pot.

Mae looked over at Trudy. She was laughing at something the round-cheeked woman said and talking in her animated way. Mae had always admired that about Trudy—her ability to talk to anyone. Trudy laughed again, and her eyes met Mae's.

"This is fun," she mouthed. Mae nodded and turned back to stirring.

Irene resumed her teaching role a few minutes later, taking the wooden spoon from Mae. "Looks like we're ready." She pulled a long ladle from an assortment of utensils neatly laid out on the counter like surgical instruments and began to dip the tomatoes into a jar she had just pulled from a pot of boiling water. When the tomatoes reached about a half inch from the top of the jar, she took a rubber spatula and slid it neatly up and down inside the jar. "This is to release any air bubbles. Then I put in some lemon juice to make sure I have enough acid. You can put it on top. The boiling action will mix it in as it processes." After she added the lemon juice, Minnie carefully wiped the outside and the rim of the jar and secured the top. Then setting six jars of tomatoes into the hot water of the pressure cooker, Lillian Biddle twisted the lid on the odd-looking pot so it was secure. The women stood around waiting for the little black knob on top to start rocking.

"It should start rocking pretty quickly here. Tomatoes need to get up to pressure, and then they're done, but if you're going to use a boiling water bath, you're going to want to let them boil for a good thirty-five, forty minutes. Always let the pressure come down on its own in the canner. You can't get it open until it does anyway. When I first started, I made the mistake of taking the knob off so I could get the jars out quicker, but that sucked the juice right out of my jars, and I had to toss the whole batch."

After the jars of hot tomatoes were all lined up on the counter, sounds of popping filled the air as each of the lids snapped tight.

It was closing in on nine o'clock when the snack was finally served. Mae was having a hard time keeping her eyes open, while the other women seemed to be gearing up for the night. She glanced around at the faces and wondered how all these retired women could have so much pep when all she wanted to do was lie down for the night.

Irene Jenkins was telling about a fire at a hog shed on Highway 36 when Trudy nudged Mae. Mae started and her head shot up. To her relief, everyone seemed focused on Irene.

"That boy always dreamed of being fire captain. Ever since Vern Elwood's family died in that fire. It's a good fit for Jake."

"Don't you worry about him?" Trudy asked.

"Of course I do. But there's nothing he'd rather do. I couldn't keep him away from it if I tried. Last week he came upon the Schmidt boys playing with matches down by the creamery. Oh, he really tore into them. But you can bet they won't do that again, not after Jake told them about some of the horrible fires he's seen." Heads bobbed around the table. No one was ready to call it a night. Mae looked at her watch—ten o'clock.

"I think I'm going to have to head on home," Mae said. "I'm getting up to milk cows with Peter."

"You're milking cows?" Lillian asked.

"Yeah. It's kinda fun."

"You couldn't get me in a milk shed," Mary Shrupp said. "When Jerry and I got married I told him the farm was all his as long as I could keep working at the hospital."

"I've never even seen a calf born," Lillian put in.

"I used to drive the tractor some during haying," Virginia said.

Mae glanced at her watch again, hoping for another lull in the conversation. Her eyes drooped. Finally, unable to stay awake, Mae pushed her chair back and said, "Thank you for a lovely evening, Irene. I really need to head out."

"Good night, everybody," Trudy said, following her.

Once they were in the car and headed down the dusty road into the starry night, Trudy said, "That was a hoot." She looked over at Mae. "You okay?"

"I'm fine. Just a little tired."

"Again?"

"It's nothing. Just getting up too early, I guess."

Trudy nodded. "I had a lot of fun tonight. Thanks for bringing me along. There was a bug on one of the tomatoes, and Minnie told me that when she was first married she watched her mother-in-law eat a ladybug right out of her salad. She just watched her, never even told her it was there!"

"How do you do that?" Mae said.

"Do what?"

"Get people to talk to you so easily."

"I don't know. I just talk myself. Why?"

"Oh," Mae said, "no reason."

Mae looked into the spangled sky. The moon was hazy behind a few wispy clouds. She could stand to be a little more like Trudy, she thought. She might even find herself liking it.

The next day Mae drove up to St. Paul to see her old doctor. She'd thought about going to see Virginia's doctor in Lake Emily, but the last thing she needed was the rumor mill churning out something about her being on her deathbed. She felt silly for going at all. She'd been a little tired, that was it. He'd probably give her one look and send her home with some placebo to ensure she wouldn't waste his time again.

She passed the exit for home and felt a twinge of longing. Maybe enough time had passed; maybe her mother and she could start over again, she thought. She could stop and have a quiet cup of afternoon coffee with her mom. It would be nice to sit and chat, tell her about the farm and all that she was learning.

Mae turned onto Snelling Avenue and into the parking lot of the doctor's office. She walked up the straight sidewalk to the sterile-looking brick building. She stopped at the front desk to let the receptionist know she was there.

"According to our records, you don't have any insurance," the woman behind the desk said.

"That's right," Mae replied. "You can bill me directly." Then she took her seat and picked up the latest copy of *Ladies' Home Journal.* The waiting room was bustling. Next to her a mother read to her two-year-old daughter, a chubby cherub with long, curly blond hair. Mae smiled at the sight and lifted her magazine to read about the latest discovery for reducing cellulite in thighs.

"Mae Morgan," a nurse called.

Mae set the magazine down and reached for her purse as she stood to follow the blue scrub–clad nurse through the maze of rooms in the back. After her weigh-in, they settled in a little cubicle of an exam room with an assortment of certificates and diplomas spread across the walls.

"So you're tired. Is that all?"

"Um, no…I've been kind of sick to my stomach off and on. I threw up a few times. I think I might be getting the flu." The nurse grunted, her eyes never leaving her chart.

The woman took a quick blood pressure and temp check, saying only, "The doctor will be in soon," then closed the door and left the room.

Mae breathed a sigh of relief that the nurse was gone. She knew this illness was all in her head. This was ridiculous, driving two hours to be told she was fine.

After what seemed an eternity, the door creaked open with a quiet knock as Dr. Newton came in. A shy man who always averted his gaze, he reminded Mae of Mr. Magoo, his head too big for his skinny body and thick glasses that made his eyes appear huge. He held out a hand to shake, then took his stool on wheels.

"You've been tired?" he began.

"I know. Everybody's tired," Mae said. "But this is a different kind of tired. Sometimes I feel as if I'll fall right over if I don't go lie down. I can't get through an afternoon without a two-hour nap. I used to nap sometimes but never more than half an hour." Mae realized she was babbling.

"You've been queasy too? When was the last time you had your period?"

Mae's face blanched, and for a moment she couldn't think. "Uh, my period? You think I'm pregnant?"

"Unless there's some evidence to the contrary."

"I'm kind of irregular. But I guess it's been…" She stopped to think back. "May. I had my last period in May." If a two-by-four had struck her, Mae couldn't have been more stunned. "It was May," she repeated.

"Let's start with a pregnancy test and go from there." He handed her a cup and pointed her down the hall to the nearest bathroom.

As Mae sat in the exam room, waiting for the results to come back, her mind paced frantically. What if she was pregnant? How would Peter react? How would they pay for it, especially without any insurance? He was already stressed out about money. This wasn't the right time, so soon after taking over the farm. They hadn't even been married a whole year yet. What if the baby wasn't healthy? A jumble of worries tumbled through her mind in a kaleidoscope of fear. Mae put her head in her hands.

The door opened and Mr. Magoo returned. He sat across from her and placed the folder on the small table. "Well, we know what's causing your fatigue, Mae." His eyes brightened. "You're going to have a baby."

Mae stopped breathing. Stared at the doctor like a deer in the headlights.

"Mae?" Dr. Newton repeated. She came to, lifting her eyes to his.

"A baby," she murmured. "How did this happen?"

He raised a brow.

"Never mind," she said. She took a deep breath. "What now?"

"Now we set you up for prenatal visits. Get you on a healthy diet, vitamins. Do you know an ob-gyn?"

"Actually, we moved to Lake Emily in April. I should probably find someone down there."

Dr. Newton nodded his head. "Not a bad idea." He stood to go, holding out a hand to Mae. She shook it woodenly as he said, "Congratulations, Mae."

She gave him a weak smile. "Thanks."

Somehow Mae made it to her Jeep and collapsed behind the wheel, staring straight ahead, oblivious of anything around her. She started the car, but the thought of driving all the way home seemed more than she could endure. She had to talk to someone. Perhaps her mother would be home.

Mae drove the short distance, pulling into her parents' driveway. Her stepdad's BMW was parked in front of the garage. She rang the bell, and after a few long moments, Paul came to the door.

"Mae!" he said. "Come in!" His greeting warmed her. Maybe this wasn't a bad idea after all. He looked behind her, obviously to see if Peter had come along.

"I was in the neighborhood," Mae said as she stepped into the entry lined in white ceramic tile.

His expression sobered. "Your mother should be back from shopping in an hour or so. It's probably not a good idea for you to stay long."

"Oh" was all Mae could get out. She felt as if the wind had been knocked from her lungs. Her stomach turned with the rejection of his words.

"She loves you, honey. She really does, but what you said really hurt her—"

"Hurt her? Did she mention what she said to me?"

He put a hand on her shoulder. "I'm not trying to upset you, Mae. But she is my wife. I have to protect her."

Mae shook off his hand. "Fine!" she almost shouted. Hot tears burned in her eyes, and she turned to leave.

"Mae!" Paul called, but she ran outside and got in the car, slammed the door, and revved the engine. She threw it into reverse and jerked backward into the quiet street, then shoved it into drive and sped away. The tears came freely, so that she could barely make out the road as she drove. She wiped them away with the back of her hand.

How could she have been stupid enough to think her mother

would be happy to see her again? Paul was actually talking about protecting her mother from her!

Mae thought about the tiny life she was carrying, and another wave of tears came.

At least she had Peter and Trudy—and Virginia. The thought came with a comforting warmth. She could tell Virginia all about it, and she wouldn't judge or criticize.

A car honked behind her, and Mae glanced up, realizing she'd been stopped at a green light. She hit the gas, and her old neighborhood ambled by, small shops, convenience stores, and eateries tucked here and there along the dirty-looking sidewalks, strangers hurrying up and down. This wasn't home, Mae realized. It would never be home again.

Peter looked like a mounted bass, frozen in time, his mouth gaping, eyes wide.

"Peter, aren't you going to say anything?"

"I…I…," he began. "Are you sure?"

Mae nodded. "Yes. The doctor told me himself."

"But…" He stared her in the eyes for a long moment, studying her, his lips bending into a smile. "We're going to have a baby," he said.

"Yes, Peter. That's what I've been telling you."

His grin grew, and he reached to swing her around. When he finally put her down, he said, "This is good."

"Really?" She felt a weight lift from her chest, and tears of relief began to form in her eyes. Peter bent to kiss her.

"Don't cry, honey. This is good news. A blessing from God."

Mae buried her head in his chest and let herself sob. Then, sniffling, she said, "I'm so glad you feel that way."

"Is that why you're crying?" He lifted her chin.

Mae took a deep breath. "No. I stopped to see Mom and Paul."

"And…?"

"Paul told me I had to leave. He didn't want Mom to find me there."

"I'm sorry." He stroked the back of his hand along her cheek, his eyes soft, loving. "You and your mother may never have the friendship that you want. I know that's difficult to consider, but in the meantime, I don't want you to make yourself vulnerable to being hurt again. Next time take me along. I'll look out for you even when your mom and stepdad won't. That's what husbands do. And let's pray about it—God knows about broken relationships."

Mae rested her head on his chest for a long time, letting the strength of his love heal her wounded heart.

ELLA ROSENBERG

Maureen Johnson and her daughter, Ella, had been driving for ten hours when the smoke started to roll from under the hood. They were still a good two hours from Lake Emily. Maureen had known the Model T was on its last legs when she started out, but she didn't have much choice. Her ma was sick, and the doctor didn't think she'd make it another day. She had to get Ella home to see her grandmother one last time. Maureen stepped out of the car and opened the hood and stood there, looking at the labyrinth of tubes and belts.

"Ma," seven-year-old Ella said from inside the car, "are we going to have to sit here long? I'm thirsty."

Maureen looked around. "I'm sorry, honey, but there isn't any water. You're going to have to wait."

"But I'm dying!" she whined.

"I think you'll live." Maureen turned her head as a truck heading the other way pulled up alongside them. An elderly couple peered out the driver's window.

"Hello. I'm Orbe Hagemann, and this is my wife, Ona." He leaned back so Maureen could see a small, round-cheeked woman in the passenger seat. "You got car troubles?" the man said.

"I sure do," Maureen replied. The man turned the vehicle around and parked on the shoulder, then went to look under the hood with Maureen.

"It overheated, I think," Maureen explained. The man lowered his head to gaze deeper into the maze.

"*Could be your thermostat,*" he said. "*Or a hose.*" He squeezed a radiator hose. "*Can't do much for it here.*" He scratched his head in thought. "*There's a filling station up a ways. I could take you up there. See if they can help.*"

"*Oh, thank you,*" Maureen said. "*Let me get my daughter. Ella,*" she called, walking closer to the back door. "*This nice man is going to take us for a little drive to get the car fixed.*"

They climbed onto the bed of the truck, which rumbled off to the gas station. When they arrived, there wasn't a soul in sight. Orbe peered in the dark windows.

"*Looks like they aren't open,*" Orbe said, coming to the back of the truck where Maureen and Ella waited. "*Where is it you were headed to?*"

"*Lake Emily, Minnesota,*" Maureen said.

Orbe scratched his head again. "*Minnesota you say?*"

Maureen nodded.

"*My gramma's real sick and we want to see her 'fore she passes,*" Ella added.

Maureen gave her a scolding look. They didn't need to be burdening these strangers with their problems.

Orbe's wife got out of the front and walked around to them. She pulled Orbe aside and whispered something in his ear. Then she nodded her head and motioned for him to say something. He turned back to Maureen and Ella.

"*Seeing as how you're stranded and all, the wife and I would like to take you the rest of the way to see your family. Give me a number where I can call you, and I'll get your car taken care of tomorrow.*"

Maureen opened her mouth to protest, but just then the old woman leaned down to whisper something into Ella's ear and the image of Maureen's ill mother holding Ella returned to Maureen. She felt herself choke up. "*I*"—Maureen turned to Orbe—"*I don't know how to thank you.*"

"*That's not something you need to concern yourself with.*"

twenty-two

Virginia and Ella sat at the little table in Virginia's dining room. It was another hot July day. The air conditioner hummed in its window home. "Snip," Virginia called to the cat who was hiding under the couch, had been hiding under the couch ever since Ella walked in the front door.

"Here, kitty, kitty, kitty," Virginia kept repeating.

"I never thought I'd see this," Ella said seriously.

"What?" Virginia lifted her gray head.

"I didn't know you even liked cats."

"I like cats. And he's coming around."

"He is?"

The pair of blue eyes stared at Virginia from beneath the couch. "I guess I'm the needy one," she admitted, rising and coming to sit at the table. She gave a heavy sigh. "I miss Roy."

"Of course you do," Ella said.

Tears filled Virginia's eyes. "It is getting better, you know. Most of the time I can put it aside, as long as I keep myself busy. But everything's changed; even the way life looks to me has changed."

"I know," Ella said. "I know. It's hard. There's no getting around it." She reached a hand across the table to her friend. "You could use a little diversion—why don't you come with me this afternoon? I'm reading with my book buddy at the library. That always does me good, seeing Sean's face light up when I read with him."

"I don't want to be a tagalong," Virginia said.

"That's something you're going to have to outgrow. Accept kindness wherever it's offered."

Lake Emily's library was a small white Gothic-style house that had been donated to the town in the 1930s to hold its meager book collection. Shelves lined the walls of the small rooms that led from one to the next, and a faint musty smell of old books, leather, and ink lingered in the air. When Ella and Virginia walked in the front door, several heads turned toward them.

The librarian, Alva Endicott, sat in her usual spot at the front desk, wearing rhinestone-studded horn-rimmed glasses, her hands covered in rings. Her white hair was pulled back in a French braid, and she was busily checking in books. The narrow aisles gave the building a claustrophobic feel. Two tables at the far end served those who chose to do their reading there, and another squat table covered with puzzles kept the children happy. The library hummed in little clusters of adult-child pairings. Two teenage girls sat at one of the tables gazing at magazines, and an old gentleman read at the other, his glasses propped precariously at the end of his nose.

Ella led Virginia to the children's book section where a blond-haired boy sat engrossed in a book. "Hi, Mrs. Rosenberg," he lifted his head and said sweetly.

"Virginia, I'd like you to meet Sean Hedden, my book buddy for the summer." Sean held out a small hand to shake with Virginia.

"Pleased to meet you, Sean," Virginia said.

"My pleasure," the little man replied.

"Aren't you polite?" Virginia said.

"My mother always says to 'spect your elders," Sean said.

"Are you ready to pick up where we left off?" Ella asked.

"Yes ma'am." He held up a copy of *Where the Red Fern Grows*.

Ella took the seat next to Sean and motioned for Virginia to do likewise. They sat together for almost an hour on the squat chairs. The old reading to the young, the young reading to the old. It was a communion of sorts, Virginia thought, each offering their gift to the experience—Sean, his joyful exuberance at hearing the story for the first time, Ella and Virginia, an appreciation for the brevity of that exuberance in the span of life.

Sean's eyes were wide when Virginia read about the red fern growing on the graves of the two hunting dogs. "That's so sad," he said.

When it was time to leave, Sean saw his mother waiting patiently at the entrance to the library. He jumped up to run to her but then turned and said, "Thank you, Mrs. Morgan and Mrs. Rosenberg."

His smile filled the room. Ella gave Mrs. Hedden a wave, and the nine-year-old was gone.

"He's a good boy," Ella said.

"This was fun," Virginia said. "Thank you. I'm glad you brought me along."

"You should sign up for your own book buddy," Ella suggested.

"I think I'd like that."

When they reached the front desk, Alva Endicott looked up from checking in books. "Can I help you girls with something?" Alva said.

"Virginia's wondering if you have any book buddies yet to assign," Ella said.

Alva's face darkened. "I have only one child that I haven't placed, and I'm afraid she's a bit of a problem. I don't know if you could handle her, Virginia."

"Who is it?" Virginia asked.

"Jessie Wise."

Ella made a small noise in the back of her throat.

"Do you know her?" Virginia asked Ella.

"I know of her," Ella said. "Her mother died last year in a car accident."

Virginia turned back to the librarian. "Sign me up. If I can't help a troubled cat, maybe I can help someone who really matters."

Virginia was nervous about her first meeting with Jessie. Everyone she'd asked had said Jessie was "disruptive," "unkempt," and worse, "trouble." Virginia decided not to make a judgment before she met the girl. Maybe she had set herself up for trouble, maybe not.

Virginia had been waiting for fifteen minutes when Jessie sauntered into the library. Her cheeks were a blotchy red, and her blond hair hadn't been combed in months—snarls and tangles jutted from the back of her head. Her shirt was faded and hanging loosely on her thin frame, and her jeans were an assortment of tears.

"Jessie, Jessie Wise?" Virginia said quietly.

"Yeah?" the girl replied. She slouched and stared at the ground.

"I'm Virginia Morgan. I guess we're going to be book buddies. Come on over here and let's get to know each other," Virginia said as authoritatively as she dared. The nine-year-old walked over and slumped into the seat beside Virginia.

"Is this gonna be like school?" Jessie said. "I hate school. They make me do things I don't want to do."

"Like what?" Virginia asked.

"They make me sit by Cory Todd. And they put me in the hall for no reason at all."

"I won't make you do anything you don't want, but we will read." There was a long pause. "I heard you've had a pretty rough year." The girl's face turned away, and Virginia was afraid she'd gone too far.

"Where'd you hear that?"

"Oh, around."

"I'll be okay," she said, straightening her shoulders.

"What would you like us to read first?" Virginia asked, deciding that changing the subject was probably her safest route.

"This was my dad's idea, you know. I don't read too good."

"We can work on that," Virginia said. "I used to be a pretty poor reader myself, but now it's one of my favorite things to do."

"Huh," the girl grunted.

"Come sit closer." Virginia patted the chair next to her. Jessie scooted over. "I pulled a few of my favorites off the shelves," Virginia said. "But we don't have to read any of these if they don't spark your interest."

They settled on *Little House in the Big Woods* by Laura Ingalls Wilder when Jessie, after a look at the cover of *Charlotte's Web,* said, "I don't want to read some dumb pig story."

"Why don't you start," Virginia said. Jessie crossed her arms over her chest. "Or I can," Virginia finished.

Once upon a time, sixty years ago, a little girl lived in the Big Woods of Wisconsin, in a little gray house made of logs...

When she finished the first page, she moved the book in front of Jessie, and the girl reluctantly took it. "You don't need to feel shy with me," Virginia said. "I won't say a word if you mess up...as long as you don't say anything when I mess up."

Clearing her throat, Jessie began, "There were no roads. There were no p-people. There were only trees and the wild an-i-mals who had their homes among them. W-olves lived in the Big Woods..."

Virginia read a page and then Jessie read a page, sounding out each new word and taking long moments on many. When finally Jessie would finish a page, a little grin would overtake her, making her dirt-smudged face shine with joy.

After they'd finished the first chapter, Jessie said, "Them girls had a real nice mom and dad." She kicked her feet back and forth under her chair. "My mom died last year."

"My husband died too," Virginia said. Jessie lifted surprised eyes, and Virginia was afraid she wouldn't be able to contain the emotion she felt at the sorrow she saw there.

"I'm sorry," Jessie said.

"Me too." Virginia placed a hand on Jessie's, and they sat in silence for a moment. "Do you want to pick a different book?"

"No. I like this family."

Virginia opened the book again and began the next chapter.

Five o'clock came all too quickly. Jessie's dad never appeared to take her home. "I'll walk," Jessie said. "Dad's probably at work late again."

"I can drop you off," Virginia offered. "It wouldn't be a bother at all."

Jessie shrugged her shoulders. "Okay. If you want."

The house on Elm Street was totally dark when they got there. Jessie pulled out a key hanging on a chain around her neck to let herself in and turned to go.

"Maybe I should meet your father," Virginia said, coming up to the door with her.

"He's not home."

"But you don't want to wait for him all by yourself. Do you know what time he's coming?"

"Nope."

"What do you do for supper?"

"I make my own."

Virginia didn't like this one bit. She went into the house. In the kitchen there was a pile of dirty dishes in the sink, and the counters were cluttered with an old loaf of bread, crumbs, a used butter knife, a stack of bills, and a variety of candidates for junk-drawer status.

Virginia peered in the fridge. It was empty except for a shelf of condiments in the door, a half-gallon of milk, and a package of bacon. She moved to the cupboards that seemed to be better supplied, though mostly with junk food. Jessie grabbed a package of chips and a bowl and went over to the table.

"That's your supper?"

Jessie gave her a blank look. "You need fruits and vegetables and protein." Virginia dug in the cupboard until she found a can of tuna and a can of peas. "This is a start," she said. "Here's some mushroom soup. Bring those chips over. We can use them."

Jessie brought the bag over, her little face curious.

"Now, you see," Virginia said, "we have all the ingredients for a good meal. Do you have a casserole dish?" Jessie reached beneath the counter for a covered bowl and handed it to Virginia, who was busy opening the cans.

"Okay, first you put in a layer of the peas, then the tuna, then some of the mushroom soup. Now we crumble potato chips over that. Here, help me crumble these." The girl broke a few chips and looked at the concoction doubtfully. "Now we'll do another layer until we use up all the ingredients. Make sure we have lots of chips on top so they can get a nice golden brown, and we'll bake that for forty minutes." She set the oven for the correct temperature and slid the dish in.

"I've never seen food like that before," Jessie said.

"Like what?"

"Oh, all mixed up like it's confused."

Virginia laughed. "You'll like it, you wait. This was my son David's favorite dish. Now…" She touched Jessie's hair. "Let's see if we can do something about that hair."

Once Virginia had gotten through the tangle of hair, she and Jessie decided to play a game of Trouble while they waited for supper to be done.

Just as the timer went off and the smell of tuna hotdish filled the house, the front door opened and a man in his late thirties entered with a bag of groceries in one hand and a case of beer in the other. "Jessie, what are you cooking? Haven't I told you not to turn the oven on?" Mr. Wise said, his words slightly slurred.

"I'm afraid that's my fault, Mr. Wise." Virginia stood up as he came around the corner. "I was showing Jessie how to make hotdish."

"And you are…?" His eyebrows knit in obvious confusion, and Virginia could smell alcohol and smoke on his breath from across the small room.

"Virginia Morgan."

"She's my book buddy, Dad," Jessie cut in, her voice anxious. She glanced from him to Virginia.

His face relaxed. "I'm sorry. I forgot all about that." He set the groceries down and leaned to give Jessie a kiss on the forehead. "I would've picked her up, but—"

"You had to work late," Jessie finished for him.

"Yeah," he said. "Something smells good. What is it?"

"A little something we threw together," Virginia said. "I should probably go now that you're home and all."

"Please stay," he said. His eyes were kind, despite the deadened sadness that lingered there. "You can't make us a meal and then leave before it gets eaten. Besides you need to tell me how reading went." Virginia looked over at Jessie's dark eyes, twinkling with hope.

"Well…I suppose," Virginia finally said.

* * *

"You know," Virginia began once the dishes were washed and put away, "I only live a couple blocks from here. Jessie could come over when you have to work late…so she wouldn't have to be alone. I'm all alone too. The company would be good for me. That is," she turned to Jessie, "if you wouldn't mind being cooped up with an old woman and her cat who hides under the couch all day."

"Could I, Dad?" Jessie asked her father.

"That's very kind of you," Mr. Wise said. Jessie beamed. "But I don't think we can afford it."

"Oh no! I wouldn't accept any pay. You'd be doing an old lady a favor."

Mr. Wise looked at Jessie. "Well, I guess that would be okay," he said.

Jessie grinned and placed her small hand in Virginia's.

This was a good thing, Virginia thought. A very good thing.

"How can I not tell them?" Mae asked, disbelieving.

"I'm not saying you shouldn't tell your mom about the baby. I just don't want to see you hurt. How about if I call?"

Mae handed Peter the phone, watching expectantly as he dialed.

"Hello, Paul," Peter began. "How've you been?" There was a pause as he answered. Mae watched, hopeful.

"Oh, she's doing well. Actually, that's why I've called." Her stepdad had asked about her—that was a good sign, wasn't it? "I have a little news… We're going to have a baby in February. Well…yes sir. It is soon. But we're excited." Peter was quiet while Paul went on. She watched as Peter's face turned red. Mae felt a ball well up in her chest, as if she couldn't take a full breath.

"Listen," Peter interrupted. "I called to let you know. You can pass the information along to Catherine. And…" Peter's eyes squinted hard, and Mae could sense that he was trying not to give the man a piece of his mind. She shook her head and Peter finally said, "Good-bye," and hung up the phone. Her tears began to fall then.

"I'm sorry," Peter said, pulling her to him. "Now they know. Next time we'll write a letter."

twenty-three

August arrived the next day hot and muggy. Mae and Peter had decided to wait a little while before telling anyone at Lake Emily that she was pregnant. They wanted to keep it their little secret as long as they could, before letting the outside world intrude.

Mae was chopping tomatoes when Peter came in the back door. The screen slammed shut behind him.

"I haven't been farming for long," he said, "but I think we've got a bumper crop out there." He was grinning, a sparkle in his blue eyes. "Mr. Biddle even commented on how great our corn looks. And I've got some other great news."

Mae stopped and turned to him expectantly.

"Milk prices look like they're starting to rise—we might actually make it."

"That's great, honey," Mae said as she wiped the lip of a Mason jar she'd just filled with tomatoes from the garden. She'd managed to put up some tomatoes, green beans, and pickled beets. And Trudy had become an expert at making a garlicky pickle that Peter absolutely loved. The multicolored jars stood on the cupboard shelf as proud testament to their diligent labor.

"Come on, let's go take a walk," Peter said.

"It's hot out there, and I'm *pregnant*," she whispered the last word.

"Please. I want to celebrate."

"I could think of other ways to celebrate," Mae said. Peter lifted his eyebrows, and she swatted him.

"I'm in the middle of a batch of tomatoes. I can't go for a walk."

"Trudy can finish it for you. Come on. You need to take a break anyway." He grinned wide as he grabbed her apron strings and pulled the knot loose.

She rolled her eyes. "All right," she said. "Let me go tell Trudes."

As she left, the phone rang and Peter picked it up.

"Hello," Peter said.

"Peter? Hey, it's Dad."

"Dad? Where are you?" The sound of his father's voice stirred the embers of anger as images of his grandfather's funeral flashed through Peter's mind. "I'm back in St. Paul. Just flew in today from Singapore. I was thinking of coming down to spend a few days in Lake Emily. See how you're keeping the old place going, see Mom."

"Oh…okay."

"You don't mind, do you? I tell you, being on the road gets old after a while. But I have some great shots of Beijing, the Great Wall, all kinds of incredible places."

"That'd be nice." Peter hoped he sounded more excited than he felt. He'd been on those tours "seeing the world," and it had never done much for him, except to make him miss home. "When are you coming down?"

"Thought I'd drive out tomorrow. Mom invited me to stay at her place, so I'll do that."

"Grandma will be glad to have you," Peter said. How was it Peter could be so clear about what Mae should do with her mother, but when it came to his own father, he felt confused, so much like the boy in front of that snowball bush on Confirmation Sunday. There were so many disappointments that lingered, so many promises unkept.

"I'll see you tomorrow sometime?" David Morgan asked.

"Yeah, Dad. That'll be good." As he hung up the phone, Mae returned to the kitchen. "Who was that?"

"Dad. He's back from his tour."

"You don't look happy."

"I'm trying to figure out exactly what I feel." He lifted his eyes to hers.

"Come on." She reached for his hand. "You were going to take me for a walk."

She pulled him out the door. Cicadas droned loudly as they walked toward the orchard, and grasshoppers bounded off the path with each footfall. "What did he say?" Mae prompted.

"Nothing really. He was nice. He's always nice... I don't know." He looked up at the azure sky filled with fluffy clouds. "He and I are very different."

"And that's a problem?"

Peter turned to gaze into her chocolate eyes. "I want to see him. I'm even excited about it, but I'm still angry that he didn't come home, that he left us to handle Grandpa's funeral without him. And I'm afraid he'll tell me that this is all crazy, taking over the farm, like your mom did."

"This isn't crazy. We're doing a great job."

"It's how I feel. I'm afraid I'm a disappointment to him, settling for farming."

"Give your dad a chance. At least he isn't telling you that you have to leave because your mom can't stand the sight of you."

"I'm sorry."

"Don't be. I'm learning from it. No matter what, God won't push me away. That's a good lesson, even if it is a hard one."

Peter squeezed her hand. "I won't push you away either."

One of the cows was due to drop a calf any day. Peter had been keeping a close eye on her all week, going out to check at all hours. There was something wrong. He'd checked all his books, but he couldn't pinpoint what it was.

On Wednesday there had been a bloody discharge with a sour smell. He wasn't sure if it was a normal part of delivery or not. Thursday she collapsed, refusing to get up to come to the feeding trough. Finally at four o'clock he called Dr. Klein. Half an hour later the short, round-faced vet was there.

Peter was pacing outside the barn. He led the way as he filled the doctor in on the details. The man leaned over the heifer as she lay on her side and listened to her heart and then the calf's. His face was grim.

"She's not been right," Peter said while the vet moved toward the back of the animal.

"Calf's dead," he said matter-of-factly. "We'll have to pull it out. The mother isn't doing too good either. We might lose her."

Peter moved closer and leaned down to the moaning cow. He'd been prepared to lose a calf, but the idea of losing a good milker hadn't crossed his mind.

The vet pulled long gloves from his pocket, putting them on to reach inside for the calf's front legs. His arm disappeared up to his biceps. "It's way back," Mark said, grunting with the effort as he tugged. "We're gonna need the chains."

By now Mae and Trudy had come to see what was going on.

"The calf is dead. We have to get it out," Peter explained to Mae.

She moved to see the suffering heifer, noting the white star on her forehead. "She's the one who always watches us milk."

Peter nodded. "You're not going to want to see this," he said. Her face reflected the concern he felt. She turned to go, whispering to Trudy before the two went back into the house.

The vet returned from the truck with the small chains and again reached inside the heifer to wrap it around the calf's forelegs. "Take it slow," he instructed Peter as he handed him the end. "The calf'll come."

Peter pulled as Mark guided the hooves out. The mother lay, unresponsive to the pressure, and slowly the little legs emerged, then the head and body. Her calf was a perfectly formed heifer calf, dead for a while by the look of her. Peter returned to the cow's side, patting her leathery skin.

"I'm sorry, Peter," Dr. Klein said.

"That's farming," Peter replied seriously.

"Unfortunately."

"What about the heifer?"

"I don't know." Mark scratched his head. "She's hot, infection most likely. I can give you an antibiotic for her, but it's hard to tell how far gone she is."

"Let's give her the shot. Then we'll wait and see," Peter said, lifting his head to look at the vet. "Thanks for coming out."

Peter walked him to the back of the truck once they'd finished with the shot. Mark pulled out a hose and a brush and sprayed his hands to wash them, then brushed off his rubber boots, scrubbing them with the brush before tossing it back into its tray in the truck bed and saying, "Let me know if anything changes."

Peter stood in the driveway as he pulled out. Farming was one big gamble, and he was betting on things he had no control over.

Peter went back into the barn to sit vigil. Mae brought his supper out, but he couldn't bring himself to eat much. He stroked the heifer's side, willing her to get up, but she lay there.

At bedtime Mae came and sat with him. "How's she doing?" Mae asked.

"Hard to tell."

"What can I do to help?" She put a hand on his back and rubbed his aching muscles.

"That's a good start," he said, turning toward her. She rubbed for a while, then they sat in silence and watched.

"Why don't you head on up to bed," Peter said, looking at Mae's tired expression. "There isn't much we can do but wait. I'll sit up with her." Mae leaned to kiss him good night, then left for the house's amber glow.

The barn felt cold and lonely as he sat. The other cows milled about, unaffected by their friend's plight. The clock ticked on the wall accompanied by low moos and tails flicking.

At two o'clock the heifer died.

Peter was spent. He sat at his grandfather's roll-top desk the following day and stared at the numbers in his ledger. He didn't have the twelve hundred to two thousand dollars to replace the dead heifer or the calf, and it would be a year before one of the yearling heifers would be mature enough to milk. He doubted the bank would extend any more credit to him anyway.

Mae poked her head around the corner from the hallway. "Are you okay?"

"No," he said honestly.

Mae came into the room and sat on the bed's crocheted coverlet. "Some things happen. You've been working so hard to make everything perfect, but everything can't always be perfect."

"It's discouraging." They sat in quiet for a moment.

"There'll be other heifers," Mae said hopefully.

"Every time we hit a bad spot it affects us personally. It's not like a big corporation having a bad day in the market. My paycheck would be the same no matter what. You know, I figured out what I made after we got the check from the peas. I made two dollars an hour—two dollars!"

"Sounds like you're thinking of quitting."

Peter stared out the window at the pasture and rich fields beyond. "If it was just about money…maybe. But this isn't about money for me." He paused. "Do *you* want us to give up?" He looked Mae square in the eyes.

"When I found out we were having this baby," she began, rubbing her hand along her belly, "and I stopped to see Mom and Paul, I was so upset by what Paul said. Afterward I was sitting there at a stoplight and I realized that St. Paul isn't my home anymore. Lake Emily is. Here with you and our child. I'll admit that I moved here to get away, but I'm starting to feel at home here. Let's at least wait and see what this season brings."

DAVID MORGAN

"I'm afraid the news isn't good." Dr. Mielke gestured for David and Laura Morgan to take a seat in one of his office chairs opposite the desk.

Laura's brow furrowed. She glanced nervously at her husband. She seemed so frail, David thought. She wasn't the same spunky cheerleader he'd fallen in love with in high school. She still had that same sparkle in her eyes, but she'd gotten so thin, no doubt from all her worry over not being able to conceive again. David squeezed her hand.

The doctor's eyes flicked from Laura to David. He wiped his bottom lip with the side of his index finger.

"It's more than we thought," the doctor said. "Your pap smear came back positive. We'll need more tests to determine if you have cancer."

David felt suddenly as if he couldn't breathe.

"I don't understand," Laura said.

"I'm sorry," Dr. Mielke said. "It's a possibility that's the reason you haven't been able to have another child."

"There could be a mistake, right?" David said.

"Yes, there could be. Let's hope so."

"So…what do we do now?" Laura asked.

Dr. Mielke held up his hands. "It's premature for anything really. It all depends on the tests, and, if it is cancer, how far it's progressed."

How could they be having this conversation? Laura was fine. They'd go home to Peter, and she could be a mom again. He thought about the coming tour he was scheduled to take, a four-month jaunt across the southern states. He'd have to cancel that. He'd cancel everything to get her well again.

As they walked outside to the car, Laura slipped her small hand in David's. "I'm sorry that we're not going to have another baby," she whispered.

"I don't care about that," he said. "I love you."

A tear slipped down her cheek. "How do we tell Peter?"

"We don't tell him anything, because there is nothing to tell him. We don't know that you have cancer." David's eyes stung. He couldn't bear to tell their only child that his mother might be dying. "We'll take this one step at a time. And we'll plan on you getting better."

twenty-four

Thursday evening, David and Virginia came over for supper. Peter had milked a little early so he would be sure to be done by the time they got there. Mae had been cleaning all day. Everything was just so. She'd prepared a roast chicken with scalloped potatoes, creamed corn, and crusty homemade rolls that filled the house with their tempting aroma. The table was set all in white—a white damask cloth and napkins, white place settings. Mae lit the long tapers as the doorbell rang.

"You ready?" Mae said to Peter.

"Ready as I'll ever be."

She smiled nervously. "How will he take the news about the baby?" she asked, placing a hand on her stomach.

"I guarantee he'll be thrilled," Peter said. "He was already hinting about grandchildren at our wedding."

Mae went to open the door for Virginia and David. Virginia held a pan of lemon bars and paused for a hug before bustling in to set them on the counter. Peter's dad had the same lean frame as Peter, albeit shorter. His graying hair was cropped short, giving him a youthful appearance.

"Everything looks beautiful, dear," Virginia said to Mae, sweeping her eyes along the dining room glowing with candles.

Mae held out her hand to David. "Hello, Mr. Morgan," she said.

"'Dad' would be okay by me," he said.

"Okay," Mae smiled, looking over at Peter. "You remember my sister, Trudy, from the wedding." She pointed to Trudy who had just come downstairs. She moved forward to shake his hand.

"Hey, Dad," Trudy said and gave David a big hug. David laughed.

"Peter, the fields look great. Nice, straight rows." David winked as he turned to his son, offering a hand.

Peter shook it in a firm grip. "Thanks."

"No doubt about that. Too bad Grandpa isn't here to see it. He would've been thrilled," he said, looking over at Virginia.

"I've wished that myself," Peter whispered.

"It isn't the same without him, is it?" David said, his voice cracking. There was an awkward silence.

"Why don't we all take a seat?" Mae broke in, taking Virginia's hand and leading her to the head of the table.

"It smells wonderful, Mae," David said. "I hope you haven't gone to too much bother."

Mae blushed and said, "It's roast chicken—not homegrown, mind you—and scalloped potatoes. No trouble at all." They all took their seats, then held hands as Peter said the blessing.

"So how's it going with your book buddy, Grandma?" Peter asked as he passed the platter of meat.

"Jessie's a peach. She's been coming over in the afternoons while her dad's at work. She's so enchanted. She stares at my cuckoo clock as if she can't imagine a bird living in that little door, and she has my Snip all tamed." Virginia smiled wide. "All she needed was a little attention. Poor girl. She's been through too much for her age."

"You sound smitten," Trudy said.

"I guess I am. She helps me see things fresh. Do you think it's too late to raise a rabbit for 4-H? I know there's only a few weeks before the fair, but it would be so good for her. You always liked 4-H, David."

"You were in 4-H, Dad?" Peter asked.

"Sure I was." David took a roll from the breadbasket. "I did some woodworking projects, usually had a calf or rabbits or chickens to show."

"You never told me that," Peter said.

"Sure I did." David shrugged.

"I think Jessie needs something to engage that mind of hers," Virginia went on. "She's so creative, but it's all bottled up in that energetic body."

"There's the talent show," David said.

"What kind of talent are we talking about?" Trudy said.

"Oh," Virginia said. "A little of everything; singing, dancing, that kind of thing."

"That sounds like a hoot. Any interpretive dance?" Trudy said. Mae raised an eyebrow and shook her head in warning.

"We'll wait to explore her artistic side," Virginia said. "I thought we could start small. Then do whatever interests her next year."

David turned to Mae. "I hear you play the cello."

"A little," she confessed.

"She's being modest," Trudy cut in. "She's really good, and she's got great pipes too."

"Maybe we can play together after supper. My violin's in the car."

"Sure," Mae said.

After the table was cleared and everyone gathered in the living room for coffee and lemon bars, Mae brought down her cello. She rosined her bow and tuned the strings. David had retrieved his violin from the car along with some sheet music. "Tchaikovsky okay?" David asked. "Fifth Symphony."

Mae reached for the copy, looking it over. Soon the low, mournful cello blended with the higher flight of the violin in a sweet interlacing of notes. It was a tender song that lilted like a lazy cloud on a summer's day.

The night stilled except for their song, and the grandfather clock keeping time in the hallway. Peter sat back in the recliner, watching Mae. She seemed enraptured by the song, and he remembered watching her play at concerts in college. Her long, delicate fingers flew above the strings as the bow brought forth its rich sound. He felt a tug on his heart. She had a definite gift for music. He'd always known that, but now, gazing at her beautiful face, he felt guilty keeping such talent all to himself.

When the song ended, the listeners applauded. "That was lovely," Virginia said.

"You're very good," David said to Mae. "Have you ever thought of auditioning for the symphony?"

She blushed. "It's a pretty far drive these days."

David and Mae sat and talked music for a long while, their instruments in hand. Then David passed around photos of his trip to China. "Now, that speck there is me on the Great Wall," David said, pointing at the photo and handing it to his mother.

Mae shot Peter a glance, tilting her head toward David, her eyes reminding him that they had news to share.

"Um. Dad, Grandma…Trudy," Peter said. "We sort of have a little announcement to make." His hands fidgeted in his lap.

The three faces lifted, and Virginia set her coffee cup on the table, a spark in her eye. Peter drew a deep breath and took Mae's hand. "We're going to have a baby."

Virginia clapped a hand to her chest, and David sat with his mouth open.

"I'm going to be an aunt! I'm going to be an aunt," Trudy chanted like a four-year-old as she jumped up and down. "This is great. I'll spoil her rotten and send her home to you stuffed with candy."

"Her?"

"It's got to be a girl," Trudy said. "Girls are just…better."

"Hey," Peter said. "I think a little boy would be nice."

"If it's nothing like you," Trudy teased.

"Whatever God gives is a blessing," Virginia added. "That's all that matters. When are you due, dear?"

"February," Mae said.

"This calls for a celebration," David said. "After all, how often do I become a grandpa for the first time?" He picked up his violin and played an embellished rendition of "Happy Birthday."

"You know, you've really upset me," Virginia said to Mae with a grin.

"Why?"

"I'm far too young to be a great-grandmother. I'll have to write your Aunt Sarah, Peter, to tell her the news. She'll be so thrilled."

"Do you have any names picked out?" Trudy asked.

"We haven't even thought about it," Peter confessed.

"Trudy's a good name," Trudy said. Everyone laughed.

"Well, you have plenty of time to decide," Virginia said. "What a blessing." Peter looked over at his grandmother's pale eyes. They had a misty quality, and he knew she was missing Grandpa Roy. He missed him too.

Around ten o'clock, Peter said, "Well, if you'll excuse me. I've got a heifer that I need to check on. She looked like she was going to drop today." He got up then and said good night before heading out the back door. Mae wanted to go talk to him but decided to let him be alone for a while.

"You know, I should head home too," Virginia said, looking over at David.

"Fine by me," David said. "Now that I'm going to be a grandpa, I'm feeling suddenly older." He held out a hand to Mae, then pulled her into a hug. "I'm glad you two are doing so well here. My concert schedule doesn't pick up again for a couple of months, so maybe I can be of some help. I'd be happy to drive down from St. Paul for the next haying."

"I'll let Peter know you offered," Mae said. "And thank you. I enjoyed tonight—playing Tchaikovsky."

Trudy stood in line and shook David's hand like a vacuum cleaner salesman. "Great to see you again, Dad," she said, punching him in the other arm. "Maybe we can get these two up to St. Paul some time for a concert or something."

"Sounds like a plan."

Virginia reached to hug Mae good-bye. "You get some sleep, dear," Virginia said. "Take care of my great-grandchild."

After David's taillights disappeared down the drive and Trudy insisted on doing the dishes herself, Mae slipped on her boots and went out to the barn to find Peter. The main lights were off, and Mae could see Peter in the back, a lone bulb lit behind him. He was sitting on a stool by a black Holstein with a white spot on the end of her tail. She lay on the ground, heavy with calf, and Peter ran his hand along her back as her tail flicked back and forth. Mae stood watching him. He was so serene, sitting in the yellow light. After a few minutes, Peter looked up.

"Hey," Mae said.

"Hi." His gaze returned to the cow.

"We had a good visit, don't you think?"

"Wasn't bad."

"Are you still mad at your dad for missing the funeral?"

"Yeah…I don't know. You know, I've been mad at him for so many things—for moving constantly, putting his music before me and Mom, keeping me from Grandpa and Grandma while we were on endless tours… Somehow it seems more distant to me now. Maybe I'm growing up." He shrugged. There was a long silence, and their attention returned to the heifer.

"She's going to deliver soon," Peter said. "I wanted to be here."

Mae's mind flicked to the one that died.

There was another long silence, then Peter said, "Do you wish you'd pursued music after college?"

"Is that what this is about? Because I'm not about to leave you to go—"

"No. I don't mean that. I know you'd never leave me."

Mae pulled up a stool next to him, put her arms around his shoulders, and rested her head next to his.

"If being a good cellist is my greatest attainment," she began, "I don't know…it seems pretty hollow to me. Life has taken on a much deeper meaning somehow." She rubbed her hand on her stomach. "I don't want the kind of life that goes with being a musician. Don't get me wrong—I admire your dad. But running from performance to performance, calling you and the baby on the phone to say, 'Mommy loves you' but not seeing you because my life is too hectic… It doesn't appeal to me. If it was just about playing pretty music, I'd say sure, let me play. But it's about a lot more than that. It's about the kind of person I want to be, what kinds of things I value in life." She lifted her eyes to his. "It isn't what my heart desires."

"So what does your heart desire?" Peter's eyes searched Mae's.

"A quiet, simple life here with you, with us. That's all. I want our baby to grow up knowing she's loved by us and by God. I want to be together, by your side, making this farm a success. That's what gives me true joy."

Peter's face relaxed with her words, and he leaned his body toward hers and ran a finger along her cheek. "Your mom was right, you know. You do deserve the best."

"I have the best right here."

The heifer moaned low, and Peter turned to look at her. The cow lifted her head from the hay, then let it drop back down. "She doesn't sound happy," Mae said, then stopped speaking when she saw small, dark hooves emerge. "Shouldn't we call the vet or something?"

"Only if she runs into trouble. I'd rather not spend the money if we don't need to." The mother let out a loud bawl. Peter and Mae stood, side by side, mesmerized, as the small forelegs appeared and then the little head. The calf's face was covered in a shiny film, and it was hard for Mae to make out exactly where its eyes and nose were. After another push the shoulders emerged, and within seconds the small calf was mostly out, its hind legs alone left inside the heifer's womb. The cow turned her head and began licking, cleaning her baby with her long, scratchy tongue. Shiny black eyes peered around and the calf let out a pitiful mew. When the mother finished bathing her newborn, she stood, and the calf's hind legs plopped to the ground. The cow turned slowly to lick again, swiping the soft fur into little tufted cowlicks on the calf's back.

After a few minutes, the calf made its first efforts to stand, putting his little rump into the air and then raising up on pencil-thin, knobby knees before plunking back onto the soft hay. After a dozen more tries he was finally up, standing frozen on wobbly legs as if afraid a gust of wind would knock him over. Then he hopped, a little uncoordinated hop that moved him next to his mother. She sniffed his bottom, nudging him to nurse, and he bunted at her udder, pushing hard to find the teat, then taking a long, thirsty sip.

"That was incredible," Mae said to Peter as he turned out the light and slipped an arm around Mae's waist. "Can I keep him?"

"We can't afford a two-thousand-pound pet. We'd have to slaughter him eventually."

"I'll cross that bridge when I come to it."

"It's for me?" Jessie's eyes were huge as she held the soft brown rabbit closely to her chest. "For real?"

"Yes ma'am," Virginia said. "I thought maybe you would like to show him at the county fair."

"The fair?" Jessie looked at her, questioning. "Isn't that for country kids?" Then her shoulders slumped. "I don't know if my dad's gonna let me keep a bunny at our house." She stroked the Rex's soft brown fur.

"We can keep him here," Virginia said. "I put up a cage for him in the backyard in a nice shady spot. That is, if it's okay with you. You can come over to take care of him. He's still your rabbit, of course. I'll expect you to be responsible. And it's okay with your father—I already asked him." She gave Jessie a wink.

"Really?" Jessie's eyes danced. She buried her face in the animal's soft coat and closed her eyes. Her expression held such an angelic joy that Virginia felt her heart swell. "What do I need to do?" Jessie said.

"Well, first"—Virginia pulled a 4-H handbook on rabbit care from behind her back—"we'll start with this. It tells us pretty much everything we need to know."

"More reading?"

"You're a good reader, Jessie. You're just impatient with yourself." Virginia opened the book to the front and said, "Why don't you start?"

"Your rabbit's home," Jessie began, and together they read about cages and bedding and water bottles and all the care Jessie's bunny would need.

"What should I name him?" Jessie asked after a while.

"What name do you like?"

Jessie twisted her face up, thinking it over. "I've never thought about what names I like before. What was your husband's name?"

"Roy."

"Maybe I could call him Roy." Virginia lifted a doubtful eyebrow. "Or how about Flopsy?" Jessie amended. "Like Peter Rabbit's brother?"

"That sounds better, more fitting for a rabbit." Virginia was relieved.

"I like Flopsy," Jessie said. "His ears look flopsy, don't you think?" The rabbit nibbled on a piece of carrot Jessie held, and his little nose twitched from side to side.

"I think he likes you," Virginia said.

"How can you tell?" Jessie lifted him up to look him in the eyes.

"He's not trying to get away from you."

Jessie put him back in the crook of her arm and smiled adoringly at Virginia. "This is the best present I ever got. Thanks."

Virginia reached over and stroked Jessie's hair. "I can't remember getting someone their best present ever before."

Mae wished she could find relief from the warmth without having to stay in air conditioning all afternoon. She'd come out of the queasy phase of her pregnancy only to be more tired than ever. She'd go to bed as soon as supper dishes were done and sleep straight through to ten o'clock the next morning. Peter told her not to worry about the morning milking. He said that if the baby needed her to rest, she should accommodate it. She was still able to milk in the evenings, as well as run errands in the afternoons. The Suzie Qs assured her it would get better, that she'd find more energy to get things done as the pregnancy progressed, but right now she felt pretty much useless. Trudy had pitched in with laundry and cleaning and weeding and harvesting in the garden, but Mae hated not being able to do all the work by herself.

Mae was washing dishes when Bert Biddle's pickup raised dust on the long driveway. She pulled back the kitchen curtain and watched him get out and head into the barn.

"Who was that?" Trudy came into the room.

"The nice brother," Mae said.

"What do you mean by that?"

"Nothing. Bert's not as flashy as Fred."

"You think Fred's flashy?" Trudy said.

"Relatively speaking—Bert isn't quite so…"

"Self-occupied?"

Mae raised a brow at her words.

"Yeah," Trudy said. "It's been bugging me. All he talks about is himself. It gets old fast. I like Bert, but he's so shy it's hard to get him to talk."

"You know, you are going back to St. Paul before too long."

"I don't mind a long-distance relationship, not if there's husband potential there."

"Well, dear, you're going to have to make up your mind."

Peter heard the barn door slam, and he leaned on the handle of the pitchfork, taking a break from mucking out a stall. Dust motes floated like diamonds in the shafts of warm sunlight that found the dark interior through cracks in the siding. The warm air smelled of sweet hay. Bert Biddle's green cap came into view. Peter straightened.

"Bert, what can I do for you?"

"I was wondering if you're taking any cows to the fair," Bert said quietly.

"I hadn't really thought about it. I suppose not. You taking some?"

"Every year. We usually borrow Roy's big trailer so we don't have to take three trips. I was hoping to use it again if that's okay with you."

"Sure you can use it," Peter said.

"If you need it, I can bring it back right away," Bert offered.

"No. That's okay. Keep it there."

"You think you and Mae… and… ah, Trudy will be comin' down to the fair?"

"I suppose so," Peter said. "It's a good chance to get out and see what the neighbors are up to."

"I suppose." Bert glanced out the side window toward the house.

"Was there something else, Bert?"

"No…uh…just wondering about that trailer."

"Go ahead and take it now if you want. That would be fine."

"Great," Bert said. "I guess I better get on home then. Ma will have supper on soon." He ducked his head in a nod and turned to go, his green cap disappearing behind one of the barn's whitewashed walls.

Mae was inspecting her rows of canned goods. With Virginia's help, she and Trudy had put up three dozen pints of beets, four dozen quarts of tomatoes, and another four dozen pints of green beans. She'd made apple butter and canned that along with apple pie filling and applesauce. She'd put up pickles and made strawberry jam that would never last until next summer the way Peter was eating it. The orderly rows, colorful and cheery on her shelves, gave Mae a feeling of true accomplishment. By milking, doing chores, and putting up food, she was doing her part to ease their financial load, even if she hadn't been able to land a job.

She had regained much of the energy she'd been lacking during the earlier part of her pregnancy. She felt almost energized at times, and she was back to milking in the mornings with Peter, feeding the calves, and keeping up with the farm duties. She'd put on almost fifteen pounds already. At this rate, she thought, she'd put on a good forty, fifty pounds by the time she was ready to deliver.

Mae had no idea what the judges at the fair would be looking for, but she'd followed the directions in her *Putting Food By* book, and Virginia had given her plenty of sage advice.

Peter came in the back door. "Whatcha doing?" he asked.

"Looking at my hard work," Mae said. "What should I enter in the fair?"

"Definitely the strawberry jam," Peter said. "I could eat that at every meal. You could try a little of everything, couldn't you?"

Mae tapped her chin. "You know, I never imagined myself as someone who would like farming. But here I am milking cows, getting my hands dirty in the garden, canning fruit and vegetables. What do you think of raising honeybees? I read that bees increase the yield in the orchard and garden."

"As long as I don't have to do anything with them," Peter said with a laugh.

Mae slugged him. "Oh, I need to make my calf his bottle of milk replacer, " she said.

"That calf is a nuisance," Peter chuckled. "He won't let me walk in the pasture without slobbering on my leg."

"He's just looking for his bottle," Mae said.

"He's a spoiled baby. You like taking care of that calf, don't you?" Peter said as he slipped his arms around Mae's expanding waist from behind and leaned to give her a kiss on the neck.

"I do," she said. "It's good practice for Junior here." She patted her stomach and turned toward him. "What do you think of the name Missy?"

"Are you serious? That's not a name, it's a form of address—Mr. and Missy. I prefer Electra."

"Peter, be serious!"

"I am serious," he said teasingly. He kissed her again. Mae put her hands on his neck and drew him closer.

Mid-August was time for the Le Sueur County fair in Le Center, Minnesota. Everyone went. The fair was a cacophony of scents and noises and sights. Fat old women sold cotton candy and corn dogs. Bent gray men stood at angles talking of weather and farming next to the Quonset sheds that housed the horses and cows. Children zigzagged with their playmates across the midway and through the animal exhibits. Cows and horses and sheep waited for inspection in neat rows. Big fans blew the warm air across the stalls. Their owners napped in lawn chairs beside them while others kept busy, sweeping and shoveling, bringing water and food, pampering their animals as they never would at home.

Mae had brought a box of her best canned goods to enter—her strawberry jam, rhubarb, apple pie filling, tomatoes, and raspberry jam. Peter had disappeared to wander through the livestock exhibits while Mae went to register.

Mae entered the small white building that hosted the women's categories. Ladies hovered like bees around honeysuckle, setting doilies under their prized recipes and adjusting them so that they sat just so. Mae moved down the aisle where beautiful quilts awaited examination, and stitched pillows and pictures of all kinds were arranged for their coming out. Women whispered over their competitors' work, pointing discreetly.

Mae pulled out the tags that she'd carefully inscribed with the information the judges required. She taped them to the tops of her jars, rims removed so that the judges could see that her seals were perfect. Virginia had told her that was important. "You can have the best recipe in the world, but if your seal is bad they won't even consider it." Mae set each jar in its place, her name and entry proudly printed on the front label. Then she walked around to see what others had brought. When she was on the other side of the divider between the narrow aisles, she heard someone say her name.

"Mae Morgan," the woman's voice said. "Who's that?"

"Oh, she's that Peter Morgan's wife," a second voice said. Mae didn't recognize the voices. "They just moved from St. Paul. Took over Roy and Virginia's place."

"St. Paul," the first woman scoffed. "What is she doing entering strawberry jam in the fair? Outsiders think they can jump right in."

Mae felt her heart sink. Why was it every time she tried something new, she was reminded of how much she didn't fit in here?

"She's a nice enough girl," the second voice said. Mae must know who this person was. She tried to look through the cracks in the divider, but all she saw was someone's gray head. "Maybe she'll give you a run for your money this year. Much as that rubs you the wrong way…"

Someone tapped Mae's shoulder, and her heart leapt. She turned and was relieved to see Virginia and Jessie. "We thought we'd find you in here," Virginia said.

"I got Flopsy all set up," Jessie said, beaming like a headlight.

"When is the judging?" Mae asked her.

"This afternoon. Virginia and I have been practicing how to talk to the judges, and she says I'm a natural."

"Oh really?" Mae said.

"Yep. And Flopsy is the best bunny of all of them. Philip Huber has this huge rabbit that looks like it needs to lose weight. Isn't that what you said, Virginia?"

Virginia turned red, then patted Jessie's shoulder. "We need to be good sports, Jessie," Virginia said.

"Uh-huh," Mae added dubiously.

"Where are your entries?" Virginia said.

"Oh, around the other side," Mae said.

Virginia led them around the wall. The women were gone.

"They look wonderful," Virginia said, inspecting them carefully. "Especially that strawberry jam."

Virginia stood nervously to the side of the ring while Jessie, a white piece of paper with the number 189 pinned to her back, waited in line with the other children. The judges moved from child to child, stooping down to talk to the smaller ones, asking questions about their animals and how to care for them. Jessie was standing as Virginia had coached her, at full attention, her back straight, quietly awaiting her turn with the judges, with an immaculately groomed Flopsy clutched in her small hands. Virginia rehearsed the procedure in her head.

Number 188, a dark-haired girl with long pigtails, was next. As the judge leaned down to talk to her, the rabbit leapt from her hands and scampered to the side of the judging area. She chased it into a corner and picked up the terrified rabbit as she sobbed quietly. The gray-haired judge gently walked her back and squatted down to talk with her, taking extra minutes until the tears gave way to a smile.

Then came Jessie's turn. Virginia felt her stomach knot, and she placed a hand on it. Jessie grinned at the judges and held Flopsy out when asked. She showed them his nails and teeth and sat him on all fours. Virginia could see the girl's mouth moving as she quietly answered each question. Finally she picked him up, and the judges probed and petted the soft brown fur before moving on to the next child.

When it came time for the judges to announce the winners, the children formed a semicircle waiting for the announcement. Some stroked their rabbits, their little brows furrowed, while others giggled mischievously with their neighbors. Virginia didn't recognize most of the children, but most of the last names were known to her, the children and grandchildren of farmers from around the county.

"Jessie Wise," the judge's husky voice finally called out. "Second place." He held out the red ribbon proudly.

Jessie's mouth dropped open as she shook the judge's hand and reached for her prize. Smiling, she looked over at Virginia and held the ribbon up high, mouthing, "I got second!" The judges thanked the contestants for all their hard work, and Jessie returned Flopsy safely to his cage where he munched passively on a carrot. Jessie ran back to Virginia.

"I got second. I got red!" Jessie jumped up and down.

"Congratulations," Virginia said, giving her a hearty hug. "You must've really impressed them."

"Does this mean I take Flopsy to the state fair?" Her eyes were wide.

"No, dear. Grand Champion and Reserve Champion get that honor. But it means you did really well."

Jessie held the ribbon up against the light and gazed at it. "I've never won anything before in my life," Jessie said. "Thank you." She threw her nine-year-old arms around Virginia again as Virginia stooped her cheek over the girl's head.

When she pulled back, Virginia asked, "We can enter more categories next year if you like. There's pretty much a contest for everything."

"Could I draw pictures?"

"Sure, you could do that."

"I can draw good pictures. And maybe…" Her mind was scrambling with possibilities.

"Jessie!" Susan Warner from Jessie's 4-H group came up behind her. "You got second!" Her voice was as excited as Jessie's. She held up her own white ribbon.

"You got a ribbon too," Jessie said.

"It's only third place though."

"Still, it's a prize." They basked in the glow of their triumph. Susan whispered in Jessie's ear, and Jessie asked, "Virginia, could we go look at the chickens?"

"I'll see you at the grandstand in an hour, okay?" The girls bounced away.

twenty-five

T he crowd of old and young, fat and skinny, began gathering at the grandstand for the annual talent show. This was the one time each year when anyone who dared could climb onstage and perform while an audience of proud parents and grandparents and embarrassed children looked on. There were the perennial dance troupes—little girls in tights and tutus who always won the audience's hearts—and the over-bearing mother-child combos who seemed more like professional lounge acts. There were the roamers, people who hopped from county fair to county fair, hoping the competition would be weak enough to send them to the state fair and eventually launch their careers with a record company.

But Virginia's favorites were her neighbors from Lake Emily. One year Alva Endicott, the librarian, got up and played a Whitney Houston song on the accordion that was truly inspired. And last year Mayor Olsen did a tap dance routine that made jaws drop, although more from the sight of such a short, round person flying on tap shoes than from any true Sammy Davis Jr. aspirations. Virginia had never unearthed any such talents in herself, although she had been told she could tell a good joke every now and again. There was a thought—an old woman telling Sven-and-Ole jokes to a crowd of Svens and Oles.

Trudy waved vigorously at Virginia as she inched down the crowded bleacher row to where she sat.

"Hey," Trudy said. Her curly red hair was pulled back into a thick wiry ponytail. She wore a long, loose yellow cotton dress and sandals, and her freckled cheeks were red from the sun. "Have I missed anything? I was painting my car and I forgot the time."

Virginia patted the spot next to her. "You were painting your car?"

"You'll love it," she said as she sat down. "I have these scenes all sketched out. It'll be great. Where's Mae?"

"I haven't seen her since before lunch. Jessie got a red ribbon."

"Good for her!"

Mae and Peter sidled up to them. "How'd the judging go?" Virginia asked Mae.

"Five white ribbons and one blue," Mae said as they took the seats on the other side of Virginia.

"That's wonderful!" Virginia said. "I bet the blue was your strawberry jam."

"Actually, it was the rhubarb. There were only three entries in that category."

"Well, it's a start. You've got some tough competition in Lake Emily. Some of these ladies have been entering the same recipe thirty years, and they win every time." She patted Mae's knee.

Jessie came up and squirmed her way between Mae and Virginia.

"I got red," she held up her ribbon and gave Mae and Peter a look-see before showing it to Trudy.

"That's super, punkin," Trudy said.

"Next year I'm gonna draw some pictures," she informed Trudy.

"Really? I like to draw too," Trudy said excitedly. "You'll have to show me some of your pictures."

A tall, thin woman took the stage. "Good evening," she enunciated into the microphone as it squealed with reverb. People covered their ears at the noise, and she motioned for the sound man to turn it down before continuing. "I'd like to welcome you to the thirty-third annual Le Sueur County talent contest. We have a great lineup of local talent this year. But first I'd like to introduce you to our judges." When the judges had been properly acknowledged, she continued, "Our first contestant is from Le Center. Please welcome Joshua Clarke as he sings 'Danny Boy.'"

The crowd erupted in applause as a little boy about six years old in a blue three-piece suit took the stage. His hair was slicked back, and he held the microphone so close to his mouth that the words all muddled together. His hand gestures were well rehearsed—he'd throw his free arm out at the start of the chorus and draw it in as the melody grew quiet. His three-year-old sister was apparently sitting right behind Virginia because she sang the whole tune in perfect unison with her big brother, only slightly better, Virginia thought. Joshua walked the full length of the stage, gazing into faces in the audience, and when the song ended, he knelt down on one knee with both arms extended. The audience whistled and cheered in a wild ovation.

Next the Lake City Dancers tap, tap, tapped to "Yankee Doodle" in perfect time except for a little blonde on the end who lost her red-white-and-blue top hat three times. Their cheesy smiles never dimmed as they bounced off the stage, their arms out and hands shaking like tambourines.

A woman in a long flowing dress sang Bette Midler's "Wind Beneath My Wings," and a skinny teenage boy with a dog collar around his neck played a drum solo, his hair flying as he moved his head to the heavy metal beat. A cowboy in black jeans and boots acted out a gunfight scene from *High Noon,* moving back and forth and switching hats to play the parts of villain and lawman as each faced the other for their shootout.

"Next," the emcee said, "we have Bert Biddle playing 'Rocky Mountain Rodeo' on his banjo." Trudy's head shot up.

"Bert plays the banjo?" she mouthed to Virginia.

"People surprise you all the time." Virginia smiled.

Bert took center stage. He was wearing a white shirt with dark jeans and his Sunday boots. He glanced up at the crowd and nodded, catching Trudy's eye and turning beet red before lowering his gaze to his banjo. The piece began slowly, building momentum with each measure. His fingers picked in perfect time, leaving the crowd hushed as the tempo increased. Once the music reached an impossible pace, the song returned to a quiet soliloquy, each note carefully sustained and measured to create a sweet calm as the song ended. Bert dipped his head and exited as the audience began whistling and cheering.

A few minutes later, Trudy looked up to see Bert making his way to her across the grandstand. "Do you mind if I sit with you?" he asked Trudy as Virginia scooted over to make room.

"You were amazing," Trudy whispered. "I didn't know you could play like that! Have you been playing long?"

"It's nothing," he said.

"Are you kidding? If I could play like that I'd be out on the road with Dolly Parton."

Bert smiled.

"So why did you enter the talent contest?" Trudy said.

A woman in front of Trudy turned and said, "Sh!" finger to lips.

"Sorry," Trudy whispered. "Can we get out of here?" she said to Bert.

As the next act finished and the clapping began, they scooted off the stand.

"So…," Trudy said as they walked the fairgrounds, "you never answered my question—why did you enter the talent contest?"

"My ma wanted me to. She thinks I could be like Peter's dad. I wanted her to stop nagging me. How many banjos have you seen in the St. Paul orchestra?" He laughed. Trudy noticed the dimple in his right cheek, like a deep parenthesis. She imagined there was a lot about Bert that she'd never noticed before.

"Wouldn't your ma want you to stick around to run the farm?"

"I suppose… For the most part. But she wouldn't mind having a famous son either."

"And do you want to leave?"

"No. I'm a farmer."

"What would you do if some talent agent discovered you and wanted to give you a big contract in Nashville?"

"I wouldn't tell my ma! Honestly, it's not really something I think about."

She looked up into his blue, blue eyes. "So what *do* you think about, Bert Biddle?"

Bert's Adam's apple bobbed in a swallow. "I think about a lot of things," he said. "The cows and my family, music…and well, lately, you…" He said it so quietly Trudy wasn't certain if she'd heard him correctly. He glanced away.

"You like hot beefs?" He nodded to the 4-H food stand. "My treat."

"Okay."

Inside was a bustling of activity as the production line of 4-H'ers delivered hot beef sandwiches, hot dogs, chips, and assorted pop to the public. "Three hot beefs," Bert said to the scrawny kid behind the counter. "I'll take a bag of the barbecue chips and a Pepsi. Trudy, would you like chips or pop?"

"A Pepsi for me too," she said. They moved down the line and took their trays to one of the long picnic tables where families gathered over their meals. Bert reached for her hand. "May I say grace?"

"Sure." She bowed her head.

"Dear Lord," he began softly, "thank you for food. For all the things that you give us. For Trudy…" He paused, then cleared his throat. "Amen." When he was done, his face was flushed, and he stared at his food.

"Amen," Trudy said sincerely. "So tell me about you—you farm… you play the banjo… What else?"

"Not much to say, really." He took a big bite of his hot beef. The sauce dribbled onto his chin, and he wiped it off with a napkin. "What about you? You're from St. Paul—do you like it there?"

"I suppose. It's home, you know? I went to school there and have a lot of friends…"

Bert shifted in his seat. "You're an art teacher?" Bert said.

"I love art," Trudy began as she took another bite of her sandwich. "Especially folk art—it's so rich in character. But all kinds of art, really. I'm pretty eclectic. Grandma Moses really gets me going, but the Impressionists are fun too. I was painting my car today. I had this idea to depict all the cool stuff in Minnesota—like a map, you know—only on my car. I'm putting St. Paul and Minneapolis on the hood. I thought I'd put Lake Emily on the trunk, like with a cow and fields of corn and stuff. Hey, maybe I could get a picture of you on your tractor to work from. That'd be perfect!" As she talked, Bert's grin grew until it split his face. "What's so funny?"

"Nothin'," he said. "I've never met anyone like you."

Her eyes met his, and electricity arced between them. "What do you enjoy, Bert Biddle?"

"Can't say as I have a lot of hobbies, 'cept for my banjo, of course. Farming keeps me pretty busy. I do like to look at tractors. They've got some really nice ones here."

"I'm not much of a tractor driver."

"I heard about that… But it takes practice. When I was first learning, I took down Ma's whole clothesline. She wasn't happy about that, especially with all our Sunday clothes covered with tire tracks."

"I bet she wasn't!" Trudy laughed. "I had to steer clear of Peter for a while too." Their eyes met again.

"Well." Bert reached for Trudy's food tray. "If you're done, would you like to take in the fair?"

They stopped at the 4-H building first, inspecting the displays from tomorrow's geniuses that ranged from woodworking projects—dressers, bookshelves, oak clocks—to button collections, flower arrangements, photographs and drawings, garden produce, and sewing projects.

They ambled toward the tall farm machinery parked in the center of the fairgrounds. Trudy climbed on a big green tractor and made motor sounds, pretending she was plowing. Bert explained the stereo system that would have been envied by any teenage boy, and how the Global Positioning Unit, or GPU, as he called it, was used to tell them where to fertilize in their own fields. Trudy took Bert's hand in hers as they strolled through the barns full of horses, sheep, swine, and cattle. She stopped to pet and talk to every animal that stuck its head out for a scratch.

"This is Duke," Bert said in the cattle barn, "our Angus bull." They walked over to a tall animal with a brass nose ring. He was bigger than any heifer Trudy had ever seen before.

"Is he mean?"

"Naw. He's a big kitten." Bert scratched the bull between the ears, and he nudged closer and pushed his nose into Bert's chest, shoving Bert backward. Bert swatted him on the neck. "He's from a long line of champions, along with these two." He tilted his head toward the next stall where two heifers munched hay. "Peggy and Sue," he finished. "Mom named them." He leaned down and picked up a galvanized bucket, then said, "I'll show you how to milk the old-fashioned way." He went to clean the bucket, then walked next to Peggy, plopping a stool beside her udder. Trudy watched over his shoulder. "Get a good grip up high and squeeze down like you're emptying a tube of tooth-paste. Don't pull from the end." He demonstrated for a few long squirts. "Wanna try?"

"Um…okay." Trudy took the seat and reached for the soft flesh.

Peggy obviously knew someone new was at her side because she flicked her tail at Trudy's back. "Stop that," Trudy scolded and patted her. Then she reached her forefinger and thumb around each teat and pulled down. She was rewarded with a thick, rich stream of white.

"I did it!" she grinned at Bert, who was squatting next to her. His face reflected her joy, and for a moment they froze, eyes searching. Peggy flicked her tail again and Trudy jumped. "Hey!" she said and slapped the cow's side. "Should I keep milking?" Trudy asked Bert.

"If you want," Bert said. "I need to milk her anyway."

She squeezed and pulled until the bucket was almost full. Then, holding it up, she said, "What now?"

He led her to a big holding tank and reached for the bucket in her hands. Their hands touched and lingered briefly.

"There you are!" the voice of Fred Biddle interrupted. "Mae said you might be here." He was looking at Trudy. "I finished chores at home, Bert. It looks like you haven't finished the chores here," he said.

Bert fidgeted.

"Well, actually, Fred," Trudy said, "I was helping Bert with the chores. Maybe we'll run into you later?"

"Oh," Fred stammered, "well, okay." He shot his brother an accusing look. Trudy reached for the bucket and turned away from him.

"We still need to milk Sue, right?" she said over her shoulder.

"Let's walk the midway," Peter whispered into Mae's ear once the talent contest was over.

Darkness had descended, and now the fairgrounds were lit by gaudy carnival lights twirling high in the air. The carnies cajoled brave young men to show off their skills for the ladies. Children and teenagers lined up for rides. The squeals and screams of nervous riders dotted the air as the more daring took on the Ride of Doom. Cotton candy and caramel apples and fried cheese curds filled hungry, happy faces attached to heavy Midwest bodies. Mae tucked her hand into the crook of Peter's arm and pulled herself close to him as they walked.

"Want to go on a ride?" Peter pointed at the Tilt-a-Whirl.

"I'm pregnant."

"And…?"

"I don't think it's a good idea. Some of those rides can set off labor."

"Okay…" He gave her a disbelieving look, then tilted his chin straight ahead. "How about the Ferris wheel?"

Mae gazed up at the towering ride. "That I think I can do."

They got in line and waited for their turn. Peter recognized Jerry Shrupp and his wife getting off the ride. "J. D. Shrupp!" Peter said.

Jerry lifted his head and smiled in recognition as he walked in his trademark limp toward Peter. "David Morgan's boy." He pulled Mary along. "No one's called me J. D. since your dad. I heard he was in town last week."

The women exchanged nods.

"He sure was, just got back from a tour of Asia. Said he wanted to look you up when he's down next from St. Paul."

"Well, you tell him to stop on by. Good man, your dad. Mary tells me Mae's been milking with you." Jerry looked over at Mae. "Nothing like a good woman to lighten the load, I always say."

Mary blushed and said, "Everything's going well with the pregnancy, I hope."

"We're doing fine," Mae said to the nurse. "I'm finally feeling a little more energy. Not so tired as I was in June and July."

"That's how it goes sometimes," Mary agreed.

"Next," the Ferris wheel attendant called to Mae and Peter as he stood holding the bobbing compartment door open.

"I guess that's us," Peter said to the Shrupps. "I'll tell Dad you said hi."

"You give us a call if you need anything," Jerry said, reaching for his wife's hand.

"Thanks, Mr. Shrupp," Peter said, turning to walk up the ramp. They got onto the ride and fastened the bar that ran the length of the seat.

"Jerry's a good guy. I remember him coming to the farm whenever Dad and I were visiting. He and I would play ball."

The wheel jerked around just above the rooftops of the surrounding buildings to let the next riders on. Their carriage rocked with the movement.

"This really is your hometown, isn't it?" Mae said. Peter stared out across the colored lights of the midway to the Quonset huts that housed the animals of the fair and to the darkened fields surrounded by even darker woods beyond.

"It feels like home." He reached for her hand. She leaned back and put her head on his shoulder as the seat rocked to a start and they began their musical ride into the heavens.

twenty six

The two Als had been known throughout Lake Emily for their arguments in their high-school days, but as they'd passed from their twenties into their thirties, the fights had grown fewer and further between. Tonight was time for a reunion. Fred had been seething ever since he spied Trudy and Bert milking Peggy and flirting at the tank. He'd watched their hands touch and then linger. He'd seen the look Trudy had given Bert. She'd never looked at him like that, not even after their helicopter ride.

Fred parked his truck next to the barn and stalked up to the rambling Biddle house. The light was on in the kitchen, and Fred could see his mother standing over the sink doing dishes. He threw the back door open and stomped into the cluttered entryway.

"What's got your undies in a bunch?" Lillian said.

"Bert home?"

"No. I did see him at the fair with that Ploog girl. He took first in the talent contest but wasn't even around to accept the prize. I was so embarrassed. I don't understand what's gotten into him lately—"

"I'm going up to my room," Fred interrupted. His face felt warm. He turned and marched up the stairs.

"Do you want a snack?" he heard his mother's faint voice as he reached the top.

"No," he grunted as his eyes caught Bert's open door. He walked into the room and turned on the light. It was pretty much the same as it had been in high school—Minnesota Twins pennants and his senior picture on the wall next to Fred's, a couple of hockey trophies. Fred scrutinized the room, getting angrier by the moment. Bert's dresser was covered with an assortment of items from his pockets—change, a black comb, wadded-up gum wrappers. Fred shifted his view when he spied an old notebook on the window sill. Fred picked it up and moved closer to the lamp on the nightstand, trying to decipher Bert's scribbles. A pen marked the page where Bert had stopped writing.

"What do you think you're doing?" Bert's voice boomed angrily into the room. Fred started.

"What were *you* doing?" Fred threw down the book. "Slobbering all over Trudy at the fair!"

"There's no law says I can't spend time with her."

"If you were a real man, you wouldn't steal your brother's girl." Fred's voice rose a couple decibels.

"You don't own her! Trudy can spend time with whoever she wants." Bert drew closer, his face red, veins bulging. "Maybe she likes spending time with someone who knows how to treat a woman!" They were nose to nose.

That was when the first blow came—a quick, swift punch to Bert's right cheek, knocking him back. For a moment he stood stunned, blood seeping from his nose.

But Fred wasn't done yet. He felt anger boil through his skull, and he threw himself headlong at his brother, pushing Bert to the bed, punching repeatedly as he did, Bert returning blow for blow.

Within moments the door flew open and Lillian's piercing shriek split the room. "Stop it!" Panting from her run up the stairs, she yanked Fred away from Bert. "What do you boys think you're doing?" Her face was flushed, and she looked ready to throw a punch or two herself.

"Nothing!" Fred shouted.

"Is this fuss about that girl Trudy?" She glanced from one to the other. "I ought to knock your heads together. You're grown men, for goodness' sake! Fighting over a girl…"

ANNETTE PULASKI

Warren Wilkes had been working on the checkout lane at the Piggly Wiggly for three hours. He couldn't wait for his shift to end so he could meet his friends David Morgan and Jerry Shrupp at the lake for their own private 1970 graduation celebration. They were going to take a night swim, maybe see what late movie was playing at the theater, and stop at the Dairy Queen in St. Peter afterward. He looked at his watch for the hundredth time. Sometimes this job really put a damper on his life.

Annette Pulaski came in with her little daughter, Molly. She went to get a cart and slipped the scrawny four-year-old into the seat. The woman wasn't that old, in her midtwenties, but she looked very tired with dark circles under her eyes. Her hair hung in long, discouraged strings. Warren had heard that her husband had lost his job at the cannery, and from the looks of Annette and their daughter, he hadn't found a new job.

"Warren." Mr. Schneider, the store manager, tapped Warren on the shoulder, talking in a low whisper. "Pulaskis have used up their credit here. If she tries to charge, you'll need to tell her it's cash or nothing."

"Okay, Mr. Schneider," Warren said uneasily. "I'll tell her."

The overweight polyester-clad manager blew his nose into a cloth handkerchief and slunk back to his office overlooking the store. Warren turned to greet the next customer.

When Annette pushed the cart to Warren's checkout lane, her daughter Molly began whining for a piece of candy. "No, honey," he heard Annette whisper. "You know Mommy doesn't have money for treats."

Warren began to ring up the sale—a loaf of bread, a gallon of milk, two containers of orange juice, bananas, a package of chicken, and a bag of rice.

"That'll be $8.47," he said.

"Can I put this on our account?" Annette asked tentatively.

Warren glanced toward the manager's window. He could see Mr. Schneider's hovering form behind the glass.

"I'm sorry, Mrs. Pulaski," Warren said. "Mr. Schneider says we can't extend any more credit to you."

"Oh." Her face fell and tears brimmed on the edge of her bottom lids. Annette blinked hard. "I suppose I should put all this stuff back then."

"Don't you worry about that, ma'am," Warren said, hoping his voice conveyed the sympathy he felt. "I'll take care of it for you. It's pretty slow around here."

"Um…okay," she said. She lifted her daughter out of the cart. "We better go, Molly. Daddy'll be waiting for us." Then she left, almost running for the doorway.

Warren felt his face flush hot. He wished he could tell Mr. Schneider what he thought of his "business practices." He pulled the cart to the side and waited on the next customer. Finally, it was time to go home. Warren bagged up the groceries that Mrs. Pulaski had brought to the front and rang up the sale again. He pulled the money from his pocket and paid the bill, then went out to his car and set the bag on the backseat.

He followed the quiet Lake Emily streets to the Pulaskis' house on Second Street. It was a meager pillbox with a bed of daffodils blooming in a flower bed along the front sidewalk. Warren rang the bell and waited. Mr. Pulaski's tall frame appeared in the doorway.

"Warren, what can I do for you?" he asked.

"Hey, Mr. Pulaski, your wife left this at the grocery store, and I thought I'd bring it by," Warren said.

"That's funny," he said. "She never mentioned anything about it." He reached for the bag.

"Oh." Warren searched his pocket and pulled out a root beer sucker. "This is for Molly." The older man took it, a puzzled expression on his face.

"She'll appreciate that," he said before closing the door. "Annette," Warren could hear the man call to his wife.

Warren returned to his car. Maybe he and the guys could skip the movie, he decided. A midnight swim would be plenty of celebrating for one night.

twenty-seven

The Suzie Qs planned a baby shower for Mae in lieu of their August meeting. Since Trudy would be leaving soon for school, they decided to hold the event early. It had been roughly thirty years since any member had had a baby, so this was definitely an occasion to celebrate. Annette Pulaski had offered to host the shower since she still had her daughter Molly's cradle that they could decorate and fill with gifts. She took great pains to create an atmosphere in her bungalow-style house worthy of Martha Stewart. She baked scones and whipped cream. She brewed three different flavors of coffee. A lovely rose topiary was set in the middle of a hand-crocheted tablecloth, and the cradle was festooned with pink and blue balloons and little bouquets fashioned from baby booties.

Lillian Biddle brought a chocolate Bundt cake with coconut icing, and Ella Rosenberg contributed her famous cinnamon rolls, each as big as a small car. Trudy brought a large collage of photos of Mae's and Peter's growing-up years that she displayed on an easel in the corner with little blurbs that said things like, "Will the baby look like him" next to a picture of Peter with his face full of chocolate cake "or her" and a picture depicting a five-year-old Mae, smiling proudly with scissors in hand after a self-inflicted haircut.

By the time they heard the crunch of gravel in the driveway, they were ready for a party. Each woman grabbed a sign Trudy had brought for them to hold up and took their places. The doorbell rang, and Annette went to answer it. As she flung the door open, the women threw up their cards that read "Happy Baby" and "Surprise."

Mae's mouth fell open in shock, and her face lit in a bright smile. "You guys!" she said. Virginia stepped forward and put a Hawaiian lei over her head.

"Everyone has to have a baby shower," Virginia said, drawing Mae into the festive living room. When Mae saw the cradle piled high with gifts and decorations, she put her hand over her mouth. "This is too much."

"You sit down and let us spoil you," Irene Jenkins said, giving her a hug. Mae obeyed, taking the chair of honor that was decorated with crepe paper streamers and helium balloons.

"First, a game," Trudy said. From behind her chair she pulled a small board with fifteen baby pictures that Virginia had collected. "Each of us has to guess whose baby picture is whose," Trudy directed as she handed out pencils and index cards. They passed the board around the room, and the ladies chattered among themselves. "Won't the old black-and-white shots give us away?" Mary Shrupp said in her petite voice.

"Your picture won't be as old as some of ours," Lillian Biddle said to Mary. "Mae and Trudy will be easy, since their pictures are probably in color."

"Oh, I wouldn't be so sure," Trudy said, raising an eyebrow.

"Ron can't tell our own kids' baby pictures apart anymore—isn't that awful?" Annette said. "I have to tell him who is who."

"When you've got nine kids, it's easy to understand," said Virginia. "I've got two, and I mix them up. That's definitely you, Lillian," she said pointing to one of the shots.

"Speaking of forgetfulness, did you hear about Millie Johnson?" Irene Jenkins said. "They found out she has the Alzheimer's. That's why she's been doing all those odd things. I heard she put her car keys in the freezer, and it took two months to find them. Poor Millie. It must be difficult for her to know she's losing her memory."

"I heard Melvin's been looking into nursing homes. Just in case," Lillian continued. "Seems a little premature to me. Already thinking of putting her away."

"I don't know about that," Virginia said. "It's practical to learn what's out there instead of waiting until you've got an emergency on your hands."

"Still," Lillian huffed, "I wouldn't want Willie doing that until I'm at least gone enough to not know that he was doing it."

"How are Millie's spirits?" Mary asked.

"She's as chipper as ever," Irene said. "Some things even Alzheimer's has a hard time putting down." Sympathetic heads nodded.

"This has to be you, Minnie," Irene said, referring to a shot of a three-year-old sitting on a step and holding a gray kitten. "I can see your son Warren in those pretty eyes."

"Otto's family always thought he looked more like Otto," Minnie said.

"How long has it been since Warren died?" Annette asked. "He was such a nice boy."

"Twenty-nine years," Minnie said quietly, "since we got the telegram that he was missing in action. You never stop holding out hope though…" Her voice trailed away.

Next they went around the room, and each lady confessed which baby shot was hers. When the board reached Trudy, she pointed out a photo of a chubby naked baby lying on a bearskin rug. "This baldie would be me," she said. "And this"—she pointed to a blond-headed baby with deep dimples—"is Mae before her hair turned dark. Isn't she cute?"

When the game was over, Virginia was declared the winner with ten correct guesses.

The party moved on to the opening of gifts. Virginia recorded each item and who it was from while Trudy taped all the ribbons to a paper plate.

"Isn't that ribbon thing usually for bridal showers?" Mary asked, turning to Lillian. "You know, the bride carries the paper plate bouquet down the aisle at the rehearsal?"

"It's for a mobile," Trudy defended. "The baby can look at the pretty colors from her crib."

"So you think it's a girl?" Annette asked.

"I'm sure of it," Trudy said. Mae held up a beautiful baby quilt from Irene, no doubt handmade. She mouthed "thank you" and passed it around the circle for all the women to see. "I just have a sense about these things," Trudy put in. "My girlfriend Libby has five kids, and I've known what each one would be. It's all in how happy she is. Some people think it's how you carry the baby, but that makes no sense to me because the shape of your uterus is the shape of your uterus. How could that change with each kid? And some people say they can tell by whether you get sick or not, that it has to do with hormones and that stuff. The way I figure it, when you're having a girl, you're happy, and when you're having a boy, you're grumpy."

Mae held up a diaper bag filled with every possible supply she would ever need. That too went around the circle for the women to inspect.

When the unwrapping was finished, Mae had quite a stash of baby goodies—onesies, p.j.'s, beautiful handmade quilts, booties, and smocked outfits, pacifiers, teddy bears, diapers, a diaper pail, a car seat, and a baby swing. Mae couldn't imagine needing another thing. In clothes alone they'd have enough to last until the baby was in kindergarten.

When all the gifts were neatly laid out for display, the celebration moved to the dining room as the ladies took their seats behind steaming cups of coffee. "Virginia told me you're drinking tea these days,"

Annette said to Mae. "I have yours over here." She led Mae to the head of the table.

"Thank you." Mae took the cup gratefully. "It's so odd, but my tastes have changed since I got pregnant. I never liked tea before, and now I actually crave the stuff."

"I was that way with pistachios," Mary said. "And only while I was pregnant. Now I don't touch them."

"Have you had a lot of morning sickness?" Annette asked.

"Not too much. I got a little green when I was first pregnant. That phase passed quickly, then I became so tired all the time." Heads bobbed knowingly. "But now I'm feeling pretty good and getting huge!" She patted her rounded belly.

Trudy and Lillian reached for the creamer simultaneously. "You take cream too?" Lillian said.

"Love the stuff," Trudy said.

"I was always the only Suzie Q not to drink my coffee black. You go ahead," Lillian offered, watching her closely.

Trudy poured a little of the white cream from the mouth of the cow-shaped pitcher. "Ooh, that's so cute!" Trudy exclaimed, examining the pitcher more closely.

"Did you hear Jim Miller broke his leg down at the Chuckwagon?" Lillian resumed the conversation for any who cared to listen. "He was roofing and backed right off it. Could've killed himself."

"You don't say," Ella said.

"Well, I tell you what, he broke that leg but good," Lillian said, "I heard he flew off that roof like a chicken off a pile of hay. Vernon Elwood saw the whole thing. Had to call the ambulance. And now they say he needs surgery. Something about putting a pin in his thigh." The ladies gasped. Lillian took a long drink of her coffee, savoring the attention.

"Estelle Martin had another angiogram," Mary put in.

"That's her second in six months!" Lillian said. "Maybe now she'll go on a diet, lose some of that weight."

Annette said, "Maybe Estelle figures she can clog those arteries back up and go back in every six months."

"Sounds like a good plan to me," Trudy put in. "This dessert is delicious, Annette." The women laughed.

They talked like girls at a sleepover until late into the night, when at last they succumbed to the hour and their old age. They stood together, accompanied by the scraping of chairs on the hardwood floor, thanking Annette for the lovely evening.

Mae glowed in the warmth of the night. Who would've thought these women would throw her a shower? Perhaps she had finally found her place here.

"Are you sure you want to do this?" Mae asked for the sixth time as she watched Trudy brush her long hair.

"I don't know what you're so worried about. What could possibly happen?"

"Lillian might chop up your body and feed it to the cows."

"Ha-ha. It's a simple dinner at the Biddles, not the Addams family."

"Are they going to draw straws for you? Or will Mama decide who gets you?"

"You know, you're a very judgmental person sometimes. I'm not liking that about you."

"Come on, Trudy, they've got something up their sleeves."

"They're nice folks being neighborly."

"If that were true, Peter and I would be going over since technically we're the neighbors."

"You're making this out to be more than it is. All this tension isn't good for the little squirt. We've had a nice summer, gotten to know each other a little bit, had some laughs. That's all. Can you help me with this?" She turned her back to Mae and pointed to the top button on her dress. Trudy was beautiful in the pale green linen with a trim sleeveless top and a long flowing skirt. She liked the way it "swished" when she walked.

"Are you sure they're going to be this dressy?"

"Have you noticed how these farm women dress up when they go out for a night on the town? You really need to pay more attention, Mae. And buy a redder lipstick."

LILLIAN AND WILL BIDDLE

Lillian Swenson had everything arranged. Her mother had arrived from Marshall, Minnesota, the night before for the rehearsal and dinner. Lillian's satin dress was pressed and waited patiently on the back of her closet door. It was a classic style with a simple cut, long and straight, no lace. The reception hall and chapel were decorated and ready. After her appointment with the hairdresser this afternoon, everything would be set.

She thought about her father, so far away in Florida, and wished for the hundredth time he could be here. She hadn't seen him in five years. After the divorce, he had all but disappeared from her life, except for the occasional letter telling her he missed his "little girl."

Lillian felt an ache that he would miss the most important day of her life as he had missed so many other important days—her first date, prom, high-school graduation... She'd invited him, but he was always "too far away," "too low on cash" in some trailer court near the ocean. "Could you ever forgive me for walking out on you and your mom?" She wondered how many beers he'd had when he wrote that letter.

A knock sounded on her apartment door. "Lillian, guess who's here to see his bride?" a deep voice teased.

Willie Biddle, Lillian's fiancé, poked his handsome face inside the room. Lillian shrieked. "You're not supposed to see me today!" She ran to put the dress back in the closet.

"Since when are you superstitious?" Willie grinned.

"I'm not. But still, isn't there some kind of rule?"

"Come here," Willie said, drawing her into his arms and giving her a

warm kiss on the lips. "I had to say good morning. I'm so happy this day is finally here."

"Me too." She rested her head contentedly on his chest. "But I'm nervous!"

"Not me. I want to get this over with so we can go on our honeymoon."

Lillian slugged him in the arm. "Willie!" She felt a blush creep up her neck.

He smiled broadly. "You can't blame a guy. Come on, do you have time to go take a walk with your boyfriend?"

"I suppose I could fit you in."

Another knock sounded. "Who is it?" Lillian's roommate, Darlene, came in.

"Sorry to interrupt, but there's a man outside asking for you."

"A man?" Lillian looked questioningly at Willie. She went over to the window of her second-story bedroom and pulled the curtain back to look.

There he stood. A single small yellow suitcase in one hand. That familiar, slightly stooped stance, and an old brown suit coat hanging limply on his once sturdy frame, a weathered hat leaning to one side of his head.

"Dad," Lillian whispered, putting a hand over her mouth. Tears stung her nose, and she ran down the stairs and out the front door. She pulled him into a fierce hug. He seemed so thin. His face was dark and wrinkled. Alcohol lingered on his breath, and tears welled in his red-rimmed eyes.

"I didn't know if you wanted your old man around for your big day," he said hoarsely.

"Of course I do—" She began to sob, shaking as they stood on the sidewalk. Willie made his way out the door. Wiping her face, Lillian said, "Dad, I'd like you to meet my fiancé, Willie Biddle."

Willie stepped up and reached for the older man's hand. "It's a pleasure to meet you, sir." Lillian stood between them staring from the older man to the younger.

"You take care of my little girl," her father said. "I haven't done much of a job of it, but she deserves the best."

twenty-eight

When Trudy pulled into Lillian and Willie Biddle's driveway, a small terrier greeted her, yapping and snarling, a definite display of poor manners. "Nice doggy," she murmured in the calmest voice she could muster.

"Down, Bullet," Fred yelled. The dog ran under the picnic table and stared at him with big eyes. Fred turned back to Trudy and said, "Hey, don't you look nice."

Trudy smiled at the compliment.

"Ma made a pork roast." He opened the screen door for her to enter through the kitchen. The turn-of-the-century house had heavy moldings and beveled-glass doors. It was cluttered with piles of old magazines and sewing projects in various stages of completion. A sewing machine sat on a card table to one side of the kitchen table, and the counters sported an array of gadgets—a bread machine, two mixers, a blender, an iced-tea maker, a pasta machine. "Ma likes to cook," Fred said as if reading Trudy's thoughts.

"Lucky for you."

"Why do you think I live at home?" Fred chortled.

Lillian bustled into the room and saw Trudy. "Oh, you're here already?" She reached up to the lone curler still in the back of her hair and pulled it out in one swift move.

"Am I early?" Trudy asked.

"No," Fred said. "Ma's running late as usual."

"Fred!" Lillian scolded. She turned to Trudy. "Fred can give you a little tour of the place while I finish up here." She looked pointedly at her son.

"Oh yeah, sure," Fred said. He led Trudy through the house, its floors sloping from one room to the next.

"Where's Bert?" Trudy asked.

"He had other things to do," Fred said. Trudy felt a sharp disappointment.

The living room had a genuine "parlor" feel with a floral couch, doilies, and old-fashioned glass lamps with roses painted on their shades. Trudy trailed behind and stopped to look at an Impressionist painting of a small girl in a field of lilies. "That's beautiful," she commented.

"Bert got that for Ma," Fred said. "You ask me, it looks like a little kid's picture." He laughed with a sort of cackle and walked into the adjacent hallway.

"What kind of art do you like?" Trudy asked. He looked at her as if she'd spoken Japanese to him, his mouth slightly ajar. His brow furrowed in pained caveman thought.

"I'm not much for paintings."

Trudy didn't comment.

"There you are." Lillian came down the hall. "I've got supper on the table and your father finally got in from doing who knows what. We'll be eating soon."

"It smells good," Trudy said, following her back to the formal dining room.

"It ought to, as much time as I put into it."

The table was set with pink rose-patterned china and a silver service complete with a candelabra that held five white tapers.

"This is lovely," Trudy said.

Lillian beamed with pleasure and went back to the kitchen. Willie came in and held out a hand to Trudy. "I don't think we've officially met. Will Biddle."

"Trudy Ploog," Trudy pumped his hand. "Thanks for having me."

"Bert tells us you're an art teacher," Willie said as they took their seats. Lillian set salt and pepper shakers on the table and took the lids from the serving dishes.

"Yes," Trudy said. "I've been teaching kindergarten through sixth for seven years now."

Fred placed an arm across the back of Trudy's chair, and she felt an awkward shiver squirm up her spine.

"Would you say the blessing?" Lillian said to Fred as she sat down.

He gave his mother a blank stare, then closed his eyes and lowered his head and said, "Come, Lord Jesus, be our guest. Let these gifts to us be blessed. Amen." They raised their heads and began passing around the bowls of steaming boiled potatoes and roast pork and peas.

"You must like children then?" Lillian said. She passed the potatoes to Willie.

"Uh, sure," Trudy said, looking uncertainly at Fred.

"Peas?" Willie offered a bowl.

"No thanks," Trudy said. "I'm not a big fan of peas."

"Peas are pretty much the bread and butter in this county," Lillian said in a scolding tone. Trudy stiffened in her chair.

"Well, I guess I could give them another chance," she said, taking the bowl and putting a spoonful on her plate, careful not to let them touch her other food. "So…" Trudy looked for a safe topic. "Is it a good year for farming?" she asked, turning toward Willie.

"Not bad," he said. "Fred and Bert really are the ones in charge these days."

"It's better," Fred jumped in, "now that's Bert's back here full time.

Kinda put a crimp in things to have him switch-hitting over at the Morgans."

Lillian cleared her throat and passed Fred another look. Trudy put a slab of roast pork on her plate.

"Have you lived in St. Paul all your life?" Willie asked.

"Pretty much," Trudy said. "My mom and stepdad still live there." She took a bite of the peas and tried not to spit them out.

"How do they taste?" Lillian said.

"Better than creamed peas," she said. Lillian raised a dubious eyebrow at Fred.

Dessert couldn't come soon enough. Trudy felt like a prisoner being interrogated in some South American jail. It was all she could do to keep from hiking up her dress and sprinting for the back door. She repeatedly tried to steer the conversation to the Biddles, asking how they became farmers, what the boys were like as children, what sorts of hobbies they liked, but each time, their talk returned to her. Did she attend church regularly? What denomination? Did she believe in infant baptism? Was she having a good summer in Lake Emily? She smiled politely at each question and tried to answer as generically as possibly. All the while Lillian covertly gave Fred looks that asked, "What were you thinking?"

"Let's have coffee in the parlor," Lillian said after clearing the dessert plates. They sat on the dainty couches while Lillian poured.

"What's Bert up to tonight?" Trudy asked.

"Well, he…uh…he had other plans," Lillian stammered.

"What kind of plans?"

"He didn't really say, did he, Willie?" Lillian said.

Willie lifted his head in obvious surprise that he was being included in the conversation and said, "What would I know? That boy's been moody all week."

Trudy hoped that meant what she thought it meant. She let herself enjoy a small smile.

Trudy drove home as twilight was settling in. She wasn't sure what to make of their meal. Everyone was on edge, although Willie seemed as confused as she felt.

She rounded the corner at the old German cemetery and noticed Bert's pickup truck parked near a tall headstone. The tailgate was down, and he was sitting with his back to the road. She pulled up next to the entrance, a tall, black wrought-iron gate covered in scrollwork. It was a picturesque sight worth stopping to enjoy, the way the setting sun cast long shadows across the headstones. As she quietly shut her car door, Trudy heard the sounds of banjo music dancing in the still air. She walked closer and waited while he played.

"Hi," she said when there was a lull in the music.

Bert lifted his head and glanced over at her. He mumbled something she couldn't make out.

"I saw you out here and had to stop. It's so pretty." Still no response. She turned and admired the long shadows that spread between the headstones. "I missed you at supper."

"I needed to get out of the house."

"Away from me?"

His eyes darted over to hers, and she could see the embarrassment on his face. She turned back to the sunset. "I'd love to paint this."

"It's beautiful," he said.

She glanced over and caught him gazing not at the scenery but at her. The sun had dipped lower, and it was almost totally dark except for the outline of his face. "So why did you have to get out of the house?"

"I promised."

"What did you promise?"

"Fred is in love with you. I don't want to hurt him." But his eyes betrayed him.

"What if I don't love Fred?"

Bert stared at the banjo on his lap as if her statement was impossible for him to comprehend. "He's my brother...," Bert said.

"It isn't Fred who draws me." She moved closer, and Bert hesitated, as if he wanted to move away from her, but her pull made it impossible. She reached for the banjo and gently set it aside, then looked at his lips and leaned in, inviting his kiss. His mouth touched hers softly, sending tingles up her arms. He pulled back suddenly, fear in his eyes.

"I'm sorry," Bert insisted. "I promised."

Trudy felt her face flush. "And what did Fred promise you? He isn't the only person with feelings," Trudy finished.

"I don't want to hurt you, but—," Bert began.

"I'm leaving for St. Paul next week," Trudy interrupted. "So you don't have to worry about hurting me." She turned and stalked away, the music of the night silenced.

Peter had just hitched the hay wagon behind the baler when his dad pulled up and got out of his car. "Morning," David Morgan called. Peter gave a wave. "Mae mentioned that you were haying today, so I thought I'd come down and see if you could use some help."

"Sure."

David hopped onto the wagon and walked toward the front.

"It's been a long time," David said, breathing in the fresh air deeply. "When did you mow?"

"Last Wednesday. Raked on Friday and again on Monday. Should be dry by now. Thankfully we haven't had any rain."

David nodded. "So what would you like me to do?"

"Do you remember how to drive?"

"It's like riding a bike," David said. "You sure you don't want me stacking bales?"

"I wouldn't want you wrecking your back—you're getting old, you know, Grandpa."

"I'm fifty! That is still pretty sprightly."

Peter grinned. "The fact that you used the word 'sprightly' proves my point. Drive to the north eighty."

David moved to the seat and popped the tractor into first. The machine pulled out smoothly. Peter rode on the empty wagon, bracing himself as it jostled back and forth as they moved between the tall fields of corn. The sun was warm on his back, a torch in the morning sky. Frogs croaked loudly, and the thick stalks rustled with grasshoppers.

David pulled the train of machinery up to the first row of hay and engaged the power take-off. He moved slowly along the raked piles. Soon the first bale came up the ramp, and Peter hefted the seventy-pound block to the back of the wagon. He moved with ease, the rhythm of the job a constant beat. He thought of his first time baling with Bert and how exhausted he'd been. A lot could change in a summer. He'd changed this summer, he realized.

He alternated the stack as Bert had taught him. Soon the pile was towering high and Peter was a good ten feet above the surrounding landscape. Sweat dripped down his back and off the end of his nose. But he felt good.

"Dad!" Peter shouted above the noise of the baler. David turned his head back. "Lunchtime. Let's take this load in and finish this afternoon." His dad nodded, turned off the power take-off, and pulled a U-turn to unhitch the baler and hitch the wagon on alone, then they headed back toward the lane to home.

The view for Peter was different from the ride out. Instead of the dark sheltering enclosure of the corn, he could see the whole river valley from atop the pile. Lake Emily's silver water tower shimmered above the treetops. The lake itself was a pale blue. Jewels of sunlight danced on its surface, a ribbon in a quilt of green. This land never kept still. There was always something new to discover, some facet Peter had never noticed before. The view was always shifting, like so much of life.

David pulled up to the tall side door of the barn that led to the hayloft and jumped down from the tractor. "It goes a lot faster with two people," Peter said. "Last time I had to stop every few yards to go and stack myself."

"That's crazy!" David said. "You should partner up with somebody. That's what Dad always did with Willie Biddle. Why don't you toss 'em down, and I'll start hauling them inside. You look winded."

Peter carefully dropped each bale squarely so it wouldn't break apart hitting the ground. When there was a big pile collected on the bottom, Peter climbed down and hauled them inside with his dad. Both men were breathing hard and were wet with perspiration. The exertion felt good, and it was comforting to be working side by side, father and son in the kinship of labor. The pile inside the barn was tall and beautiful. Clean, sweet, fresh hay that smelled of goodness and health, a winter without worries. It gave a deep satisfaction. A few bales had burst open on the ground, the firstfruits for the animals to taste, and their remnants trailed at the opening to the barn.

"Let's get lunch before we go tackle the rest," Peter said. David was huffing, his face gleaming with moisture.

"That sounds wonderful." David leaned his hands on his knees, catching his breath. "You think Mae has some iced tea in the house?"

"Always does." He glanced at his dad as they walked. This was a first, Peter thought, a day together, working hard.

"There's nothing as gratifying as a day of haying," David said. "I've missed it."

Peter looked at him, truly surprised at his comment. "Not even a concert solo?"

David smiled. "That's gratifying too, but not in the same way. Working until you sweat does something for the soul…"

"I thought you hated farming."

David stopped walking and stared at his son. "Why would you think that?"

"You didn't exactly stick around to follow in your dad's footsteps," Peter said.

David gazed at the sky and began speaking. "Peter, that was one of the hardest decisions of my life, leaving this farm. It was Dad who convinced me to join the orchestra. I loved it here, but he knew I had a greater passion, a gift for music. He said he'd never forgive himself if I settled for less than what I was born for. I don't know if staying here would've been better, but I do know that I've enjoyed my life and what I've done. I wouldn't have chosen for your mother to die… But I always loved farming."

"I thought we traveled so much to get away from here, to get away from the memories." Peter paused. "I didn't know what you'd think of me taking over—whether you'd be pleased or think I had wasted those years of education."

"Peter." David waited until Peter's gaze lifted. "I know I don't say this much, but I am proud of you no matter what you choose to do. I haven't always communicated that. One of my failings as a father, I guess."

Peter felt his heart squeeze at his father's words, and he cleared his throat. "I've been mad at you…for missing the funeral…"

"You've been mad at me for a lot of things," David said.

"It wasn't that I thought you weren't a good father...I just...I wanted us to be a regular family."

"It was tough without your mother."

"Yes." It was a whisper.

"I tried, Peter." David lifted his gaze to the sprawling lawn. "I want you to be happy, and seeing you and Mae here, I know that you are. Your grandpa would be so proud to know another Morgan is milking his cows and tending his fields."

"I only hope I can do a good job of it. We lost a heifer and a calf last month, and my pea crop barely covered my costs. If the corn and beans don't do well, I don't know if we'll be able to pay back our operating loan and meet expenses, much less make any kind of a profit."

David put his arm across his son's shoulders as they went into the house. "Now you're talking like a true farmer."

Fred's white pickup pulled into the driveway. Trudy saw him coming, but she made no move to go greet him. She wasn't looking forward to this.

"Hey, Tru-udes." Mae walked out onto the porch a dishtowel in her hands. "Look who's here."

"I know," Trudy said. "Do I have to see him? Could you tell him I died?"

"You're not helping yourself if you avoid this."

Trudy sighed dramatically. "You're not helping yourself if you avoid this," she mimicked. "Sometimes you're very irritating." She got up and walked down the porch steps, the screen door slamming behind her. The August sun was tucked behind patchy clouds, giving the landscape a dotted look. Fred was standing next to his truck when he turned and gave her a toothy grin. A huge bouquet of flowers peeked from behind his back. Trudy groaned as she slipped on her shoes.

"Hey, good lookin'," he said.

"Fred, you and I need to talk..."

"I brought you something." Fred pulled the flowers from behind his back. Trudy gave him a halfhearted smile.

"They're nice, Fred. But I really can't accept them."

His face fell like an anvil off a cliff. "What's wrong with them?" He looked at the daisy and baby's breath bouquet.

"Nothing. The flowers are lovely. It's just that—"

"It's Bert, isn't it? That weasel—"

"It isn't Bert!" Trudy was almost shouting. "It's me. I just don't have those kinds of feelings for you."

Fred took a step back, his mouth ajar.

"I don't want to hurt your feelings," Trudy continued, "but it isn't fair to you..."

"Wait a minute," Fred said.

Trudy stopped.

"Did you think I was trying to romance you?"

"Well..." Trudy was perplexed. "I... Yes, I did."

"You're not really my type, Trudy. You're nice and everything, but I like more refined women."

"I can't believe the summer's already gone!" Mae said as Trudy loaded her last suitcase into the backseat of her Pacer. Trudy had painted tiny caricatures of the capitol building in St. Paul along with Mickey's Dining Car, the Walker Art Center with its trademark spoon and cherry on the hood, and representing Minneapolis, the Foshay Tower and the Metrodome, and then south to the Mall of America in front of the left windshield wiper. She'd eventually get to the rest of the state, but she'd have to do a lot of driving to make sure she captured all the sights of

Minnesota. She couldn't very well paint Split Rock Lighthouse without first visiting it. She had painted a cute square brick farmhouse for Peter and Mae's place and the towers of the Farmers' Elevator in town and an empty tractor in a field. She hadn't been able to bring herself to put Bert in the driver's seat.

"It's been a trip," Trudy said. "And it's been wonderful." She leaned down to Mae's stomach and said, "Now, you take care of your mommy for Auntie Trudy." Then she stood up and gave her sister a long hug.

"What are you going to do about Bert?" Mae asked.

"What can I do? You were right, you know. It was all a bad idea."

"I hate being right if it means you're hurt."

"I'll be okay." She glanced toward the barn. "Tell Peter I'll see him around, and thank him for putting up with me. He isn't still mad at me for knocking over the telephone pole, is he?"

"Are you kidding? He loves you. He's totally forgotten it."

There was a long silence before Trudy said, "Well, I guess I'd better get going. If you hear about any teaching jobs in Lake Emily, call me."

Mae gave her another hug. "I'm going to miss you."

"I'll miss you too, but I'm not far away. We'll do weekends."

"It's not the same as having you here whenever I want you," Mae said.

Trudy opened the door of her car and sat down.

"When this baby comes I expect you to come for at least a week," Mae said.

Trudy saluted and said, "Yes ma'am." Then she gave a little wave and backed the Pacer from its spot. All too soon she was raising dust on the dirt road as the car became a speck in the distance.

Mae sighed and went back into the house. Everything was still. Sunlight streamed into the living room through the sheer curtains.

"Now what?" she said to the empty house.

* * *

The chickens had quickly gotten fat over the summer, and now that fall was here, the day to butcher had arrived. Virginia said that between the two of them they could process half the flock in a day. Mae couldn't imagine killing and dressing fifty birds all in the space of a few hours, but she was glad it would be over quickly. The thought of actually cutting an animal's head off gave her the willies.

At seven o'clock Virginia pulled up in her white Oldsmobile and got out. She had on an old coat, a housedress that peeked beneath the jacket's hem, and ratty sneakers. Her gray perm was covered in a bandanna. Mae slipped on her own coat, which she couldn't button over her growing pregnancy, and went out to meet her.

"What do you think you're doing?" Virginia said, pointing to the Playtex Living Gloves on Mae's hands.

"I'm ready for butchering."

"You're going to have to get your hands dirty, dear," Virginia said, a definite smirk on her face.

Mae scrunched up her nose and took off the gloves. "You want a cup of coffee first?"

"Nope," Virginia said. "We've got work to do. You don't seem very eager."

"I'm okay," Mae said.

"Is everything ready?" Virginia pulled a full-length apron from the car and tied it around her waist, then handed two more to Mae.

"Yep," Mae said, putting the old red gingham apron atop her layers and leading Virginia to the coop. She had moved the picnic table close to the yard, and on it she had placed a hatchet and a block of wood with two nails about an inch apart. A huge enamelware pot of water simmered on the Coleman stove. There were five-gallon pails for feathers and scraps, a propane torch and matches, sharp knives, two cutting boards, a pile of clean rags, freezer paper, and tape. Next to the table was a fifty-gallon plastic tub of cold water.

Virginia looked the collection over and nodded. "That'll work."

"How are we going to catch them?" Mae asked, remembering the hen in her kitchen.

"You'll see," Virginia said. She walked over to the chickens' yard and opened the gate to let herself and Mae in. Closing it behind them, Virginia walked to the coop door, reaching just inside and pulling out a long metal rod with a crook in one end and a wooden handle on the other. "This is our secret weapon," she said with a raised eyebrow. "Just watch." The chickens contentedly pecked at the ground. Scout began pacing outside the fence, whining and yelping. Soon he had the chickens whipped into a frenzy; they squawked and ran-flew back and forth across the pen. "Put Scout on the back porch, or I'll never be able to catch them. I'll wait until you get back," Virginia said to Mae as a wave of white feathers streaked past her. Mae grabbed the dog by the collar and left.

When she returned, Virginia was stalking a cluster of fat hens. In a flash, Virginia slipped the rod between the birds, flipped the crook around a leg, and pulled the old girl upside down by her foot. She squawked to protest this assault on her dignity, and the other jailbirds clucked madly until she was out of sight, then returned to pecking the dirt as though nothing had happened.

Virginia held the bird's legs in one hand and carried her upside down to the chopping block. The wings flopped out wide, but Virginia tucked them back. The hen had given up her complaining, and Virginia rested its neck between the two nails on the block and pulled on its feet to stretch the neck out. The bird opened its eyes wide in curiosity as Virginia lifted the hatchet, and with one hard *whack* the head plunked to the ground, mouth open and eyes blinking.

Blood spurted out of the headless creature like a fire hose, and Virginia tossed the hen down and said, "We've gotta wait until she's done twitching, or she'll make a mess all over."

The specter flipped and flopped and squirted for a good thirty seconds before finally coming to rest at Mae's feet. Green-faced, she grimaced.

"All set," Virginia said with a twinkle in her eye. Mae reached for the legs, and the bird gave a final twitch. She shuddered, hoping her weak stomach wouldn't give way. "Dip it for ten, fifteen seconds in the hot water," Virginia instructed. When Mae pulled the dripping animal out, Virginia tugged on some of the feathers and they came out easily. Virginia said, "Good. Now you can pluck."

Mae ran her hands along the chicken's breast, pinching and pulling feathers which lifted out like dandelion fluff, coating her hands in a thick layer. Within a few minutes the old girl was naked. Virginia cut off the feet and then showed Mae where to insert the knife to gut it. Virginia followed the rib cage to the backbone, careful not to cut too deeply. Then Virginia pushed her thick hands up inside, and in one moment pulled all the innards out. She moved swiftly with the knife to remove the gullet and neck.

Once it looked pretty much like any store-bought chicken, Virginia reached for the propane torch and matches. She held the carcass up to the September sunlight, and Mae could see tiny hairs all over its flesh. "We have to burn off these pinfeathers." Virginia lit the torch and ran it along the bird's body. The hairs flamed and curled quickly, filling the air with a sharp smell. Then Virginia dropped the chicken into the ice-cold tub to soak. "Now we're ready for the rest." She wiped her hands on her old apron and handed the long rod to Mae. "Your turn."

Mae took a deep breath and turned toward the chicken yard. Only forty-nine more to go…

* * *

When they'd finished half the hens, they took a lunch break. Mae washed her hands in the sink after filling the laundry tub with soapy water and putting in her apron to soak. She would wear the fresh one for the next round. Then she put on a pot of coffee and joined Virginia at the kitchen table for BLTs.

"Do you ever get used to it?" Mae asked. "That smell really bothers me—when I'm pulling out the insides."

"You're pregnant. Smells always bothered me when I was pregnant too. But when you see those white packages of the best-tasting chicken you've ever had all lined up in your freezer, you'll change your mind," Virginia said.

"Why don't the other chickens run away from us after watching us kill their friends?"

"They're stupid, Mae. Sometimes I used to find chickens who had hung themselves from the string on the light. One hung itself from a rake! Another managed to get the string from the feedbags tied around her tongue. I didn't even know chickens had tongues until I saw that."

Mae laughed.

The coffee gurgled its last, and the rich aroma filled the air. Mae got up to pour a cup for Virginia, then she poured herself some tomato juice. "I've been drinking a lot of this lately." Mae held up her glass.

"When I was pregnant with David I couldn't get enough garlic toast. Funniest thing. But that was what I craved. Roy would be down here at six in the morning putting a batch under the broiler so I could have some." She smiled across her coffee. "Good memories," she said.

"I've been craving Cap'n Crunch cereal too," Mae said. "I went and got one of those huge boxes of it, and I've been hoarding it for myself." She smiled shyly. "I even hid it so Peter couldn't find it!"

"Enjoy it now, dear," Virginia said. "This is your time."

Once they finished lunch dishes, they put on their spare aprons and went out to resume the carnage. Virginia pulled the birds they'd already butchered from the cold water, letting them drip before patting them dry. They packaged some whole, and others they cut into legs and wings and breasts so Mae would have a good variety to choose from. Virginia carefully wrote the date and contents on each package, and Mae took armloads down to the freezer in the basement. Mae changed the water in the big tub, added a fresh bag of ice, and changed the water in the dipping pot. This they did every few birds because it got dirty quickly with blood and feathers.

The afternoon had warmed, and Mae soon forgot the gruesomeness of their task and simply enjoyed the companionship.

When she hauled the last armload to the freezer, the women stood, staring at the neatly stacked rows—wings and drumsticks, thighs and breasts. And of course whole chickens for roasting and soups.

"You should take some of these home," Mae said.

"Oh no," Virginia insisted, patting her hand. "It would take me a whole week to eat one. It was a fun day. You can invite me for chicken dinner sometime—that'll be payment enough."

"Okay, how about next Sunday after church?"

Virginia smiled. "I'll be here. When do you want to butcher the rest?"

"I don't even want to think about the rest!"

Slowly the plants in the garden began to wither. The pumpkins blazed bright orange, and Mae put up thirty pints of pie filling for the cold days ahead. The tomatoes and beans turned brown, and, thankfully, the zucchini at last stopped sending forth its abundant fruit.

Mae chopped up the dried stalks with a long machete and added them to the compost heap behind the chicken coop. The tomato cages were neatly stacked in the garden shed along with the terra cotta pots that had given up their petunias and pansies. The squash was touched by the first frost and added its wonderful sweet taste to the table. Mae finished digging the rest of her potatoes and onions and carrots and stored them in the root cellar that Virginia had faithfully maintained, layering each in moist sand along with the beets and turnips and rutabagas she'd laid up earlier. It was amazing to her how much of her produce would keep for months simply by resting in this dark, cool place.

The garden was bare now, rows of black, tilled earth where there had been lush green. Even the grass was turning brown.

When cold winter days came, they would never be lacking for good, healthy food. She had followed *The Have-More Plan* book's instructions for gardening perfectly, even going overboard when it came to canning and freezing. Where Mrs. Robinson recommended a hundred quarts of canned goods per family member, Mae had put up a hundred and twenty-five quarts. She reasoned that it would give her an excuse to have a lot of company in the coming months when the work waned and they would again have time to visit.

She sat at the gray Formica-and-chrome kitchen table, a cup of tea steaming before her. She felt the baby kick and patted her stomach where little feet nudged. It was a curious thing, pregnancy. Everything changed with it, her emotions, reactions, energy level, even whether she liked tea or not.

Last night Peter had come in and found her at the kitchen sink, crying. "Honey, what is it?" he'd said, a worried expression on his face.

"I can't reach the sink!" she'd sobbed. He'd taken the washcloth from her hands and held her in his arms.

Mae lifted the mug and took a sip. She wondered what else would change once this child was actually in her arms. Would the baby change their small family? Who would he or she look like? Who would it grow up to be?

Peter came in the back door and put his chore coat on the hook by the back bench.

"It's getting cold out there. Time for harvest soon," he said. He went to the cupboard for a mug and poured coffee from the thermos Mae kept for him each morning. As he sat down, Mae felt another sharp kick in her belly. "Oh my!" she squealed and placed a hand on her stomach.

"What's wrong?"

Mae grabbed his hand and placed it on her stomach. "Wait," she said. They were both still, waiting for another boot. Peter lowered his head to her stomach as if willing the baby to move again. And then it happened. A bump of flesh as an elbow or a knee changed position. Peter's eyes grew wide.

"No different than a calf," Peter teased.

"Oh, you!" Mae protested. "I'm not a cow."

October third was Grandparent's Day at the elementary school. Jessie had called the week before to invite Virginia to serve as her surrogate. Virginia stopped to register at the front table and then navigated the brightly tiled corridors to the third-grade hall. When she knocked on Mr. Odegaard's door and came in, Jessie's little face took on a grin. "Jessie, would you please introduce your guest to the class?" her teacher asked.

Jessie stood up next to her desk when Virginia drew near and in a loud, rehearsed voice announced, "This is my grandparent for the day, Virginia Morgan. She isn't my real grandma because my real grandma died. But she's just like the real thing."

The class greeted her with a "Good morning, Mrs. Morgan."

"Good morning." Virginia nodded in return. A dozen other gray-haired heads dutifully exchanged greetings with her and returned to the construction-paper and macaroni-noodle art that they were gluing together.

Jessie scrunched up her nose at the self-portrait she'd drawn and said, "We're supposed to glue the noodles for hair. I think it looks dumb, like my hair is in rollers."

"We'll give it a shot anyway, okay? Maybe it could be me—my hair's in rollers all the time." That brought a smile to Jessie's face. They spent the next hour finishing their project and reading as a class from *Trumpet of the Swans.* Then they went to lunch where Virginia stood in line with Jessie and took a tray and a pint of chocolate milk in a paper carton.

"You like chocolate too?" Jessie pointed to her own tray.

"It's better than vanilla any day, don't you think?"

"Vanilla?"

"The white milk."

Jessie nodded as the hair-netted cook plopped four chicken nuggets, a big spoonful of Tater Tots, and green beans onto each tray.

"M'm. Looks good," Virginia said. Jessie looked at her in disbelief. They sat at the squat tables and talked about their morning. Some of the children who'd had no grandparent that day came and sat with them, looking at Virginia with curious eyes.

When lunch was over, the bell rang and it was time to return for the afternoon session. Mr. Odegaard instructed the children to get out the essays they had written for Grandparents' Day. One by one the children walked to the front of the class to read their papers. Many talked about gray hair and Christmas presents and what it was like to go fishing with Grandpa. When each concluded, polite applause would usher the reader back to his seat.

Finally, it was Jessie's turn. She took her place at the front, turned, and nervously tucked her blond hair behind her ears. She held the paper shakily and then, taking a deep breath and raising her chin, she began to read, "What a grandma is to me," she began. Her eyes darted to Virginia, then back to her page. "A grandmother is a friend. A person who sits and reads with me even though I'm not very good at reading. But she says I'm getting better. She bakes cookies and tells silly jokes. She reminds me to brush my hair and taught me to make hotdish. She bought me a bunny and helped me earn my very first ribbon at the fair. Some grandmothers come when you're born. But my Virginia came when my mom died. Her Roy died too. She is my friend and is like a real grandma to me." Jessie's eyes flicked to her teacher and then to Virginia before she returned to her seat. Virginia could barely focus for the tears that swam in her eyes.

The class applauded. Jessie returned to her chair beside Virginia and leaned toward her as the next reader went up to the front. "Was that okay?" she asked.

"That was fine, dear, just fine."

The harvest began. With chores twice a day, Mae's and Peter's hours were long, getting up at 5:30 A.M. to begin, done with milking at 8:00, then to the fields until the evening when they'd milk again from 6:00 to 8:00. Then Peter went back to the fields as late as his exhaustion would allow. Mae caught up on household duties in the evenings, shuttled meals between the house and the fields, and, once their silos were full, hauled corn to the elevator to sell each time Peter filled the back of the old 1963 Chevy grain truck.

The work was exhausting, but Peter couldn't keep from smiling. To float above a golden sea that waved in the breeze, to see the combine spit out dusty chaff as the truck bed filled with golden corn, to watch the landscape transformed by the work of his hands—there was nothing as satisfying in the world. He pictured himself sitting behind a stuffy desk, counseling parents on why their spoiled child was bullying others—and he felt relief and gratitude that he hadn't pursued that line of work. This was what he'd been born to do. He could sense that as clearly as his father knew his own passion for the violin. This was his place in the world as it had been his grandfather's.

He could feel God's pleasure here. He supposed some people could feel close to God in St. Paul amid the old beautiful churches, but to Peter, the sun, the wind, and the sky spoke far more profoundly than anything man could make.

Peter turned a corner and headed up the next row when he saw a deer at the edge of the woods bordering the field. He stopped the combine, content to watch. The deer lifted its head and stared straight at him, motionless. It flicked its tail, and then after a long moment, lowered its head to eat. Peter sat and watched for a long while before the doe lifted her head again and loped off into the dark woods.

It was nearing noon, and the combine was almost full, so he headed toward the lane where the truck waited for its refill. He pulled the machine next to the truck and positioned the auger that would transfer the corn from one vehicle to the other. The smell of turned earth and dry field corn filled his senses. He could see Mae coming toward him in the pickup, no doubt with a lunch on the seat beside her. She parked and got out, her wicker picnic basket in hand, her walk a definite waddle in her fifth month of pregnancy. Peter climbed down to meet her.

"How's it going?" she asked. She laid the food out on the hood of the pickup.

"I've got another load to take to town."

Mae nodded.

"You look tired," Peter said, inspecting the circles under her eyes. "Are you getting enough sleep?"

"I sleep when you sleep." She handed him a plate of macaroni casserole and a fork.

"The only difference is, I'm not carrying our first child."

"Okay, maybe I have been pushing it a little bit," Mae admitted. "I'll get a nap in after lunch. But you need someone to haul that corn." Mae served a plate for herself, and Peter said a prayer over their little meal.

"Why don't I take this load in?" Peter said.

"I'm okay." Mae reached for his hand. "Really."

Peter took a deep breath and gazed across the field. "I saw a deer over there a bit ago. She stood and watched me for the longest time." Mae lifted her eyes to look too.

They ate their meal. Swallows dipped and swooped over the field, and the sun turned a burnished copper in the western sky, coating the landscape in a pumpkin light. The air was still warm but carried a hint of the cold to come.

VIRGINIA MORGAN

It was a hot June day in the canning factory. Virginia Bjork had been sorting peas all morning as the big conveyor moved a sea of peas before her and into the cannery. She wiped the sweat from her neck with her handkerchief and glanced across the belt. A girl of about fourteen with big blue eyes was staring at her. She wore a tattered dress, and her light brown hair hung in sweaty strings across her eyes and face. Her gaze shifted as soon as she noticed that Virginia had seen her.

"My name's Virginia," Virginia offered while her hands kept at her task.

"I'm Ida," the girl said quietly, her eyes back on her work.

"Have you worked here long?" Virginia asked.

"A couple, no, three years," Ida said. Virginia was saddened that someone so young needed to take such hard work. But these were hard times with the Depression in full swing—it wasn't an uncommon story.

"That's a pretty dress," Ida said. It was almost a whisper, so Virginia wasn't sure if she'd heard correctly. She looked down at her simple, flowered print covered by a full apron.

"Thank you," she said.

Ida nodded. "You must be real good at sewing."

"I don't sew at all," Virginia confessed. "I can't even stitch a button on to save my life."

Ida's mouth dropped in astonishment. "You mean it's store-bought? You must be wealthy."

"No." Virginia smiled. "Where I come from a lot of people buy store-bought clothes."

"Where's that?"

"St. Paul." The girl's eyes widened. "Still, it's a real pretty dress," she said again.

A shadow appeared in the open doorway, and Virginia turned to see who was there. He was a handsome man, not particularly tall, but tall enough. He had a strong jaw and pale, pale blue eyes. As soon as he glanced Virginia's direction, his face lit in a broad smile. He ambled over, and Virginia felt her face flame and her heart skip a beat.

"Hey, sis," he directed to Ida.

The girl grinned broadly, and she said, "Roy! What are you doing here?"

"Thought I'd share lunch with my baby sister." He held up a black pail.

"This is my new friend Virginia. She's from St. Paul," she said.

The man turned toward Virginia and held out a hand. "Roy Morgan. Pleased to meet you." His grip was strong and firm.

"Would you like to join us for lunch?" he asked. "There's always plenty to share."

twenty-nine

Mae was paging through her *Taste of Lake Emily Cookbook,* a gift from Virginia, the next afternoon, looking for a good recipe for supper. She had felt short of breath through the day, and her stomach hurt. It would grow hard and firm, and she felt as though the baby was pushing down on her pelvis. Mae got a drink of water and tried lying down, but that did nothing to ease her discomfort. Then she went to the bathroom and noticed that she was bleeding. As the pain increased, she went out to the barn where Peter had begun getting the cows ready for milking.

"Peter?" she said. He lifted his head from his work. "I think something's wrong."

Immediately, Peter was on the phone to Dr. Mielke, describing Mae's symptoms. When he hung up, Peter's face was pale. "We need to get to the hospital. Doctor Mielke says you might be in premature labor."

A dark pall overtook them both. Peter led her by the elbow to the Jeep. Mae felt too scared to even talk. She was only five and a half months pregnant, yet with each kick and movement she had fallen in love. She put her hands on her stomach, trying to feel the baby moving. Her stomach hardened again. *Oh, Lord,* her heart cried out, *don't let this happen. Keep our baby safe. Please.*

Peter looked over at her, his eyes searching as the Jeep flew toward town. When they reached the hospital, Peter commanded, "Stay here," and ran inside.

A moment later Mary Shrupp appeared, pushing a wheelchair. "Mae," she said gently, "come sit in the chair."

"I can walk," Mae protested.

"Not today," Mary replied, helping her into the chair. They moved quickly to an exam room where Dr. Mielke was waiting. His bushy gray eyebrows furrowed in concern as he pressed on Mae's stomach.

"Your water hasn't broken, has it?" the old doctor asked.

"I don't think so. But I'm bleeding."

"When did the pain start?"

"Oh." Mae thought. "Maybe an hour ago." The look of fear on Peter's face kept her from saying more.

"Okay. I'll take a look," he said. Mary took Mae's blood pressure. Then the doctor listened to the baby's heartbeat. He was dead silent as he moved the stethoscope repeatedly across her belly. Then he wrapped the tubes around the back of his neck and said, "Peter, can I have a word with you outside?"

Mae looked at him, panic in her throat. "What is it?" she demanded. "You have to tell me!"

Dr. Mielke glanced from Peter to Mae uncertainly. "I think we need to do an ultrasound."

"Why?" Mae asked.

"I can't find a heartbeat," he said simply, his gray eyes clouded.

Mae was stunned. She couldn't speak, couldn't breathe, only felt hot tears form in her eyes.

"You could be mistaken, couldn't you?" Peter asked.

"That's why I want the ultrasound. We need to make sure."

Mae reached for Peter's hand. She felt a terror she'd never imagined before, a raging pain that ran willy-nilly through her consciousness. "No, no, no" she moaned as the tears rolled in a torrent down her cheeks. Peter pulled her to himself, their grief mingling.

Moments later Mae was being wheeled to a dark room where they transferred her to another bed. The technician, a plain-looking middle-aged woman, squeezed the clear jelly onto Mae's abdomen and moved the probe across the surface of her stomach. Mae's face was glued to the monitor, hoping to catch a glimpse of a healthy, beating heart, but the technician turned the screen away as she kept moving the probe. Mae stared at the woman's face, and after a few minutes she knew.

Another contraction swelled across her belly and Mae cried through the pain. The doctor talked in low whispers to the woman. Then he came and stood at Mae's side, looking down at her with a kindness Mae couldn't bear to see. "I'm sorry."

Her heart wanted to scream with those words, to thrash out and grasp anything that could possibly change them.

"We may have to do a C-section, but your body seems to be doing the work so far. We'll see." There was a deep kindness in the old doctor's eyes as he studied Mae. "How are you holding up?"

Mae felt numb. How could she ever withstand labor, to endure this pain without the promise of a baby to hold? This was all happening too fast. Mae felt swallowed up, suffocated. Their baby was gone, this life she'd felt beneath her own flesh, that she'd talked to with each movement. Tears cascaded down her cheeks, and she looked up at Peter. The expression on his face tore at her heart—his own raw pain exposed. She squeezed his hand.

"I don't know, Doctor. I don't know if I can do this."

Peter held Mae and rubbed her back, all the while praying for a miracle. But they were all out of miracles for today.

By eleven that evening it was over. Peter and Mae held their still baby girl, stroked her soft cheek. So tiny. She was so tiny. Their little

Laura Morgan would never breathe, would never laugh and play and feel her daddy's arms around her.

Doctor Mielke said he didn't know what had gone wrong, and right now Peter didn't need to know. At least Mae was okay. That was all that mattered.

"You're exhausted," Peter said while Mae stared up at him with empty eyes. "You need to rest."

"I'm sorry," she whispered.

"Don't be sorry." He stroked her hair, his own heart weeping. "Don't be sorry." He felt another wave of tears begin. "I'm glad you're okay. I couldn't handle losing you too." They held each other for a long time, their grief a river of sorrow.

"Your mom can take care of her in heaven," Mae said. Peter nodded mutely.

When he pulled back there was a soft rapping on the door.

Peter turned to see who it was. There stood Virginia, her face filled with concern. "Grandma," Peter said. She moved close to the bed and reached for Peter's hand.

"Mary called," she said.

"I'm sorry. I should've—"

"No. You had more important things to consider," Virginia said. "I'm sorry, so sorry."

"I was milking—," Peter said, then stopped. "Oh no. I never milked the cows. I forgot all about it." He ran his hands through his tousled hair.

"You go," Mae said. "Virginia's here. I'll be okay. You have to milk." He looked at her uncertainly, hardly able to bear the thought of leaving her.

"I can't," he said. "I need to be here with you."

"You have to go, Peter," Mae insisted.

"I'll take care of her," Virginia said.

* * *

The drive to the farm was torture. Peter almost turned around twice.

When he pulled onto the gravel drive, he was surprised to see a blue pickup and a burgundy sedan parked by the house. The sedan he recognized as his father's; the other he couldn't place. He walked into the barn and stopped, staring at the sight that met his eyes.

The cows he had lined up for the first round of milking were milling about with the rest, and the equipment was put neatly away. Peter checked the tank. It was obvious that someone had milked.

He walked up to the house. A light in the living room glowed through the lace curtains. When he came in the back door, Peter saw his father and Jerry Shrupp sitting at the kitchen table talking.

"What's going on?" Peter asked.

"Is Mae okay?" David asked, rising to walk over to his son.

"We lost the baby. But Mae's okay, at least physically." He choked out the words.

"I'm so sorry," David said. He pulled his son to him in a long embrace, and Peter felt hot tears slip from his eyes.

"Go back to the hospital," David said. "We have it covered here. Mae needs you, Son."

Peter nodded his head and turned to go. Then he turned back. "Dad?" David's eyes were glued to his. "Thanks."

"Whatever you need—I'm here for you. Don't worry about the farm. Go be with Mae. She's more important. I'll be here as long as you need me."

When Peter returned to the hospital it was 1:00 A.M. Virginia and Pastor Hickey were sitting outside Mae's room on green vinyl chairs talking in low voices. They glanced up when Peter drew near.

"Pastor came to pray with us," Virginia said.

Peter nodded to the man in greeting and whispered, "Thank you," then glanced toward the door.

"She's sleeping," Virginia said, reaching for his hand.

He took a seat next to his grandmother and put his head in his hands. He inhaled deeply and let the breath out in a long gust. Pastor Hickey reached across and placed a hand on Peter's shoulder.

"Loss is never easy. May I pray with you?" he offered.

"I'd like that," Peter said, looking at the man's face.

Pastor Hickey lowered his head and began. "Father, Peter and Mae need your comfort right now, and your strength. You know what it's like to lose a child, the pain and grief that comes with that. So console them as only you can. We know that you are always here. Don't let the whys crowd out the knowledge that you've never left their side, never will leave their side. But be a constant strength to them, and in the coming days help them. Help Peter to be strong for Mae and to mourn. Bring healing even in this hard time. Amen."

They lifted their heads, and Virginia placed her arm around Peter's shoulder and held him for a long while.

"Are you sure she's sleeping?" Peter said, wiping his tears.

"She's exhausted." Virginia's expression reflected her own weariness.

"So, what happens now?" Peter said.

"You take each moment as it comes," Pastor Hickey said. Peter stared unseeing at the quilt that hung on the wall across the tiled hall.

"We wanted this baby so badly…"

"Of course you did," Virginia said.

"But now we have to plan a funeral," Peter finished.

"We could see if the cemetery would let us bury her with Roy. If that would be okay with you."

"Yeah," Peter said. "She'll be near Mom then too." His mind

couldn't comprehend that they were even having this conversation. This was supposed to be a time of joy, welcoming a new baby into their family. How could this have happened? How? It was all his fault. If only he hadn't allowed Mae to work so hard... Peter suddenly felt very tired.

When Peter brought Mae home the next morning, David's car was still in the drive along with Bert Biddle's truck. The door to the barn was propped open. Peter helped Mae up the stairs, then pulled back the blankets and took off her shoes. "I'm okay, Peter," Mae insisted.

"I know, but I need to take care of you." He fluffed her pillows, avoiding her gaze.

"Peter," Mae said again, grabbing his arm. He sat on the bed next to her. "Stop blaming yourself."

He looked her in the eyes, the depth of her emotion sending darts to his heart. "It is my fault. If you hadn't been working so hard...up all hours—" His words broke off.

She ran her fingers along the hair on his forehead.

"I wanted to help you," she said. "That isn't why the baby died. It isn't. The doctor said it could be any number of reasons. We don't know why she died. Don't blame yourself."

Peter rested his head on her shoulder and whispered into her hair, "I love you, Mae."

Once Mae was asleep and the sound of her even breathing stilled the room, Peter slipped out to the barn. His father was cleaning the milk tank, his back to the door. Peter could hear Bert up in the loft.

"Dad?" Peter said. "We're home."

David turned to his son, dark circles under his eyes. "You okay?"

303

Peter shrugged his shoulders. "I can take over here now that—"

"Don't rush it," David interrupted. "I meant it when I said I'd stay as long as you need me. I told my conductor I'm taking a leave."

"Dad, you don't have to—"

"Yes, I do. And you need to let me."

Bert came up behind them. "Everyone's fed," he said.

Peter turned to Bert. "Hey," Bert said simply.

"Don't you have a harvest to bring in at your place?" Peter asked.

"Dad and Fred have it covered."

"See? There's nothing for you to worry about out here," David said. "You've got a wife who needs you."

That afternoon the meals started arriving—hot dishes, soups, Jell-O salads, and bars. Some in glass casserole dishes, others in plastic containers, all labeled with names on masking tape. Irene Jenkins, the fire chief's mother from the Suzie Qs, was the first to arrive, bearing a green bean Tater Tot hotdish still warm from the oven. She stood on the back steps, hot pads and towels wrapped around the bowl.

Peter opened the door at her knock. "Hello, Peter, I'm Irene from the extension group. I heard about your loss. I'm so sorry. I thought you folks might need a little supper about now. It's still hot, or if you have something already made, you can heat it up for tomorrow." She held the bowl toward him. Peter didn't know what to say. He'd never had someone bring him a meal out of the blue before.

"Thank you," he finally said.

"Well, here."

Peter took it.

Then Irene said, "I have some bars out in the car for dessert."

She disappeared to retrieve the treat. He set the hotdish on a trivet

on the counter, and Irene returned bearing an aluminum pan of chocolate chip cookie bars, which she handed to Peter.

"I don't want to disturb Mae's rest, so you just tell her that Irene said
hi and that we're praying for her on the prayer chain." She turned to go.

The next meal came less than an hour later. Virginia's friend Ella
brought a complete chicken dinner—homemade lemon chicken, mashed
potatoes with chicken gravy, coleslaw, rolls. It was enough food to feed
a family of twelve.

For the next two days the meals came. They came from church
members, extension members. Delicious homemade food, and always
plenty to feed them for two or three days. "We know people would do
the same for us," was all they'd say.

And then there was Virginia. She was an ever-faithful presence. She
shooed away any who came while Mae got her much needed rest, kept
the house cleaned and the laundry done, and filled their home with rich
smelling baked goods, and she seasoned it all with her comforting words
of wisdom.

Trudy had come to help with the preparations, her usually jovial self
subdued by her sister's grief. She, Peter, and Virginia planned a small
graveside service. Peter chose a tiny coffin for his daughter. Trudy suggested having one bouquet of flowers on the casket, tiny peach roses
with baby's breath. There would be no obituary, no radio announcement. The service would be for those closest to Mae and Peter, those
who could comfort them best.

They buried their little Laura on the same day Mae's milk came in. It
was a small gathering, Peter and Mae, Virginia, David and Trudy, Fred
and Bert Biddle, Ella Rosenberg, and the Shrupps, along with Pastor
Hickey. As the service was about to start, a black SUV pulled into the

cemetery, and Mae watched her mother and Paul emerge and slowly approach them. Her mother's glance met hers, and tears stung Mae's eyes. Catherine gave a sympathetic smile, the lines of her face marking her shared grief.

The chill October breeze ruffled Mae's hair. She stood, staring down at the brown pile of dirt. She pulled her jacket tighter around herself. Pastor Hickey read the familiar words, "The Lord is my shepherd…" Mae's thoughts drifted, and she watched a squirrel climb a large oak tree and chatter in its loud voice. Mae closed her eyes and let the tears trail down her face.

Life would still go on, she knew. Tomorrow would come, and she would still be on this earth. And she would have to find a purpose, a reason to keep breathing, even though her broken heart told her to give up. She gazed over at Peter and Virginia, their faces intent on the pastor's words.

She knew Peter was suffering as much as she was, and yet she felt powerless to help him. How could she when she couldn't even help herself?

Trudy hoped their mother's presence would encourage Mae. But from the expression on her face, Mae was still far away. Trudy hadn't been able to reach her since she'd come down from St. Paul. She scanned the faces around the small circle gathered in the cemetery as the pastor finished the benediction. Bert Biddle's eyes met hers, and he moved over to her as the group began to disperse in a silent exit.

"Thanks for coming," Trudy said.

"I'm sorry," he said. She wasn't sure if he was talking about the baby or their last encounter. The intensity of his stare held her. Soon the cars had left, and they were alone in the quiet of the headstones and oak trees. "Are you going to be staying with Peter and Mae for a while?"

"Yeah, I think so...the rest of this week anyway. I need to be here for Mae." Her gaze shifted to the mound of dark earth, then back to Bert. "Why don't you come out? We can talk."

Mae had gone upstairs to get changed when she heard a knock at the bedroom door. "Come in," she said. The door opened slowly, tentatively. Catherine met her daughter's gaze, and Mae burst into tears. "Mom."

Catherine stepped inside. "Trudy called to tell us about the baby."

Mae looked toward the ceiling with blurred eyes. "She was beautiful," Mae whispered. "Had all her fingers and toes complete with nails. Eight and a half inches long."

"I'm sorry," Catherine said, moving next to the bed.

"We named her Laura," Mae continued. "After Peter's mother."

Catherine's eyes brimmed with tears. "You look tired," she said.

"I am." Mae sat down on the bed and fidgeted with the coverlet's contours.

"I'll let you rest," Catherine said. "I needed to see you."

Mae gazed at her mother's sad face. "I needed to see you too," she whispered. There was so much Mae wanted to say.

"We need to get back to St. Paul," Catherine said. "Would it be okay if I called you?"

Mae nodded, and Catherine closed the door. She sat staring at where her mother had stood. She didn't know what to feel anymore. She wanted to hope that her mother's presence here meant they were turning a corner in their relationship, but right now hope was an elusive ghost.

That evening as Mae sat in her bedroom, Virginia poked her head inside. "Do you want to talk?" Virginia said. Mae nodded and motioned for her to take a seat.

Virginia moved slowly to the chair by the bed and sat thoughtfully.

"It's going to be hard for a long time," Virginia began, her head bent down. "You'll always wonder what it would've been like if she'd lived, who she would've looked like, what her interests and abilities would've been." Mae studied Virginia's wrinkled face as she spoke. "You'll be glad that you didn't know her so well, that somehow that will make you mourn her less. Then you'll feel guilty for feeling that way." Her eyes glimmered with tears, and her gaze seemed focused on nothing in particular as she lifted her head. "Wondering about who she would've been is almost harder than being grateful for the fifty-seven years you had with your husband…" Her words faded away, and Virginia's gaze met Mae's.

"When did you lose your baby?" Mae said.

"Three years after Sarah was born," Virginia said. "I wasn't as far along as you were, but it never goes away, the pain. Not really. But healing comes in the small things. Like when Peter was born, when you joined our family. It's all part of the give-and-take of life. But God is faithful. He never turns his back on us."

thirty

Mae had been up since six. The morning air had called her to come sit on the front porch, so she had taken a quilt, wrapped it around herself, and sat in Virginia's old rocker as the birds chirped across the front lawn. The leaves on the trees had nearly all fallen now. The river valley was filled with a cool gray mist that floated upward as the breeze kissed the valley. The events of the past days all seemed unreal. Yet the pain was all too real. A blue jay dove toward the bird feeder and bullied the other birds away, took up residence, and feasted on sunflower seeds.

"God," she whispered into the air, "why do I feel so alone?" The flower beds shivered, their now-brown blooms sending little seeds to the earth. A chickadee called out in a trill, answered by another. The little table at her elbow held a worn Bible. Mae picked it up and turned to Matthew, looking for some word of encouragement. Reaching chapter 11, verse 28, she read, "Come to me, all of you who are weary and carry heavy burdens, and I will give you rest. Take my yoke upon you. Let me teach you, because I am humble and gentle, and you will find rest for your souls. For my yoke fits perfectly, and the burden I give you is light."

Mae closed her eyes, and a sting of tears filled her nostrils. Virginia's words resonated. God was here and he loved her. He loved their baby too, and now little Laura was with him in heaven. She breathed deeply and let the tears fall.

"I need you too," Mae prayed. "Lord Jesus, I need you too."

* * *

"Hey," Peter whispered, opening the screen door with a squeak.

Mae looked up. "Hi," she said softly as he took the rocking chair next to her.

His brow was lined with worry. "What are you doing?"

"Thinking. Praying." She was quiet for a while. "I'm going to be okay, Peter. You will too." Peter held her hand and touched the Bible in her lap.

"You haven't been in the fields," Mae said. "If we're going to pay off that debt, you're going to have to finish the harvest."

"You've needed me." He stopped and amended. "We needed each other."

"I haven't exactly been here for you."

"You've been here."

"But if we're going to farm here for the next forty years we're going to have to work hard."

Peter reached for her hand. "I don't know if my heart's in it anymore," he said. "This life might be too hard for us. Maybe we should consider moving back to St. Paul. I could take a regular job to pay off the debt. Grandma could sell to someone else."

Mae stared off to the neighboring fields that stretched for miles. She could see the silver glint of Lake Emily's water tower just on the horizon. She took a deep breath. "Peter, this would've happened no matter where we lived. I know that you love me. I also know that there's nothing in this world that fits you better than farming. I see that passion in your eyes as surely as Virginia saw it in Roy's eyes all those years. It's what you were born to do."

Peter took her hand and stared deeply into her eyes. "But I want you to be happy too."

"We're home, Peter. That makes me happy. This pain in our hearts will heal. I could sense a hint of it this morning. We have to be patient. And when I'm feeling up to it again, I'll be out there with you in the barn and the fields because I'm your wife and I'm happy being with you."

Peter kissed her hand. "We'll have another baby," he whispered.

"Someday. Just not *this* baby."

The sound of machinery echoed in the distance, and Peter looked up. "Someone's working early," Peter said. On the dirt road he could see dust rising above the corn. He stood and shaded his eyes against the morning sun.

As the rumbling drew closer, David came out the front door to join him. "What's going on?" he asked.

"I'm not sure," Peter answered. The procession of giants—two combines, one John Deere green and the other a Massey Ferguson—passed the house and grove, turning into Peter's field.

"Looks like Vernon Elwood in the John Deere. He was a friend of Grandpa's," David said, "and J. D. Shrupp in the other."

Then two semis with grain trailers pulled into the drive, and Peter and David went out to meet them.

Mel Johnson, the usher from church, climbed down. Peter could see Bert Biddle waiting in the driver's seat of the second. "Heard you've been having a go of it out here," Mel yelled above the roar of the engines. "Thought we'd see if you could use a few extra hands to get the harvest in." Mel's face crinkled in a smile. "Your grandpa was a good man, Peter. From what I hear, his grandson is made of the same stuff."

Peter felt like crying.

Mel climbed back into the old truck. "Should have her done

tomorrow, day after at the latest," he said and pulled the door shut. He put the machine in gear and chugged toward the fields of corn.

Bert Biddle climbed down and reached a hand to Peter. "You know, I noticed that you don't seem to have one of these." He held up a new green seed cap with the word "Trelay" stitched across the front in yellow. "Every farmer needs one."

Peter took it reverently and placed it on his head. "Thanks, Bert," he said. "How do I look?"

"Like a farmer."

"Then I guess I'd better get out in those fields."